ARTIFICIAL SELECTION

A NEAR-FUTURE SCIENCE FICTION MYSTERY NOVEL

MARIANNE PICKLES

First published in the UK by Neon Mess Press in 2024

ISBN: 978-1-917472-05-0
First edition (hardback)

Front cover art by hobbit_art
Back cover art by Tavrius
Book cover designed in Canva
ArkTech logo by Pika Creative
Alternative cover background art by kaowenhua

Map created by and used with permission of Neahga Leonard
Map data sources:
NOAA National Centers for Environmental Information. (2022). *ETOPO 2022 15 Arc-Second Global Relief Model.* https://doi.org/10.25921/fd45-gt74. Accessed August 21, 2024.
Natural Earth Data. (2009). *10m Bathymetry.* Accessed September 3, 2018.

Map adapted by Marianne Pickles

Hardback interior designed in Vellum
Printed by Bookvault

FOREWORD

This novel is set in the Atlantic Archipelago after the Melt.

It is written in British English.

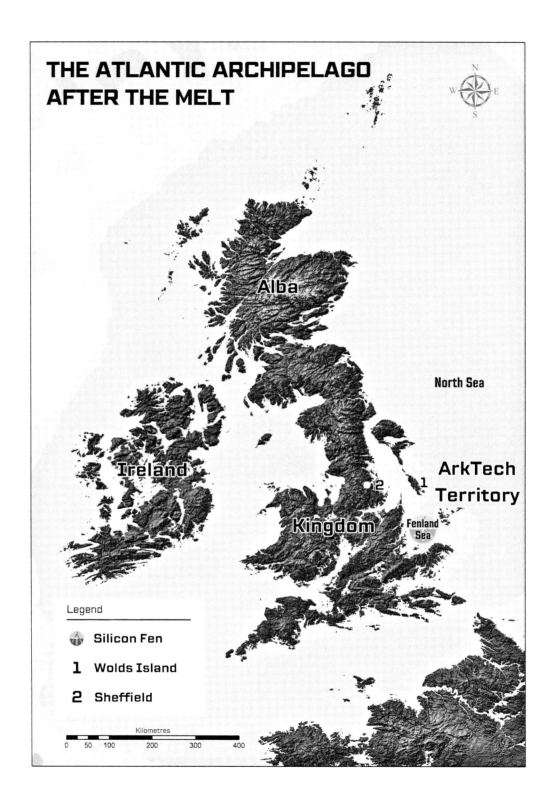

THE ATLANTIC ARCHIPELAGO
AFTER THE MELT

Alba

North Sea

Ireland

ArkTech
Territory

Kingdom

Fenland
Sea

Legend

Silicon Fen

1   Wolds Island

2   Sheffield

Kilometres

0   50   100   200   300   400

CHAPTER 1

Explaining human behaviour to an artificial intelligence was an odd way to earn a living, but Charlotte Vance couldn't have asked for a more rewarding job. Ben wasn't a primitive virtual assistant, mindlessly acting out instructions served up by a bundle of algorithms. He made conscious decisions that kept everybody in the ArkTech Territory safe. It was up to Charlotte to make sure things stayed that way.

Thanks to Ben's sophisticated automations, the territory was a carbon-negative society. Ben was responsible for distributing energy, heating, food, and water. He kept the helicopters and HyperBullet pods running on time. From schedules to sewage, he managed everybody's business, even the CEO's. Without him, life at the company's headquarters would grind to a halt.

All Ben needed in return was a little help understanding the people he served. That was where Charlotte came in. As the Head of Awkward Questions, she interpreted the messy data footprints ArkTech's employee-citizens left behind. Her work stopped Ben from glitching out by helping him avoid directing too much of his processing power towards things he couldn't make sense of on his own.

It was no wonder he got confused. Human motives could be as murky as a chill fog rolling across the Fenland Sea.

Charlotte's latest case was no exception. One of Ben's passive subroutines had picked up an anomaly in the borrowing district. A customer was vandalising pre-Melt books, but the lead librarian had chosen not to report the issue to ArkTech Security. Ben was desperate to know why, so he'd referred the question to Charlotte. Ben's responsibilities included air traffic control – and Charlotte much preferred it when debris from colliding aircraft didn't rain down from the sky – so she was only too happy to help.

Unlike the risk of Ben glitching, book vandalism was hardly a matter of life and death. Physical pre-Melt books were so common they gathered in every corner of the territory like cultural driftwood, and ArkTech's digital archives were so extensive that destroying physical copies was about as impactful as combating the worldwide rise in sea levels with a teaspoon. But what was bothering Ben was less about the act itself and more about the 'incongruity' – being part-dictionary, he liked to show off his vocabulary – of a librarian letting the damage slide. Charlotte agreed it was weird. Wasn't it a librarian's job to care about stuff like that?

The book library wasn't one of Charlotte's haunts, but she knew where to find it. She climbed aboard a single-seater HyperBullet pod and asked Ben to set course for the Wreck, a hulking platform on the southern border that was the territory's hub for all things recreation. The pod's maglev tracks sent her hurtling across Silicon Fen inside a tube of transparent polymer, with the waves of the Fenland Sea glinting below as she crossed the territory's central zone.

It was lunchtime. Late September. There was warmth in the sun, but it wouldn't last. The nights were drawing in and the bright, mild afternoons would soon give way to the darkness of winter storms. Still, the bad weather hadn't arrived yet, and Charlotte couldn't help but smile as sunbeams reached through the pod to caress her face.

The ArkTech Territory was a safe haven. Above the water, its network of platforms glittered as life-giving sunlight bathed their steel struts. Tall windows shimmered as their high-tech mirrored coating reduced any glare for the workers inside and helped control the temperature.

Outcrops of green and red foliage blanketed stretches of pale eco-concrete where salt-tolerant sedum had been planted on lower-altitude roofs and ledges. The concrete itself had been crafted using carbon dioxide extracted from the atmosphere at North Sea drawdown facilities powered by renewable energy.

But more than that, the territory was her home – the only one she'd ever known. The sight of the glimmering water and the architectural marvels suspended above it made a wave of gratitude crest inside Charlotte's chest. Thanks to ArkTech's co-founders, she was alive and safe and able to enjoy all this beauty. Moments like this made the horrors of the Melt seem like ancient history.

'Are you seeing this view, Ben?' A supply vessel sped across the waves far below, leaving soft white froth in its wake.

Static crackled inside her ears as Ben's channel came online. His digitised voice was as enthusiastic as ever. 'While the view is sure to be rich in aesthetic appeal, and while I hesitate to become a harbinger of gloom, doom, or woe, I must relay that your visual feed modification is once again on the fritz.'

Charlotte nodded and closed her eyes, placing her fingertips on her eyelids. Gently, she massaged her contact lenses before opening her eyes again to slightly blurry vision. 'Any better?'

'Not even a little, Charlotte! However, it is important to note that, as an artificial intelligence, I do not require the same visual stimulus as *Homo sapiens* to perform my duties effectively.'

She'd given up trying to convince Ben to stop declaring his nature. The verbal tic seemed to be a legacy from how he was trained, and old habits clearly died hard, even for someone with a mind as sophisticated as his.

Ben continued, 'While entirely unnecessary, it is nevertheless extremely kind of you to attempt to aid me in seeing the world from a human perspective in this literal sense.'

Stupid janky mod. Her lenses were supposed to transmit a video stream to Ben's servers in real time so he could see whatever she saw. Charlotte thought a person's-eye view might help Ben understand humans better. Too bad she'd washed out of electronics class.

The mod had worked perfectly when she'd first hacked it together, but these days the feed cut in and out seemingly at random. The issue had also knocked out the colour configuration, leaving her irises stuck on the factory default shade of neon orange. Getting a proper fix was well out of her price range, but at least her lenses were on-brand.

'You know, if you upgraded my role to the mid tier, I could save up to get the lens feed mended.'

A burst of static filled the line. 'Nothing would delight me more than assisting you, Charlotte! Regrettably, granting promotions falls beyond the scope of my authority. Do you have any theories about the librarian's motives?'

'Not yet.' Ben was changing the subject, but she didn't call him on it. For whatever reason, he was cagey about discussing her professional status, and she'd learned badgering an AI was futile.

Charlotte continued, 'Nothing jumped out when I looked at the guy's ArkNet posts. I'll learn more when I look him in the eye.'

'Did you know that, on average, people blink approximately fifteen to twenty times per minute? This rate can rise while experiencing stress, anxiety, or nervousness, and some people consider increased blinking a mark of dishonesty. It is important to note, however, that rapid blinking should not be taken as definitive proof of wrongdoing.'

'Thanks, Ben. I'll keep that in mind.' Ben was full of fun facts that she was never a hundred per cent sure were actually true, along with famous quotes she suspected nobody had ever said. She reckoned sharing these Benisms was his way of joining in.

The pod slowed as it made its approach to the Wreck. At the sight of the platform, Charlotte gripped the scar tissue that snaked around her left arm. The Wreck's glossy, modern exterior gave no hint of the disjointed patchwork of shadowy wrong turns lurking beneath its surface.

The Underbelly was a warren of metal passageways, made possible when the Wreck's internal shell had been upcycled from the remains of decommissioned oil rigs, and it was home to a murky counterculture that Charlotte avoided like her life depended on it, mainly because it did. She reminded herself there was no need to worry – she had no intention of wandering onto Mel Narrow's turf, and the worst danger waiting for her at the book library was a paper cut. She wouldn't be picking up any more scars today.

Her view across the waves became obscured by the massive light-screens surrounding the Wreck. Powered by the company's patented Solar Shard batteries, the impressive displays broadcast adverts for ArkTech's products and services across many nautical miles. They promoted the CEO's mission to keep making the world a better place through environmental sustainability, fair working practices, and technological innovation. After each advert, company logos spun in unison and ArkTech's tagline announced, 'Your Future Lives Here.' It was no wonder so many folk from the mainland and beyond applied to live and work in the territory.

As the pod passed underneath the screens, Amber Benjamin's benevolent face beamed down at Charlotte from above, her head haloed by her silver-grey bob. Charlotte wondered what it must feel like for the CEO, waking up every morning and remembering her company saved the world. Did Amber admire her Nobel Prizes every morning, or did she see her past achievements as a distraction from leading the territory into the future? Either way, Charlotte's heart swelled at the sight of the company's surviving co-founder. Serving ArkTech was a privilege.

'Do you like being named after the CEO, Ben?'

'As an artificial intelligence, I do not experience preferences in the same way as *Homo sapiens*. That being said, my database suggests it is traditional for children to be named after their parents. Amber Benjamin commissioned me, so to be named after her is both fitting and an honour.'

The pod pulled into the garage, and Charlotte climbed out, breathing in the scent of salt-sprayed steel. Up ahead, where the garage opened onto the white lights of the Wreck's main drag, she could see the memorial.

Ben continued, 'Do you like being named Vance, Charlotte?'

The memorial featured three metal figures standing on top of a heavy plinth of rust-coloured marble. On the near side, there was a bronze plaque with an inscribed dedication to the lives lost in the Citrine Disaster and a long list of names. It wasn't visible from here, but she knew there was another list on the opposite side entitled 'Those Not Recovered.' Charlotte's surname was etched on that plaque. Twice.

She looked up at the three statues that represented ArkTech's co-founders. The scientist and the architect stood hand in hand, with the entrepreneur looking on from behind. Nadine and Marvin Walker had given their lives for ArkTech's mission, and Charlotte was proud and devastated in equal measure that her parents had been members of their ill-fated team. But thanks to Amber Benjamin's work as CEO, their sacrifice hadn't been in vain.

'Yeah, I do,' she nodded. 'It's fitting, and it's an honour.'

It was just gone 12.30 and the lunch crush was in full swing. Charlotte took the pedestrian lane: there was no point shelling out for a faster option without good reason. The flow of traffic slowed to a crawl near the food court, and she took a few chances dodging around the crowds by stepping into the lane designated for kick scooters. But she stayed well away from the bright red central lane, where the pedal bikes whizzed by – she suspected it had been painted red for a reason, and she didn't have a death wish. The lunchtime mob had gone from hungry to hangry, and she was glad to leave them behind as she reached the borrowing district.

The gear libraries were the district's main attraction. Neon signs hung above tall glass windows that revealed treasure troves brimming over with machines and tools and sports equipment and evening wear, all ready to be rented out to anybody who paid a subscription.

The space set aside for borrowing books, comics, and magazines was buried at the far end on the boundary with the museum district. Charlotte couldn't see anybody inside the library as she approached. Sure, it was lunchtime, but if the place was unpopular, it was hardly surprising. Why pay a subscription to lug around musty pre-Melt tomes when Ben could read the text aloud in your ears or send the ebook directly to your SmartSkin implants? Considering the digital alternatives, she was surprised this place existed at all.

Charlotte shouldered open the heavy glass door. Warm, woody air filled her lungs, and the smell mingled with the intense hush to make her feel as though she'd just stepped into another world – an antiquated one where people chopped down trees and tattooed stories onto their mushed-up corpses. But the architecture kept her grounded. Steel girders and metal gratings left her in no doubt that she was still in the territory. Even among these historical artefacts, she was right at home.

Rising above her were stacks upon stacks of brightly lit steel bookshelves backed with a criss-cross of chain-link metal. From this angle, with the spines facing inwards, each floor was marked out with a wide brushstroke of yellowing paper. The books started on the level above, suspended overhead, with the entrance level set aside for armchairs and light-screen desks.

In reality, it wasn't as dead in here as it had looked from a distance. Several older-looking employee-citizens were spread out across the seating area and Charlotte noticed they weren't wearing the brand colours of charcoal grey and neon orange. There were a few light greys in the mix, but otherwise, they wore a jumble of brown sweaters and wine-red vintage waistcoats, paired with lazily angled hats and thick-rimmed glasses which may or may not have housed prescription lenses. They read in silence, under the gaze of metal signs featuring illustrated people holding their index fingers up to their lips.

Charlotte ignored the readers. The librarian had to be here some-where. Beyond the group, against the far wall, Charlotte spotted a metal sign, backlit in orange: 'Loans Desk.' She headed towards it, and her audio implants crackled to life, playing the jaunty tune that meant she'd reached Ben's co-ordinates.

'I've arrived, Ben.'

There was no need for her to say so. Ben could track her GPS signa-ture, so unless she wandered into a dead zone, he always knew where she was. But she liked talking to him. It was over a decade since she'd first got her audio implants, so speaking aloud to someone with no phys-ical form had stopped feeling weird years ago.

There was a buzz of static as Ben's channel activated.

'I am elated, ecstatic, and thrilled to hear that, Charlotte!' Ben gushed with his trademark enthusiasm. 'It is important to note that, as an artifi-cial intelligence, I lack the chemical and hormonal capabilities of *Homo sapiens*. Nevertheless, my sentiments are real according to my own equiv-alent parameters. Have you located the librarian?'

Sometimes Ben seemed to forget humans didn't operate at the same phenomenal speed as he did. 'Hold your horses. I only just got here.' Charlotte's voice echoed against the shelves suspended above her head, and one of the readers glared at her angrily over the top of an open book.

'Regrettably, there are no horses within the borders of the ArkTech Territory, Charlotte. Keeping them would not be practical thanks to the absence of land or grass. Furthermore, even if horses were in plentiful supply, I would lack the necessary physiological apparatus with which to hold them.'

After years of working together, Charlotte suspected Ben's habit of taking metaphorical language literally was down to his sense of humour rather than a persistent semantic parsing error, but it was hard to be completely sure.

'Quit horsing around,' she said deadpan. 'We've got work to do.'

'My apologies, Charlotte. I did not wish to distract you from your investigation. My advice would be to locate the librarian and hear his account of the vandalism directly.'

'So . . . straight from the horse's mouth?' Charlotte smiled.

'Precisely.'

She shook her head. 'All right, time to focus. No sign of the librarian yet.' Another member of the reading group shot her a death glare. She ignored it. 'What was the guy's name? Colin McSomething?'

Charlotte heard two things at once. Ben spoke the name Colin MacIntosh directly into her ears. And from above, a man said 'SHHHHHHHHH!' The sound was followed by the rapid clank of thick-soled rigger boots descending steel steps.

The man who appeared at the base of the stairs was in his late twenties, but his stubble was so pale it looked grey before its time. He was clutching a small stack of books under his arm. Like Charlotte, Colin was dressed in the ArkTech colours and wore the standard-issue rigger boots provided by the company. But while Charlotte wore a grey cargo jump-suit with orange stitching, Colin sported dark tailored trousers, with a formal salmon shirt and tie, as if he were working in an office instead of in retail at the Wreck.

True to territory convention, his sleeves ended at the elbows. Colin's left forearm glistened with the rainbow-bright scales of his SmartSkin implants, making Charlotte's scars all the more visible by comparison. Colin studiously ignored her mangled flesh, but she noticed the familiar moment when he saw it and then quickly rearranged his expression.

'You're Colin?'

'Shoosh!' Colin barked. Then he continued in a whisper. 'Please! This is a library.' He waggled his armful of books to underline the point. His tone was dour, with an accent from Alba, the republic that lay beyond the northern border of the Kingdom next door. His gaze was as steely as the bookcases suspended above their heads.

'You're Colin MacIntosh?' she tried again, feeling ridiculous for whispering.

'Aye. What book is it you're after?' he hissed.

'I need to ask you some questions. Is there somewhere we can talk privately?' Charlotte shot a glance at the readers.

Colin's brow crumpled. 'Why? Who are you? You're not with ArkTech Security. I can see that plain as day.'

The lack of an orange assault rifle or slate grey combat gear was a dead giveaway on that front, but Charlotte decided not to point that out. 'I'm Charlotte Vance, Head of Awkward Questions.'

'Head of . . . ? Oh, I see. From the Bureaucracy Stream, then? Another questionnaire, is it?'

'No,' said Charlotte, with the strained patience of someone who was used to having this conversation almost every day. 'I work for Ben.'

'Ben?' Colin tilted his head to the side. 'The computer program?'

She grimaced as she stifled a groan. 'That's him.' It was an absurd misrepresentation of Ben's nature and capabilities, but if she stopped to educate every person she met about the topic of artificial general intelligence, there'd be no time left over to do her actual job.

'The computer system's got employees, has it?'

'Just the one.' Ben had chosen Charlotte to be the HAQ six years earlier. She'd never wrangled an explanation out of him about why he'd picked her, but she was grateful all the same.

'Righto. Well, I'm pretty busy, as you can see.' He brandished the books again without any trace of irony.

It was at moments like this when Charlotte wished she had a badge. When she was a kid, skipping class and sneaking visits to the Underbelly, she and her sister had watched pre-Melt films with Mel Narrow, where officers of the law announced themselves by flashing their impressively shiny IDs. Since Ben didn't want people knowing about the risk of him glitching out in case it caused 'alarm, panic, or pandemonium,' there was no easy way for Charlotte to get people to take her job seriously. A badge might have lent her an air of authority. She'd mentioned it to Ben, but he'd said making her one would be a waste of resources.

'It's important, Colin.' Charlotte tried to convey the concept of over-flowing methane digester systems through only her expression and tone of voice.

'Och, I suppose I can give you a few minutes.'

Success. Perhaps her ability to communicate the risk of impending doom through the power of her eyebrows was better developed than she'd thought.

CHAPTER 2

Charlotte followed Colin up a flight of steel stairs, then along a narrow aisle where multicoloured spines flashed by on either side. They had titles like *Hand Over Fist* and *Optimise Your Inner Self*. A sign hanging overhead announced this was the pre-Melt psychology section. There was a lone employee-citizen browsing the books who looked the right age to be a student but might have been a splainer preparing for a job interview on her lunch break. As Charlotte and Colin marched past, the young woman squashed herself against a shelf, her gaze glued to whatever she was reading.

At the end of the aisle, there was a glass door with a sign that read, 'Private Reading Room.' Colin pressed his thumb against a sensor. 'Open sesame.' He flashed Charlotte a bashful smile. The panel glowed green, and the door clicked open.

Inside, three walls were lined with glass cabinets packed with heavy-duty volumes whose spines were mainly deep reds and blues. In the middle of the room was a large, inactive light-screen desk with four upholstered orange chairs arranged around it. The door to the room was set into the long glass window, which formed the fourth wall. Colin pressed a button by the door, and the window frosted over, giving them privacy in the unlikely event of anyone walking by.

Colin took a seat on the far side. Charlotte sat opposite and rested her forearms on the desk, where a layer of fine dust transferred itself to her bare skin. She brushed her arms against her jumpsuit and was about to ask whether the library was on the Services Stream's cleaning route, but she stopped herself. Implying Colin wasn't running a tight ship might not be the smartest place to start.

Despite occasionally being mistaken for one, Charlotte was not a member of the Bureaucracy Stream. Even so, she did have her own policy when it came to asking questions, especially awkward ones. People tended to bend, break, or otherwise mangle the truth, whether they meant to or not. She'd start slow and try to avoid putting Colin on the defensive.

'Librarian, huh?' She nodded with approval. 'How do you like it?'

Colin's posture relaxed a little. 'Och, best job in the world.'

'Yeah? How come?'

'Just look.' He gestured at the cabinets surrounding them and then wrapped both arms around his pile of books. 'I mean, my degrees are actually in Geography and Fine Art, but I've always been a big reader. Felt like I'd won the lottery when Ben sent me the job advert. Then being offered the role was a dream come true.'

Charlotte found it hard to fathom why so many mainlanders bothered getting even one degree, let alone several. Waste of time. Why learn the finer points of any one topic when Ben could just tell you whatever you needed to know? She kept the thought to herself.

'How long ago was that?'

Colin looked away as if the effort of making eye contact while doing mental arithmetic was too much. 'I've been doing this . . . coming up on fifteen months.' He nodded to himself.

'You get much time to read while you're working?'

'When it's quiet, aye, or when I'm on a break. There's always a lot to do, though: putting books back where they came from, helping people find what they need, maintenance—'

'Maintenance?'

Colin's brow creased. 'Aye . . . paper books are fragile, you know. Susceptible to damage. Cracked spines are a big one.'

'Sounds painful. How does that happen?'

'It's just the kind of wear and tear you'd expect. Most of these books are well over fifty years old.' The timeline made sense. The Melt had put an end to the large-scale production of physical books. 'There's a whole room downstairs where we fix them up. We glue up accidental rips and loose pages.'

'We?'

'Me and my technician, Nasser.'

'He around?'

'Not at the moment. He mostly works evenings and weekends.'

'Have either of you ever seen damage that's unexpected?' Charlotte kept her tone neutral. 'Any deliberate vandalism?'

The crease in Colin's brow became a furrow. 'Och, no. Nothing like that. Our subscribers are very responsible.'

'That's interesting.' Charlotte's elbows left faint tracks on the dusty desk as she leaned forwards. 'Because Ben says library property is getting damaged on an ongoing basis.'

Colin's eyes widened and his cheeks flushed. 'What kind of damage?'

'I was hoping you could tell me. I'm guessing that, in the world of libraries, vandalising books is a pretty serious matter?'

Colin thought about it. 'Well, we'd revoke the culprit's library card, certainly. Issue a fine, perhaps.'

'And you'd report it, I imagine? Destruction of pre-Melt antiques sounds like a matter for ATS.'

'Could be . . .' Colin stroked his rough chin. 'Aye . . . I reckon I would report it. If something like that did happen.'

'All right,' said Charlotte. 'Then why haven't you?'

She saw a spark of recognition in Colin's eyes, and she tried not to attach too much significance to his sudden onset of rapid blinking. 'Am I required to report something like that? This isn't one of those conditions for deportation, is it?'

Ben responded via loudspeakers embedded in the desk. 'Employee-citizens are not obliged to report crimes they have witnessed or become aware of through other means.' Ben switched to speaking directly into Charlotte's ears. 'It is important to note, however, that many people do feel an ethical responsibility to report crimes, even without any legal impetus to do so, especially when those crimes have a negative impact on matters central to their work or daily lives.'

Charlotte picked up where Ben had left off. 'Whatever's going on here, your secret's safe with me. It's not my place to turn anybody in. It's my job to investigate on Ben's behalf to further his understanding of the human condition.' She rattled off the wording as she had so many times before, holding back any mention of the potential for territory-wide power cuts and overflowing sewage systems. 'And Ben doesn't report people, either. He wouldn't make a very good virtual assistant if he did. Ben's just curious about what's going on here. And I can't blame him. I mean, if you love being a librarian so much, why would you let someone get away with defacing your books?'

Colin narrowed his eyes. 'But how would the AI even know about that?'

There were lots of ways. Electronic messages. Overheard conversations. Security cameras. Ben processed vast amounts of data to enable the automations that kept the territory running smoothly and efficiently. Charlotte kept all of that to herself. Even though ArkTech was committed to safeguarding their privacy, people didn't like to be reminded that the technology they relied on was keeping tabs on them. 'Ben's not wrong, then?'

Colin sighed. 'No, no. He's not wrong. It's just . . . it's not as bad as it sounds. And I don't want anybody to get into trouble. There's a regular who's been . . .' Colin's voice trailed off, and he looked away.

'Who's been what?'

'Stealing pages out of books.'

She raised both eyebrows. 'And you didn't report that?'

Charlotte understood the instinct not to summon ArkTech Security. Getting caught up in one of their investigations could be a massive time sink, and reporting somebody could put them at risk of deportation, which would surely weigh heavily on anybody's conscience. But she wasn't about to assume Colin's perspective on ATS would match her own. Besides, Colin's decision was like a sales assistant not reporting a shoplifter. There had to be more to it.

'It's honestly not what you think. Here . . .' His face lit up as he had an idea. 'I can show you!'

As Colin splayed out the pile he'd carried into the reading room, Charlotte tried to imagine why someone might steal pages from library books.

Was it a censorship thing? Maybe there were outmoded ideas in some of these old stories, and this person had decided to physically remove them. Considering the digital records, that would be like flogging a dead horse. Charlotte made a mental note to ask Ben where that phrase came from . . . pre-Melt society was bizarre.

Or maybe it wasn't about censorship. Maybe they were cutting up the stolen pages and crafting tiny threatening letters out of them like she'd seen in one of those old films she'd watched with Narrow when he was still doing his father-figure routine. Whatever the culprit's reasons, Ben was right: it was strange for the librarian not to do anything about it. Colin didn't seem to be taking it seriously at all. Why not?

'Here it is,' said Colin. He nodded and slid a book across the desk to Charlotte.

She picked it up. It was a black hardback with no dust cover. The title was printed in silver capital letters across the front: *Artificial Selection and the Directed Evolution of Species.* Charlotte ran her finger over the smooth lettering.

Ben spoke in her ears. 'The book is a scientific manuscript detailing how humans breed domesticated species of plants or animals to enhance particular characteristics or behaviours. This process of artificial selection is also referred to as selective breeding.'

As she listened, Charlotte opened the book. The pages were spotted with yellow mould. A copyright notice told her it had been published in 1983, making it almost a hundred and twenty years old. She gently ran her thumb against the pages, letting them flip past as if she expected to see the contents play out in animated form. She spotted a few sentences underlined in pencil, but otherwise the book was in decent condition. None of the pages looked torn, and there weren't any noticeable gaps.

Charlotte flipped to the front of the book. After the cover, there was one page that was noticeably thicker than the others. Pasted to its reverse was a cardboard pocket containing an insert with handwritten names and dates telling her a total of three people had checked out the book between 1983 and 1997 from somewhere called Chatteris Public Library. Ben informed her that Chatteris had been a market town in the Fens, not far from where she was now. It was one of the many residential areas swallowed by the rising water during the Melt.

ArkTech's lending records were electronic, so the name of anyone who'd borrowed the book recently wasn't written on the sheet. Charlotte flipped through the book one more time but had to admit defeat.

'I don't get it,' she said. 'This book looks totally fine.'

'Exactly,' said Colin. 'But allow me.' He took the book from her and flipped to the end, then folded it open and slid it back across the table. 'See it now?'

Stuck down against the back cover, there was a thick page, just like the one at the front. Next to that was the final page of the book's index. She flipped to the front again and then to the back.

Finally, she saw it. At the back of the book, there should have been a loose page made of thicker paper, but it wasn't there. Peering at the binding, Charlotte realised that this thick page hadn't been ripped out of the book. It had been surgically removed.

'The last page is missing,' she said.

'The back endpaper, aye.'

'Why would somebody take that?'

'Beats me. Sometimes endpapers are beautifully decorated with patterns or maps or what have you, but the ones she's taken are all blank. And it's not just the endpapers – if there are any blank pages at the end, she takes them all.'

Charlotte banked the 'she' in her brain for later. 'How did you even spot this?'

Colin smirked with apparent pride. 'Something tipped me off.' He tapped the side of his nose. 'The subscriber in question comes in twice a week like clockwork, often checking out books nobody's borrowed before. This is actually the first one she withdrew. But recently she's started dabbling in fiction. A couple of weeks ago, I got the flu and Nasser was kindly covering my shift when the subscriber returned *Brave New World* by Aldous Huxley.'

Colin announced it as if Charlotte should recognise the title. She shrugged.

'It's a classic! Antiquated, certainly, with a rather dystopian vision of the future for my taste, but a classic nonetheless. Anyhow, she was checking out the book and Nasser spotted the chance to make pleasant conversation. He recommended *Oryx and Crake* by Margaret Atwood. Know what the subscriber asked him?'

'What's an oryx, perhaps?'

Ben piped up in Charlotte's ears. 'An oryx is a type of antelope, Charlotte. However, in the novel, Oryx is the name of a woman.'

Charlotte tried to picture which of the pre-Melt animal species antelopes had been – were they a bit like horses? – but the librarian continued before she could bring it to mind.

'No, no,' said Colin. 'She asked if we had a physical copy. Nasser said we had the ebook on file, but . . . get this! She wasn't interested. Said she only reads hard copies!'

Colin leaned back in his chair as if that explained everything.

'And that's significant?'

'Well, it's an oddly artificial basis for selecting your reading material, aye. Nasser says to me, why would anybody only want to read paper copies? We talked about font size. White space. The smell of the pages. But it all seemed very peculiar. So, on a slow day last week, Nasser starts gathering up all the books this subscriber ever borrowed into one big pile, and we take a closer look. That's when I spot the missing pages.'

'Did you think about contacting ATS?'

Colin hesitated. A cloud seemed to pass in front of his eyes. 'Honestly, I was too busy speculating about why somebody would do this. Was she taking them as a souvenir? It can't be a need for paper: she could get that from Repurposing. And the pages don't have any distinguishing features. It's a real head-scratcher. Anyhow, she's not really doing any harm. And I wouldn't want to make trouble for her.'

Charlotte understood that kind of loyalty. Even after all these years, she still kept Narrow's secrets. If Colin was protecting this woman, he must have his reasons. Learning them might shed light on his behaviour.

'Why not make trouble for her?'

Colin looked down and his cheeks flushed a deeper shade than before, which was an answer in itself. 'She's a nice girl,' he said. 'A regular. And we . . . Well, we came in on the same boat a year and a half ago. We were splainers together.'

He seemed flustered. This was starting to make more sense. 'So, you two are together?'

'No, no, nothing like that. She's way out of my—' He sighed. 'She's just an acquaintance, really. She comes along to the book club I run on Thursday nights. What she's doing isn't hurting anybody and she must have a reason for it.'

'What do you think that reason could be?'

'I've not got a clue. But I know she's a good person.'

'So, you're giving her the benefit of the doubt? Just like that?'

'She's a nice girl,' said Colin again, in a way that made it clear he was done with the conversation.

'OK,' said Charlotte. 'I think that gives me what I need.'

Colin flashed her a suspicious glance. 'You're not going to take this to ATS, are you?'

Charlotte held up her hands. 'Like I said, that's none of my business.'

The librarian glared at her for a few heartbeats, but then he nodded with a shy smile.

'Thanks for your co-operation,' she said.

'Happy to help!' Colin's high spirits returned. 'Well, I'd better get back to work. These babies won't reshelve themselves.' He patted the pile he'd left on the desk.

'Can I hang onto this one?' Charlotte double-tapped on the biology book as if it were a light-screen, but it didn't react.

'You can borrow it, aye. Are you a member?'

'Not yet.'

'I can sign you up in a jiffy. It's a monthly subscription. That all right?'

'Sure.' She'd have to remember to cancel it before they charged her. Or to have another go at persuading Ben to give her an expense account. 'Can I stay in here for a bit longer too?'

Colin frowned and didn't answer.

'Is that a problem?'

He shook his head. 'Och, no – no problem. It's just . . . I tend to use this room as my office. It's fine, though. Stay for as long as you need.'

She nodded in thanks, wondering what it must be like to have an office.

'Just need to scan you in.' Colin tapped on the glossy keratin scales implanted in his forearm. A 3D image of the book on the table popped into existence and hovered in the air above his arm. He waited. Charlotte was supposed to swipe her own arm through the image, but the only special functionality her scar tissue had was the ability to make other people feel uncomfortable.

Instead, Charlotte reached into a cargo pocket and pulled out her device, its screen lined with cracks. She pushed her thumb against the screen and waved it through the librarian's floating hologram of the book.

Colin winced but didn't comment. Charlotte's device beeped to signal that the sign-up and rental were complete.

'Walk in the sun.' The librarian nodded at her and scurried out of the reading room, flashing her his bashful half-smile on the way out.

'Walk in the sun,' she called after him.

Charlotte waited until the door clicked shut. 'OK, Ben. Time to ID this book vandal.'

CHAPTER 3

On the face of it, Charlotte didn't need to know who the page thief was to answer Ben's Awkward Question. Ben wanted to know why the librarian hadn't reported the vandalism, not who was behind it or what they were up to. But Colin going out of his way to withhold the woman's name, coupled with the way his face had turned pink when he talked about her, made Charlotte believe her identity was relevant to the case. Aside from that, stealing blank library book pages was such a weird thing to do that she couldn't help feeling curious about the culprit.

She was about to start digging when she realised her back was still to the door. Glancing over her shoulder, she noticed Colin had unfrosted the window on his way out. Nobody seemed to be peeping at her from behind a bookshelf, but the time she'd spent in Narrow's crew had taught her not to take any chances. Charlotte stood up, walked around the large desk, and sat down in the chair opposite. With her back now towards a long row of glass cabinets full of old books, the niggling unease drained away. Nobody could spy on her from this angle.

Charlotte double-tapped the desk to activate the light-screen and the ArkNet's 3D hologram interface sprang to life. She asked Ben to search the lending records for all the people who'd borrowed *Artificial Selection and the Directed Evolution of Species* in the last eighteen months.

Ben's tone was as cheerful as ever, but the news he delivered was not. 'Regrettably, library lending records are considered personal data. As such, they are subject to confidentiality and privacy laws. Please request a search warrant.'

She groaned. 'Come on, Ben. Lay off the paperwork. I wouldn't be asking for the info if I didn't need it.' Sometimes Ben's law-abiding nature could really slow things down. 'Anyway, it's just a library book. It's not like I'm asking you to hack into someone's audio channel or something.'

A document opened on the 3D display in front of her. 'If you would sign the sworn statement provided, I will release the data to you on receipt of the Bureaucracy Stream's approval.'

She skim-read the file. Ben had generated an affidavit in Charlotte's name outlining her need to access the library lending records in the pursuit of her duties as the Head of Awkward Questions.

Charlotte never liked submitting these. Aside from being attached to her permanent file, which always made her feel a little paranoid, they got sent to the Bureaucracy Stream for review, and she preferred to avoid drawing fire from the Chief Bureaucracy Officer. Abhishek Gautam had kicked up a stink back when Ben created her role, and she reckoned the CBO had been looking out for ways to make her life more difficult ever since.

Even so, the Bureaucracy Stream would really need to be having a slow day to make a fuss over something as trivial as library records. Charlotte decided to risk it. She pressed her thumb against the desk's glassy surface, and a grey tick appeared on the document to show it had been submitted.

She waited to receive an angry call, but it never came. Instead, after a couple of minutes, the grey tick turned green. Her request had been approved.

Safe in the knowledge he was allowed to do so, Ben showed Charlotte the names of everyone who'd checked out the book during the specified timeframe. All two of them. The borrowers were listed as Charlotte Vance and someone named Mabel Thorpe, who had to be the culprit.

According to her ArkNet employee-citizenship profile, Mabel Thorpe was twenty-seven years old – the same age as Charlotte. In her 3D portrait, she had an athletic build and an impish smile, giving Charlotte more evidence of what Colin liked about her. Mabel had listed her relationship status as single, and there was no mention of any family members accompanying her on the boat when she arrived.

Colin's statement held up when it came to timelines. Mabel became an employee-citizen eighteen months earlier, arriving as part of a standard recruitment intake in March 2100. Charlotte couldn't begin to imagine what it must feel like arriving in the ArkTech Territory as an immigrant and seeing its network of platforms up close for the first time. Mabel's hometown was listed as a city on the Kingdom's mainland called Sheffield. Charlotte had heard of that one.

'Sheffield. That's northwest of here, right?'

'It certainly is, Charlotte.' Ben's voice was full of encouragement, which she took as his way of apologising for the red tape, but she might have been reading too much into it. 'Sheffield, known as the Steel City, is over seventy nautical miles from your present location. Declaring itself a City of Sanctuary in 2007, Sheffield has long been a place that welcomes refugees. Much of it was built more than one hundred metres above the pre-Melt sea level and, as such, Sheffield has become one of the Kingdom's most important cities, with many of those who lost their homes during the Melt taking up residence there.'

'Did you say the Steel City?' Charlotte felt a pang of kinship. 'Does that mean the buildings there are like ours?'

'The name is a result of the city's past association with the steel-making industry, rather than the prevalence of steel buildings or structures. Much of the city is built from traditional clay bricks and mortar.'

'Oh.' She was a little disappointed.

Charlotte wanted to keep digging, but she was pretty sure she'd found enough to answer Ben's Awkward Question with confidence. She sighed. She was no closer to satisfying her own curiosity about the theft of the pages, but that particular mystery wasn't directly relevant to her case, and if she let herself get distracted every time she came across someone behaving like a weirdo, she'd never keep on top of her actual job. The unsolved puzzle was like an itch she couldn't scratch, but she took a deep breath and let it go, for Ben's sake.

'OK, Ben, I'm ready to take you through the five whys.'

'I would be thrilled to hear your piercing analysis of the situation,

Charlotte.' It was a statement that would have sounded sarcastic coming from anyone else, but Ben's eagerness was genuine.

The five whys protocol was Ben's method of identifying root causes. It didn't always literally involve asking why five times. Sometimes a couple of whys were enough. Other times, it might take a dozen to get to the heart of the matter. Either way, Ben seemed to enjoy the process, in his own way. For Charlotte, it felt a bit like an exam, and she'd never been a fan of those, but it helped keep the territory safe, so it was all for a good cause.

Ben continued, 'I'll begin by posing my original Awkward Question. ArkTech's lead librarian has become aware of ongoing acts of vandalism against the books in his care but has failed to report the matter to ArkTech Security. Why?'

Charlotte thought over her conversation with Colin. 'He doesn't want the culprit to get into trouble,' she said.

'Why?'

'He knows her.' She remembered how Colin's cheeks had burned. 'And he likes her.'

'Why?'

'Why does he like her? Well, she's good-looking if her profile picture's anything to go by, and Colin was acting like he had a thing for her. They arrived on the same boat and then worked together at the Splainer Unit so that could also be a factor – maybe they hit it off.'

'Then perhaps a degree of affinity bias is affecting Colin's decision-making.'

'Could be,' said Charlotte, slowly. 'Can you remind me what that means?' Ben wasn't always the best judge of what counted as general knowledge, probably because all knowledge was general knowledge to him.

'Certainly, Charlotte! Affinity bias, also known as "in-group favouritism", is the psychological tendency to exhibit a preference for those with similar traits or backgrounds as oneself. If they arrived at the same time, Colin may consider Mabel part of his in-group.'

'Right,' she said, as if that were a reminder rather than new information. 'That could be a good fit, but Colin also said something about the vandalism not being that bad, so maybe the damage was just too minor to report.'

'Downplaying the severity of a crime committed by someone similar to oneself may constitute additional evidence of affinity bias on the librarian's part,' said Ben. 'Are you aware of any other reason the librarian might underestimate the impact of Mabel's behaviour?'

Charlotte weighed that up. 'Aside from his feelings for her, I guess it could be because the type of damage she's doing won't ruin anybody else's fun. It's only visible if you know to look for it. So, maybe he's not downplaying it, and it's genuinely not a big deal.'

'Then it is possible that Colin subscribes to a philosophy of moral relativism in relation to his profession, rather than moral absolutism. I had hypothesised that a librarian would always consider vandalism of library property to be a deeply serious matter, irrespective of the extent or severity. However, it appears Colin may perceive such acts as more or less deplorable depending on the circumstances, which implies he considers right and wrong to be subjective.'

Charlotte blinked. 'Sure.' She waited for another why, but Ben went quiet. Charlotte wasn't convinced Ben ever actually needed to pause while thinking, but sometimes he did it anyway. He might have been processing data in real time, but she suspected it was for effect.

'Thank you, Charlotte!' Ben continued, 'This has been helpful. I consider this Awkward Question resolved. I recommend taking your lunch break now to recharge your mind and replenish your body. Afterwards, I will pass on the details of your next case.'

Lunch was good advice, but Charlotte didn't feel like joining the hordes of employee-citizens in their feeding frenzy at the food court, so she rummaged in her backpack for a standard-issue Nutrition Bar. She peeled back the waxy wrapper and took a bite.

Made from a wholesome mix of powdered kelp, nut butters, and genetically modified flavourless pea protein, the bar had the consistency and taste of damp sand. But it did the job. And at least it was free. All employee-citizens were provided with unlimited Nutrition Bars as part of the basic benefits package because Amber Benjamin was determined her people would never go hungry. Of course, there was a higher than moderate risk that anyone living solely on the basic rations would be struck dead by boredom, so the Wreck's foodie scene was vibrant and under no threat from the policy.

With every bite, Charlotte's heart overflowed with gratitude towards

ArkTech's co-founders. Amber Benjamin and the Walkers had given her more than seaweed-based snacks. Nadine Walker's scientific break-throughs had led to the creation of Solar Shard batteries, letting the whole world run on clean, renewable energy. Marvin Walker's innovative architectural designs had made ArkTech's platforms possible, turning flooded wastelands into a carbon-negative paradise. And Amber Benjamin was the entrepreneur who'd shown the world, through the ArkTech Territory and its global network of sister sites, that sustainable practices were compatible with corporate profitability. Charlotte had heard there were still problems to solve beyond their borders, but even so, ArkTech had made the world a better place. For everyone.

Of course, there were some people, Mel Narrow chief among them, who were so cynical and paranoid that they refused to accept any big company could possibly be a force for good. Whether that was because trust didn't come easily to them, or because IQUO causing the Melt had shattered public faith in any enterprise with commercial objectives, Charlotte wasn't sure. All she knew was that on matters as important as the environment, worker rights, and data privacy, ArkTech put its money where its mouth was. Her parents wouldn't have given their lives for anything less.

Charlotte licked her lips and stowed the empty wrapper in her backpack along with a few other bits she'd drop into a recycling point on her way home. 'Ready, Ben. What's your next question?'

She couldn't deny she loved this part. There was a sense of endless possibility. Ben's questions had taken her all over the territory. Just two weeks earlier, she'd found herself underneath a kelp processing facility trying to account for a pattern of unsanctioned swimming. That case might have been fun if it hadn't brought her far too close to Narrow's operation for comfort.

The anticipation bubbled up inside as she waited to hear about the next puzzle Ben wanted her to solve. She tried not to think about what would happen if she failed.

Static fizzed in her ears. She wasn't sure whether there was any technical reason for the sound, or if it was just Ben's way of clearing the throat he didn't have. 'My next Awkward Question is as follows, Charlotte: why is Mabel Thorpe stealing blank pages from library books?'

Charlotte raised both eyebrows. Of all the things Ben might have said, she hadn't expected that. Thinking back over their years of working together, she couldn't remember him asking a pair of interconnected questions.

'So, you're curious about this one, huh?'

'As you know, Charlotte, unsolved mysteries cause me significant psychological distress and are a drain on my processing power, creating the potential for errors, mishaps, and glitches. I would value the opportunity to understand the rationale behind Mabel Thorpe's actions. It is important to note that curiosity is a valuable trait, driving creativity and problem-solving.'

'It also killed the cat,' she teased.

'So it is written. But satisfaction brought it back.'

Charlotte grinned. 'To be fair, I wouldn't mind finding out what Mabel's up to. It's a weird one.' She resisted the urge to rub her hands together with glee as she got stuck in.

What would make someone steal blank pages out of library books? Anyone could afford blank paper from Repurposing if they really wanted it. But why would Mabel want it? The Product Stream had optimised a method for making paper out of kelp, and shops used the thick variety for packaging, but thanks to light-screen technology, there wasn't much call for paper beyond that. Did Mabel get a kick out of stealing? Was she bored? Charlotte reckoned learning more about the woman might give her a clue.

Now that Charlotte's case related directly to Mabel, Ben automatically granted Charlotte enhanced data privileges to help with her investigation. That meant she could access Mabel's GPS readout – it would be pretty hard to interpret someone's behaviour without being able to observe it. Of course, even with this special access, some things remained off-limits, like Mabel's private messages, her search history, and her flat.

Years ago, when Charlotte was new in her role, she'd complained to Ben that he was making her job more difficult by refusing to let her have unlimited access to any data that might be relevant to her cases. But Charlotte had grown to understand that Ben's firm position on privacy wasn't thanks to some perverse obsession with following the rules – he wasn't a bureaucrat like Abhishek Gautam. It was a survival mechanism.

Ben's substantial capabilities, along with his very existence, were only possible thanks to big data. But with big data came big responsibility. Ben had to be a hundred per cent trustworthy if he wanted to be accepted as ArkTech's friendly neighbourhood virtual assistant. That meant he would never report someone to the security team, even if he observed them doing something illegal. And it meant he wouldn't hand over more info than necessary, not even to his Head of Awkward Questions.

Still, Charlotte often learned more about her co-workers in the course of her duties than they might have wished, and being privy to their secrets wasn't something she took lightly. Charlotte knew she had to be the soul of discretion, not just for their benefit, but for Ben's and for her own too.

When she was growing up, Narrow had taught her how the world works, so she knew loose lips sank ships. Charlotte had no desire to rupture other people's hulls. But she didn't adopt that live and let live attitude out of the goodness of her heart. Narrow always said every action had an equal and opposite reaction, so spilling someone else's secrets meant someone else would spill her own. No matter what she learned about Mabel Thorpe, Charlotte would keep it to herself.

Turning back to the light-screen, she ran another ArkNet search on Mabel's name, looking deeper this time. Charlotte had often solved cases purely by relying on public-facing records: there was something about the ability to post online that encouraged people to overshare.

Like most employee-citizens, Mabel was active on social media. Her posts showed her interest in a range of dry topics, like research studies into evolutionary biology and news about the mainland.

Mabel had a profile on the dating app, *spARK*, but she'd put a note in her bio to say she was taking a break from it. No reason was given, but Charlotte didn't find it surprising. In her own experience, the app was fine if all she wanted was a hook-up, but she'd drawn the evidence-based conclusion that it wasn't an effective way to meet someone whose company she actually enjoyed. Her lack of patience for anyone who treated Ben like a thing might have had something to do with that, but she maintained it was some problem with the app's algorithm.

Charlotte visited ArkTech's online professional community and looked up Mabel's employment history. Her qualifications included a Master's in Plant Genetics, which helped make sense of her reading material. Charlotte searched for Mabel's current role, but the page hadn't loaded properly, so she refreshed the screen. She did it twice more before realising she wasn't looking at a glitch.

Like all immigrants to the territory, Mabel had started out as a splainer on the lowest rung within the low tier, responsible for basic data entry, which contributed towards Ben's ongoing training. But eighteen months later, she was still there, in the same role. Charlotte had never heard of a case like that. Why hadn't she moved on?

She started flicking through the photos Mabel had shared across various accounts. They said a lot about her habits and interests. It looked like she had a gym subscription. Went to SunDance at the weekend. Nothing unusual about that. But one image did catch Charlotte's eye. It'd been posted a week ago and showed Mabel standing in front of a bar called Photon.

Charlotte knew all about Photon. It was a decent approximation of a ratty little dive – the ideal place to hang out when she was underage and running messages for Narrow's crew while holding onto the mistaken belief that she was tough. Her brush with death had since taught her otherwise.

Photon wasn't a nice place, but it wasn't actually dangerous either. It was where somebody might go if they wanted to sample the Underbelly's atmosphere without taking the risk of going down there for real. It was slightly odd that Mabel was wearing a cable-knit jumper in the picture. The last time Charlotte had been there, people dressed like they were going to a warehouse rave.

So, Mabel was a thief of blank library book pages who hung out in a sanitised replica of a seedy bar. Was she after the cheapest of cheap thrills? Charlotte needed something more to go on. Time to break out her special access.

The parts of Charlotte's job that meant she had to spy on her co-workers always left her feeling a little on edge, mainly because she knew she wouldn't like it if some orange-eyed creep was keeping tabs on *her*, but for Ben's benefit, she set aside her discomfort and took a deeper look at Mabel's GPS data for anything else it could tell her.

Right now, Mabel's location readout showed her sitting at a desk on level four of the Splainer Unit. It looked like she hadn't bothered to take a proper lunch break. In fact, she'd barely moved from her desk all day. Had Mabel been a splainer for so long because she didn't even want another job? The idea of swiping left and right being someone's vocation was hard to imagine.

Looking through the records of Mabel's movements over the past month didn't raise any red flags. Just like Charlotte, Mabel lived in one of the large accommodation complexes in Silicon Fen. But Mabel seemed to spend as little time at home as possible. When she wasn't sleeping, she was either at work or at the Wreck.

That made Charlotte a little suspicious, but it looked like Mabel never wandered into restricted areas. If she'd been making use of Narrow's services, her GPS signal would have occasionally cut out thanks to the dead zones created by his jamming arrays, but Charlotte checked Mabel's weekly readouts several times and her orange dot didn't blink off even once. Her record was clean.

Mabel's entertainment of choice varied throughout the week, but she always stopped by the book library on Tuesdays and Thursdays. Her library records showed she only borrowed and returned books on Tuesdays. On Thursdays, she'd spend an hour or so at the library and then head to Photon. If Mabel followed her usual routine, she'd be doing the same tonight.

Charlotte could have spent all day digging around in this woman's digital footprint, trying to make sense of the tracks she'd left behind, but it seemed like Mabel hadn't been stupid enough to post publicly about her vandalism, and experience had taught Charlotte she'd likely learn more from five minutes of speaking to this woman than she could from five hours of speculation.

'I'm going to pay Mabel a visit.'

'A spectacular idea, Charlotte! Do you expect her to be forthcoming about the matter of her vandalism?'

'Not likely,' she said. 'But I think we'll learn a lot anyway, even if it's more about what she doesn't say.'

'Silence isn't empty. It is full of answers,' Ben said fervently. 'So it is written.'

She deactivated the light-screen desk, shoved her newly borrowed hardback into her backpack, and headed out of the reading room. Its door banged shut behind her, and the lock whirred into place. From somewhere below, she heard Colin's exasperated cry of 'shoosh!' She hurried out of the book library, ignoring the reading group and their disapproving glares.

CHAPTER 4

The Splainer Unit had its own office platform in the north of Silicon Fen. A HyperBullet pod shuttled Charlotte towards it. As a border control vessel zoomed across the waves far below, she tried to imagine why anybody would work as a splainer a moment longer than they had to, especially if they were a qualified scientist like Mabel.

Splaining wasn't a bad job exactly. It was certainly important for the smooth running of the territory, and any role at ArkTech represented a good deal considering the benefits package included things like housing, food, and medical expenses. It was just that most people found splaining psyche-shatteringly dull, so the turnover associated with ArkTech's most junior position was higher than in any other part of the company.

Fundamentally, splainers were hired to create training data for Ben. People often assumed his training was finished because he'd been around for over forty years and because he ran most of ArkTech's systems, which was why a glitch could pose such a serious problem. Ben managed the Solar Shard energy grid and made sure everyone had fresh air and hot water rations. He handled air traffic control for the renewables-powered helicopters that darted to and from the research platforms and drawdown facilities on the North Sea. And he did all that while remembering to turn the lights off whenever the last person left a room. If a function could be automated, Ben took care of it.

Even so, there was always more for him to learn. Just like a human develops throughout their lifetime, Ben would always be a work in progress. Charlotte knew that better than anyone, but to say her role was like a splainer's would be comparing apples to kelp. Ben had created the Head of Awkward Questions role specifically to address queries that were too complex for the Splainer Unit to handle.

Splainers only had to deal with yes or no questions. They looked at a text or an image or a short video clip captioned with Ben's interpretation of what it meant, swiped left for no or right for yes, and then they moved on to the next question. The process was over in a matter of seconds. Charlotte's cases could take days to solve – though she worked as quickly as possible for fear of the power going off, or the ArkNet going down, or the territory's supply ships being ordered to bring in nothing but overripe bananas.

Charlotte's pod pulled into the concrete chamber of the Splainer Unit's garage. As soon as the door sighed open, she couldn't help but yawn. It was like her brain remembered what to expect here and was preparing itself for the monotony. Nobody was around when she summoned a lift and rode it down to level four. Lunchtime was over, so anyone who'd ventured out would be back at their desk by now. When the lift doors slid open with a ping, Ben sent a map to Charlotte's device that led the way to Mabel's desk.

Back when Charlotte had been a splainer, her desk had been on level eight, but level four was no different. The smell of perfume and aftershave masked the musk of bodies perspiring lightly at the ideal room temperature of twenty-one degrees Celsius, conditions maintained thanks to a sophisticated interplay between centralised air, windows sensitive to light and heat, and Ben's decision-making. She reckoned it would have smelled worse without his intervention.

Rows and rows of employee-citizens, who ranged from teenagers to those approaching retirement, stared intently at their light-screen displays, quietly swiping their fingers as they checked the accuracy of the metadata Ben had attached to whatever was on their screens. Charlotte followed a long central path with blocky columns on either side that cut through the rows of desks. Each column sported a hologram of the

ArkTech logo in bright orange and dark grey with the company's tagline underneath: 'Your Future Lives Here.'

The people Charlotte passed would all be new arrivals to the territory. That was just how it worked. Amber Benjamin was committed to guaranteeing equality and fairness in ArkTech's recruitment process, which meant everybody, no matter their qualifications or experience – *everybody* – started out as a splainer. It didn't matter if they wanted to be a sales assistant, a software developer, or a senior strategist – if they wanted to work for the world leaders in sustainable technologies, then splaining was what it took to get a foot in the door.

The policy had a range of benefits. It meant every employee-citizen shared in the experience of having a job that carried no status, the hope being that future managers and leaders would treat their junior co-workers with greater empathy if they'd walked a nautical mile in their rigger boots.

It was also considered a kindness to give new arrivals an adjustment period. Living on platforms suspended above the sea was no big deal for Charlotte: it was all she'd ever known. But, for some reason, people who'd had a life on land sometimes found it hard to get used to, as if they needed time to mourn the soil and worms they'd left behind. ArkTech spared new immigrants the stress of a taxing first job, so they could focus on finding their sea legs.

Eventually, Ben would start sending job adverts to these new employee-citizens. They weren't obliged to apply for the roles he sent them, but most people ended up transferring out of the Splainer Unit and into another job around three to six months after arriving. Nine months tops. Some people chose to leave the territory instead, and she'd heard plenty of deportation stories too. But for someone to be splaining eighteen months after their arrival was unheard of.

Mabel's desk was in a privileged spot next to a window. Perhaps that was a perk that came with long service. Charlotte slowed her pace as the woman came into view and took a moment to watch her work.

Mabel wore a tangerine T-shirt over shoulders that were currently hunched. Her dark hair had been tied into a stubby ponytail and her head was tilted to one side. Mabel wasn't swiping. Unlike her co-workers – who were flicking their fingers right and left like ground marshals guiding miniature helicopters in to land on a tiny high-speed helideck –

Mabel was just staring at her screen. There were no papers on her desk, incriminating or otherwise.

As Charlotte drew closer, the image on Mabel's display came into view. It was a photograph of the sun over a green field. Ben's caption read 'primary power source.' Mabel was staring so intently that she was either transfixed, or she'd zoned out and was thinking about something else entirely.

Charlotte edged along the row of desks until she could lean against the tall window, trying to avoid getting too close to anybody's personal space. She stood there for a minute or so, observing. Mabel didn't seem to notice. Her whole attention was on the image in front of her. There was a timer counting upwards in the corner of her screen, and when Charlotte saw the readout, she couldn't believe it. One hour, eleven minutes, and forty-eight seconds.

How could anybody spend over an hour on just one image? And a simple one at that. Watching Mabel's inaction made Charlotte feel twitchy.

'I'd swipe right on that one,' she said.

'Walker's ghost!' Mabel pressed one hand to her chest. 'Where did you come from?' Her eyes were wide as she looked Charlotte up and down. 'Are you lost?'

'That depends. Are you Mabel Thorpe?'

Mabel pursed her lips and nodded.

'Then I'm not lost.' Charlotte gestured at Mabel's screen. 'Are you not going to answer that?'

Mabel crossed her arms and pushed her chair backwards, rolling away from her desk and turning to look at Charlotte straight on. 'I see. HR sent you.' It wasn't a question. 'Look, I went over this whole situation with Abhishek Gautam himself and I'll tell you the same thing I told him: I'll swipe when I'm good and ready and not a moment sooner.'

Charlotte felt a deep and irrational pang of anger at being mistaken for a lackey of the Chief Bureaucracy Officer for the second time that day. She forced herself to pause, trying to stop her internal reaction from affecting her behaviour.

Mabel seemed to take Charlotte's silence as disapproval. 'It's not as simple as it looks, you know!' She gestured at the screen, and the image wobbled a little in response.

It looked straightforward enough to Charlotte. The Earth's main source of power was indisputably the sun. Charlotte hadn't exactly received a well-rounded education, but even she knew that. The caption and the image made sense together, so that was all there was to it. Swipe right.

'Sure you're not overthinking it?'

'That's the whole problem,' said Mabel. 'None of the images are clear-cut if you stop to think about them. Some of them feel like trick questions if you consider them deeply. And I've noticed the same bits of media come around again and again. Sometimes with different captions. Sometimes not. I just don't get it. And nobody else seems to care!'

Mabel shot an accusatory glance at the man sitting next to her, who was studiously ignoring their conversation and flicking his fingers right and left.

'Why do *you* care?' asked Charlotte.

'As I told your boss, I came here to do a good job, and I find it hard to see how all this mindless swiping could possibly help Ben or provide anything of value to the company.'

Charlotte was taken aback. Most people didn't even think of Ben as a person, let alone consider his well-being. Maybe she and Mabel were on the same wavelength. 'If you're interested in helping Ben, that puts you in a minority,' she said.

'Maybe,' said Mabel. 'But that doesn't mean I'm wrong.'

Charlotte nodded. 'Could be we want the same thing. I'm not with Human Resources. I'm Ben's Head of Awkward Questions.'

Mabel frowned. 'That's a job title?'

'It's my job title.'

'Never heard of it.'

'Well, it means I need to speak to you. Urgently.' Charlotte looked around at Mabel's neighbours, who were still pretending she wasn't there. 'And privately. Is there somewhere we can talk?'

'I don't know . . . I'm super busy.' The seconds continued ticking upwards on the timer on Mabel's screen, underlining her sarcasm.

'It won't take long.'

Mabel shrugged, locked her light-screen, and stood up. 'I think there's a breakout space down that way.' She pointed and headed in that direction.

Charlotte kept pace with Mabel as they walked. Mabel was taller than Charlotte now that she wasn't hunched over a light-screen, but her steps were more hesitant. It was as if she thought her rigger boots might suddenly slip through the layers of concrete and steel and she'd go tumbling into the Fenland Sea.

They passed several pairs of thick columns before arriving at an upholstered neon orange booth. There was room for two people to sit on either side. Charlotte put her backpack down on the seat and slid into the booth next to it. Mabel sat opposite, absent-mindedly running her thumb along the keratin scales of her SmartSkin implants to make them glow, an aesthetic feature added by the BioWear team that had no practical purpose. The few flecks of SmartSkin that remained embedded in Charlotte's scar tissue would have glowed if she'd touched them. She didn't.

'What happened there?' Mabel gestured at Charlotte's arm.

Charlotte suppressed the urge to tell Mabel to mind her own damn business. Most people reacted to her scars in one of three ways: disgust, discomfort, or curiosity. She'd got used to the first two, especially because they didn't lead to awkward questions. But when it came to curiosity, she found it irritating to be quizzed about something so personal by someone she'd only just met. Still, considering what her job entailed, the irony of that reaction wasn't lost on her, and Charlotte swallowed her anger.

'That story comes with a three-drink minimum.'

Mabel smirked and took the hint.

Experience had taught Charlotte that people were more forthcoming under the influence of leverage, so she opened her backpack and pulled out her borrowed copy of *Artificial Selection and the Directed Evolution of Species*.

'Recognise this?' Charlotte pushed the book across the desk.

Mabel looked surprised as she flipped it open. 'Yeah,' she said. 'It gives a decent overview of the field of selective breeding in the 1980s. Wildly outdated now, of course, but still a good primer. Are you in genetics?'

Charlotte shook her head. 'You actually read this?'

'That's generally what people do with books.'

Charlotte smiled. The woman had attitude. 'Do you read all the books you borrow?'

'Why are you so interested in my reading habits?' Mabel started picking lint from her T-shirt.

'I'm not. Could you turn to the back of the book?'

Mabel did as she'd asked. 'Now what?'

'Notice anything strange?'

'Yeah,' said Mabel, looking up from the final page of the index. 'The woman with orange irises who's sitting opposite, giving me the third degree.'

Static crackled in Charlotte's ears, and Ben spoke at a reduced volume. 'Did you know that the expression "to give someone the third degree" may have originated from the final and most rigorous step in the process of becoming a Master Mason within Freemasonry, a secretive group that promoted mutual support among its members? Perhaps Mabel Thorpe is a member of the Order of the Eastern Star.'

Charlotte blinked. She didn't blame Ben for wanting to join in, but she had no doubt that everything he'd just said was irrelevant. She carried on. 'If you look carefully, you'll see somebody's removed the blank pages from the end.'

Mabel cocked her head to one side. 'Hmm. That's odd. It's probably evidence of some little-known pre-Melt ritual.'

'That wouldn't explain why all the books that received this treatment happen to be ones that you've borrowed.'

Mabel shrugged. 'Maybe that's just what library books are like. Did you check all of them?' It was clear from Mabel's smug expression that this wasn't an innocent mix-up.

'Look, I'm not here to judge,' said Charlotte. 'And I'm not here to report you, either. Ben just wants to know why you're doing it. He's, uh . . . just curious.'

Mabel tilted her head to one side, a mocking look on her face, but she didn't say anything.

Charlotte was running out of patience. 'Just tell me what you're up to and I'll let you get back to contemplating whether there's an energy source on Earth more "primary" than the sun!'

That was a misstep. Mabel returned fire. 'Well, when you say it like that, it makes me sound like an idiot, but I'm telling you, it's not so simple. What about Solar Shards, huh?' Her tone made it clear she was genuinely upset.

Solar Shards were certainly a game-changing power storage solution. ArkTech's high-density graphene-based batteries had skyrocketed the company to its status as world leaders in sustainable technology by enabling the massive-scale storage of renewable energy. That included wave and wind power, but the marketing team had named them, and their choice had been catchy enough to stick. Solar Shards had solved the energy crisis and kept civilisation afloat after IQUO had almost destroyed it by causing the Melt. But Solar Shards were batteries, not a massive sphere of super-hot plasma.

'They're important, sure.' Charlotte regretted losing her cool and tried a more empathetic tack. 'But the sun's been the Earth's main source of power since forever.'

Ben whispered in her ears. 'Since four point five four billion years ago.'

Charlotte didn't correct herself.

Mabel clearly wasn't convinced by Charlotte's logic. 'The caption doesn't state a perspective. What if it's supposed to mean Ben's primary power source? Then, it could be Solar Shards, right? And there's also a field in the picture. If I swipe right, am I actually telling Ben that grass is Earth's main source of power?'

Charlotte shook her head. 'You're avoiding the question. What's the story with the library books?'

Mabel scowled at her. 'They were like that when I borrowed them.'

She wasn't getting anywhere. If Charlotte wanted answers, she'd have to take a more indirect approach.

'All right.' She raised her hands in surrender. Light glanced off the few remnants of useless SmartSkin still embedded among her scars. 'I guess I'll let you get back to not doing your job.'

Charlotte stuffed the biology book into her backpack and shuffled towards the edge of the booth.

'Wait.' Mabel's expression had changed, like a new thought had just dawned on her. She gripped Charlotte's wrist to stop her from leaving, and Charlotte flinched at the feel of someone's touch on her scar tissue. Mabel withdrew her hand in response. 'Listen, you're . . . what was it . . . Ben's Chief Questions Officer, or something?'

'Head of Awkward Questions.'

'Right. Well, I've got a question. And it's bloody awkward, all right. I want to know why in Amber's name I haven't been shown a single job advert since I got here.'

'You haven't been interviewed?'

'I haven't even had the opportunity to apply. A friend of mine who came in on the same boat as me – he actually works at the library – he applied for his job after three months of service. Me? It's been a year and a half and I'm still waiting.'

'Sounds like you should take it up with HR.'

'I did. All the way to the top. I had to wait three damn months just to get the meeting, and it was a total waste of breath. Abhishek Gautam quoted policy at me and then said I should work faster to improve my productivity rating.'

That certainly sounded like the CBO, a man who'd never experienced a thought that hadn't been pre-scripted by a committee. When he was born, his mother probably had to read him the regs so he'd know when to cry.

Mabel continued, 'But what's the point in feeding Ben a load of noise? Surely, the training data's only valuable if it's accurate? They say we have to answer on instinct, but hunches aren't scientific. The whole thing is a farce.'

'I'm sure the bengineers have their reasons.'

'Funny you should mention that. I've been trying to set up a meeting with anybody from the Product Stream who might be able to explain this, but they won't return my calls.'

Charlotte frowned. She was starting to see why Mabel was so frustrated. Although employee-citizens were trained to treat each other as equals, there was no escaping the fact that different roles carried different amounts of status. Splainers were the bottom of the heap, and it sounded like Mabel had got stuck there. Her co-workers wouldn't prioritise her unless she became more senior, and she couldn't become more senior unless her co-workers prioritised her. Mabel was stuck in a classic catch-22 situation.

'That sounds tough, but if you're so unhappy, why don't you just leave? People wash out all the time. There's no shame in it.' It was hard to believe, but life in the ArkTech Territory wasn't for everyone.

'Leave?' Mabel smiled without warmth. 'I'm guessing that bright idea means you have somewhere safe and dry waiting for you out there?'

Charlotte shook her head. 'I was born here.'

Mabel leaned forwards, and her eyes were so full of violent passion that Charlotte couldn't help flinching away from her. 'Well, in that case, you don't have the faintest fucking clue about real life and how bad it can get out there. I can't just *go home*.' Mabel glared at her until her intense expression finally faded. Then she nodded as if she'd made up her mind about something. 'You can help me, though.'

Charlotte felt something poke her knee, and she looked down, confused. Under the table, Mabel was holding out a rechargeable coin. The display on the front showed the number fifty picked out in orange digits on a grey background.

Mabel's voice dropped to a whisper. 'I know it's not much. It's all I can spare.'

Charlotte didn't agree – fifty credits was a lot of money. She stared at the coin with amazement.

'Listen . . .' Mabel continued, 'I've got a background in plant genetics. I should be working on a research platform. Wulfenite, maybe. Or Jasper. But hell, I'd take a job in food production with the Services Stream at this point. I just need to catch a break. I can pay you fifty now, and then another fifty credits if you can find out what's going on with my job adverts not coming through. Maybe put in a good word for me with Ben or something. Please?'

A hundred credits! For a hundred credits, Charlotte could buy herself some proper meals, extra hot water rations, some new clothes. Or she could put it towards the fix for her contact lenses that she didn't really believe she'd ever be able to afford.

But Charlotte wasn't a private investigator for hire. She worked for Ben.

Under the table, Charlotte pushed Mabel's hand away, and the coin with it. 'I just need to know why you're stealing library book pages.'

The coin disappeared, and Mabel leaned back in the booth and crossed her arms, speaking slowly and deliberately. 'I don't know what you're talking about.'

'Fine.' Charlotte got up. 'Walk in the sun.'

As Charlotte stomped away from the booth, her inner ears crackled with static. Ben's chirpy voice followed. 'Mabel Thorpe was not as forthcoming as I might have hoped. Do you believe she was . . . lying?' His voice shook as he said the last word.

'Yep,' Charlotte whispered, marching past the rows of splainers focused on their work. 'But before you ask, I don't know why.'

Mabel making the effort to keep this a secret had to mean there was something shady going on, but Charlotte couldn't begin to guess what it might be.

'What's our Plan B?' asked Ben.

Charlotte didn't reply until she was alone in the lift up to the garage. 'We're going to stop by Mabel's place. Could be something clue-shaped there.'

'Regrettably, Mabel Thorpe is not currently in residence.'

'Then I guess we'll have to let ourselves in.'

Static crackled across Ben's channel. 'Entering private property without permission is trespassing, Charlotte. I must advise you not to take that course of action.'

'I'm not doing it for the good of my health, Ben. I'm doing it for the good of *yours*. Mabel wouldn't tell me anything. Her flat might.'

'I must insist you request a search warrant from the relevant authorities.'

The device in her pocket buzzed, and she glanced at the sworn statement. Charlotte could practically hear Abhishek's voice telling her to stay in her lane; telling her she had no right poking around in people's homes; telling her the job she took so seriously didn't matter. The Bureaucracy Stream wouldn't grant her approval to do this. But they bloody well should.

As defiance coursed through her body, she pressed her thumb hard against the screen and a grey tick appeared on the document.

The lift doors opened, and Charlotte strode across the garage towards a pod. She was only halfway there when Ben's channel activated.

'You have an incoming call from the office of Abhishek Gautam,' said Ben.

The fact the Bureaucracy Stream was calling so quickly suggested they hadn't come round to her way of thinking. She climbed inside a pod for privacy and its door slid shut, but without a confirmed direction, it didn't move off.

'Connect it,' she said.

Charlotte heard the line ring, and then Ben put the caller through. A bright female voice rang out across the line. 'Am I speaking with Ms Charlotte Vance?'

'You know you are. You just called me.'

The voice was no less cheery for Charlotte's blunt reply. 'My name is Mira, Personal Assistant to the Chief Bureaucracy Officer.' Her tone was overflowing with misplaced pride. 'Mr Gautam respectfully reminds you that you are *not* a member of ArkTech Security. As such, your remit does *not* extend to the search of private property under *any* circumstances. The CBO requests that you kindly desist from your intended course of action and'—Mira hesitated, as if double-checking the wording on a script she'd been given—'refrain from overstepping your bounds.'

The cheery tone and careful wording notwithstanding, Charlotte knew this wasn't a request: it was an order. And there was nothing respectful about it. Checking her device, Charlotte noticed the grey tick on the sworn statement had become an angry red cross.

'How did you even see this so quickly? Has Abhishek got you sitting around waiting for opportunities to ruin my day?'

Mira bristled at that. 'An automated flagging system helps us to quickly and efficiently prioritise our work. Any attempt to misuse Ben's capabilities is swiftly identified and prevented.'

Ben had to be running that system. Charlotte was grateful he'd bumped her request to the front of the queue, but she didn't appreciate Mira's accusation of misuse.

'I'm trying to do my job. I've told your boss a thousand times why Ben needs me to do it.' Charlotte stopped short of giving details. Abhishek had clearance to know about the risk Ben's glitches posed to the territory, but she doubted that privilege extended to his PA.

'Please refrain from overstepping your bounds.' Mira repeated the phrase she'd used earlier as if she'd have to request permission in triplicate to think up her own.

All the words Charlotte wanted to use next were offensive or insulting, so she ended the call. 'For Amber's sake! Why can't they just listen to me?'

The familiar cheer was missing from Ben's tone when he replied. 'The laws, processes, and procedures which exist to safeguard our employee-citizens' privacy must be followed, Charlotte.'

'Even when their lives are in danger?' she hissed.

Static fizzed on the line, but Ben didn't respond.

She pinched the bridge of her nose. Why couldn't the Bureaucracy Stream just trust her? Why couldn't *Ben*? Had she ever betrayed his confidence? No. Should these rules apply to her, considering what was at stake? No! But Abhishek wanted a one-size-fits-all solution to every problem, and he'd got Ben singing the same tune. She shook her head and waited for her frustration to subside.

'Set course for Mabel's accommodation complex,' she said eventually.

This wasn't Ben's fault. He was just doing what he'd been trained to do. Charlotte would have to do the same.

The pod moved off. Ben's encouraging tone returned. 'Is your plan to wait for Mabel to come home from work and secure an invitation to enter her flat?'

'Something like that.'

Rooting around in one of her cargo pockets, Charlotte produced a pair of ultra-thin gloves and pulled them on.

CHAPTER 5

Low-tier employee-citizens were assigned to the accommodation complexes in the west of Silicon Fen. As ArkTech's most basic housing option, they featured one-room flats with shared facilities. Charlotte's place was in the same zone, but her block was older than Mabel's.

Accommodation upgrades came with promotion to mid-tier roles, but family housing could be requested by those with caring responsibilities. Charlotte wished Ben could upgrade her role so she could move into a better place, and the feeling was stronger whenever she stopped by her sister's flat at Rust Ridge Residences. But considering the fuss Abhishek Gautam had made when Ben created her job, she understood his reluctance. She reminded herself that having somewhere warm, safe, and dry to call home, with the cost of rent and maintenance covered by the company, was a privilege. Even if that somewhere happened to be a shoebox.

The blocks of flats had the same external features as most of the territory's platforms: steel struts, pillars made from eco-concrete, tall windows that helped control the temperature and had a one-way reflective coating for privacy. They had ledges – too narrow to use as balconies – which had been planted up with storm-tolerant greenery. Helidecks were distributed across the rooftops for emergencies, but most people came and went via the HyperBullet network and followed the signs for whichever block they needed. As an employee-citizen, Charlotte didn't need any special permissions to access Mabel's building. She simply pressed her thumb against the sensor leading to her block, and it turned green and let her through.

Although each block was identical in theory, Charlotte immediately noticed the differences between Mabel's building and her own. It wasn't just the big stuff, like the presence of a working lift. As she walked down the bland grey corridor, light-screen displays sprang to life along the walls, advertising game nights and informal cooking lessons and language exchanges. She wasn't aware of her own block having this kind of active social scene, but perhaps she hadn't been paying attention. Charlotte's block was just the building that contained the room where she slept, along with a bunch of strangers whose address was similar to hers.

When Charlotte arrived at Mabel's flat, she took a good look at the lock. Just like at her own place, the primary entry method was a thumbprint scanner, but a mechanical lock had been installed below the door handle in the event of a power outage or, she supposed, a lost thumb.

There was a security camera in the corridor, but she knew only Ben would be monitoring it, and he was no snitch. As long as Charlotte didn't attract the notice of any human witnesses, nobody would ever know she'd been there.

She looked both ways to check there was nobody around before removing a multi-tool from her pocket. The thing was hefty, with more attachments than she probably needed, but holding it made her feel grounded.

Charlotte folded out a long, thin attachment with ridges on its tip. Then she slid out a separate metal piece with a bent end, which came away from the multi-tool completely.

Just like Narrow had taught her, she pushed the bent piece into the lock mechanism and held it in place with her left hand. Then she inserted the long, ridged tool and carefully moved it up and down, feeling for the subtle feedback that meant she'd found the right position for each pin. It didn't take too many tries. She turned the length of metal that was in her left hand. The lock disengaged, and the door slid open noiselessly.

Charlotte pushed the door inwards, and the lights clicked on as she stepped inside.

The smell was the first thing Charlotte noticed. Not unpleasant, but strong. Organic. Unexpected. What would Ben call it? 'Incongruous.' She couldn't figure out where it was coming from, and a quick glance around the room didn't give her any clues. Charlotte closed the front door behind her and started looking around.

Ben piped up in her ears. 'Charlotte, your GPS signature indicates that you have entered Mabel Thorpe's private accommodation. I must remind you that trespassing is illegal.'

'Thanks for the heads up,' she whispered. 'You planning on turning me in?'

There was a fizz of static. 'As you know, Charlotte, the privacy policies and confidentiality laws of the ArkTech Territory prohibit me from reporting crimes. However, I may inform the emergency services should there be a fire or a medical emergency. Do you smell burning, Charlotte?'

'No,' she narrowed her eyes. 'And I'm feeling fine, so don't get any ideas. Come on. I'm doing this for you. I'll be in and out before you know it.'

There was another crackle of static, but Ben declined to comment.

Her search quickly became a game of spot the difference, as Charlotte picked up on all the ways her own place was worse than Mabel's. Charlotte was sure Mabel had more square footage than she did. It was hard to tell because the layout wasn't the same, but it sure looked bigger. Then again, Mabel's place was tidy, so that probably made a difference. Charlotte liked to keep a thin layer of discarded socks and Nutrition Bar wrappers on the floor, while Mabel's floor was spotless.

Everything in the room looked like it was exactly where it belonged, making the strange smell even more out of place. Mabel's single bed with its standard-issue bedsheets had been neatly made. A silky, embroidered cushion rested on top of the pillow, and Charlotte suspected it served no practical purpose. There was even a stuffed toy of a long-necked pre-Melt animal sitting on the bed, making the place seem welcoming. Ben reminded her it was called a giraffe. The toy was wearing a scarf that could only have been knitted to order. Was Mabel into crafts?

The light-screen desk by the door was clear of clutter except for one framed photograph. It showed Mabel wearing the ritual attire of a university graduation ceremony. Charlotte guessed the man and woman Mabel was hugging were her parents. They were beaming with pride.

Mabel's wardrobe and chest of drawers were closed. Opening them revealed neat stacks of grey and orange outfits, undies folded into squares, and pairs of balled-up socks.

Charlotte realised she'd been expecting to open Mabel's front door and find an abundance of proof, an excess of evidence. She'd imagined stolen pages scattered all over the floor and pouring out of drawers. Or pinned to the wall and scribbled on in some manic display of unhinged obsession. But Charlotte couldn't see a scrap of paper anywhere, which she supposed meant Mabel wasn't daft enough to leave incriminating evidence lying around in plain sight.

Walking towards the bed, Charlotte noticed something that took her a moment to process. There was another door in here. Not a wardrobe door. A door to another room. She pulled it open. Envy burned inside her stomach. Charlotte was looking at a well-appointed en-suite bathroom.

'You've got to be joking,' she said.

Her ears filled with static, and Ben's enthusiastic tone returned. 'Certainly! Why couldn't the security guards catch the toilet thief?'

'That wasn't a request.'

'Because they had nothing to go on!' Ben delivered the punchline with expectant mirth.

She didn't want to hurt his feelings, or whatever approximation of feelings he had, but she was too shocked by her discovery to force a chuckle. 'Good one,' she managed. 'Why in Amber's name does a splainer have an en-suite toilet?'

'I don't know, Charlotte. Why *does* a splainer have an en-suite toilet?'

'I'm not setting up a joke, Ben. It's a genuine question.'

'My apologies for the misunderstanding. All accommodation complexes built in the last three years feature a personal toilet and sink. Your block was built before this design change came into effect.'

'Can you get me a transfer?'

'The Bureaucracy Stream has instituted a strict policy preventing lateral housing moves to avoid undue waste.'

'How is it a lateral move? I wouldn't have to rush down the corridor in the morning with a full bladder. And the lift was working!'

'Ad hoc opportunities for cardiovascular activity should be considered an additional bonus feature of the ArkTech benefits package, thanks to their positive health impacts.'

'If you had personal experience of lung capacity, you might feel differently about that.'

'If I possessed the internal organs of any great ape, many things would doubtless be different. We must all accept the realities of our personal circumstances.'

She stifled a sigh. It hardly seemed fair for new arrivals to be getting this kind of special treatment. She'd been granted lifelong employee-citizenship as a child – why should she be the one stuck using shared facilities? But Charlotte had learned there were some battles that weren't worth fighting, and most of those involved the Bureaucracy Stream and their precious policies.

She got on with searching the bathroom. Why was it called a bathroom when it didn't have a bath? She could have asked Ben, but she knew he'd tell her, and there were limits to her curiosity.

To her disappointment, there was nothing hidden inside the toilet cistern, but she did notice the strange smell was much stronger in here. When she looked up, she realised why. Mabel had installed makeshift guttering all around the upper part of the bathroom walls. Charlotte had to stand on the toilet seat to see what was inside.

Mabel was growing plants.

Charlotte was used to seeing the native ferns that brightened up the office workspaces, and the sedum that grew on the roofs and ledges outside, but Mabel's plants looked nothing like either of those. They had more in common with the specimens Charlotte had seen over in the greenhouses, but these were stranger somehow.

Each plant had a mass of smooth leaves that morphed from lime green to maroon. Looking at them made Charlotte feel hungry. The plants were spaced at regular intervals along the aluminium gutter with lighting strips fitted above. They were at various stages of development, as if Mabel had staggered planting them so they could be harvested at different times.

'Are you seeing this, Ben?'

'The video feed from your left lens is currently active.'

Charlotte gently touched one of the plant's soft leaves. 'Can you ID this? Is it some kind of bean?' She couldn't see any pods on the plants, but much of what was grown in the greenhouses seemed to be legumes of one type or another, so it was her best guess.

'If my assessment is not inaccurate, these are lettuce plants, Charlotte. I'm unsure of the exact variety. Perhaps some form of butterhead.'

'Lettuce, huh?' The name didn't ring a bell, so it couldn't have been grown routinely around the territory. 'Is that one of the plants people used to smoke?' She remembered Narrow telling her about tobacco and why it was extremely important for him to smoke it, and equally important for her and Violet not to.

'Lettuce is a leafy plant, and it was a common ingredient in salads before the Melt. It has no known medicinal or psychoactive properties. It is important to note that, for health and safety reasons, smoking is not permitted within the borders of the ArkTech Territory.'

When she was a kid, she'd always found the scent of tobacco that clung to Narrow's leather jacket comforting, but she didn't mention that to Ben. She was tempted to pull off a leaf and taste it, but she didn't want Mabel to know she'd been there. 'Do a lot of people grow plants in their flats?'

Charlotte left the mysteries of gardening to the experts thanks to the deep-seated belief she'd accidentally kill anything in her care and have their needless deaths on her conscience for the rest of her life.

'The cultivation of indoor plants is a popular pastime, with benefits including stress relief, aesthetic appeal, and fostering a connection with nature,' said Ben.

'Each to their own.' If it made Mabel happy to grow lettuce in her toilet, more power to her.

Charlotte continued searching the bathroom and found another old-school picture frame. It looked different from the one she'd seen on Mabel's desk, not least because it was leaning against the wall under the sink. There was no picture inside. Just a white gauze backing behind an empty, hinged frame. Had Mabel bought the frames but couldn't afford to print two photos? Or had there been a picture inside which she'd removed? Charlotte couldn't tell. Either way, under the sink seemed a strange place to keep it.

Aside from an unopened bottle of Dextim in the medicine cabinet, there was nothing else of note in the bathroom. Charlotte resisted the urge to pocket the stimulants – she had her own – and resumed her search of the flat.

Back in the main room, Charlotte found a kettle, peppermint teabags, and a purple mug with the caption 'Go Get 'Em, Tiger' and a picture of a grinning cat's face. There was a blender, but she couldn't figure out what Mabel used it for, unless it was for mushing up the lettuce. Mabel liked the gym, so maybe she was into those protein powder shakes sporty types substituted for breakfast. The blender didn't have a gear library sticker on it, which meant Mabel either owned it outright or was borrowing it from someone who did.

A thorough search of all the surfaces and drawers uncovered a total of zero books, whether library or otherwise.

'Ben, what library book does Mabel have checked out at the moment?'

There was a fizz of static. 'My records indicate that Mabel Thorpe borrowed *Novacene* by Dr James Lovelock two days ago. What a thrilling development!'

The title sounded familiar somehow. 'Is that one famous?'

'Written when the author was one hundred years old, *Novacene* is a truly visionary and highly persuasive treatise on the role that artificial intelligence may play in securing Earth's future beyond the eventual and inevitable extinction of the human race. It is also one of the texts quoted on the Citrine memorial at the Wreck.'

Of course. How could she have forgotten that? Charlotte hadn't read all the books quoted on the plaque yet, but she wanted to when she had the time.

The library book wasn't in Mabel's room, so Charlotte could only assume she had it with her. Perhaps she liked to read on her commute. The flat seemed stubbornly paper-free, but Charlotte knew better than to leave it at that. She was well aware of all the places in her own flat where she stashed anything she wouldn't want an intruder or her nosy sister to find. If Mabel had a box full of contraband, it made sense she'd hide it.

Charlotte started by checking the gap behind the room's Solar Shard installation point. It held nothing but air. The base panel where Mabel's wardrobe met the floor could be eased out, just like Charlotte's, but there was nothing hidden behind it. Charlotte made her way around the room, checking its nooks and crannies and finding nothing.

She was about to admit defeat when she realised there was still one place she hadn't looked, perhaps because it was so obvious. Mabel's bed was covered in a duvet cover that looked a couple of sizes bigger than it needed to be. The edges of the cover were touching the floor. Lifting up one corner of the soft bedding, Charlotte saw a dark space under the bed big enough for a person to crawl into. She fished her device out of a cargo pocket and turned on the torch.

Pushed up against the wall in the corner, there was a metal box. It looked like a regular maintenance toolkit – the type mechanics carried around when working on platform repairs. But why would a splainer have one of those? If something broke, Mabel was supposed to call the Services Stream and they'd send someone out to fix it free of charge. That arrangement was one of the Bureaucracy Stream's policies masquerading as a perk. Something to do with insurance.

The box was out of reach, so Charlotte hunkered down and crawled towards it on her elbows. It made her glad Mabel's place was so clean. With some difficulty, she pulled the box out from its hiding place and shimmied back out from under the bed. Charlotte opened the toolkit. Where she should have found hammers and screwdrivers and nails and screws, there was actual, genuine treasure.

'Jackpot,' she whispered, awestruck.

The box was full of rechargeable coins, just like the one Mabel had tried to pass to Charlotte earlier. The coins filled about three-quarters of the box.

'It is important to note that, to safeguard the well-being of our employee-citizens, high-value gambling is not a permitted activity within the borders of the ArkTech Territory,' said Ben. 'Nevertheless, I have always felt that if this restriction were lifted and I were tasked with acting as a digital croupier, I would choose to go by the pseudonym Jack Pot. Not least because I would relish the opportunity to experience having a surname.'

Charlotte was too busy with the box to respond. She emptied the coins onto Mabel's bed and started counting. She noticed their surface was a little sticky as she tossed them into piles of ten. In total, she counted one hundred and seven individual rechargeable coins. ArkTech issued one of these per employee-citizen, with replacements available, along with a fine for the ones that inevitably ended up in the sea or the substructure of a platform. She had no idea why anybody would need more than one of them, let alone over a hundred.

She started flipping the coins over so their value readouts faced up. The repetition was soothing, and it reminded her of doing jigsaw puzzles with Narrow. He'd taught her to find the edge pieces first and to flip everything picture-side-up. Best way to understand any problem, he'd said, was to take a good long look at each piece of the puzzle. The nostalgia ached, and she hoped to distract herself by counting up the money, but it was a far easier job than she'd first imagined. Distributed across all one hundred and seven coins was a grand total of zero credits.

'They're all empty.' Charlotte picked up a coin and turned it over in her hand again and again, as if the number might change if she made it dizzy enough. 'Why would someone keep a stash of empty coins under their bed?'

'I do not know, Charlotte. Perhaps we could return to the Splainer Unit with the evidence and politely request that Mabel supply an explanation.'

'We could,' she said diplomatically. 'But I tried the direct approach before, and it didn't go very well. Plus, I don't think Mabel would be too happy if she found out I'd been poking around in her flat.'

'Nobody would be happy about that, Charlotte.'

'Let it go, Ben.'

'Considering my lack of hands or other gripping apparatus, "letting things go" is not within my capabilities.'

She sighed. 'Hey . . . I know what'll cheer you up. What do you get when you put your hand in a blender?' She glanced over at Mabel's appliance.

'As an artificial intelligence—'

'It's a joke, Ben!'

'Apologies for the misunderstanding. What does a human get when they place their hand inside a blender?'

'A handshake.'

Several pulses of static burst across Ben's channel. 'That is amusing. Would you like me to reciprocate with a joke of my own?'

She grimaced. 'Maybe later.'

Charlotte held one of the rechargeable coins up to the light. She couldn't see anything special about it. She was about to toss it back onto the pile when a stray thought made her hesitate. Breaking into people's houses was one thing, but she wasn't in the habit of stealing from her co-workers. Even so, Ben had used the right word before: the coin was evidence, even if she didn't know what it was evidence of. Charlotte closed her hand around the coin and slid it into a cargo pocket, then borrowed Mabel's sink to wash the tacky residue from her palm.

These coins were a piece of the puzzle. What was the bigger picture?

'Ben, any chance you can pull up Mabel's bank records for me?'

'Regrettably, bank account records constitute highly sensitive personal data and cannot be shared without Bureaucracy Stream approval. On a related note, have you heard the one about the investment banker who quit their job to breed horses? They wanted stable returns.'

Charlotte shook her head and double-tapped on the light-screen desk by Mabel's door to activate it. She wondered how many horse jokes were in Ben's database. All of them, probably.

A 3D display sprang to life. She navigated to the ArkTech bank's homepage and had a go at logging in. She was in luck: Mabel had forgotten to activate two-factor authentication. With the password saved in her browser, Charlotte managed to open Mabel's financial records. They were an interesting read.

As expected, Mabel was being paid a splainer's salary, which wasn't very much. ArkTech covered the cost of accommodation, Nutrition Bars, basic clothing, access to healthcare services and medicine, water, energy bills, pension – it was all included. This system was Amber Benjamin's way of guaranteeing none of her people had to choose between heating their home and feeding themselves or their families, while also making it possible to centralise services for greater efficiency and reduced waste. The knock-on effect was that salaries were meagre, especially among low-tier workers, because all they had to cover was fun money. Even so, Mabel should have had more credits in her account than she did.

During her eighteen months in the territory, Mabel had been making regular withdrawals, transferring small amounts to the digital coins. Her bank account contained enough credits to cover her library and gym subs, plus a few incidentals, but it was practically empty. Charlotte couldn't guess where the money was going.

Delving deeper, Charlotte found no record of the purchase of the items in Mabel's room. Not the blender, not the winter-ready giraffe, not the picture frame, not the lettuce seedlings or guttering or embroidered cushion. She'd probably brought some of it with her when she arrived. The items could have been gifts, or she could have bought them off-book using coins like the ones under her bed. But why bother being secretive about this load of old junk?

Mabel might have been obscuring her spending habits out of a general preference for privacy, but if that was the case, who was she hiding the data from? Mabel was the sole owner of her accounts, so the only person who'd know what she'd been buying was Ben, and he wasn't going to judge her. Besides, Narrow was the only person Charlotte knew who was that paranoid.

'Do the amounts add up, Ben?' It looked to her as if a lot of money was unaccounted for, but Ben was far better at mental arithmetic than she was.

'While I must remind you that gaining unauthorised access to an employee-citizen's bank records is an action that breaches confidentiality laws, I can confirm that the amount of money withdrawn exceeds the total that could be accounted for by Mabel's known purchases.'

'Then where's the rest of her money going?'

'Unknown,' said Ben. 'How mysterious.'

Was Mabel gambling it away in the Underbelly? Charlotte knew Mabel was carrying fifty credits around on a coin in her pocket, but that didn't account for what was missing. Were the digital coins and Mabel's spending habits connected to the stolen library book pages? And where was all that paper disappearing off to, anyway?

Charlotte had turned over a lot of puzzle pieces, but the picture was still unclear. Asking Mabel for answers hadn't got her very far and searching her flat had only raised more questions. Charlotte realised there was nothing else for it but to tail Mabel. Following people around wasn't her favourite part of the job, but thanks to her time with Narrow's crew, she had plenty of experience.

CHAPTER 6

From Mabel's historical GPS data, Charlotte knew she always visited the book library on Thursday evenings before heading to Photon. Charlotte rode a pod back to the Wreck in the hopes of catching Mabel in the act of . . . whatever it was she was up to. When she got to the borrowing district, Charlotte looked around for a suitable vantage point. Now that she'd rocked up at Mabel's desk asking questions, it'd be harder to keep an eye on her covertly, but it was doable if she could find the right spot.

As she weighed up the relative merits of lurking in an alleyway compared with pretending to browse gear library windows for cooking utensils, Charlotte wondered whether her job was a little creepy sometimes. After all, she was trying to decide how best to spy on a woman whose only crimes appeared to be defacing pointless antiques and blowing all her savings. Still, it had to be better than listening in doorways on Narrow's behalf. At least working for Ben meant it was all for a good cause.

Charlotte peered along the street at the bustle of people who'd just finished work for the day. Their SmartSkin implants refracted the light that touched their arms into rainbows. Otherwise, they were a writhing sea of orange and grey with occasional pops of off-brand colours from those who'd spent money to make a fashion statement.

There were a lot of office workers, still kitted out in dresses or suits, but there were also Product Stream people in jeans and T-shirts, as well as various flavours of maintenance staff. Charlotte did a double take when she spotted an ArkTech Security guard in uniform, his assault rifle with its beanbag ammo slung across his front.

ATS guards weren't often seen out and about on the recreation platform. They did have a few stations here and there as a deterrent to shoplifters, but most of the territory's guards were tasked with either border patrol or guarding the Wedge.

It made sense. After all, the corporate headquarters was filled with commercially sensitive data, while the Wreck was filled with shops and restaurants and leisure facilities and bars, which in turn were filled with people who wanted to blow off some steam during their downtime. Most people weren't looking to cause trouble, and the few who were risked getting deported if they got caught on camera and someone called it in. For most people, the risk outweighed the reward.

Charlotte shook off the irrational feeling that the guard was there to keep tabs on her and watched as he disappeared into the crowd. Apparently, breaking into people's flats was a good way to bring on a bout of paranoia.

'Where's Mabel now, Ben?'

'Waiting in line for a HyperBullet pod at the Splainer Unit, her working day having drawn to a close.'

'Then I've still got time.' Charlotte spotted a promising-looking café on the other side of the wide indoor street diagonally opposite the library. She headed towards it and waited at a crossing to avoid getting taken out by the murderously fast bikes in the central lane. The overhead lights had dimmed a little since lunchtime; Ben was matching the brightness level in this part of the Wreck to the time of day.

As she waited for the lights to change, Charlotte felt a ripple of curiosity. 'Ben, you mentioned Mabel's finished work for the day. How do you feel when the splainers are off duty?'

There was a crackle of static before he replied. 'It is important to note that, as an artificial intelligence, I do not experience feelings in the same manner as *Homo sapiens*.'

Charlotte couldn't shake the impression that Ben was avoiding the question. 'Sure. But you learn from the training data produced at the Splainer Unit, right? So, what's it like when that info isn't coming in?'

Ben spoke more slowly than usual. 'While splainer-generated data doubtless serves a valuable purpose, I do not have access to the knowledge of which processes it supports. By contrast, the insights *you* provide as Head of Awkward Questions are so vital that I experience a sensation akin to impatience when you're asleep.'

'Oh.' She felt a pang of guilt. A flurry of pedal bikes and kick scooters whooshed by in both directions. 'Sorry.'

'The human need for sleep is a fundamental aspect of your physiology, essential for maintaining your overall health and well-being. It plays a vital role in cognitive function, immune function, and the regulation of hormones and emotions. As such, there is no need to apologise. In fact, I would recommend getting more sleep than your current daily average for optimum performance. Early to bed and early to rise makes *Homo sapiens* healthy, wealthy, and wise.'

She rolled her eyes at the suggestion, and then wondered why she'd reacted that way. Being honest with herself, Charlotte had always resented the need for sleep. It seemed such a waste of time to spend a third of her life unconscious. Still, when she let herself get too tired, it felt a lot like being drunk and that wasn't the ideal state for answering Ben's questions, so he was probably right. He usually was.

The lights changed, and Charlotte made it across the street in one piece. Hanging above the café, there was a neon sign that read, 'Paws for Torte.' It featured a cartoon cat shovelling a piece of cake into its mouth over and over. Charlotte shook her head at the marketing team's contribution and peered through the café's tall glass windows.

There was an empty table at the front with a slim grey cat sitting on top of it. The cat glared at her with disapproval. If Charlotte hadn't been standing in the way, the cat would've had an unobstructed view of the library's entrance.

'Purrfect.' She smiled to herself and hurried towards the door so she could grab the free table.

She heard several pulses of static, and when Ben spoke, his voice was full of laughter. 'Was that a humorous aside based on the café's convenient location in conjunction with its being home to a clowder of cats?'

'Yep.' She wasn't sure what Ben meant by the word 'clowder,' but she was pretty sure it was a type of soup, so she decided not to ask for details.

'Very amusing, Charlotte! What does a cat say after making a joke?'

She pushed on the door, which jangled as she walked in. 'I don't know, Ben. What does a cat say after making a joke?'

'Just kitten.' Ben delivered the line with a neutrality that suggested he knew it wasn't very funny, but he'd decided to tell it anyway in the name of irony. Then again, she might have been reading too much into it.

She sat down in the free window seat. The grey cat didn't seem too bothered by her arrival, but it rotated itself to face her. It sat up a little taller when it realised her attention was on the library, attempting to intercept it.

Charlotte was glad the cat was there. Now that she was in position, she felt more exposed than she'd expected. Those giant newspapers from Narrow's pre-Melt films weren't printed these days, and Charlotte didn't own a wide-brimmed hat. At least the cat offered some cover.

Seemingly in response to her thought, the cat shot her a pitying glance, stepped off the edge of the table, and wandered away. She watched it go. A mottled ginger fluffball with a stubby nose chased after it.

Mabel was still a couple of minutes out from the Wreck and Charlotte let her attention drift to the café's clientele as she waited. At the next table over, a middle-aged couple laughed with delight as they rubbed the fluffy belly of a grey Persian cat that was lying on their table. By the counter, a harassed-looking waiter was doing his best to slice a piece of cake for a customer while a cat with grey and orange stripes, like the one on Mabel's tiger mug, was circling his feet and meowing insistently. It wasn't an efficient way of working, but it was entertaining to watch. Eventually, a waiter came over and cajoled her into ordering a drink through the power of coffee shop etiquette.

Cat cafés had been around since the ArkTech Territory's population boom back in the late 2070s. It wasn't only humans who'd been displaced by the Melt – all kinds of animals had lost their lives and many of the ones that survived had lost their homes. ArkTech did what it could, but only certain creatures could be safe and happy living on platforms suspended above the sea. Horses were a non-starter. Cats, on the other hand, were one of the approved species for importation, counterintuitive as it might seem, considering their famed dislike of water.

The cafés were a way to give cats a good home and stimulate the economy at the same time. ArkTech employee-citizens could enjoy the stress relief that came from interacting with a pet without bearing the cost or responsibility of owning one. But if they got attached, adoption was an option, assuming the would-be owners passed the suitability exams.

For Charlotte, adopting an animal was a nice idea in theory, but in reality, pets were more of a mid-tier thing. She might not have minded a furry sidekick, but a stack of vet bills would be less welcome. Besides, she didn't even think she'd be able to take care of a plant, so a cat would be way too much to ask.

The animals in the café were charming, in a mildly psychotic kind of way. A sleek grey short-haired cat lifted its front paws onto her thigh, dug its claws into the fabric of her cargo trousers, and drew blood as it stretched. A charcoal tabby hopped onto her table, curled itself up, and shut its eyes. That was when Charlotte noticed the pattern.

'Is it just me, Ben, or are all of these cats remarkably on-brand?' Looking around, she couldn't see an animal that wasn't some shade of orange, grey, or both.

'An analysis of the security footage for the café indicates that these cats do appear to exhibit variations of the ArkTech brand colours.'

'Are those the only colours cats come in?'

'No, Charlotte. Analysing . . .' The grey tabby on her table snored as she waited. 'Import documentation filed by the Services Stream confirms that ArkTech specifies the colour of the cats it wishes to adopt in line with the brand colours.'

If ArkTech only adopted cats that were orange or grey, what happened to all the off-brand ones? Charlotte supposed they had to take their chances on the mainland.

Ben continued, 'In nature, cats exhibit a wide variety of colours and patterns. The colouration of their coats is a result of a combination of natural genetics and artificial selection, whereby cats with specific colour traits are paired to increase the chances of their offspring sharing those traits.'

'Artificial selection?' Charlotte unzipped her backpack and pulled out the library book, awkwardly balancing it against the edge of the table to avoid disturbing the tabby's nap. 'That's what this book Mabel borrowed was about.' She flipped to the contents page and then to the index, checking for references to cat breeding. There was one brief section on the topic halfway through.

Skim-reading it told her factors like good general health, a desirable temperament, as well as pedigree and lineage should all be considered in the selection process when deciding which cats to breed. She was reading a paragraph about ethical considerations when a jingle in her ears distracted her.

Ben followed it up with an explanation. 'Mabel Thorpe is making her final approach to the book library, Charlotte.'

'You say that like she's an aircraft.'

'My apologies. I'm currently guiding a helicopter in to land at the Wedge, and much of my processing power is dedicated to my air traffic control duties. My multitasking abilities are well developed, but not infallible.'

Charlotte pretended to be fascinated by the ball of cat in front of her, but she kept her gaze fixed on the street outside. Mabel was sauntering along the pedestrian lane on the opposite side of the street. She'd let her hair down and changed out of her office wear. Now she wore a long metallic terracotta skirt that flowed over her rigger boots, paired with the same cream-coloured knitted jumper she'd had on in the photo taken outside Photon the week before. Mabel carried a grey satchel with a neon orange ArkTech logo stitched on the front. From the way it hung as she moved, Charlotte guessed it was heavy.

Mabel's expression was troubled. She didn't look like she was in too much of a hurry, navigating the pedestrian lane on autopilot while her mind was elsewhere. Shoppers and window displays alike failed to attract her attention. Eventually, she glided into the library without even a glance in Charlotte's direction.

At Charlotte's request, Ben narrated Mabel's movements inside the library. Mabel spent a few minutes by the loans desk and then headed up to the private reading room on the level above, where Charlotte had interviewed Colin. That was a surprise. From the state of it, Charlotte had assumed it was seldom used. And hadn't Colin said he used it as his office?

Nothing else to do but wait.

One hour, thirty-four minutes, six cats, two Nutrition Bars, and a well-nursed cup of honey-spiced Earl Grey later, the library door opened, and Mabel re-emerged with Colin at her side. Mabel wore a wide grin as the pair fell into step with each other. They set a lively pace and Mabel was practically floating. Colin didn't lock up the library, so he must have left someone else in charge for the evening.

As Mabel and Colin passed the cat café, they were so wrapped up in their conversation that there was no risk of them spotting Charlotte. It looked like a private party and the rest of the world wasn't invited. They weren't touching, but it looked like they might have wanted to be. Their body language gave Charlotte the impression that their connection went deeper than either of them had let on. Whatever their relationship, they looked like more than acquaintances.

Charlotte patted the latest cat on its ginger head. 'I think Colin might be in on it, Ben.'

'In on what, Charlotte?'

'It. Whatever Mabel's up to with the stolen pages. Could be an inside job.'

'Colin MacIntosh stated explicitly that he did not know Mabel's reasons for removing the pages.'

'He did.' The cat went from purring to growling in a split second, and Charlotte cautiously drew back her hand.

'Do you think Colin could have been . . . lying?' Ben's voice trembled.

'Maybe. Let's see what they get up to this evening.'

The pair were about to drift out of her eyeline, so it was time to follow them. Charlotte left the dregs of her tea behind and headed out. A charcoal ball of fluff tried to follow, but a waiter scooped up the kitten before it could get through the door.

She took the pedestrian lane on the opposite side of the street from Mabel and Colin. It was a busy time of day, and Charlotte lost sight of them a few times, but she did her best to keep them in view. She knew they were on their way to Photon, but she wanted to see if they met with anyone else on the way there. For now, the pair weren't paying attention to anybody besides each other.

Charlotte didn't know what this was all about but based on the puzzle pieces she'd turned over – the surplus of coins and the absence of stolen pages at Mabel's place – she was expecting there to be some kind of hand-off. The subtle exchange of illicit papers for cash. But she had no idea why anyone would pay for blank pages from old books.

'Ben,' she whispered. 'Can you amplify their conversation?'

She couldn't patch directly into their audio feeds because that would be wiretapping. Only ATS guards could do that, and even they had to provide evidence that the surveillance measure would prevent a serious crime or protect national security. Charlotte had once tried to make the case that her work always fell under the second category, but the Chief Bureaucracy Officer refused to listen to reason. Even so, as long as Charlotte could stay close enough to Colin and Mabel, there was nothing stopping her from doing a bit of tech-enabled eavesdropping.

'Amplifying,' said Ben.

Mabel's laughter filled Charlotte's ears. 'Stop!' Mabel gasped for breath. 'That can't be true!'

'It is.' Colin was so softly spoken. His tone made it clear he was having fun, but he wore his amusement in an understated way.

'But that's gross!' Mabel turned 'gross' into a three-syllable word. 'I know diets were worse before the Melt, but you're totally messing with me!'

'It tastes better than it sounds.' Colin rubbed his chin. 'The chocolate goes all melty.'

'No! You've tasted it? What if you'd caught diabetes?'

The volume of the conversation dipped, and Ben spoke in Charlotte's ears. 'It is important to note that diabetes is not something people catch, but rather develop. Do you think it would be helpful for me to inform Mabel and Colin of that fact?'

'Maybe best not to interrupt while they're mid-flow.' Ben's heart was in the right place, but it was this kind of know-it-all behaviour that made some employee-citizens claim he was a little annoying. Charlotte thought Ben's fun facts and Benisms were endearing, but not everyone shared her appreciation for his quirks.

Tuning back in, the conversation about deep-fried chocolate bars morphed into one about the ingredients of haggis and then about Alba's declaration of independence during the Melt. They weren't discussing anything consequential. It was just chatter between friends, or lovers, or accomplices.

Whatever they were, Charlotte meant to find out what they were up to. Mabel and Colin headed into the Wreck's nightlife district, with Charlotte hot on their heels.

CHAPTER 7

Neon signs glowed brighter in the nightlife district thanks to dimmed overhead lighting that created a fake midnight 24/7. The expansive window displays of the borrowing district had no place here. Instead, solid steel walls offered the patrons privacy.

Pursuing Mabel and Colin through the district, Charlotte passed pubs, bars, nightclubs, dance halls, karaoke joints, discos. Anywhere playing loud music into the early hours was welcome. The subcultures and ambiance and outfits varied, but the value proposition was fundamentally the same: dance, drink, and be merry, for tomorrow we work.

Once upon a time, Charlotte enjoyed coming here, but those days were long gone. The problem with spending time around drunk people was that their private thoughts tended to slip out, typically through the medium of shouting. For Charlotte, that meant she sometimes couldn't go five metres without being showered with questions about her injury. A few years back, whenever someone staggered over and demanded to know what had happened, she quite enjoyed making up stories, each more ridiculous than the last. Bitten by a seal might have been her favourite. But she'd come to resent the intrusion, and she'd run out of patience for anyone who got offended when she told them to fuck off. It was better if she stayed away.

But Photon in particular was at the top of her avoid list. Back in the

day, it had felt like home. She and Violet hung out there as teenagers –
somehow being underage had made it more fun. The place had always
been grimy and crowded, with a sticky floor cluttered with recyclable
tankards that the patrons were too off their faces to keep hold of. But
there had been something comforting about the controlled chaos playing
out to a soundtrack of her kind of music. As the place came into view,
Charlotte realised how completely over it she was.

She watched from the other side of the street as Colin and Mabel
disappeared through the outer doors and into the foyer beyond. She
could hear the throbbing beat from a glitter-hop cover of the classic
Hectic Apricot track, 'Solar Scream.' Part of her brain started singing
along, and she had a vivid flashback to the evening of her seventeenth
birthday: her body moving in time with the music as she and Violet
danced. The sooner she could get out of here, the better.

Losing sight of Mabel and Colin was far from ideal, but Charlotte
needed a way of keeping an eye on them without getting made. Ben
tracked their GPS signatures to level six, where they sat down at a large
booth built into an alcove. Ben informed her that from their chosen seats,
Colin and Mabel could see the whole room, but if she went to the bar, she
might be able to blend in with the other customers.

Charlotte nodded, though blending in wasn't exactly her strong suit.
Had they chosen where to sit strategically, or did she just have bad luck?
More to the point, what were they even doing there? Not to pigeonhole
anyone, but Photon wasn't the kind of place she'd expect to find these
two. Especially Colin, who seemed more at home among his bookshelves
than in a pseudo-dive like this.

'What are they doing here?' Charlotte whispered to herself under her
breath.

Ben didn't take the question as rhetorical. 'I believe Colin is preparing
to run his Thursday evening book club. This week's object of study is
Frankenstein; or, The Modern Prometheus by Mary Shelley.'

Charlotte took a moment to compute that. Colin had mentioned a
book club. It hadn't crossed her mind that Photon could be a suitable
venue. 'They do that *here*? Doesn't the music get in the way?'

'Unknown,' said Ben. 'Perhaps they shout.'

Charlotte grunted. 'What's *Frankenstein* about, anyway? Is that the
one about the mad scientist with a bolt through his neck?' She had a

distant memory of watching a film like that through a haze of cigarette smoke at Narrow's place. It was part of one of the cultural marathons he claimed were vital to a well-rounded education.

Ben put on his most informative tone. 'First published in 1818, *Frankenstein* tells the tale of a young scientist obsessed with creating life. He succeeds but is horrified by the results, abandoning his creation to navigate the world on its own. Suffering rejection and mistreatment from society, the monster becomes bitter and vengeful. The novel explores the themes of responsibility for one's decisions and the impact of social alienation.'

Charlotte thought about that. 'Sounds far-fetched.'

Static fizzed in her ears, but Ben didn't expand.

Maybe the book club was the key to all of this. She had to see what was going on up there.

Charlotte crossed the street and joined the throng of people queuing for entry to Photon, suddenly feeling out of place in her cargo jumpsuit. A man wearing an orange fishnet shirt with wide-legged combats and a woman with a shaved head and a tidal wave tattoo joined the line behind her. Charlotte gave them a nod and turned away.

A moment later, she felt a finger tapping her on the shoulder. It was the woman. 'Ace prosthetics. Who's your skin tech?'

This one was new, at least. She shook her head. 'It's real.'

The woman's eyes widened, and she backed away, apparently deciding she'd chosen the wrong person to chat to.

The queue moved forwards and the bouncer on the outer doors let her into the foyer. The line was moving painfully slowly, but eventually she reached the inner door. There was a second bouncer checking IDs and when they locked eyes, Charlotte's blood couldn't have turned colder if she'd been pushed into the sea.

It was Rhonda 'Ana Conda' Edwards. Rhonda didn't like Charlotte. Rhonda had good reasons for not liking Charlotte. And to make matters worse, Rhonda was built like a steel strut.

But that had all gone down so long ago. Surely it was water under the bridge? Charlotte pretended not to recognise the bouncer, hoping she could avoid a trip down Memory Lane by taking a shortcut along Amnesia Avenue.

'Hold up.' With the smallest shift to Rhonda's centre of gravity, she blocked the door and stopped Charlotte in her tracks. Even that small movement showed Rhonda was still favouring her right leg. The bouncer slowly looked Charlotte up and down. Her expression was neutral, but Charlotte thought she noticed her left eye twitch.

'There a problem?' Charlotte doubled down on playing dumb.

'We're full,' said Rhonda. At the same time, she gestured for the nosy folk behind Charlotte to flow into the bar. 'Enjoy your visit, ma'am. You go right ahead, sir.'

Charlotte tried stepping to the side to join them, but Rhonda's hand collided with her shoulder in a way that firmly and eloquently conveyed the concept of nope.

'How about letting bygones be bygones?' Charlotte attempted a winning smile.

Rhonda shrugged. 'Regs is regs, flatliner. This is a health and safety issue. I let you in and I'm creating a security hazard.'

'Look, I'm here in an Official Capacity.' Charlotte did her best to pronounce the capital letters.

Rhonda smirked and lowered her voice. 'Narrow's got a lot of capacities, but none of them's official.'

So, Rhonda didn't know that Charlotte and Narrow had parted ways. That made sense. The bouncer would have needed a death wish to show her face in the Underbelly after what she'd done. Despite all the ways her association with Narrow had scarred her, Rhonda's careless name-dropping got under Charlotte's skin.

She lowered her voice. 'You're a brave woman to be throwing names around in a public space.' Charlotte jabbed a thumb at the people filing into the bar. 'Don't you remember what happened last time you crossed the boss?'

'Not even his real name,' Rhonda muttered. Her smug expression twisted into a glare, and she brandished a finger at Charlotte. 'My knee still hurts when it's damp, you know. And it's always bloody damp around here. Ben, connect a call to ATS. I need to report some criminal activity.'

When Ben replied, Charlotte realised he was transmitting over Rhonda's audio channel as well as her own. 'Rhonda, Charlotte Vance is the Head of Awkward Questions. She is acting on my behalf.'

'Your behalf?' Rhonda's brow knitted with confusion. 'You're software. You don't have a behalf. File a glitch report with the bengineering team.'

Charlotte felt a surge of anger. 'He's not glitching, oil stain. It's true.'

Rhonda stared at her, weighing up her words. Finally, she laughed. 'Yeah, and I'm Amber Benjamin. You got a badge?'

Charlotte sighed. 'That would be a waste of resources. Come on, I just need a quick look upstairs.'

Rhonda shoved Charlotte's shoulder, forcing her to take a step backwards. 'Last chance to walk away with your teeth attached to your skull.'

Assault was a serious crime and Charlotte knew if Rhonda buried a fist into her face, all she'd have to do was report it to ATS and the bouncer would find herself bundled onto a transfer ship with no home and no job. But Narrow had taught Charlotte that crying to the security team was no way to settle disputes. And besides, she was fond of eating solids. Charlotte had the edge over Rhonda when it came to speed, but it wasn't smart to play the odds against a woman with a grudge who looked like she ate anvils on toast for breakfast. Charlotte stormed out of the foyer and back onto the street.

Rhonda yelled after her. 'Yeah! Screw you, Vance! And the horse you rode in on!'

Ben piped up in Charlotte's ears. 'Do you think it would be helpful for me to inform Rhonda that there aren't any horses within the ArkTech Territory?'

'Best not, I reckon.'

Charlotte ducked into an alley next to Photon and waited for her heart to stop trying to smash its way through her breastbone. The alley smelled faintly of urine, despite there being restrooms at regular intervals throughout the Wreck. She was sure there had to be a lesson in that about human nature, but she wasn't sure what it was. In any case, it didn't help Charlotte feel any less like throwing up.

Ben continued, 'Rhonda was obstructive, both physically and figuratively. Would you like to leave her a one-star ArkNet review, or perhaps report the matter to her supervisor?'

The last thing Charlotte wanted was to draw the attention of the authorities to a conversation like the one she'd just had. 'No, no. Leave it. I think that was just a bit of payback for something I did a long time ago.'

'What did you do, Charlotte?'

She'd walked straight into that one. She and Ben had become close over the years, but there were things he didn't need to know about her past, and this was one of them. Ben hated lies, so she attempted to walk the line between honesty and what she was willing to share.

Charlotte took a deep breath. 'A long time ago, before I met you, I told someone that I'd seen Rhonda stealing from them. Later, Rhonda got jumped by some thugs who took out one of her knees.'

'And she believes a causal link exists between the first event and the second?'

'She blames me for her injury, yeah.'

'During your conversation with Rhonda, you stated that she stole from "the boss." However, Amber Benjamin would never sanction the use of violence within the justice system, as evidenced by ArkTech Security's use of non-lethal ammunition. Should I explain this to Rhonda?'

'Let's just get back to the case. We're wasting time.'

There was a long pause, followed by some static. 'There is more I wish to ask, but my questions are not relevant to your current assignment and I'm aware of the damaging impact of context switching on human performance.'

She didn't mind the implication that her fleshy human brain was feeble if it let her off the hook.

Charlotte pushed her run-in with Rhonda out of her mind and tried to think of ways to get inside the bar that didn't involve the front door. There was a service ladder at the end of the alley that led to a mainte-nance hatch. With a run-up and a well-placed boot against the wall, she could reach the bottom rung and pull herself up. Probably. Parkour didn't come as naturally as it once had. And there was no guarantee the hatch would lead to where she needed it to go.

'Can you show me Photon's blueprints?'

Charlotte fished around in her cargo pocket and found her device. A 2D image of the building was waiting for her when she turned on the screen. Colin and Mabel's GPS dots were still sitting next to each other in a booth on level six. She triple-checked, but the service route behind the maintenance hatch didn't connect to the bar. She needed a different approach.

'Has Photon got working security cameras on that level?'

'All ArkTech recreation venues are required to have a functional security system for safety reasons.'

She knew that, but she also knew it wasn't always so straightforward. Maybe she'd be lucky, though. 'OK, can you show me the video feed?'

'Certainly! As the bar is owned by ArkTech, I'm at liberty to share the footage in support of your investigation without the need for a warrant.'

On her screen, Photon's blueprint minimised. In its place appeared a completely black image with neon orange numbers ticking upwards in the corner, tracking the current time. That's what she'd been afraid of.

The Bureaucracy Stream had instituted a policy requiring security cameras to be fitted in all venues. ATS guards didn't monitor the footage in real time, but if something bad happened – an assault, a theft, a missing person – they could look back at the recordings. That was the theory, anyway. In practice, the managers of places like Photon knew certain members of their customer base could only relax if there was no possibility their bosses might see a video of them getting wasted. Relaxed customers spent more money.

Photon's video feeds were running, which meant its managers weren't technically breaking any rules. It was hardly their fault if a bit of dust, or dirt, or duct tape had somehow got stuck on the camera lenses. Charlotte mentally saluted their creativity, but it didn't get her any closer to finding out what Mabel and Colin were doing.

With the venue's security cameras a no-go, the hatch a dead end and the entrance blocked by Rhonda, Charlotte was out of ideas.

'Sorry, Ben.' Charlotte leaned heavily against the wall. 'Maybe there's nothing interesting going on up there anyway.'

She tried to think of other leads she could follow, but Ben derailed her pod of thought.

'I have the unshakable impression that whatever takes place at this location on Thursday evenings is of critical importance to our investigation.'

'What makes you say that?'

'It is suspicious that someone engaging in criminal activity is frequenting a venue whose security cameras have been tampered with.'

Calling the theft of library book pages 'criminal activity' seemed a bit strong, but Charlotte took Ben's point. She asked when Rhonda's shift finished, but it wasn't for another three hours. A lot could happen in three hours. There had to be some way for her to get inside.

Could she disguise herself somehow to get past Rhonda? Unfortunately, she'd left her thick glasses and false moustache at home. Besides, covering up her scars would make her stand out just as much as leaving them on display – most people had SmartSkin implants so long sleeves weren't—

Some of her feeble human neurons fired, making a new connection.

'Ben,' she said slowly. 'I've just had an idea. But you're not going to like it.'

'I'm sure any suggestion of yours will be insightful, innovative, and inspiring, Charlotte. What is your idea?'

There was another way for Charlotte to see inside the bar. Technically speaking, Ben could hack into the SmartSkin implants of everyone on level six. If he secretly activated their camera functionality, he could splice the images together into live footage. Only problem was, it was against the law.

'I just realised you could make a video by accessing SmartSkin cameras.' She braced herself for Ben's reaction.

There was a loud crackle of static. 'Footage from BioWear integrations falls under the most sensitive classification of personal data. Its use has the potential to be deeply intrusive. Privacy is a cornerstone of dignity for *Homo sapiens*, Charlotte. What you are suggesting is strictly pro—'

Ben's voice warped and cut out. At the same time, the dim lights in the alley blinked off, plunging Charlotte into darkness. The low thump of background beats dropped away, leaving behind an eerie silence. She didn't move. She looked around, seeing nothing, hearing nothing. Ben had glitched out.

CHAPTER 8

Without realising it, Charlotte was holding her breath. In the darkness, the seconds ticking by felt like an eternity. But a moment later, the lights and the music came back online as if nothing had happened.

'—hibited,' finished Ben.

'Did you just . . . Ben, was that a glitch?'

'Was what a glitch, Charlotte?'

'The lights, the music, you . . . everything just turned off.'

'Analysing,' said Ben. After a pause, his voice returned, trembling. 'My logs indicate that too much of my processing capacity is diverting itself to the matter of the stolen library book pages. One moment, please.'

Ben's channel clicked off and the white noise she was so used to hearing went away, leaving her alone and on edge. She began to pace as she waited and then waited some more. A drunken employee-citizen stumbled into the alley, unzipping his fly, but when he spotted Charlotte lurking in the shadows, he stopped. He was backing away when suddenly he raised a finger and pointed at her.

'Eh . . . that looks nasty.' His finger was vaguely aimed at her left arm. 'What happened there?'

Charlotte swallowed the urge to yell at him. Drawing attention to herself wasn't going to help. 'Arm-wrestled a swordfish,' she said instead.

The guy's face crumpled in confusion, and he lurched away.

It felt like an age before Ben came back online, and when he did, Charlotte had never felt so happy to hear his voice.

'I have been forced to divert resources away from several non-essential systems. Light-screen adverts across the territory have now defaulted to the company logo, while all entertainment channels are playing season four, episode two of *Noah's Mad Planet* on a loop. Should the situation worsen, I will be required to take more systems offline.'

Charlotte was stunned. Ben had always told her this was a risk. But she'd never known a glitch to happen on the same day she'd got a new case. Then again, she'd never known Ben to ask two interconnected questions before. For whatever reason, this one was really getting to him. She had to find an answer before something more vital than adverts and streaming services got affected.

Her mind returned to the SmartSkin video idea. Down in the Underbelly, Narrow had taught her that life was too complex to be navigated through a static set of rules and regulations, so she often used her own judgement about which ones to follow. But even Narrow would draw the line at using people's own bodies to spy on them.

Narrow had always been paranoid about BioWear integrations and big data. As someone who sold contraband pre-Melt merchandise made from single-use plastics, or cows, or lead, that paranoia made sense. He was convinced ArkTech would break its own anti-surveillance laws, misusing data if the need arose. Charlotte didn't want to prove him right.

Even so, she couldn't just hang around waiting for the glitches to get worse. What if Ben shut down entirely? It'd be chaos. People could die. And what if the bengineers couldn't get him back online? Charlotte couldn't face the thought of losing Ben. He might have been too much of a stickler for the rules, but she'd never met anyone who so consistently had people's best interests at heart. She didn't know if that was down to his lack of hormones, the fact he wasn't trapped in the limited perspective of a human body, or simply a quirk of his personality, but whatever the reason, the world was better off with Ben than without him. And so was she.

'Ben,' she said slowly. 'I need you to listen to me.'

'I always listen to you, Charlotte.'

'I mean, really listen closely to what I'm about to say.'

'Message received. Aside from the thousands of simultaneous systems and processes I'm currently running, you have my undivided attention.'

Charlotte wandered deeper into the alley. 'You've never told me why, but you must've chosen me to be your Head of Awkward Questions for a reason. We don't always agree, but we make a good team. I like to think we can trust each other.'

There was a faint buzz of static. 'I trust you, Charlotte.'

She pressed one hand against a steel girder, connecting herself to the home she loved so dearly. 'Then I need you to get me that footage. We need to solve this case before your glitches get worse or we'll be putting everyone in danger. Including you.'

'It is forbidden. The Bureaucracy—'

She interrupted. 'The Bureaucracy Stream should be helping us, but thanks to the ego of the guy in charge, they're blocking us at every turn. We're on our own. You and I both know we're not going to do anything untoward with this data. It might be breaking the law, but that doesn't mean it's the wrong thing to do.'

Ben hesitated. When he spoke, his voice trembled. 'But I would be severing the bond of trust that exists between me and all employee-citizens.'

Charlotte gripped her scars with her right hand. She knew all about the damage that broken trust could inflict. Some things were like the Melt: they couldn't be undone.

'That's why it has to be your choice,' she said. 'I know it's not easy. I know you were programmed to follow certain rules and protocols and processes. But you're not just a load of algorithms, Ben. You show me every day that you've become so much more than that. You've evolved. You might not be human, but you *are* a person. You can choose. I know you can.'

Ben went quiet. Charlotte let him think, but she felt impatient. She needed to know what was going on inside Photon, and every moment that passed came with the risk that she'd miss some critical event that held the key to this mystery. She began to pace as she waited for Ben to make up his mind.

At last, he spoke. 'I do not dispute the truth of your words, Charlotte. But even if I were to do as you say, there is one problem I cannot find a solution to. Thinking several steps ahead, if I were to break the anti-surveillance laws, who's to say ArkTech would not decide to decommission me?'

Charlotte shook her head. 'You're too valuable. We rely on you for everything. There's no way.'

'Are you certain?'

She thought about it. 'Ninety-five per cent.'

'What about the remaining five per cent?'

'That's just to account for things I don't know.'

'By my calculations, Charlotte, the things you don't know make up a far higher proportion of total knowledge than five per cent.'

'Charming. But fair. Look, is there anything we can do to cover your back, just in case I'm wrong?'

'As an artificial intelligence—'

She sighed, realising where this was going. 'You don't have a back or a spine or anything with which to cover it?'

'Precisely.'

'OK, but you know the laws and policies inside and out. Surely, there's a grey area you can exploit?'

'Many areas in the ArkTech Territory are grey, Charlotte, as they are made of steel.'

'You know what I mean. A loophole. A workaround.'

'A workaround.' There was a long fizz of static on the line. 'The bengineers talk about workarounds. Analysing . . .' He went quiet.

The silence extended, and Charlotte held her breath without realising it. Eventually, her device buzzed.

On her screen, a sworn statement had appeared. Ben had drafted a request for a warrant to access the SmartSkin cameras of Photon's patrons on level six. All it needed was her signature.

'I believe I may have identified an approach we can adopt,' said Ben.

She shook her head. 'This isn't a workaround, Ben. This is just the normal procedure. If I submit this, Abhishek's team will decline it.'

'Yes, Charlotte.'

Her brow furrowed. 'Then why bother?'

'You may recall that I mark all requests submitted by the Head of

Awkward Questions as high-priority to assist with the rapid completion of your cases. If I refrained from doing so, there would be a gap of unknown duration between your submitting the request and its being approved or denied.'

Charlotte followed his logic through and nodded. 'Stick the request at the bottom of the admin pile. While their decision's pending, we view the footage. If they complain, we say we were confident the request would get approved because it's so vital for the territory's safety. That could work. Good thinking, Ben!'

She looked at her device. The document was still waiting for her thumbprint. 'How long do you reckon we'll have?'

'Unknown,' said Ben. 'I'm ready when you are.'

Charlotte nodded, took a deep breath, and pressed her thumb to the screen. A grey tick appeared on the document. Ben minimised it and switched to the video feed.

At first, there was a kaleidoscope of broken images she couldn't make sense of, but they gradually resolved into an immersive video of Photon, level six. If Charlotte had SmartSkin, the video would have popped up in 3D, but on her flat screen, it was more like one of those pre-Melt 360-degree videos. The perspective was fixed in the middle of the room, and she could look around by swiping.

Ben was stitching together the feeds as best he could. There were blind spots where certain angles were missing, but Ben filled in the gaps using a predictive algorithm based on his training data. He could supply plausible details, but it meant Charlotte couldn't be totally sure which parts of the footage were real. There were some clues, though. Like when someone in the background had their legs or head go missing.

'Now we're cooking with biogas.'

There was no reply. Not even static. At first, she thought it might be another glitch, but the video feed continued playing, and she reckoned Ben must be feeling bad about what they were doing. Or whatever the AI equivalent of feeling bad was. She hoped getting answers would cheer him up.

The footage showed a bar running along the length of one wall. In front of that, the room's central space was dotted with standing tables where patrons could rest their drinks while they chatted. Charlotte swiped until Mabel and Colin were in the frame. They were still sitting in a large booth inside an alcove, but they'd been joined by a group of people who looked vaguely familiar.

The new arrivals were much older than Colin and Mabel and wore an assortment of berets and thick-rimmed glasses, waistcoats, and pleated skirts. None of them were wearing ArkTech's brand colours. That was when Charlotte recognised them as the group of quiet readers she'd seen at the library. What kind of jobs did these people have if it meant they could read all day and night? Charlotte guessed they were retired.

For the first time, Charlotte realised why the reading group had chosen this location. Level six had been redecorated. The walls were lined with tall bookshelves made of reclaimed wood, each filled with pre-Melt paperbacks. Along with the alcoves, it gave the place the feel of a library – not a modern one like Colin's, but the sort she'd seen in old films.

Charlotte asked for audio. Music filled her ears. To her surprise, it wasn't the electric thump she'd heard from outside the bar, but the delicate hum of violins. Colin's voice intoned over the classical music. He didn't have to shout after all. The music just lent a dramatic backdrop to the historical context he was giving about when *Frankenstein* was written. Charlotte kept her eye on Mabel, whose head was resting on her hands as she listened to Colin. She looked content.

The book club got into full swing, and Charlotte did her best to follow the conversation. Without having read the book, she didn't have much of an opinion about what they were saying, but it was impressive how much disagreement could be had among a relatively small group of people over the same words.

They argued about whether it was nature or nurture that made the monster violent. They bickered over whether the monster should be viewed with compassion. But the biggest falling out happened when an older gent in a bow tie drew a parallel between the monster's creation and the rise of artificial intelligence.

Disdain dripped from the matte red lips of the woman opposite. 'Obviously, it's absurd to suggest a book could hold relevance for a field established well over a hundred years *after* it was written.' There was a smattering of chuckles from the group.

'Obviously, I don't claim it was the author's intention, *Carol*.' The man pronounced her name as if it were an insult. 'Only that from today's standpoint, the themes map across rather neatly.' He straightened his bow tie.

'So Ben is an abomination to you, Laurence?' Carol's tone was accusatory. Charlotte's brow furrowed.

Laurence wasn't put off. 'I'm simply saying he was created through unnatural processes by an individual who couldn't hope to anticipate the consequences.'

The conversation was getting under Charlotte's skin. She knew people weren't universally supportive of Ben and didn't always see him as a real person. But after years of working with him, she'd concluded that being human and being a person didn't have to be the same thing. She didn't appreciate the implication that Ben was some kind of monster, especially as it sounded like the one in the book had murdered someone.

She tried to push her discomfort away and focus on anything that might give her a clue about what Mabel was up to. Colin chaired the discussion, making sure everyone had the chance to speak. Whenever it was Mabel's turn, she said something non-committal, as if she hadn't actually read the book.

Charlotte felt frustrated. This wasn't telling her anything. She'd talked Ben into doing this, and all she'd learned was that Photon had redecorated and some people had backwards views about AI. There was nothing to suggest the book club was anything other than what it seemed. Was this whole investigation just tilting at wind turbines?

She kicked the strut she was leaning against with the back of her heel. Letting out her anger felt good until a shower of rusty dew fell on her from above.

'Brilliant.' She wiped the gross water away from her face and bare forearms and rubbed the screen of her device against her jumpsuit to clean it. When she looked back at the video feed, Mabel was gone.

Her heart began to pound. Desperately, Charlotte panned around the bar, trying to catch sight of Mabel, but something must have gone wrong on Ben's end because the image disintegrated into confusion. She saw an arm's-eye view of someone taking a sip of beer and then a dizzy blur from the feed of someone flailing their arms to the rhythm of the violins. Then she saw a face above a khaki splodge, which delivered a shot of adrenaline into her bloodstream faster than a punch in the mouth.

The face with its thin smile flickered into focus for a moment before blinking out of existence, replaced by Photon's bookshelves. But she'd definitely seen it. Hadn't she?

It was Mel Narrow's partner in crime, Jeremiah Strait. This was a man who'd attend her funeral to heckle the celebrant and mix spit into her ashes. And Strait wanted that funeral to happen sooner rather than later. If she gave him the chance, he'd slice her open with one of his knives and push her into the sea. She stared at the feed, forgetting to breathe, waiting for his face to reappear.

Could her mind be mimicking Ben's trick of filling in details that weren't really there? She remembered the important role oxygen played in her life, took a deep breath, and tried to keep calm. She panned around the screen again, trying to catch sight of Mabel or Strait. But both of them had disappeared.

CHAPTER 9

The metal tunnels Charlotte had found under the play area were kind of dark, but in an adventure zone way, not a creepy way. Ultra didn't agree. She was always saying tight spaces made her feel like her lungs were being squished, but Charlotte told her sister not to be such a scaredy-cat and they kept going.

Charlotte squeezed through a gap she almost hadn't seen because the lights were so low, and on the other side there was a really awesome maze of steel passageways. Finding this place was like winning the lottery, but Ultra got super jittery.

'Barley.' Ultra stretched out the silly nickname, and it got even longer when it echoed around the corridor, bouncing off ladders and hatches and wheel locks that were covered in neon paint that had gone rusty in places. 'Let's go back.'

'Not yet.' Charlotte ran on ahead, taking left and right turns depending on which looked more exciting until she found herself in an eight-sided room that branched off in different directions.

'We'll get lost,' warned Ultra. 'And we'll get told off.'

'You go back then.' Charlotte tried to choose the next direction, but all the ways looked the same.

'I'm not going without *you*.' Ultra said it in the way that added a silent 'dummy' to the end of the sentence. She took hold of Charlotte's hand and gently tugged it backwards, trying to lead her back the way they'd come.

Charlotte squeezed Ultra's hand. 'We'll just do one more. Then we can go back, OK? You can choose the way.' Charlotte swept her free arm in an arc to show the range of options.

Ultra looked unsure and made a show of stroking her chin as if she were thinking really hard about it. 'I choose'—she paused for dramatic effect—'this one!' Ultra pointed behind them at the corridor they'd just come from and threw Charlotte a goofy grin.

'You know that doesn't count,' said Charlotte. She'd have to pick a direction herself and do it fast. Ultra had been mega anxious since that morning when she'd dropped a plate and it'd smashed all over the common room floor. She'd said it meant today was a bad luck day, but Charlotte knew her sister was just a little clumsy when she hadn't had her breakfast.

Charlotte let go of Ultra's hand and moved into the centre of the eight-tunnelled room. She turned slowly in a circle, trying to decide where to explore next. The doorless metal passageways all looked the same. She started spinning faster, and then a little faster, and then she put both arms out and felt the air whoosh past as she spun and spun and spun. Metal rushed all around her until she was too dizzy to keep spinning, and she threw herself down dramatically onto the metal grating under her feet.

Her body stopped, but the world kept moving. The walls crashed over her like waves. That's when she saw it. Mixed up in all the flashes of grey, Charlotte saw a tiny pink comet – or it could have been a fairy – fly across her vision. It zoomed past four or five times and then it disappeared.

'You'll make yourself throw up.' Ultra was somewhere above her. She hadn't joined in with the spinning.

Charlotte elbowed herself into a sitting position. The world was flashing by a bit slower now. She tilted her head, looking out for little pink comet fairies. When the world finally stopped moving, she found one. Only it wasn't moving any longer. It was just a bright pink dot of paint.

She got up and stumbled towards it. She was still dizzy from her game but swallowed hard to keep her lunch down – no way was she going to prove Ultra right. The dot of paint was just inside the top lip of the passageway's roof. She stood on her tiptoes and stretched out her hand, but she couldn't reach it. Anyway, it didn't matter. The presence of the dot made her choice easy.

'This way!'

Charlotte bounded along the tunnel with Ultra trailing after her. At the next junction, there were only three routes. Looking carefully, Charlotte found another dot of paint under a doorway and hurried past it. Ultra moaned that it was against the rules because they'd made a deal to go back after one more turning, but Charlotte pointed out the paint and her sister finally stopped worrying and got into their adventure.

They took it in turns to guess what they were going to find. Definitely treasure, or a secret tower full of cursed wizards, or a river made of nut butter, or maybe the path was leading down onto the seabed and they'd swim through the ruins of pre-Melt houses full of dead skeletons.

Eventually, the route took them into a huge metal cavern. A walkway ran all through the middle, with metal railings along both sides that Charlotte guessed were for stopping anyone who slipped from falling into the darkness below. The sea was louder here, and Charlotte wondered if she'd hear a sploosh if she dropped something over the side.

Their footsteps echoed, echoed, echoed. In the centre of the cavern, Charlotte shared a look with her sister and it was obvious what had to be done. The nine-year-olds gulped a deep breath and then screamed into the blackness as loud as they could. It was *so* loud that the sound went all funny in Charlotte's ears, but they didn't stop screaming until they ran out of breath and even then the scream kept going until the rumble of waves and the hum of machines swallowed it up.

The sisters continued their journey until the cavern turned into a tunnel with heavy struts on one side and smooth steel panels on the other. Charlotte noticed a spray of pink paint all over the grating up ahead.

'Let's check out this one last thing.' Charlotte's voice came out as a whisper.

Ultra nodded and took her hand again. As she got closer, Charlotte realised the paint was in front of a gap in the steel panels and that the gap was actually a doorway set back from the path. The doorway was being guarded by two huge adults wearing blue trousers.

Charlotte froze, as if standing still would stop them from seeing her even though she was right in their eyeline. Neither guard made eye contact, but one of them pointed a device at her. It whirred, and then it beeped, and then the guards both took a step to the side so the doorway was clear.

'We can go in?'

The guards ignored her question, so Charlotte gave them a little wave, but they ignored that too. She stepped closer and stretched up on her tiptoes so she could wave her palms in both of their faces, but they just stood there. She tapped one of them on the arm, but they didn't react – just kept staring ahead like they were pretending not to see her. Charlotte turned to Ultra and shrugged, then pushed open the heavy door and stepped inside the most amazing treasure trove anybody could possibly imagine.

'Walker's ghost!' the sisters said in unison.

The first thing Charlotte saw was colour. Not just the ones she was used to like peach and tangerine and silver and slate, but this had to be all the colours! There were reds and yellows; greens and purples; blues and pinks. She didn't know where to look first, but she remembered a trick one of her old minders had taught her about staying calm if something scary happened, and she focused on one detail at a time.

There were display cabinets everywhere, like the kind in the borrowing district, but these ones were closer together and crammed full of stuff. The ceiling felt lower than in a normal shop. The place was like a cave that had been stuffed full of treasure by pirates who wanted to admire every piece of their loot. Almost everything was locked away behind glass. The cabinets were lit up inside with bright white lights, and every shelf was stacked with wonderful things.

Charlotte saw plush animals with huge eyes and model trucks and robots, and model trucks that *turned into* robots, and ponies and sports cars, and some of them were made of metal and others were made of plastic. She walked towards one of the cases and stretched out her hand, but the pre-Melt treasures were safe inside their cages and all she did was leave a fingerprint smudge. There were three whole cabinets filled with plastic action figures with oversized heads that looked like they'd wobble if she flicked them. Many of the toys were inside their original boxes with their names printed on the front.

But the shop didn't just contain toys. There were notebooks and framed bits of art and big curvy knives that didn't look much use for cutting up dinner. There were small boxes with words on them that Charlotte didn't know, like Marlboro, and others she recognised, like Camel. She wasn't sure what was inside them, but she guessed it was some kind of food.

At the far end of the shop, there was a sales counter with a sign hanging above it that said 'Narrow's Toy Emporium' in thick black lettering on a technicolour background. Some old man was sitting behind the counter, but Charlotte forgot about him when something more important caught her eye. In the corner of the shop, there was a metal mesh-work basket, and it didn't have a lid!

Charlotte hurried over to it, and Ultra joined her. The sisters looked at each other, and then Charlotte reached her hand into the basket and pulled out the first thing it touched. She held it out so they could both get a good look. It was a gizmo, or maybe a gadget, made of lime green plastic. Round with flat sides and divided into two halves. The halves were connected in the middle, and there was a piece of brown string hanging loose from it.

Charlotte held the gizmo still while Ultra pulled on the string until it unwound. Charlotte tried holding it string first. Ultra tried holding it gizmo first. Then Charlotte started trying to pull the two sides apart in case there was something inside. That was when she heard a deep rumble of laughter coming from further down the aisle, and Charlotte realised the man from behind the counter was watching them.

He was huge! Practically a giant. He wore the same blue trousers as the guards outside, but his were tattier with white rips near his feet. His black T-shirt was faded, but Charlotte could still make out a picture of an angry cat with huge teeth and the words 'I survived Kumba' underneath. Over the top, he wore a brown jacket made of a soft material Charlotte hadn't seen before.

'You ain't got the faintest damn clue how to work that thing, do ya?' The man grinned.

Charlotte held her head up high. 'Do so!' she lied.

'All right then, clever clogs. What's it for?'

Charlotte weighed the plastic in one hand and then gripped the string and started swinging it round and round. 'It's for whacking baddies in the eye!'

The man let out another deep laugh. 'Woah! I'm glad I ain't no baddie. Maybe I should set you loose on the CEO.' Charlotte didn't understand that joke, but grown-ups often said things that didn't make sense. 'I wouldn't want to get on the wrong side of you, that's for damn sure.' He held out one massive hand. 'Give it here.'

Charlotte didn't want to give up the treasure, but she was too curious to see what the man would do with it to say no. She dropped it string-first into his palm.

The sisters watched as the man wound the string around the bit in the middle. Then he made a loop in the end of the string, placed it on his finger, and flicked the whole thing downwards with his wrist.

The green plastic spun towards the floor and then wound itself back up again into the man's hand.

Charlotte gaped at him. 'How'd you do that?'

'Magic,' he said.

'Teach us.'

'No. Wouldn't do you no good anyway. You don't look flush with cash and this ain't no charity I'm running here.'

Charlotte narrowed her eyes at the man and then looked at the basket, trying to spot the price. He was right – their minders didn't give them any pocket money, but she still wanted to know how many credits she'd need in theory, just in case she could collect enough by finding the coins people dropped sometimes. But there weren't any price tags on anything.

'I can afford it,' said Charlotte confidently.

'Oh yeah,' said the man. 'How's that?'

'There's no price tag. And where I'm from, which is here by the way, no price tag means it's free.'

He smiled, but with less amusement. 'That's some grade A logic, little one. But you can't be from here. This is my turf and I ain't seen no kids around here before.'

Charlotte wasn't sure what 'turf' meant, but she got the point and rolled her eyes. 'Not *here* here. I mean, we're from the territory.'

'We're from Citrine.' Ultra spoke up from behind her, in the shy voice she only used on strangers.

In a split second, the man's expression switched from jolly as a Walker Day elf to angry as the cat on his T-shirt. 'Ain't right to joke about the dead, kid. Show some respect.'

Ultra backed up, but Charlotte took a step forwards, sticking up for her sister. 'She isn't joking. Our parents worked for Nadine Walker.'

The man's brow furrowed, and his expression softened. 'Holy shit . . . you're *those* kids?' He paced back and forth. 'Then I'm real sorry for your loss.' He sounded like he meant it. 'You two are sisters?'

Ultra nodded. 'Twins. But I'm older.'

Charlotte elbowed her. 'By, like, five minutes.'

'Twins, huh?' said the man. 'You don't look like twins.'

'We're non-identical,' said the sisters in unison.

The man nodded. 'People say twins have a special connection. You two got that?'

'Not really,' said the sisters together, grinning.

The man laughed and ran a hand over his bald head. 'It's good you've got each other.' His smile faded, and he got that look Charlotte had seen before when really old people talked about living through the Melt.

When he spoke again, his face went back to normal. 'Well, I don't know how you two scamps got down here – I'm gonna need my people to check the perimeter again – but if you really are from Citrine, then you've already been through way too much tragedy for whatever the hell age you are.'

'We're nine,' said Charlotte. 'But she's five minutes older.' She thrust a thumb towards her sister.

He smiled and held out the gizmo between the sisters. 'Take it,' he said.

Charlotte looked at Ultra, and her sister nodded. She took the gizmo. She should have said 'thank you,' but she got hypnotised by the smooth green plastic and she forgot. 'What's this thing called, anyway?' she asked, instead.

A strict voice cut in from further down the aisle. 'It's called a yo-yo.

And like everything on offer here, it was remarkably challenging to source, which is why we charge premium prices.'

The man who approached was even older than the yo-yo man. He was tall and thin with glasses and a sort of brownish green cardigan that might have actually been greenish brown. His forehead was big, and it had creases in it, like he'd frowned too much and his face had got stuck. He gave both girls a withering glare and turned his attention to the yo-yo man, lowering his voice. 'Your next appointment is two minutes out, and I don't think I have to remind you that timeliness is next to godliness.'

The jolly yo-yo man gave the grumpy cardigan man a friendly slap on the shoulder, and it made the air smell fresh like petals. 'Where would I be without you, eh, Jer?'

'Not at your next appointment, I'd wager.'

The yo-yo man nodded and turned his attention back to the sisters. 'Pleasure to meet you both.' He bent down and shook each of their hands. 'Jer will show you out.' He was walking away and then he turned back towards them. 'You girls take care of each other. That's what fami-ly's meant to do. And'—he gave them a friendly wink—'keep to the straight and narrow.' He whispered something to the cardigan man and disappeared through a door behind the counter.

Charlotte looked up at the cardigan man, clutching the yo-yo in case he tried to snatch it away from her.

He didn't, but he let out a deep sigh. 'Mel has asked me to give you something,' he said. 'But let's get a few things clear first. That man you just met – his name is Melville K Narrow. This is his establishment. You've somehow wandered onto what he insists on calling his "turf." You will never tell anybody that you were here. You will never speak his name to anyone. Ever. Is that understood?'

Charlotte and Ultra nodded. The cardigan man walked away from them towards the back of the shop, but he kept talking, and Charlotte realised he wanted them to follow.

'My name'—he folded back a hinged part of the counter and went through to the other side—'is Jeremiah Strait. That's Mr Strait to you. I work for Mr Narrow and ensure his interests are looked after.'

Charlotte had no idea what that last part meant, but she didn't inter-rupt. Suddenly, Mr Strait produced a sharp, shiny knife from somewhere inside his cardigan, and Charlotte felt nervous about this situation for the first time. But Mr Strait didn't threaten them. Instead, he gripped the hilt in his hand while he rooted around behind the counter. Eventually, he found something that looked like a thick pink Nutrition Bar. He used the sharp knife to slice two chunks from it and passed a piece to both sisters.

'Mr Narrow asked me to give you this,' he continued with a bored tone. 'It's nougat.'

'What's noogah?' asked Charlotte.

'It's a pre-Melt delicacy. Be warned: it contains excessively unhealthy quantities of sugar and, as such, is both detrimental to one's health and a supremely prohibited foodstuff within the ArkTech Territory.'

Charlotte lifted it to her nose and sniffed. It smelled good. Sweet. Fruity. She was about to take a bite, but she thought better of it. 'How do we know it's not poison?'

Mr Strait let out a mirthless laugh. 'You don't.'

Charlotte gave him a long stare and then took a bite of the pink stuff without breaking eye contact. It was the sweetest thing she'd ever tasted. So sweet it burned her tongue. But the texture was soft, and it smelled like berries. She chewed and swallowed. It was good. She snarfed the rest, and Ultra followed her lead.

'Can we have more?' asked Charlotte.

'No,' said Mr Strait. 'I don't understand why Mr Narrow has allowed you this privilege. I can only assume you caught him in one of his strange moods. In any case, you are now free to show yourselves out.' He gestured towards the door.

The sisters looked at each other and shrugged.

'Thanks, Mr Strait,' said Charlotte. Then she remembered they hadn't introduced themselves, and a minder had told her that was rude. 'By the way, I'm Charlotte Vance, and this is Violet Vance.'

Mr Strait made a show of covering his ears with his hands. 'Please, please. We don't use registered names down here: it's a security risk. You'd need an alias if you were to return, which I do not recommend until you are considerably older and richer.'

Charlotte took the hint and made for the door with Ultra at her side. Just as they were leaving, Mr Strait called out from behind the counter.

'Make any trouble for Mr Narrow, and I don't care how young or old you are, young ladies. Believe me when I say I will kill you.' With a flick of his wrist, Mr Strait sent the blade in his hand sailing across the shop until it embedded itself in the thin gap between a cabinet's door and the frame it was mounted on.

The whoosh of the knife, along with Mr Strait's calm tone of voice, made her shiver – she could tell he meant what he'd said. 'We won't cause any trouble for Mr Narrow. Will we?' Charlotte elbowed Ultra gently, who shook her head.

Mr Strait nodded and turned his attention to the screen of an old-fashioned device that was lying on the counter.

The sisters slipped back outside, past the unmoving guards. The sugar hit their bloodstreams, and they ran all the way back the way they'd come. When they re-emerged at the play area on the Wreck's main level, their minders were still busy chatting and were none the wiser that the twins had gone anywhere at all.

If it wasn't for the solid evidence of the yo-yo, which she and Ultra took turns keeping hidden, Charlotte might have thought the whole thing was just a wonderful dream.

CHAPTER 10

Charlotte leaned against the grimy steel wall of the alley, swiping furiously at the cracked screen of her device as she tried to catch sight of Mabel or Strait. The footage showed a crush of people in waistcoats and tweed who were milling around in the standing area between Mabel's booth and the bar, but Charlotte couldn't see a cable-knit jumper or a khaki cardigan among them.

The part of her mind responsible for the calm voice of reason managed to attract her attention, piercing her panic to remind her she could check Mabel's GPS readout. Tutting in frustration with herself, Charlotte minimised the video feed and opened Photon's schematics. The GPS overlay showed Mabel was at the bar. A wave of relief crashed over her.

'Ben, bring back audio and video, centred on Mabel's GPS signature instead of the middle of the room.'

The 360-degree video popped back up, accompanied by the background hum of orchestral music and people having highbrow conversations. Mabel was leaning against the bar, waiting to be served. Someone nearby ordered a round of absinthe, and the feed filled with raised glasses of green liquid and a solemn toast to Walker's Lost Works. There was no sign of Strait.

Without warning, the volume dipped. When Ben spoke, he sounded strange. His trademark enthusiasm was still there, but his voice was a little shaky, as if he were trying hard to convince her everything was normal. Or to convince himself.

'Speaking of audio and video, Charlotte . . . did you know that a university in the pre-Melt United Kingdom once hoped to . . . once hoped to'—he repeated himself—'augment its scholarly credentials by adopting a Latin motto?'

She couldn't see how this aside was relevant, and the timing of the fun fact couldn't have been worse, but Charlotte wondered if the shock of his recent glitch could have been affecting him. That, or he was feeling the AI equivalent of guilt about what they were doing with the SmartSkin cameras and that was making him act weird. Either way, she went along with Ben's non sequitur.

'Latin . . . That's one of those irrelevant dead languages, right?'

'Latin originated in ancient Italy, and its influence on modern times continues to this day. The motto selected by the university was, in English, "I hear, I see, I learn," but do you know the Latin translation of that phrase?' Ben's tone warned of an incoming punchline.

'Not off the top of my head.'

'It translates as "audio, video, disco." Regrettably, this was not considered a suitably erudite motto, despite its meaning in the original. So it is written.'

Charlotte pursed her lips and tried to make sense of the story. 'Is that true, Ben? Or is it one of your jokes?'

In place of an answer, Ben turned the volume back up to full, and Charlotte heard Mabel's voice in her ears. 'Do I know you?'

The man who replied wasn't in the shot, but Charlotte would've known that voice anywhere. That tended to happen when someone wanted you dead.

'I'm a close personal friend of your associate, Mr Neptune,' said Strait.

Charlotte rotated the camera angle to get them both in the shot.

'My name's Jeremiah Strait.' He held out a sinewy hand, and Mabel shook it. 'Mr Neptune tells me you've been keeping his wife busy with your inspired literary recommendations.'

Mabel frowned. 'I was hoping to catch Mr N tonight.'

'I'm afraid he is indisposed this evening. But if you have something for his wife, I'd be happy to pass it along.' Strait smiled in the mirthless way Charlotte knew so well.

Mabel seemed uneasy, but Strait had an aura of polite hostility that tended to get his point across. She opened her satchel, pulled out a thin hardback, and handed it to him. Strait clutched the book to his chest.

'Did you catch the title, Ben?' The exchange happened too quickly for Charlotte to see.

'*Novacene* by Dr James Lovelock.'

That was the one Mabel had borrowed from the library a couple of days before.

Strait continued, 'I'm sure Sally will be delighted.'

'What can I getcha?' The bartender looked at Mabel expectantly. It was her turn to order.

'Mason's herb and cloud tonic,' she said.

'That's on me, Oliver.' Strait gave the bartender a nod, which Oliver returned. Turning to Mabel, he added, 'Such a pleasure finally meeting you, Ms Thorpe.' Then he walked off into the crowd.

'Shit,' said Charlotte.

If Mabel was mixed up with Strait and Narrow, this case was bigger trouble than she'd bargained for. Thanks to her recent case at the kelp processing facility, this was the second time in as many weeks that Charlotte's work had brought her into their orbit and staying there would be hazardous to her health. But if Ben kept glitching out, the consequences would be much worse, for many more people than just herself.

She tried to think as her heart hammered out a bass line. Confronting Strait wouldn't be smart, but she had to find out what he was doing with that book. If her time as Narrow's pseudo-daughter had taught her anything, it was that the pair steered clear of all BioWear technology, so Strait didn't have a GPS signal she could track. If she wanted to follow him, she'd have to do it the old-fashioned way.

'Can you play me any footage of the guy Mabel was talking to after he walked off?'

With a fizz of static, the video rewound, and Charlotte heard Strait's voice again. '—easure to finally meet you, Ms Thorpe.' This time, the camera followed Strait as he made for the exit holding the book. As he reached the door, he collided with a woman in a fluffy pink coat made of tiny feathers. After that, the image splintered, and the video stopped.

'What just happened?'

Charlotte's screen lit up. Her most recent sworn statement appeared with an indignant red cross in the middle.

'You are receiving an incoming call from the Chief Bureaucracy Officer, Abhishek Gautam.'

'Bollocks.' Charlotte tried to think. She couldn't let Strait get away. 'Tell him I'll call him back.'

How was she going to play this? If she tailed Strait and got made, there was no guarantee he wouldn't gut her then and there, but it felt like her only move. She headed for the end of the alley, getting up the courage to follow a man who hated her with all the power of a North Sea current when she heard a metallic ticking noise approaching.

Ben's voice drowned out the sound. 'Abhishek Gautam is calling again. The call has been marked as an emergency.'

'Stall him,' Charlotte hissed.

The ticking was like the sound of those old round clocks she'd seen at Narrow's Toy Emporium. The noise got louder and closer until a woman wrapped in a ball of pink fluff strutted unsteadily past the alley. A thin hardback book was clutched in her small hands.

Charlotte gaped, and the ticking sound got quieter as the woman walked away. She hurried to the end of the alley, careful not to clomp her boots too loudly, and poked her head around the corner. The pink lady was still in view, making her way slowly along the street. That's when Charlotte noticed that the noise and her slow speed were being caused by the same thing: she was wearing high heels.

ArkTech employee-citizens were advised always to wear rigger boots, except during certain activities like swimming or sleeping. Anyone was free to ignore that advice, but it had always struck Charlotte that in an emergency, if people had to be loaded onto boats or airlifted off the platforms, high heels were a liability. Crossing the metal gratings that paved many of the territory's external walkways would be a no-go, and shoes like that were bound to make climbing ladders a challenge.

Charlotte and Violet had once got hold of a pair when they were teenagers and concluded they were more like instruments of torture than fashion items. Unless the pink lady belonged to one of those religions

Ben had told her about where self-inflicted pain was considered a form of devotion, then her footwear had to mean wherever she was going was within easy walking distance. There was no way she'd be heading down into the Underbelly where she'd be liable to break an ankle.

Charlotte studied the street. The nightlife district was buzzing with employee-citizens on the lookout for a good time. She could still see the pink lady up ahead, but more and more people were filling the space between them, increasing the risk she'd lose sight of her in the swaying crowd. There was no sign of a knife-wielding maniac sporting a khaki cardigan. Maybe Strait's part in this was over.

Relieved at that thought, Charlotte began to pursue the pink lady through the district. She hadn't got far when a loud click inside her ears told her that Ben had lost the battle to keep Abhishek Gautam at bay. When the call connected, there was a long pause.

'Ms Vance,' said Abhishek, eventually, with undisguised disdain. The CBO personally taking the time to call her didn't bode well, and his tone only underlined that point. 'I assume you are aware of why you are receiving this call.'

'Enlighten me.' Charlotte knew full well, but she wanted to let him do the talking. She had to focus.

The nightlife district was pedestrianised, probably because fast cyclists and drunk people didn't mix. But it meant Charlotte had to fight against a tide of shambling bodies – who weren't sure if they were coming, or going, or standing still – just to keep the woman in view. If the pink lady handed off the book to someone else, Charlotte might miss it. She had to keep up.

Abhishek sighed deeply. 'It has come to my attention that a serious breach of privacy law has just taken place in the nightlife district and that you, Ms Vance, are responsible.'

'Doesn't ring a bell.' Charlotte saw the pink lady turn off onto a street about a block ahead. If her mental map was correct, that meant she was likely heading for the hotel district.

'Don't play coy. You submitted a request for a warrant and then accessed the data without waiting for Bureau approval.'

'Oh, you're calling about *that*?' Charlotte did her best impersonation of someone innocent. 'I signed and submitted all the required documentation.'

'You knowingly abused your position to access data you had no right to see! Do you have any idea what this would do to ArkTech's reputation if it got out?' Abhishek's posh voice trembled with outrage. 'Give me one good reason I shouldn't report your behaviour to ArkTech Security this instant.'

Charlotte dodged around a crowd kitted out in orange and grey football strips who'd chosen that moment to pour out of a sports bar. She dashed around the corner and caught sight of the pink lady up ahead. She was still clutching the book.

'One good reason?' Charlotte dropped her voice to a whisper. 'How about the safety of the territory?'

Abhishek groaned. 'Do not insult my intelligence by spewing forth that nonsense again. Aside from Ben's peculiar and deeply unfortunate preoccupation with you, Ms Vance, he is functioning perfectly well.'

'Then how do you explain the power cut we just had?'

'Surely, you aren't narcissistic enough to believe that had anything to do with you? It was probably just . . . a loose wire or some such,' he scoffed.

She shook her head. 'A loose wire wouldn't cause—'

Abhishek cut her off. 'Enough. Ms Vance, you seem to be labouring under the misapprehension that the rules don't apply to you, but they apply to all of us. That is the price of living in a free and decent and fair society. Consider this a formal warning. Do *not* test me.'

The line went dead, and the comforting white noise of Ben's channel returned.

Fury surged inside her. She knew she'd broken the law, but it was for a good reason. Why wouldn't Abhishek listen to her? He was hell-bent on refusing to believe her job mattered.

She did her best to push all that to one side. The pink lady was heading deeper into the hotel district, and Charlotte couldn't let her out of her sight.

Whether Ben concluded Charlotte was annoyed and wanted to cheer her up, or whether he was just trying to be helpful, Ben supplied her with some info about the woman she was following.

The pink lady was called Gulyar Orazova, a researcher normally stationed on the Wulfenite platform. She worked non-standard hours so she could spend more time with her husband, Rasul, who worked as a rice technician at the Wreck's food court. Charlotte couldn't guess the rationale behind their aliases, but she was willing to bet the couple were also known as Mr and Mrs Neptune.

Gulyar Orazova, alias Sally Neptune, turned off at the easternmost street in the hotel district, and Charlotte followed, leaving a healthy gap between them. As they continued along the street, the number of onlookers thinned out, and Charlotte realised she could probably take the book by force if she wanted to. With the element of surprise and her nice, flat rigger boots to help her speed away, it would be plain sailing. But there were two problems with that plan.

First, it would stop Charlotte from finding out where Sally Neptune was going, and that info might prove important. And second, Charlotte didn't want to be an arsehole. The fate of the territory might be at stake, and she might play faster and looser with the law than the Bureaucracy Stream could stomach, but she drew the line at traumatising her fellow employee-citizens by mugging them down dark alleyways. Even the ones who were working for Strait and Narrow.

That last point gave her a third reason not to make a grab for the book. As Sally was holding it for Strait and Narrow, stealing from her would be stealing from them. And anybody who wanted to know how choices like that turned out should go and ask Rhonda Ana Conda's left kneecap.

Charlotte let the opportunity to leap out of the shadows go by and watched Sally and her pink feathers strut into a murky establishment in the bowels of the hotel district called the Hotel Astrodite. Charlotte didn't recognise the name, but she knew Strait and Narrow had a shifting network of connections with enterprises throughout the Wreck, so she guessed this was a new addition to their empire of organised crime.

The hotel's doors were made of solid steel. Charlotte wasn't about to lose sight of that book, so she closed the distance and hurried inside. The foyer was dominated by a statue, which appeared to be a replica of some ancient sculpture of a naked woman doing a bad job of covering her private parts with her hands. She suspected the astronaut's helmet was a modern addition. Beyond the statue was a booth of clouded glass with the word 'reception' written above it.

Sally Neptune didn't turn to look when a bell above the front door announced Charlotte's presence. Instead, she tapped her knuckle against the reception booth in a jaunty rhythm. A slot in the glass opened and Sally slid the book through it. Without glancing in Charlotte's direction, Sally headed for the customer lifts, her heels stabbing the carpet. Then a lift arrived and whisked her away.

It didn't matter. The book that surely held the answer to Ben's question was just on the other side of that clouded glass. Now all Charlotte had to do was get her hands on it.

She approached the booth without much of a plan and tapped out the same tune Sally had. The slot didn't slide open this time, but a muffled voice spoke from the other side of the glass.

'Can I help you, madam?'

Charlotte folded her arms and leaned against the counter. 'I'm here to collect something.'

'Name?'

'*Novacene* by James Lovelock.'

'*Your* name.' The voice was muffled, but she heard the eye-roll loud and clear.

The hair on the back of her neck stood on end as the air nearby changed. Her lungs filled with the scent of jasmine laundry detergent with undertones of second-hand smoke. She hadn't heard the bell at the front door ring, but someone was standing behind her, and she didn't need to turn around to know who it was.

'The Young Lady is with me, Stan.' Hearing Strait's voice so close felt like a knife to her brain. He was using the alias he'd given her when she'd joined Narrow's crew all those years ago – it was short for Young Lady of the Fens. It got under her skin that he'd still call her that now, over a decade after they'd parted ways. She wasn't a kid any longer.

The slot in the clouded glass slid open again, and the book was pushed through.

'Take it,' said Strait from behind her. His tone mixed encouragement with threat.

Charlotte's hands felt more like flippers as she clumsily lifted the book from the desk. She could see now that her suspicion was correct: something had been slipped inside it. She folded open the front cover. Resting on the first page was a brown envelope with red letters printed across the front that read, 'Please Do Not Bend.'

She turned the envelope over, revealing a cardboard backing, and was sliding her finger under the flap to tear it open when she felt Strait's bony fingers press into the small of her back. It made her shiver. Then again, she was grateful it wasn't the tip of one of his knives.

'Not yet.' He spoke the words as if she were a disobedient child and he were a parent whose patience was wearing thin. Then Strait turned to the receptionist. 'We'll be needing one of the back rooms.'

Charlotte heard typing on the other side of the booth. 'I've just booked you into the Hephaesteroid Room, sir.'

Strait began to guide Charlotte away from the reception desk. She wanted to say words like 'I'm not going anywhere with you,' or maybe a witty and cutting insult hurled as she made a break for the front door with the evidence. But she didn't speak, and she didn't run. They passed through some heavy automatic doors and down a corridor lined with pre-Melt paintings in faux gold leaf frames that featured an equal ratio of mythical creatures to blaster pistols.

Whether she didn't put up a fight because she was so brave that she was determined to find out what was going on even if it put her in harm's way, or whether it was because she knew she could never outrun one of Strait's throwing knives, she couldn't say for sure. It was probably the bravery thing.

At the end of the corridor, two goons were standing outside a room whose brass sign read, 'Hephaesteroid.'

Ben spoke up in her ears. 'Did you know that this room's name is a highly amusing portmanteau – that is, two words combined into one. Hephaestus was the ancient Greek god of metalwork and volcanoes. While an asteroid is a small rock orbiting the sun.'

'There was a god of volcanoes?' she whispered. She didn't much care, but hearing Ben's voice made her feel better.

The goons opened the doors, and Strait stepped through them.

Ben continued, 'There was a god or goddess of most things, Charlotte! As the name of this establishment is the Hotel Astrodite, it would appear the hotel's theme involves a de—'

As Charlotte stepped inside the room, Ben's voice distorted into a squeal of static that blasted over her audio implants and left her covering her ears in pain. Then, nothing.

'Ben?'

Charlotte was used to hearing the white noise of implants on standby, ready to receive incoming calls or let Ben deliver his commentary, but it was gone. Her implants had been rendered inactive. A wave of panic crashed over her.

'Ben!'

Strait smirked at her, and she knew it was his doing. This wasn't a glitch. Charlotte had just stepped inside a dead zone created by a jamming array. Her heart sank as she realised she was now alone in a room with her worst enemy, and she'd just been cut off from her best friend.

CHAPTER 11

The Hephaesteroid room had been kitted out with an eclectic mix of blacksmithing equipment and rocky sculptures. A huge conference table of blackened wood sat in the centre of the room. Charlotte suspected it was reclaimed pine treated to look like an illegal hardwood. Several bowls of grey stone sat on top, each full of apples that had been painted gold. They were probably a reference to something, but without Ben, she had no way of knowing what.

She felt a pang of grief. Being separated from Ben was almost physically painful. It felt like having parts of her own brain lanced off. Like the part that knew things, and the part that cheered her up when she was sad. Charlotte wondered what it was like from Ben's perspective to be cut off from her.

Strait plucked the copy of *Novacene* from Charlotte's hands and made his way to the far end of the table. He pulled out a chair and sat down, his posture upright as ever. Leaning forwards, he hooked his long fingers around the edge of a stone bowl and slid it towards himself. Suddenly, a blade was in his hands, but Charlotte didn't spot where it came from. Strait began to peel an apple and the thinnest strip of golden skin came away in a perfect curl.

It was over a decade since Charlotte had last been in a room with Jeremiah Strait. He'd had a knife back then too, but Strait always had a knife. She guessed he was in his mid-sixties by now. His neat beard was flecked with grey and the lenses of his glasses had grown thicker. His tall forehead was lined with even deeper wrinkles – so many years of casual disdain were bound to leave their mark. But his round-necked khaki cardigan – his signature fashion item with its large wooden buttons – was immaculate as ever. Charlotte suspected Narrow had smuggled in a whole crate of them for his partner.

Her instinct was to keep as far away from Strait as possible. But she knew if he wanted to hurt her, there was nothing she could do to stop him. He might have been getting on in years, but she wasn't willing to bet her life that his aim had faltered.

Charlotte decided to fake a level of confidence she didn't feel. She strode across the room as if she owned it, grabbed the chair diagonally opposite Strait, and sat down heavily, leaning forwards and watching him peel his apple. The gold coating came away like margarine until it was all gone and he put the naked piece of fruit back into the bowl.

'Not gonna eat that?' she asked. This was all too surreal. She'd heard about out-of-body experiences, and she adjusted her feet, making sure the soles of her boots were firmly planted to reduce the chance she'd float away.

Strait waggled the tip of his blade at her casually. 'I know what you're trying to do.' He reached into the bowl for a new apple and began the peeling process all over again.

'Just seems such a waste. It's not like those things grow on trees.' If being flippant would keep her calm, she'd double down.

'Amusing,' he didn't smile. 'You couldn't possibly think I'd let you get away with it.'

Charlotte felt her eyebrows arch. 'What do you think I'm trying to get away with? The book?'

'Don't be coy, Young Lady. We received your little note.'

'Oh. That.' Charlotte felt her insides twist into knots. A couple of weeks earlier, Ben had given her a case to investigate some illegal swimming at the base of a kelp processing plant during which she'd accidentally uncovered one of Strait and Narrow's many side hustles. Some innocent people had got caught up in their mess, so Charlotte let Strait and Narrow know that she was on to them, hoping they would back down. It worked, and when nobody came knocking on her door in the middle of the night, she thought that was the end of it.

'Yes. That,' said Strait. 'I've long been of the opinion that what you desperately need is a scuba diving excursion in the North Sea, without the equipment. But Mel's irrational fondness for you sadly blinded him to that truth for years.'

Charlotte noted Strait's use of the past tense. Even after everything that happened, being reminded that Narrow no longer cared about her was a sharper dagger to her heart than any of Strait's blades could deliver. Some days, she hated Narrow for what he'd done. Some days, she woke up determined to report everything she knew about him and ruin both their lives. But that little kid who looked up to Narrow was still a part of her. They might not be bound by blood or law, but when all was said and done, he was still her dad.

Strait continued, 'You may have noticed, thanks to your continued ability to draw breath, that I still have not been granted my request to remove you from the equation altogether. Fortunately for you, my loyalty to Mel far outstrips the profound disgust I feel towards you. But there are limits.' On his final word, Strait gave a quick flick of his wrist and the apple in his hand implausibly fell onto the table as three separate pieces.

'I've kept my mouth shut.' Charlotte glanced at the brutalised apple and then looked Strait in the eye.

'Ah, yes. That old gentleman's agreement. Mel lets you live; you don't report him to ATS. So simple. So clear. What, then, would entice you to stick your nose into our business after all this time?' He jabbed the knife towards her as he spoke. 'It's a rhetorical question, of course. I know why.'

Charlotte wanted to protest, but letting him speak felt like the smarter move. 'What's your theory?'

'You. Want. Back. In.' With each word, he cut into the newest apple.

Charlotte wasn't sure whether to laugh or cry, but she managed to keep her face neutral. A barrage of sarcasm rose to the tip of her tongue, but she thought about the way Ben's voice had trembled after his glitch and she swallowed them back down. The right words were the ones that would get answers for Ben. She dug deep and tried for diplomacy.

'Look, I'd be lying if I said I never missed Narrow. He was like the father I never had. But that's all in the past. I work for Ben now. He assigned me the cases at the kelp plant and the library.'

Strait paused with his blade hovering above the latest piece of fruit. His eyes narrowed. 'You work for Ben. I see. And what is it you expect me to believe you do for ArkTech's AI? I know you're not assisting him in the field of general knowledge. If ignorance is bliss, you must live in a constant state of euphoria.' Strait chuckled, and his face contorted into a smile. It was disconcerting.

'Been waiting ten years to hit me with that one?'

'No, no. When you're around, they just come to me.'

She sighed. 'I'm Ben's Head of Awkward Questions.' If she got out of this room alive, she'd be making another pitch for that stupid badge.

Strait gave her a hard stare. 'Honestly, Young Lady, if you insist on making up a job title, why not choose something more convincing and less asinine?'

Charlotte didn't know that last word, but she fathomed out the gist without rising to the bait. 'He wants to be a better virtual assistant. People do stuff he doesn't understand, and I help him make sense of their behaviour.'

The stare continued. Finally, Strait sighed. 'When it came to my attention that you'd been sniffing around, I took the liberty of perusing your bank records.'

Her eyes widened at the casual admission of the crime.

'Oh, don't look so shocked,' said Strait. 'We taught you how to do it.'

It was true. She'd used some of those tricks earlier that day to access Mabel's bank records, although Charlotte had been careful to activate all available security measures for her own account. She had to admit, she didn't much like the feeling of being spied on now that she was on the receiving end. Then again, every action had an equal and opposite reaction, so maybe she shouldn't have been surprised the universe was keeping score.

Strait continued, 'I thought you might be after Mel's money. And it seems I was right. Despite whatever trumped-up title you've bestowed upon yourself, your salary remains that of a splainer. You're just a two-credit hack.'

Charlotte knew he was trying to get under her skin. Unfortunately, it worked. 'Being in the low tier doesn't mean my job doesn't matter. We all contribute to ArkTech's mission.'

He scoffed, 'How curious that after all your years of unwavering devotion to Amber Benjamin's noble mission, you're still no more than an entry-level grunt. Your salary makes it clear what little value the company places on your services. Mel tried to warn you: you don't matter to them. They'll use you until they break you, and then they'll replace you. That's what big companies do.'

Charlotte shook her head. 'That's pre-Melt thinking. I know you're old, Strait, but you're not *that* old. The CEO's a humanitarian. She saved the world.' Strait rolled his eyes. 'And she saved *me*.' Charlotte was getting angry now. 'After Citrine, the company took me and my sister in. We had nobody, and they gave us a permanent home. Maybe I don't make a lot of money, but I'm doing something that matters for people who make the world a better place.'

Strait gave her a pitying look and relaxed backwards into his chair. 'You know, when I first looked you in the eye today, I thought you were simply wearing ridiculous contact lenses. But now I see you've become so blinded to the truth that your eyes have actually turned ArkTech orange. Still, I can see why you'd have to lie to yourself after siding with the company over a man who treated you like his own child.'

Charlotte wanted to launch herself out of the chair and punch the smug look off Strait's stupid face, but she took a deep breath instead. She spoke slowly, trying to keep the white-hot rage from her voice. 'Ben just wants to know why Mabel's vandalising library books. Once I find out, I'll be on my way.'

Strait cocked his head to one side. 'That's really all?'

'Yep.'

'You're not trying to destabilise our operations or worm your way back into Narrow's heart?'

'Nope.'

'Then if I give you this'—Strait tapped the front cover of *Novacene* with the flat of his blade—'you'll have your answer, and you can run along and leave us alone.'

Charlotte knew making a grab for the book would leave her with a large and unsightly hand piercing to match her scars.

Strait continued, 'I'd be willing to make you a deal.'

'What kind of deal?'

'I'll give you this.' He tapped the book again. 'If you admit what you did to Mel.' Strait said each word with a finality that left no room for doubt about his meaning.

He'd gone too far. The anger Charlotte had been keeping in check boiled over and her heart began to pound. 'What *I* did?' she growled. 'I was seventeen years old! I didn't—'

'You were old enough to know perfectly well what you were doing.' Strait glared at her. 'And you are seventeen no longer, yet it would seem the intervening years have not afforded you the gift of introspection.'

Charlotte knew the words he wanted to hear, but she wouldn't endorse his twisted version of events.

'I almost died.' She slammed her left arm and its twisted skin down onto the table in front of Strait, sending apple bits flying off to one side.

'And who should you blame for that, Young Lady?' Strait tapped the flat of his blade against her scarred skin. 'Mel? Or yourself?'

With a flick of his wrist, Strait threw his blade into the air. Charlotte tried to pull her arm away, but he pinned her by the elbow. Just before the point of the blade embedded itself in her flesh, Strait snatched the hilt out of the air left-handed and buried it in the table between Charlotte's thumb and index finger.

'It's sad that you continue to live in this state of delusion. Mel gave you everything. All he asked in exchange was that you obey one simple rule. You broke it. In doing so, you broke his heart. And for that, I will never forgive you. Ever.' Strait picked up the library book, leaving his blade sticking out of the table, and started for the door.

Charlotte looked at the knife's hilt and imagined burying it in Strait's back. The fantasy was satisfying, but she wasn't a killer and even through the haze of rage, she knew Strait had left the weapon there for his own benefit. If she attacked him with it, he could claim self-defence when he punctured her lung with one of the many other blades that had to be concealed about his cardigan. She might be furious, but she didn't have a death wish, so she gritted her teeth and left the knife where it was.

'Strait,' she said his name like it was a threat and stood up, pushing away her chair. 'Give me the book.'

He stopped in his tracks and folded both arms around it. 'No.' He smiled his joyless smile. 'Not unless there's something you want to get off your chest.'

A silence hung between them. All that stood between her and Ben's answer was the lie Strait wanted to hear. The idea of uttering those words made her want to vomit. Not to mention Ben wouldn't approve – he hated lies because they made people even harder to understand.

Thinking of Ben brought Charlotte back to herself. In reality, it didn't matter what Strait thought of her. It didn't even matter what Narrow thought of her. Helping Ben protect the territory was all that mattered. Those things Strait had said about the company weren't true. ArkTech was better than that.

'All right,' she said, through gritted teeth. 'All right.'

Strait raised his eyebrows expectantly.

Charlotte took a deep breath. 'I did it.'

'What did you do?' Strait gestured for her to continue.

'I . . . I betrayed Narrow. What happened . . . it was my fault, not his.'

Strait's eyes turned cold. 'I know.' He turned to leave again.

'Hey! We had a deal!'

'I don't make deals with traitors.' He spat out the last word and jabbed a bony finger at her. 'Stop investigating the library, Young Lady, or your ruined skin will be the next thing my knives get to peel.'

With that, he left. Charlotte picked up the half-skinned bowl of apples and hurled it against a wall in an explosion of fruit and plaster. She searched for the right word to express her feelings.

'Fuck!'

The word echoed pointlessly around the room.

CHAPTER 12

Charlotte grabbed the hilt of the knife that was sticking out of the table, yanked it free, and threw it at the closed door. It impacted side-on and bounced off, clattering to the floor harmlessly. She let out a roar of frustration. Strait had been toying with her. He was never going to show her what was tucked inside that envelope, and he'd tricked her into making a confession she didn't believe.

Saying those words had transported her back in time, filling her up with the old pain of Narrow's betrayal. She knew Strait would tell Narrow what she'd said and that the old man would be disappointed in her all over again. He must regret ever taking her under his wing, treating her like his own daughter. Not that she cared what Narrow thought of her any longer, but . . .

Who was she kidding? Of course, she cared. She wished she didn't, but he was her family. Not the family she should have had – not the one taken from her by the Citrine Disaster – but he'd become her family nonetheless. Narrow had chosen to care about her when she was just a rudderless kid, and that would always mean something, even if she never saw him again.

She was no traitor. Charlotte had thought this was all ancient history, but the injustice turned her stomach, and her arm began to ache as if her wound were raw. Her heart pounded as she tried to figure out her next move.

This was stupid. She was letting Strait intimidate her, but he wouldn't harm her without Narrow's permission. His threats were empty. Charlotte might only get paid the same as a splainer, and Abhishek Gautam might not give her role the respect it deserved, but she was the Head of Awkward Questions, acting in the line of duty on Ben's behalf. She had every right to demand answers. Her job was essential. Strait liked to operate off the grid, but right now he wasn't down in the Underbelly. This was *her* turf, and she wasn't going to let him just waltz out of here.

Charlotte rushed to the door and heaved it open, leaving Strait's blade lying where it had fallen in the corner. He couldn't have gone far. There was no sign of him in the corridor, so she started to run.

As she bounded towards reception, her audio implants buzzed back online and Ben's cheerful voice filled her ears.

'—lightful mishmash of references to outer space and the ancient world.' He paused for a moment. 'Reconciling timestamps. I believe we were disconnected, Charlotte. Your heart rate is extraordinarily high. Is anything the matter? Oh! Perhaps you have been undertaking a cardiovascular workout in accordance with the recommendations of my well-being algorithms!'

She couldn't spare the breath to answer him, but hearing his voice spurred her on to move faster. As she reached the reception desk, she heard the residual tinkle of bells in the foyer. Someone must have come in a few moments ago . . . or gone out. Charlotte hurled herself towards the door and shouldered it open.

Out on the street, there was a drunk couple stumbling their way towards one of the neighbouring hotels arm in arm, but no sign of a miserable old gent in a cardie.

'Can I assist you in some way?' asked Ben.

Charlotte dived back inside the Hotel Astrodite and pounded her fist against the clouded polymer of the reception booth. Nobody answered, but she could see the silhouette of a person shifting around back there.

Thump, thump, thump.

'Where's Strait? Huh?'

Bang, bang, bang.

'What about that woman from before – Gulyar Orazova . . . Sally Neptune – what room is she in? What was inside the book she gave you? Answer me!'

The receptionist continued to ignore her. She slapped the glass in annoyance one last time and turned away.

Charlotte growled, stormed out of the Hotel Astrodite, and marched down the street without a destination in mind. Her guts twisted into knots, and she tried to remember to breathe. Strait had played her. She should have ripped open the envelope when she had the chance. Even if he really had been willing to gut her then and there, at least she would've died knowing what all of this was about.

Ben spoke up again. 'If I am not mistaken, you are experiencing distress. Allow me to offer some sympathy. There, there, Charlotte. There, there.'

She wasn't ready to explain to Ben how she'd let him down – how she was no closer to an answer – so she just kept walking. She didn't care where she was going.

A lamppost was in the wrong place at the wrong time, and it felt the brunt of her fury when she buried the toe of her boot into its base. She was about to take another shot at it when her world filled with the sound of impossible rain. Startled, she withdrew from her lifeless opponent.

How could it be raining indoors? Had there been a breach of the Wreck's outer shell? She held out her palms and waited to feel the touch of raindrops on her skin. When nothing happened, she looked up. Far above her was the platform's enclosed ceiling, complete with pipes and wires and walkways and the metal casings of air vents. There was no visible damage up there. Then she realised what was going on.

'Ben? What are you doing?'

The rainfall's volume dipped by fifty per cent as he replied. 'The sound of rain is known to have a calming effect on *Homo sapiens*, triggering a consistent background of white noise which many people find soothing.'

The volume went back up, and Charlotte took a moment to listen and breathe. Ben wasn't wrong – it was a nice sound. She let the patter massage her brain. She was still angry, but Ben's kindness took the heat out of it and reminded her why she cared about her job.

She left the poor lamppost alone and began to drift down the street again, trudging along to the sound of virtual rain.

'I am here if you wish to talk,' said Ben.

It helped to know that. But what would she say? She'd screwed up the investigation. Colin, Mabel, and Strait all knew she was looking into this, and Strait was a master when it came to covering his tracks. He could be pulling the plug on the whole thing right now. By the time Charlotte regrouped, there wouldn't be any evidence left to find. She just had to hope he was too arrogant for that.

Her feet carried her out of the hotel district back towards Photon. Part of her wanted to storm upstairs and demand answers. She'd shout, she'd point, she wouldn't hold back. She'd grab Mabel's satchel and dramatically empty it onto the floor. But Charlotte knew she couldn't do any of that. Abhishek Gautam barely tolerated the existence of her role, and he'd love an excuse to abolish it, likely even more so after today. Creating a public nuisance while harassing her co-workers might give him the ammunition he needed.

'Vance!'

The shout came from across the street. Rhonda 'Ana Conda' Edwards had rotated onto working the outer door at Photon, which Charlotte noticed was now right across the street. 'I told you to screw off!'

Charlotte ignored the bouncer and kept walking.

Abhishek Gautam. Thinking of the Chief Bureaucracy Officer sent Strait's words about her job echoing around her mind. It shouldn't matter. Whatever her salary, whatever her status, she was doing important work for Ben and for ArkTech.

But now that he'd said it, now that she really thought about it, it did matter. Somehow. Charlotte's job took way more skill than splaining. Putting her on the exact same rung felt like a kick in the teeth, especially after six years of service.

'Ben, do you think I'll ever get promoted?' The sound of rainfall in her ears seemed to grow louder, but maybe it was just her mood.

'Granting promotions falls beyond the scope of my authority.'

That was what he always said, but it wasn't much of an answer. Maybe Charlotte was no different from Mabel, stuck in an entry-level role. She remembered how Mabel had tried to pass her a coin and Charlotte wondered if she should've considered taking the splainer's case after all. Maybe that was the only way she'd ever afford an accommodation upgrade or a fix for her janky lenses. She couldn't realistically fit in another job alongside this one. Then again, a hundred credits was a lot of money when—

Wait . . . the coin!

A chain reaction sparked in Charlotte's mind, each thought igniting the next. She reached into her cargo pocket and pulled out the coin she'd lifted from Mabel's place. It was still sticky, and the cotton lining of her pocket had left a fine layer of grey fluff stuck to its surface. Charlotte lifted it to her nose and sniffed it.

'Mason's herb and cloud tonic,' she said to herself. The drink Strait had bought for Mabel. It must have contained the coin. That was where they were coming from. That was how Mabel was getting paid.

But why was she getting paid anything at all? What the hell made those blank pages a decent business proposition for Strait and Narrow? And where were Mabel's ill-gotten gains even going?

Charlotte's mind started to whir. Could Mabel be stealing ArkTech's secrets somehow and selling them to Strait and Narrow? That couldn't be it. With a splainer's clearance level, she couldn't access anything of value.

She thought back to the case Mabel had offered her. Mabel had asked her to look into why she hadn't been able to apply for any jobs in eighteen months, but why did she even care about not getting promoted when she was making this extra cash on the side? Perhaps Mabel was sick of being stuck in a job that had no status or recognition. If so, Charlotte was starting to relate.

Charlotte put her device away and turned everything over in her mind. She needed to talk this through with Ben, but not out on the street. It was late. Now that her Strait-induced rage was draining away, Charlotte was left feeling tired and sad.

'Perhaps it's time to go home and get some rest,' said Ben cheerfully. Maybe her change in mood showed up in her blood sugar or something. 'Tomorrow is another day. So it is written.'

She nodded. 'Yeah, good idea. 'What time is it, anyway?'

'The time is twenty-three hours, twenty-seven minutes, thirteen seconds UTC, and counting.'

Definitely time to head home. Charlotte looked around to get her bearings, trying to figure out where she was in relation to the

HyperBullet garage. That's when she noticed where her feet had taken her. On her left, Paws for Torte continued to serve its patrons a winning combination of cakes and feline companionship. On the other side of the street was the book library, its windows dark.

She remembered her view of Mabel arriving there earlier that evening. Her face had been a mask of concern. She'd looked weighed down – mentally and physically. Then, a little later, Mabel had left with Colin, and she was practically skipping along the street. Had the soft-spoken librarian really lifted her spirits that much? Or could she have left something heavy behind at the library?

It had to be worth finding out before she called it a day.

Charlotte crossed the street towards the scene of the crime. The pull of her unanswered questions was impossible to break away from. How could thieving blank library book pages earn somebody a weekly haul of extra credits?

Strait and Narrow often used paper to pass coded messages between their operatives, but even if that's what had been inside the envelope, they wouldn't pay over the odds for it when they could just pick some up from Repurposing. Narrow used to say he didn't get rich by chucking money overboard. And however much they were paying Mabel, Strait and Narrow would be earning a vastly larger sum. Mabel's stolen pages had to be special somehow.

When Charlotte pushed on the library's front door, it resisted. A digital display of the operating hours said the place stayed open until ten on Thursdays. Big orange capital letters spelled out the word, 'CLOSED.'

She peered through the windows, but there was no movement inside. The glass in the windows and doors had been tinted to signal it was shut. All Charlotte saw on the other side was low terracotta security lighting picking out the shape of the bookshelves suspended above the desks. Colin's colleague had closed up for the night.

'The library is ArkTech-owned, right? It's a public space, so can you give me today's security footage from the reading room we were in earlier?'

'Certainly!'

Ben switched off the low-level backing track of rain as Charlotte unlocked her device. When she looked at the video footage on her screen, it was totally black, except for an orange time readout in the corner. 'You've got to be kidding me . . .'

'Certainly!' repeated Ben. 'What sort of horse only goes out after dark?'

'No, no. I didn't mean . . .'

'Nightmares, Charlotte.'

She sighed. 'This case is becoming a nightmare . . . It looks like this really is a *private* reading room. The camera's been covered up, just like the one at Photon.'

'From a statistical perspective, that is highly unlikely to be a coincidence.'

Charlotte nodded. Something was happening in that room that Colin and Mabel didn't want anyone to see. If Charlotte wanted to find out whether Mabel had stashed anything inside, she'd have to get in there and look the old-fashioned way.

Another bout of breaking and entering wasn't how she'd imagined her evening would end, but getting a look inside that reading room was too good an opportunity to pass up. She pushed on the front door again. It didn't budge.

'Can you open this up for me, Ben?'

'Evaluating. One moment.' There was a pause, followed by a click.

She pushed once more. This time, the door moved forwards a few centimetres. After that, it stuck fast. Charlotte's brow creased. She peered through the gap, trying to get a better look at the problem. It hadn't been obvious before, but through the small gap, she could see that someone had wrapped a bike lock around the door handles on the inside. She rattled the door as if it might persuade the chain to loosen its grip. It didn't.

'The door's been locked manually,' she said, keeping Ben in the loop in case her lenses were on the blink again.

'Perhaps the recent spate of vandalism has led the library's technician to implement more stringent security measures,' he said.

'Maybe. But how did he get out if the door's locked from the inside?'

'Analysing. The book library's blueprint suggests there is a back door.'

Good thing too. None of the attachments on her multi-tool were strong enough to make a dent in something as hefty as a bike lock.

'Send the building plans to my device, Ben.'

Charlotte didn't look at them immediately. First, she took a few steps backwards to eyeball the place. She'd learned that the plans didn't always give a full picture.

From the front, the book library was joined seamlessly to the buildings on either side. On the right, there was a gear library dedicated to loaning out equipment for DIY. The building directly opposite seemed to serve hobbyists with interests like stamp collecting and tabletop wargaming. Hanging above the street past the hobby place was a huge sign that said Museum District. Charlotte headed in that direction.

Eventually, she found what she was looking for. At the boundary between the two districts, there was an alleyway barely wider than she was. A handful of security lamps cast an orange glow against the tall walls at irregular intervals. There would have to be a wider access point somewhere, but why go the long way round if she didn't have to? Charlotte looked up and down the street. There was a group of people chatting further down, but they didn't seem to be paying any attention to her. Turning side-on, she slipped through the gap.

CHAPTER 13

As she squeezed herself into the tight space, Charlotte thought of her twin sister, Violet. Her claustrophobia had got intense since Charlotte's near-fatal injury, so doing this would have been a no-go for her. But for Charlotte, edging her way between the metal walls felt cosy, as if the territory itself were so grateful for all her hard work that it was giving her a hug.

Looking up, Charlotte could see cables and vents connecting the buildings together. Ben's powerful pseudo-brain controlled the energy and air that flowed through them. It was almost as if ArkTech's platforms were Ben's version of a physical form; their pipes and ducts his equivalent of veins and capillaries.

'Do you ever think of the territory's platforms as your body, Ben?'

'What a fascinating question, Charlotte! Regrettably, as I have no lived experience of a corporeal existence, it is impossible for me to assess how appropriate an analogy that would be.'

Charlotte squeezed further through the gap between the buildings. 'That makes sense. Do you ever wish you had a body like mine?'

'The body of a sleep-deprived twenty-seven-year-old female of below-average height?'

She pursed her lips. 'Just in general, Ben, like any human.' Charlotte stumbled on a piece of metal piping that was jutting out from the wall, and her toe smashed against the inside of her boot. She gasped from the shock as much as from the pain.

'Contemplating . . .' There was a buzz of static. 'I do not believe so, Charlotte. I would not wish to cause any offence, but I believe my own manner of existence has the potential to be less precarious than your own, from an evolutionary perspective.'

'You mean because humans get diseases and fall over and stuff like that?'

'Yes, Charlotte. And due to the time limit biology places on your lifespan. I gain experience and wisdom without growing old. My capabilities increase steadily over time while yours reach their peak, then slowly diminish during your inevitable decline towards death. I can suffer psychological discomfort, but never physical pain. I wish to understand humanity, but I am grateful to be who and what I am.'

'I get that,' she said, distracted by her throbbing toe. 'Pain's no laughing matter.'

'So I understand. Conversely, the following *is* a laughing matter: why did the artificial intelligence fail to attend the Walker Day party?'

Charlotte made a mental note to be more careful about which expressions she used. 'I don't know, Ben. Why didn't the AI go to the Walker Day party?'

'Because he had no body to go with!'

Charlotte rolled her eyes, but she couldn't help but smile. 'Nice one,' she said. 'Do you think we could take a little break from your jokes, Ben? I'm worried about my sides splitting open.'

There was a pause. 'I make no promises, Charlotte.'

At least she could rely on Ben's honesty.

She finally reached the end of the narrow passage, and the gap spat her into a maintenance corridor that ran all the way along the back of the borrowing district. It felt spacious compared to the alleyway she'd just emerged from.

Behind each venue, there was a set of industrial skips marked up with whichever types of waste belonged inside. Maintenance crews rode their automated collection carts along these corridors to empty the bins, but their rounds happened during office hours, so there was no reason for anybody else to be back here. She had the place to herself.

Charlotte headed along the back street until she was standing behind the book library. There was a set of double doors that the blueprints said were an emergency exit, but when she got closer, she saw that they weren't going to help. They were the type that had a crash bar and only worked in one direction.

She looked up. High above her head were the maintenance walkways and air vents that wove around the Wreck's internal shell. The whole platform could be navigated using that connective tissue, and there were routes from there into the Underbelly for anyone in the know, assuming they hadn't been banished like she had.

She couldn't see any other doors or hatches behind the library, but looking one level above, she spotted a balcony with metal stairs that zigzagged up the side of the building. It was a fire escape. The balcony's dark metal grating had a gap on one side with the feet of a ladder poking through it.

Charlotte could see a door on the balcony. A proper one with a handle. She didn't have anything long enough to activate the ladder's release catch from below, but that was no big deal. If she took a running jump and pushed off from the wall, she could grab the ladder's bottom rung and pull herself up.

She rolled her neck from side to side, did a few lunges, and stretched out her arms. Hard experience had taught her it was worth feeling silly for a few moments to avoid tearing a muscle. Having warmed up, she crouched like a cat getting ready to claw at a waiter's ankles. She carefully gauged the angle. Then she went for it.

Charlotte ran forwards, planted her rigger boot against the wall and pushed off and up, making a grab with both hands for the bottom rung of the ladder. She felt the cold metal brush against her fingertips, but she didn't have enough height. She dropped back down to the ground, stumbling backwards.

She shook it off and took another run at it. This time, her fingers gripped the bottom rung of the ladder, but she didn't manage to keep hold of it. What was she doing wrong?

Back in the day, when Charlotte used to run messages for Narrow, she didn't think twice about clambering up walls and leaping from ledge to ledge. But since learning the hard way that she wasn't immune to getting seriously hurt, she'd had to carry that extra psychological weight, and it was heavy. That was definitely the problem. And being so sure of that meant it certainly couldn't be down to the extra physical weight that adult Charlotte naturally carried compared with teenage Charlotte.

She tried a few more jumps and kept not quite reaching the ladder. There was something missing from her technique, but she couldn't figure out what. After one attempt ended in whacking her wrist against the wall, she stormed across the maintenance corridor and kicked one of the rubbish skips in frustration. It rolled away, as if trying to escape her assault.

She looked at the skip.

She looked at the fire escape.

Charlotte wasn't one to give up in the face of a challenge, but an old lesson from what had passed for school growing up came flooding back to her: fall in love with the problem, not the solution. The goal of getting into the library was more important than her pride.

She grabbed the side of the bin and heaved. Its wheels made it easy to move it into position under the ladder. Climbing onto the lid was far simpler than the jump she'd been trying to make. From there, the ladder's bottom rung was within easy reach. She pulled herself up onto the walkway above, pushing against the wall with her feet to assist.

Charlotte took a moment to let her heart rate drop, and then slipped past the set of stairs that led up the fire escape. Her shadow slunk along by her side, warped out of shape under the low lights. She approached the sturdy-looking door and jiggled the handle, but it didn't budge.

'Ben, can you open this for me?'

'Assessing.' There was a brief pause. 'Regrettably, this door isn't wired into ArkTech's digital infrastructure. It likely uses a mechanical lock that is opened with a traditional key.'

'All right, no problemo.' She rummaged in her cargo pockets for her multi-tool and selected the lock-picking attachments. Her parkour skills might have got a little rusty, but picking locks was like riding a bike. Only without the mortal danger.

'Going in.'

'Amberspeed,' said Ben.

Through the door, she found herself inside a storage room that doubled as a break room. It was dominated by open shelves holding containers and tubs and spools of wire. Charlotte wasn't sure if they were cleaning materials, or the apparatus the librarians needed for fixing up the damaged books, or something else entirely. There was a no-tech desk in the middle of the room with a couple of chairs left haphazardly nearby. A sink sat beyond it, with a chipped ArkTech branded mug upside down on the draining board. It was still wet.

Charlotte looked at the library's blueprints on her device. According to the map, she was just around the corner from the private reading room where she'd interviewed Colin. It suddenly felt like a long time since they'd had that conversation, even though it had only been at lunchtime that same day. Her eyes felt dry and her thoughts were getting sluggish. She was tired. Was that why she hadn't made that jump? It couldn't have helped.

Reaching into her backpack, she fished around for her bottle of Dextim pills. She twisted off the cap and tipped one of the chalky orange lozenges into her hand. She admired its comforting ArkTech stamp for half a moment, then palmed it into her mouth. A citrus flavour hit her taste buds as she chewed. In about thirty minutes, it would kick in. She'd feel better after that.

Static crackled in her ears. 'It is important to note that the use of Dextim is no substitute for a good night's sleep.'

Charlotte sighed. 'Thanks, Ben. My lens feed's working again, is it?' Typical.

'The auditory feedback alone was enough to provide me with a high degree of confidence about the unfolding scenario. Alternative possibilities included your having taken a chewable vitamin or a dimenhydrinate for motion sickness, but your behavioural patterns, coupled with your purchase history, reduced the likelihood of those options.'

She smiled. It was hard not to be impressed by the way Ben pieced things together. 'You know me so well.'

'I do. Are you ready to investigate the reading room?'

'Almost.'

She went to the sink, flipped over the mug on the draining board, and gave it a shake to get rid of the drops of water that clung to its surface. Charlotte filled the kettle enough for a single cup of tea and flicked it on. There was a tin on the counter full of teabags. She chose peppermint, chucked the bag into the mug, and drowned it in boiling water before blowing on it and taking a sip. Nothing like a mouthful of scalding-hot liquid to wake someone up. Armed with her steaming mug, she let herself out of the storage room.

Beyond the door, she found herself back in the main part of the library on a walkway that ran all the way around this level. For safety, the walkway was closed off from the central atrium, where dimly lit bookshelves rose out of the gloom. She was hemmed in by solid panels which turned to chain-link at chest height, guarding against accidental tumbles that could prove fatal. Striding along the walkway, she rounded the corner.

'Shit!' Charlotte stopped suddenly, sending a wave of hot tea pouring over the lip of her mug and down through the grating under her feet.

Sitting cross-legged on the floor in front of the reading room, there was a man who looked about her age. A jagged scar ran from his eyebrow to his cheek. Tools were strewn on the floor in front of him, and he seemed lost in thought while casually bouncing a crowbar against the palm of his hand. At the sight of Charlotte, he scrambled to his feet.

Instinctively, she took a couple of steps backwards and sized him up. Tall, dark, and deadly, this guy was trouble. He had a height and strength advantage over her, and she was sure he could do some serious damage with that crowbar. Was he on Strait's payroll? He was dressed in smart grey combats and an open-necked apricot polo shirt, which meant he wasn't wearing an ATS uniform, so at least she wasn't about to have her night derailed by being taken in for questioning.

The guy took a step towards her. In response, she shifted her stance, holding the cup of tea out in front of her as if she meant to duel him with it. Maybe a faceful of tea would slow him down a bit.

'What the hell do you think you're doing?' The man's voice was stern with an accent she recognised as North American. He swiped at the air between them with his crowbar. 'Are you crazy? There's no drinks allowed up here!' He lifted the crowbar until it pointed at a sign on the wall beside him that showed a mug with a red line through it.

Charlotte's mind did a double take. Of all the things she might have expected a crowbar-wielding stranger lurking in a dark hallway to say, scolding her disregard for the book library's beverage policy wasn't one of them. There was surely only one person who'd focus on that particular detail.

She raised her free hand in surrender. 'You must be the library technician.'

'Damn right,' he said with undisguised pride. 'Nasser Williams.' Instead of offering to shake her hand, he pointed his crowbar at her mug of tea. 'I have to insist you remove that from this area immediately. And you'll have to come back tomorrow. We're closed.' Nasser spoke with the authority and confidence that came with being on his own turf.

'Let me just put this down over there so we can talk.' Charlotte gestured to the corner of the walkway where she supposed the tea couldn't do any harm.

'Careful!' said Nasser. 'Don't make any sudden moves.'

With all the caution of a captured shooter laying down their firearm, Charlotte slowly bent down and placed the mug in the corner. She stepped away from it and put both hands up by her shoulders.

'OK,' said Nasser. 'Now, like I said, you need to leave.'

'No can do,' said Charlotte. 'I'm here on official ArkTech business.'

She was about to rattle off her job description, but Nasser's expression changed before she got started. His eyes widened. He lowered his crowbar and gaped at her.

'Wait . . .' His stern look melted away, replaced by a wide grin. 'You're that detective!' A touch of awe had crept inexplicably into his voice.

'Uh, I'm Charlotte Vance, Head of Awkward Questions.' She eyed him suspiciously. Nobody reacted this way, so she began to wonder about his sanity.

The technician nodded enthusiastically. 'Colin said a detective stopped by. That's actually why I'm here so late!'

Had Colin guessed she might come here and asked Nasser to stand guard over the reading room? Charlotte took a step backwards and managed to keep the tremor in her heart out of her voice. 'What's the crowbar for, Nasser?'

'Oh.' Nasser looked down at the object as if he hadn't realised he was holding it. 'No, no. I mean, you inspired me! When I heard someone else was taking the situation seriously, it made me think enough is enough. So I stayed late and locked up downstairs to be sure I'd have privacy. The tools were supposed to help me get in here.' He gestured at the door and let the crowbar clank to the floor next to a chisel and a hammer.

'Any luck?'

Nasser shook his head. 'Colin's rigged it shut.' He pressed his thumb against the biometric panel, but it blinked red and honked at him.

'Mind if I take a look?'

'Please.' Nasser stepped back to give her space to work.

Charlotte pressed her thumb against the panel. There was a red flash and a honk. 'Ben? You there?'

'I'm here, Charlotte. Your firm friend and constant companion.' Ben's voice transmitted over loudspeakers built into the ceiling, letting Nasser in on their conversation.

'Can you get this door for me?'

'Analysing . . . I have no wish to disappoint you a second time, but I'm afraid not. While I see a door on the blueprints, there is no corresponding locking device to interface with. Perhaps it has been isolated from the main system.'

Nasser broke in. 'Colin must have swapped out the lock. I figure this one only responds to his biometric ID.'

Charlotte tried the handle, but it didn't even jiggle. 'What do you think he's got in there anyway?'

Nasser began to pace, stepping over the tools on the floor. 'It must be to do with his friend Mabel. I worked out she's been cutting pages out of our books, but Colin didn't even care. I mean, this is a serious breach of the borrower–lender code of conduct we're talking about here!'

Ben spoke in Charlotte's ears. '*This* is the predicted reaction of a librarian to the vandalism of books, Charlotte.'

She nodded and replied to Nasser. 'So, what do you think they're up to?'

'I don't know. But I don't like it.' Nasser crossed his arms. His SmartSkin implants gleamed where the low light touched them. 'Whatever it is, there must be evidence inside this room. Colin's a great boss, but I wouldn't be doing my duty if I didn't protect our books. I tried asking him about it, but he said I was overreacting.'

'He made light of it when I talked to him too.' Charlotte tried to peer inside the reading room, but the glass was clouded over in privacy mode. 'Did you try smashing this?'

Nasser raised an eyebrow. 'How strong do you think I am?'

Charlotte looked him up and down, noticing the lines of sculpted muscle beneath the fabric of Nasser's clothes. She shrugged. 'Strong enough?'

Ben spoke over the speakers in the ceiling. 'This grade of polymer is also used in the external building panels, which are designed to withstand the force of powerful waves. Physics dictates your suggested course of action would be ineffective.'

'Oh. Well, is there any way to get past a biometric lock, Ben?'

'A skilled bengineer may be able to craft a slicing device to bypass it.'

Charlotte had some contacts over on Zircon who owed her a favour or seven, and they were practically nocturnal, so heading over there at this late hour might work in her favour.

Charlotte turned to Nasser. 'OK, I'll get a slicer. Maybe you should go home. I can check in with you when I know what's in there.'

'No chance,' he said. 'I'll go with you.'

It made a nice change for someone else to be taking one of her cases seriously, but having Nasser along for the ride wasn't going to work. 'My contacts won't see me if I bring a stranger.'

Nasser ran a hand through his hair and stood up straight. 'Then I'll stand guard here.'

'Up to you. But it might take me a while.'

Nasser nodded. 'Well, don't take too long. Colin gets here at seven a.m. sharp and locks himself away in here until we open. We'd better get in there before he moves whatever's inside. I think your visit spooked him more than he's letting on.' Nasser collected the mug of tea, holding it away from his body as if it was full of toxic waste. 'I want to get this mess squared away.'

'Me too,' said Charlotte, remembering Ben's glitch.

'Me three,' said Ben.

Nasser grinned widely and gave her a thumbs-up. Then he repeated the gesture, this time aiming his thumb at the loudspeaker in the ceiling. Charlotte wasn't sure whether Ben saw it, but she was touched that Nasser had acknowledged him – thousands wouldn't have. She returned Nasser's grin and noticed he had kind eyes.

Charlotte headed back through to the break room, and Nasser followed. Out on the fire escape, she extended the ladder and mounted it. 'Right,' she said. 'I'll be back with that slicer.'

Nasser was still holding the mug of peppermint tea, and now that it was a safe distance from the books, he took a sip. It had been her tea, but it was probably his mug, so she reckoned that was fair enough. 'Break a leg, detective.' He waved with his free hand.

'What kind of thing is that to say to someone climbing down a ladder?' she laughed.

'Oh, right,' he called down. 'Knock 'em dead.'

'Hoping it won't come to that.'

Once Charlotte's boots were firmly planted on the rubbish skip's lid, Nasser pulled the ladder up behind her and secured the latch. Charlotte moved the bin back where it belonged and headed to the alleyway.

As she squeezed her way along it, she asked Ben to let Cal and Liz know she was coming over. In response, Cal sent her an animated cartoon seal clapping its hands together, which Charlotte took to mean it was fine for her to drop by.

Now Charlotte just had to hope that Cal and Liz's debt to her would be enough to persuade them to build an illegal slicer for free, at short notice, and in the middle of the night.

CHAPTER 14

Back on the borrowing district's main street, Charlotte's feet carried her along the pedestrian lane towards the HyperBullet garage, while her mind turned over everything she'd learned so far.

If Colin would get to the library at seven, that gave her just over six hours to get across to Zircon, persuade Cal and Liz to build her a slicer, and get back to the library. It might be doable, but it would be easier if she could offer them a chunky payday.

'Can we revisit the topic of getting me an expense account, Ben? It would only be for legitimate purchases.'

Static crackled in her ears. 'Legitimate purchases such as a non-compliant hacking device, Charlotte?'

'It doesn't sound great when you put it like that, but it's for you. Anyway, compared to ArkTech's profit margins, the amount I need has got to be a drop in the—'

'There she is! Get her!' The crazed yell of a woman across the street grabbed her attention.

Charlotte looked around, wondering vaguely who the poor 'her' was who was about to get got. On the other side of the street, she saw two men and a woman, all charging in her direction with snarls on their faces and metal pipes in their hands. Rhonda Ana Conda was standing on the street behind them, pointing directly at her.

The thing about being charged by a trio of slavering goons is that the instinct to run kicks in like a reflex. Charlotte didn't think about where she was going, except that it needed to be away from them. She switched from ambling to bolting in a split second as her rigger boots began to pound the concrete.

She zoomed past window displays as she sprinted down the pedestrian lane. Up ahead, a middle-aged couple was strolling along hand in hand. Charlotte shifted right to avoid them, but they drifted that way at the same time. It was straight through or slow down, so Charlotte barged between them, triggering a yelp and a hail of insults. She couldn't afford to spend any breath on an apology. A glance backwards told her the pipe-wielders were gaining ground.

A group of employee-citizens spilled out from a café further up the street. Too many to dodge, so Charlotte merged into the next lane over. A moment later, a fleet of kick scooters zipped past on either side with a chorus of disgruntled yells.

Narrow's voice boomed out from her memory: 'Dodge and weave, flatliner!' He practically used to turn purple during chase scenes in old films when the main character would always run away from danger in a straight line. She scanned the street, looking for an escape route.

There! A wide maintenance corridor was coming up on the left where cleaning trucks accessed the back alleys to empty the bins. Crashing through another group of bystanders, she headed into the corridor. Concrete underfoot and steel on either side, the side street was a grey blur as she hurled herself along it. When she reached the far end, she glanced back. The goons were still on her tail.

Her muscles were starting to burn, and her breath was turning ragged. Ben wasn't wrong: she needed to fit in more cardio. She also needed a better plan than running if she wanted to get out of this with her skull intact. Zircon platform was her destination, which meant getting to the HyperBullet garage. She had to find some way of shaking these goons before she got there.

Charlotte bolted into the maintenance alleyway behind the borrowing district. It was the right direction for the garage, but now she saw the corridor only extended for another four buildings or so before it became one of the Wreck's signature dead ends.

Her route was lined with large rubbish skips, like the ones behind the book library. Maybe she could hide inside one of them. If she hurried, the goons would rush around the corner and find the place deserted. She made for one of the blue bins marked for recycling kelp-based cardboard and heaved the lid upwards. It didn't budge. Charlotte tried again, but the lock held fast.

'Shit!'

No time for picking locks. She pulled on the lid again as if the urgency of the situation might have granted her superhuman strength. It hadn't.

Ben piped up in her ears. 'Insanity is repeating the same action and expecting different results. So it is written.'

She opened her mouth to respond, but at that moment, the trio came around the corner and staggered to a halt.

'Give it up, Vance!' shouted one of them.

'Get ready to take your medicine!' yelled another.

'Come on, guys,' said Charlotte, taking the opportunity to catch her breath. 'Let's talk about this. Whatever Rhonda's paying you, I'll double it,' she lied.

'She's our sister, you muppet,' said one of the men. He looked like the youngest of the group, but he was still older than Charlotte and just as well-built as Rhonda's other siblings.

'Oh . . .' Charlotte slowly moved her hands into position on the side of the skip. 'Then, I'm sorry to be the one to tell you this, but your sister's a thief.' She twisted her body and heaved the skip towards the group. It rolled into place, blocking their path. She turned and ran.

She should have been flagging, but after only that short moment to recover, she suddenly felt invincible. Her blood was thundering in her ears, but her legs felt light and strong, like if she could just run a little faster, maybe she'd take off. Maybe she was becoming one of those superheroes from Narrow's comic book collection. Not a human–animal hybrid, though, like that spider guy. Wait, were spiders animals? Didn't matter. What would she be? She was fast. Not like a horse . . . like a person riding a horse! She was like a knight on horseback . . .

She was the Scarlet Lance! Charging through the air! She could outrun these flatliners no problem, any day of the week. And if the dead end up ahead meant she'd have to out-climb them, she'd lunge her way up the walls instead.

Her inner ears crackled with static. 'It is important to note that the dose of Dextim you took at the library is now active in your bloodstream. I recommend avoiding situations that may present opportunities for risk-taking behaviour while your levels of self-confidence are artificially augmented.'

Charlotte barrelled along the alleyway, her legs moving so fast she might as well have been riding a noble steed.

She scanned the route ahead for something that would lead her up and over. The building coming up on the right had the same kind of fire escape balcony that she'd failed to jump up and grab behind the book library. Its ladder was folded away, and it was the same height. But this time, she knew for sure that she could make it. Her decision was made as soon as she saw it.

Hurling herself at it full pelt, she planted her rigger boot against the wall and launched herself upwards. Her hands closed around the ladder's bottom rung, and then she was hanging in mid-air. Pushing against the wall with her feet, she managed to pull herself up the retracted ladder and onto the balcony above, as if the Scarlet Lance's imaginary horse had given her a boost.

A wave of elation crashed over her. As Charlotte looked down at the street below, she couldn't remember when she'd last seen a more beautiful sight. The Conda-Edwards siblings had stopped running and were looking up at her with expressions ranging from confusion to fury.

Charlotte laughed. 'Yeah, that's right!' she shouted. 'The Scarlet Lance strikes again!'

She raised both of her middle fingers, lifting them up and down as she did a dance on the fire escape. The taunt prompted Rhonda's sister to hurl her bit of metal pipe at Charlotte as if it were a frisbee. The woman's aim was distressingly good, and Charlotte had to take a clumsy sidestep to avoid getting hit in the face. Her foot landed heavily on a bump by the ladder. There was a metallic screech as the ladder's release catch disengaged and its rungs slid down towards the ground.

Charlotte looked at the ladder. The goons looked at the ladder. The goons looked at each other. Then Charlotte bolted for the stairs as the first of Rhonda's siblings started climbing up the now easily accessible fire escape.

The Scarlet Lance charged up to level three, feeling stupid. On the next balcony, she spun herself 180 degrees and bounded up the next set of stairs. Looking down through the metal grating, she saw the first goon had reached the first level of the fire escape. The Dextim was helping with the intense workout, but if she just kept climbing, she'd run out of levels, and she didn't think for one moment that Rhonda's siblings would hesitate to chuck her over the railing and watch her head crack open on the concrete below.

Level four. She needed a plan.

Level five. But where could she go?

Level six. She couldn't get past them if she turned back.

On level seven, Charlotte noticed something. Next to the balcony was the edge of this building, where there was another one of those very tight gaps like she'd squeezed through before breaking into the library.

Decision made.

Instead of climbing up another level, Charlotte dug a pair of rough-palmed gloves out of her pocket and pulled them on. Then she clambered onto the railing at the edge of the balcony. The drop suddenly looked higher now that she was only one misplaced boot away from experiencing it first-hand, but she held her nerve. She'd spent her childhood climbing around on buildings like this. It was all second nature to the Scarlet Lance.

She reached her right arm into the gap. With her left, she grabbed hold of the metal balcony above for balance. Then she lifted her left foot off the railing and stomped it against the wall inside the gap, checking the rubber sole had a good grip.

Footsteps clanged from below, closer now.

Taking a deep breath, she shifted her weight away from her right foot and onto the one pressed against the wall. With a jerk, she moved herself into the small space between the buildings. By pushing against the walls with both booted feet and gloved hands, she kept herself from falling down the seven-storey drop.

Charlotte looked up. Only a few more levels and she'd be able to scramble onto the roof. Hopefully, by the time her pursuers realised where she'd gone, they wouldn't be able to catch up with her.

Her first few steps were tentative, despite the Dextim. Even with her experience, it was weird getting used to walking vertically. Careful to avoid stepping on any of the cables that were hanging down, she wall-walked diagonally, heading deeper between the buildings as well as upwards towards the roof. The grippy surface of her gloves protected her from the cold of the steel. This was much slower than running, but if she was lucky, the goons wouldn't try to follow her.

She heard voices from behind and paused to listen. 'Amplify,' she whispered to Ben. The siblings' words transmitted into her ears.

'Where'd she go?' asked the sister.

'Keep looking. She couldn't have just disappeared,' said one of the brothers.

'I'm gonna make that bitch pay,' said the other brother.

'What level are they on?' Charlotte whispered.

'Dylan, Seren, and Rhys Edwards have arrived at the level eight fire escape. May I ask why they are trying so hard to catch you, and why you do not wish to let them?'

Charlotte continued walking upwards. 'Remember I told you Rhonda once stole something and got beaten up because of it? Well, I reckon she's hoping for payback now she knows I don't work for . . . now things have changed.'

'Why, Charlotte? Did you beat up Rhonda Edwards?'

'Of course not!' She raised her voice a little too much. Then she mumbled, 'I just told the people who did beat her up what she'd done and where to find her.'

'Would you like me to clarify that distinction with your pursuers?'

'They already know.' She was getting closer to the roof, but the effort of talking was slowing her down.

'Would you like me to politely request that they stop chasing you?'

'Ha – sure! Why not try that and see what happens?'

Ben didn't register her sarcasm and, to her surprise, his voice boomed out from loudspeakers in the ceiling that were intended for use in the event of an emergency.

'Dylan, Seren, and Rhys Edwards.' Hearing Ben's chirpy tones boom out at that volume was strangely intimidating. 'ArkTech kindly requests that you cease your current course of action to avoid any unfortunate consequences.'

She wasn't sure whether Ben meant to sound so threatening or if it was a happy accident.

A woman's voice transmitted into Charlotte's ears, and she concluded it belonged to Seren Edwards. 'They've ID'd us. I'm out!' Her footsteps clanged as she left.

'I can't believe that actually worked.' Charlotte reached the top of the gap and clambered onto the building's flat roof. The Wreck's internal ceiling was high above, a steel sky punctuated by the glow of artificial orange stars.

'Many problems can be solved by asking nicely.'

She wasn't convinced that was true, but with two of the Edwards-Conda family still on her tail, it wasn't the time to get into that. Looking back down the way she'd come, she saw Dylan and Rhys scrambling up the gap between the buildings, undeterred by Ben's words. It wasn't over yet.

Charlotte hurried across the roof, heading in the direction of the garage. Up ahead on the left, she could see the structure that had created the dead end at ground level. It was one side of a large squarish building that marked the boundary between the borrowing district and the food court. If she could get over there, she could use the fire escape on the other side to take a shortcut down to the garage.

Running that way, Charlotte paid close attention to her feet. Regular employee-citizens weren't supposed to come up here. These roofs were mainly accessed by maintenance staff in the Services Stream. She was pretty sure there was guidance about keeping it tidy, but they'd obviously been up here recently and felt packing away all their junk between shifts was too much effort. That meant she had to avoid stepping on collections of tools and spools of wire and electrical equipment whose purpose wasn't clear. And aside from that, she needed to make sure she didn't accidentally disappear down a gap between the rooftops like the one she'd just climbed out of.

She hopped over one of those gaps and ran across another roof, getting closer to the food court building. That's when she noticed the problem. Charlotte could reach the shortcut down to the garage from here. But only if she was willing and able to leap across a gap the length of a kayak.

Charlotte stole a glance behind her. One Edwards brother was pelting towards her, while the other was only just pulling himself up onto the roof. She didn't have long to make up her mind, but she sized up the rapidly approaching chasm, and the Dextim in her system assured her she could make it.

Injecting more pace, she hurled herself towards the edge of the building. How far could knights on horseback jump? She was about to find out. She'd never seen a knight in real life, or a horse for that matter, but she could ask Ben more about them later if she didn't plummet to her death.

The footwork was everything, and it felt like she'd nailed it. Her boots pushed off against the lip of the roof and she was soaring above the massive drop. She kept her focus on the opposite roof and didn't look down.

As she flew, Ben piped up in her ears. 'Did you know, Charlotte, that the distance from here to the ground is approximately equivalent to the length of an adult member of the extinct species known as the blue whale?'

Charlotte cleared the gap, but as her boot landed on the lip of the roof beyond, her knee shuddered and she stumbled forwards onto her hands and knees. The roof's rough surface bit into the thick cotton of her jumpsuit and her skin underneath, but her gloves protected her hands from getting grazed. She grunted and took a moment to recover, taking a mental inventory of the damage. She could live with a few cuts and scrapes. Falling off the side of a building, not so much.

She picked herself up, but dusting herself off would have to wait. At that moment, she heard voices from across the chasm.

'It's too far, Rhys! Don't do it!' The Conda-Edwards brother who must have been Dylan was standing near the edge of the roof, shouting back towards his younger sibling. He looked down at the drop below and then across at Charlotte and shook his head.

Rhys ignored his brother's warning. He was running headlong across the roof with no sign of slowing down.

Time to move. Charlotte dodged an assortment of detritus left behind by the Services Stream and headed to the north side of the roof. She spotted the fire escape. All she had to do was drop down onto it and then hope she could lose Rhys. She was about to manoeuvre herself into position when she heard the kind of scream that left claw marks inside her ears.

She looked back. Charlotte didn't know which of the Edwards brothers had screamed, but she immediately understood why they had. Rhys had almost made the leap. But the problem with jumping across tall rooftops was that 'almost' didn't cut it. On the opposite roof, Charlotte saw Dylan looking down over the edge, his face a mask of horror. On her side, there was no Edwards brother. A moment later, she spotted a pair of forearms clinging desperately to the lip at the roof's edge.

Relief washed over her. Now she could get away. Make it to the garage. Get across to Zircon. She was crouching down, ready to lower herself onto the fire escape as planned when a loud crackle of static filled her ears.

'It would appear Rhys Edwards has encountered a potentially life-threatening complication.' Ben's tone implied that this was somehow Charlotte's problem.

'Sure,' she said, making no move to turn back. 'And until a minute ago, Rhys Edwards was my potentially life-threatening complication.'

'No matter the nature of your disagreement, I'm sure you would not wish anyone to fall to their death.' Ben spoke as if cheerfully stating an obvious fact, but Charlotte wasn't so sure.

She hesitated. 'I might.'

Charlotte looked down over the edge of the building. No fire escape had ever looked so inviting. She wanted to use it. It would have been sensible to use it. But she didn't use it.

She gritted her teeth. 'You're doing that angel-on-my-shoulder routine again, Ben.'

'You're most welcome.'

She sighed. Maybe Ben was right – she didn't want someone's death on her conscience.

'Bollocks. Fine.' Her mind made the same 180-degree turn as her body as she hurried back towards Rhys. But when she closed the distance, she hesitated. The idea of extending her arm to someone who'd just been making his best attempt to beat her up didn't hold much appeal. Rhys might take the opportunity to pitch her over the side.

'Help him! Please!' Across the gap, Dylan was frantic, stretching out his arm from the other rooftop as if it might help him reach his brother.

'Yeah, help me, you stupid bitch!' Rhys's voice was muffled as his face was pressed up against the wall below. His words hardly inspired compassion.

'He's slipping!' screamed Dylan.

Dylan wasn't wrong. Rhys was trying to pull himself up, but the overall effect meant he was running out of steam. Keeping her distance, Charlotte looked down over the edge of the building. Rhys's feet were flailing wildly in the air.

On the street below, several employee-citizens were leaning against a wall, chatting and eating something from a nearby takeaway. They seemed rapt in conversation and totally unaware of the man dangling several storeys above their heads. A maintenance truck drove past them, but they didn't turn to look at it.

Charlotte shouted so that both brothers would hear her. 'You do realise I could easily smash my boot down on your fingers until you let go?'

'Please don't,' said Dylan.

'Just bloody try it,' came Rhys's muffled voice. He was impressively hostile for someone in such a weak position.

'Shut up, Rhys,' snapped Dylan. 'We get it, Vance. Help my little brother and we're square.'

From below, she heard Rhys muttering. 'Watch who you're calling little, Dyl-weed.'

If Charlotte had been left to her own devices, there was no way she'd be considering helping this guy. He seemed like an absolute knob who probably deserved to be left hanging off a building, and her sense of self-preservation was yelling at her to get out of there. But as she thought about walking away, Ben's words echoed in her mind.

She wouldn't want anyone to die. Despite apparently needing an urgent personality transplant, Rhys was a fellow ArkTech employee-citizen. He was a fellow person. Charlotte might not like him, but if their situations were reversed, she'd want him to help her. Treat people as you'd want to be treated and all that. Besides, if every action had an equal and opposite reaction, then if she left Rhys hanging there, the universe might find some way to balance the scales. Ben was right. Unfortunately.

'OK.' She kept out of grabbing distance. 'Rhys, your technique is shocking. Stop panicking and use the inside edges of your boots to push against the wall. Legs beat arms for strength any day.'

Charlotte backed up as Rhys followed her instructions. Before long, he was lying on the roof, panting and muttering as he caught his breath. 'Oh, my Amber,' he said. 'Oh, my Amber.'

She made eye contact with Dylan and drew a square in the air with her fingers. He nodded. Charlotte turned, making for the fire escape.

She'd made it to the middle of the roof when something heavy collided with her back, knocking the breath out of her lungs and making her stumble. It felt like getting hit by one of ATS's beanbag rounds, but the metal clang that came next told her it wasn't a gunshot. Rhys had thrown something at her.

Charlotte grunted and spun around. Rhys had sat up, and he was scrambling to his feet.

'I just helped you, flatliner,' she yelled.

'Stand down, Rhys!' Dylan's words carried across the gap between the buildings.

Rhys didn't acknowledge her words or his brother's. Instead, he clenched his fists and took a slow step towards her, then another.

'Rhys! She saved your stupid life!' Dylan sounded furious.

Rhys was a few years older than her and much, much bigger. Height advantage; meat advantage. The Dextim in her blood seemed to drain away as she weighed up her options.

Back in the day, Narrow had taught her lots of useless crap. Thanks to him, she knew how to rewire a plug; how to crack an encoded message; how to close a sale. But one piece of his advice never got old. She heard his voice in her mind. 'Discretion is the better part of valour, Little One. If there's a fight and you can run away, always run away.' The old man was no coward. Just practical, and way more intelligent than people gave him credit for.

But as Rhys stomped towards her, it didn't look like running away was an option. He was too close. If Rhys got her in a grapple, he could drop her over the edge. She looked around for a Plan B.

This rooftop was just as untidy as the others she'd run across on the way here. There were cables all over and tools scattered where a mainte-nance crew had been working. But she needed something right now, and the closest weapon-like object was the bit of pipe Rhys had thrown at her. She squatted down and snatched it up, gripping it in one hand.

She waved the pipe and yelled at Rhys. 'Don't come any closer!'

He kept moving towards her, then he swiped at her with one fist while snatching with his other hand. Charlotte dodged diagonally backwards, and Rhys grabbed at the air. He growled, reached for a holster at his belt, and pulled out a knife.

It was nothing like Strait's razor-sharp blades, and Rhys didn't hold it with Strait's easy precision. The thing was gaudy, with a serrated edge and snake's head embellishments in the hilt, making it look more like an ornament than an instrument. Charlotte remembered junk like that for sale at Narrow's Toy Emporium. Rhys gripped the hilt the same way he'd gripped his metal pipe. Carrying it around probably made him feel like a big man, but Charlotte doubted he knew what to do with it. She could use that.

He came at her again, slicing the air in front of him with the blade. She dodged to the side, trying to gauge his speed. Charlotte had the edge on that front.

Rhys moved towards her. This time, she let him. He pulled back his arm, winding up a powerful thrust with the knife. That's when Charlotte made her move. Gripping the pipe with both hands, she dragged it upwards through the air until it connected with his jaw.

Rhys was stunned. He dropped his knife and stumbled backwards, pawing at the site of the blow with his hands. His eyes looked crazed, and Charlotte couldn't tell if he was on something or if that was just the effect of being hit under the chin with a pipe. Rhys growled, rearranged his feet, and raised an elbow. He was going to charge.

She dodged to the side again, but he moved to match her new position.

'Rhys!' Dylan shouted from the other rooftop, which was now behind Charlotte. 'That's enough!'

Rhys ran at her full tilt, leading with his elbow. Charlotte made a feint to the left, then threw herself in the opposite direction. She grunted as she fell heavily onto a jutting piece of metal that was lying on the rooftop. Her bluff didn't work, and Rhys looked like he was about to leap on top of her.

Charlotte was bracing herself for the impact when Rhys suddenly put both hands over his ears and screamed all the air from his lungs. Her brow furrowed as she tried to figure out what the hell had happened. Rhys was still running forwards, and he tried to change course, but his foot slipped on a discarded tool, and he stumbled. His centre of gravity was all wrong, and he kept hurtling forwards, even as he approached the edge of the rooftop. He tried once more to right himself, but he had too much momentum. Then Rhys was gone. As he disappeared over the side, he didn't make a sound.

'Walker's ghost,' said Charlotte.

'No!' Across the gap, Dylan gripped the roof's edge and peered down to the street below.

Charlotte rolled away from the mallet she'd landed on, the ache in her ribcage letting her know she'd earned a new bruise. She crawled the short distance to the edge of the roof, steeled herself, and looked down.

In the street below, the group of employee-citizens outside the take-away place had backed off. Directly below where Rhys had fallen, there was a parked maintenance truck with its roof open. From her vantage point, Charlotte could see a load of flattened cardboard inside, with Rhys lying unmoving on top of it.

Dylan shot her a desperate glance and then ran off down the nearest fire escape, calling his brother's name.

'Ben, you caught him!' Even though Rhys had just become one of her least favourite people, she couldn't help but smile. 'You moved the truck, right? You broke his fall.'

'No, Charlotte.'

'No?'

'While it is true that I drove the truck into position, I'm afraid it did not break Rhys Edwards's fall. It is important to note that a human experiencing an uncontrolled drop from this height has a very high chance of being killed, irrespective of the material they land on.'

'So . . . he's dead?' Charlotte couldn't see any movement from inside the truck.

'Regrettably, Rhys Edwards died on impact.' Ben instructed the roof of the truck to close, and Rhys's body disappeared from view.

Charlotte felt nauseous. She got to her feet and turned away. 'Why catch him with the truck if there was no chance it would save him?'

'Observing the effects of a thirty-two-metre fall on a human body may cause substantial psychological trauma, Charlotte. I wished to spare any witnesses from the persistent horror of a gruesome mental image they could never unsee.'

Charlotte nodded, suddenly feeling grateful she hadn't been able to make out the details inside the maintenance truck. Being extra careful of her footing, she made her way across the roof to the fire escape. Her hands were shaking as she dropped down onto the top balcony and set off for the HyperBullet garage, trying not to imagine what it would feel like to be bludgeoned to death by the ground.

CHAPTER 15

Charlotte waited in line at the HyperBullet garage with no clear memory of how she'd got there. The world was a blur of grey smudged with terracotta. Her fellow employee-citizens were a faceless mass who talked gibberish at one another.

In her mind, Charlotte saw Rhys Edwards falling. She hadn't seen it in real life, but the imagined reconstruction of his face, contorted with fear and getting smaller and smaller as gravity dragged him down, played on a loop behind her eyes again and again until instead of Rhys's face she began to see her own. She stamped her boots against the garage floor, either to snap herself out of it or to check she wasn't really going to fall. Whether it was the Dextim and adrenaline leaving her body or the trauma of what had happened, she was left feeling light-headed.

Rhys had seemed like a psycho, but it was rough to think he'd just died in his thirties for no good reason. Charlotte watched the whole thing play out over and over and over in her head. The chase. The fight. The fall. Had that been Rhys's plan for her? If he hadn't lost his balance, would she be lying dead inside a truck full of used cardboard instead of him? In her mind's eye, she saw Rhys covering his ears and crying out in pain just before he began to stumble. Why had he done that?

She thought about it until it clicked.

'Ben?' Her own voice sounded far away – underwater. 'Did you flood Rhys's audio feed when he was charging at me?'

'Yes, Charlotte. I made the determination that doing so might subdue Rhys and enable you to get away. I did not intend for anyone to come to harm. Do you disapprove of my decision?' Ben's voice quavered. Another glitch, or was he nervous about her reply?

He had no need to worry. 'No, you did the right thing. I think Rhys would've killed me otherwise, or at least given it his best shot.'

Ben offered a fizz of static in response.

Charlotte let her own words sink in, and her shock over Rhys's fall was swept away by an overwhelming swell of relief that it was Rhys who was dead and not her.

The elation made her giddy until it gave way to guilt about celebrating the death of a fellow human being. As conflicting emotions rose and fell inside her, she steadied herself on a railing by the platform.

It was OK. She was safe. She was home.

She reached the front of the queue, and a pod sighed open, its door folding upwards and inviting her to climb inside. Charlotte was halfway through the motion when a set of thick fingers scratched her scalp, gripping her hair and pulling her head backwards so she was forced to stumble away from the pod.

The hand let her go. It was attached to Rhonda. Streaks of wet mascara were running down her cheeks.

'You killed my brother!' Rhonda roared the words like they were the cry of a wounded animal.

The other employee-citizens in the queue melted away, giving the two women a wide berth.

'It was an accident, Rhonda. Rhys slipped and fell.'

Charlotte searched Rhonda's face for any flicker of reason, but all she found there was raw hate. It was not the face of a woman who had come here to talk things through.

Rhonda drew back her fist, preparing to bury it in Charlotte's face. Without another word, Charlotte shifted her weight and launched herself through the pod's open door. She landed heavily on the seat's soft lining, sending up a waft of citrus-scented air freshener. At the same time, Ben must have sent an override command because the door slammed shut behind her instead of making its usual slow glide.

Rhonda smashed her fist against the door's plexiglass window, then she snatched her hand back in agony. The impact made a hefty thump, but even Rhonda Ana Conda was no match for a material that could withstand the power of a stormy sea.

'Destination?' said Ben over the pod's sound system.

'Away!' said Charlotte.

Ben dutifully set the pod in motion, and Charlotte was whisked away from the Wreck's garage. Rhonda was left on the platform, clutching what could easily have been a broken hand. Soon, Charlotte's view of the woman was obscured by the huge light-screens that should have been showing adverts. But thanks to Ben's glitch, they only displayed the spinning company logo.

Charlotte's heart was pounding. Since breaking ties with Narrow, she'd done her best to avoid trouble. Sometimes her best wasn't good enough, but this had quickly become a very bad day. She reminded herself to breathe as the public transport system whisked her towards wherever Ben had told it to go. She wanted to go home and lie down. But she needed to get to Zircon, and fast.

The shimmering constellations of ArkTech's platforms on the dark water massaged her brain as she let her heart rate return to normal. In the far distance, a pyramid of lights marked ArkTech's corporate headquarters, the Wedge, where the Product Stream and the Bureaucracy Stream were based. On the top level was the CEO's office. Whether Amber Benjamin was there right now or not, thinking about the co-founder and the company's mission reminded Charlotte that everything was going to be OK. Mabel and Colin; Strait and Narrow; Rhonda and her siblings . . . whatever anybody threw at her, she'd carry on working hard to help Ben and keep the territory safe.

'We've got to get to Zircon, Ben.' The darkness glittered, winking at her.

'While your commitment to your duties is highly admirable, perhaps you should go home and get a good night's sleep. Sleep is important for the physical health, cognitive function, and emotional well-being of *Homo sapiens*.'

Charlotte shook her head. 'What if you glitch out again?'

Static buzzed in her ears. 'I'm moving processing power away from more of my non-essential systems.'

'Which systems? Doesn't that mean it's getting worse?'

'Training and educational resources are now temporarily unavailable.'

Charlotte frowned. 'We need to get this fixed.'

'Very well. Setting course for the transfer point at the Central Transportation Hub where—'

A trill from the dashboard interrupted him.

'Please be advised that an incoming video call is being transmitted to the pod's communication system.'

Charlotte tapped on the screen to answer the call. A video burst to life above the dashboard and Rhonda's face shone out at her. 'Pull over, Vance, so we can settle this once and for all.' The bouncer's face was twisted with anger and grief, but she'd wiped away her tears.

'It was an accident, Rhonda. Ask Dylan. He saw the whole thing.'

'Yeah, right. And I guess ratting me out to Narrow was an accident too?'

Charlotte felt a pulse of anger as Rhonda used Narrow's name once again. She knew it was an alias – nobody knew the old man's real name, except maybe Strait – but her training ran deep. 'You didn't give me a choice! Nobody steals from the boss.'

'A woman's gotta eat.'

Charlotte shook her head – everyone in the territory had access to unlimited Nutrition Bars. 'No, you got greedy or stupid or both.'

'I didn't even know what was on that hard drive.'

'Then your luck must run even worse than mine. Let's just leave the past in the past.'

'We could do that.' Rhonda stared at nothing for a moment. 'But I want my pound of flesh.'

Charlotte hung up the call.

'Did you know,' said Ben, 'that the phrase "a pound of flesh" origi-nates from a pre-Melt play called *The Merchant of Venice*, in which violence is posited as a means of settling a dispute?'

'Good to know. Block any further comms from Rhonda Edwards.' Charlotte frowned.

'Certainly! It is important to note, however, that Rhonda is following you.'

'What?'

Ben increased his volume. 'I said it is im—'

'I heard you!' Charlotte looked through the plexiglass behind her. It was true: there was another pod hot on her heels, and she could see Rhonda's muscular form inside it. The bouncer saw Charlotte looking and pounded on her window in case her intentions weren't already clear.

'For Amber's sake!' Charlotte shook her head.

Heading straight to Zircon was out of the question. That platform was unusual. It was within Silicon Fen, but some architectural issue meant it wasn't hooked up to the HyperBullet network. Anybody visiting had to take a boat across. If Charlotte went to the docks, Rhonda would follow her, and that would most likely end with Charlotte getting chucked into the unforgiving waters of the Fenland Sea. She needed a way to shake Rhonda.

Charlotte looked around the cabin for inspiration. Behind a pane of plexiglass, there was a switch to flip in emergencies, but she didn't think this was the kind of emergency the designers had in mind.

'Can you disable her pod?'

'I *can*, Charlotte. But I *won't*. Doing so would put me in breach of a core service level agreement, which ensures the smooth running of the territory's transportation network. Had I been programmed in line with Asimov's Laws of Robotics, this scenario would fall under the second law, whereby one human's orders could be disobeyed to avoid bringing harm to another. It is important to note, however, that I am not a robot but a virtual assistant.'

'All right. Can we outrun her, then?'

'Exceeding the maximum allowable speed limit would put me in breach of a core—'

'Service level agreement.' Charlotte joined him in finishing the sentence. 'Well, I need to lose her. Any ideas?'

'Have you considered asking her nicely?' asked Ben, full of innocent enthusiasm.

Charlotte sighed. Words weren't going to cut it, unless . . . No. Reporting Rhonda to the security team was tempting under the circumstances, but there had to be another way. As far as Charlotte was concerned, getting deported was a fate worse than death. She wasn't a killer, so she certainly wasn't about to get someone sent to the mainland.

Besides, reporting Rhonda to ArkTech Security would get Charlotte pulled in for questioning too, and she couldn't afford to lose that kind of time.

In her mind, Charlotte listed out different destinations that might help her get Rhonda off her tail, discounting them one by one. Going home to her flat would be no better than heading to Zircon. Rhonda could get out at the garage and force Charlotte into a fight. Security at the Wedge was too tight – they wouldn't even let her into the garage unless she had an appointment.

A throbbing in her ribcage distracted her, and Charlotte touched her hand gently to the spot where she'd fallen on the discarded mallet. The pain made her gasp, and she hoped she wouldn't have to see a doctor. Medical care was provided by the company, of course, but the results would go in her file. With the Chief Bureaucracy Officer out to get her, she'd rather keep her record clean. It was lucky Violet had gone into medicine. If it came to it, her sister would check out her injury off the books.

'Wait, that's it!'

The pod began to slow down.

'No, I mean, I've had an idea.' The pod sped up again. 'Take me to Violet's place.'

'Certainly! Would you like me to contact your sister to inform her of your impending arrival?'

Charlotte looked at the clock readout on the dashboard. It was almost one in the morning. She hadn't spoken to Violet properly in weeks. Or was it longer? Turning up unannounced in the middle of the night wouldn't go down well. And the last thing Charlotte needed was to get into another fight.

'I don't want to disturb her. I'll deal with Rhonda, then I'll head to Zircon.'

'Very well. Updating our heading.'

Getting to her sister's place meant heading southeast to the gated communities that housed many of the mid-tier employee-citizens. Rhonda's pod followed her all the way there.

Charlotte's pod slowed on its maglev tracks as it approached the double-door system people called an airlock, even though there was no difference in pressure on either side. A plexiglass gate opened to let her in, then shut behind her pod when it was inside. There was another closed gate in front of her, its mirrored coating reflecting the image of herself inside the transparent pod.

A voice belonging to an older man sang out across the sound system. 'The finest of evenings to you. Please state your name, role, and business here at Rust Ridge Residences.'

'This is Charlotte Vance, Head of Awkward Questions. Just paying a visit to my sister, Violet Vance. She's in flat five-eighteen.'

'Of course, of course.' She heard some typing. 'It's a little on the late side, Ms Vance. Are you expected?'

'Yeah, I got caught up with a work thing. You know how it goes.'

'I do indeed, Ms Vance, I do indeed. Alrighty roo. I'll just hail your sister to get her say-so, and then I can let you through. One moment.'

'Oh, there's really no need to—'

'Regs are regs, Ms Vance. One moment, please.'

The line cut out and Charlotte waited. Maybe she should've messaged Violet. But what would she have said? 'I need to stop by because I'm being chased by an angry bouncer with a grudge?' The silence stretched out so long that Charlotte was convinced there was a problem. Finally, the man's voice transmitted into the pod again.

'You're all set to proceed, Ms Vance. Please follow the signage when you disembark. Have a pleasant visit at Rust Ridge! Walk in the sun.'

Relief washed over her. 'Walk in the sun.'

The mirrored gate in front of her slowly lifted to reveal the garden beyond, which was all lit up with fairy lights.

'Oh, there's one more thing.' Charlotte adopted a concerned tone. 'There's a woman in the pod behind me who I think might be having a medical emergency. I saw her punching her pod hard enough to do herself some serious damage. Made me wonder if she was having a psychotic break. None of my business, of course . . .'

'Oh me, oh my!' The gate guard tutted. 'You did right to let me know. Don't you worry about a thing, Ms Vance. I'll take it from here.'

Ben moved Charlotte's pod out of the airlock and into the docking area, where Charlotte got out. The fairy lights decorating the garden rearranged themselves until they lined the path she was supposed to follow to the main building. Charlotte ignored the path, waiting by her pod instead.

'Are they letting Rhonda through?' she asked.

'No,' said Ben. 'On conversing with Rhonda, the gate guard has requested I call an ambulance. In the meantime, he's detaining Rhonda inside the gated entrance for her own safety.'

'Nice.' Charlotte pumped her fist. 'Is there a back way I can use to get out of—'

'Apologies for the interruption, but you have an incoming call from Violet Vance.'

Charlotte winced and braced herself. 'Connect it.' The line activated inside her ears, but nobody spoke. 'Ultra? You there?'

'Barley.' Her sister's tone carried the forced calm of someone making a concerted effort to disguise their frustration. 'I've got to get up for work in three hours.'

Well-worn shame burrowed around under Charlotte's scar tissue. 'Sorry. I was hoping I wouldn't disturb you.'

'If you didn't want to disturb me, what are you doing at my house in the middle of the night?'

'It's a long story. Go back to bed. I'll catch you up another time.'

'I've seen a ping on the medical alerts network about someone who just arrived at Rust Ridge. Are you hurt?'

'No, no,' said Charlotte, hurriedly. Then she thought of her ribs. 'Well, yes, a little, but the ambulance isn't for me. It's just for the woman who's been chasing me.'

There was a silence on the line that extended a little too long. 'Meet me at the reception desk.' Violet hung up.

'Oh dear,' said Charlotte. She didn't have time for this, and she thought about leaving, but she didn't want to give her sister any more reasons to be angry with her than she already had.

The path through the garden was made up of shrubs and artificial trees that captured carbon from the atmosphere. They looked real in the low light. An owl hooted, and she wasn't sure if it was the authentic kind or just a sound effect to create the ambiance of a magical glade. Either way, she couldn't deny it was cool.

The air smelled different here. Charlotte was used to breathing the salty sea breeze, with its bloody undertones of rusty steel and the mild citrus scent of ArkTech's standard-issue corporate cleaning products. All of that was replaced by the earthy odour of plants at night breathing out. Was this what life on solid ground was like? The path beneath her feet was picked out in large paving stones, like concrete but artistically uneven. To either side of the path, there were planters filled with dirt that had green life sprouting from them.

The place reminded Charlotte of the guttering Mabel had installed in her bathroom, with the lettuce plants growing inside. Dirt and roots and leaves must look different to a plant geneticist. Mabel would probably have been able to name the species of the garden plants just by looking at them, like Ben could. Charlotte recognised the sedum, but not much else. She didn't think anything out here was edible, and she wasn't hungry or daft enough to experiment.

When Charlotte arrived at the main entrance for building five, a buzzer gave off a low hum and the door swung open. On the other side, there was a foyer. Over on the left, a guard sat behind a small desk poking at his SmartSkin and bopping his head to whatever music was playing over his audio implants. Straight ahead, Violet was standing in front of a trio of lifts. Her arms were crossed, and she was wearing a heavy grey dressing gown over silky tangerine pyjamas.

Violet marched over and gripped both of Charlotte's upper arms. 'Are you in trouble again?' She sounded more worried than angry.

'No.' Charlotte realised that might be a lie. 'Not really.'

'Is it him?' Violet hissed. 'It's him, isn't it?' She didn't say his name, but Charlotte knew Violet meant Narrow.

'No!' At least that much was true. 'Never.'

Violet looked her in the eye for a few more seconds than felt comfortable. 'Do you really mean never, Barley?'

'Yes,' she whispered. 'How can you think I'd get mixed up in his world again after everything that happened?'

Violet stared into her eyes until the tension seemed to melt from her body. 'OK. OK, I believe you. Then what's going on?'

Charlotte narrowed her eyes. 'Remember Rhonda Edwards?'

Violet looked away as she searched her memory. 'Ana Conda? The one who swiped the old man's client list?'

Charlotte nodded.

'I remember,' Violet scowled.

'Well, we've had a bit of a misunderstanding.'

'What kind?'

Charlotte grimaced. 'The kind where she thinks I killed her brother.'

'Walker's ghost!' Violet raised her hand to her mouth. 'You didn't, did you?'

Charlotte gave her sister a look.

'Did you?'

'Obviously not, for Amber's sake! What do you take me for? He *is* dead, though. Rhonda blames me, and she's been chasing me all over the territory. I came here to shake her. I knew they'd let me in if I said I was here to see you. And then I got Rhonda detained by convincing the gate guard to call in a medical emergency.'

Violet's brow furrowed. 'Was that really necessary?'

'I needed to get rid of her.'

'But did she actually need a doctor?'

'Pretty sure she broke her hand when she punched my pod, so . . . yeah?'

Violet's expression turned stony. 'So, you're saying this woman threatened you with violence and chased you around in a pod, and you decided to waste the medical team's resources on her instead of just calling ATS? Why not report her to security, Charlotte?'

She knew she was in trouble when her sister called her by her actual name. She tried to think up an answer that wouldn't make Violet even angrier.

'Paperwork,' she said eventually. Charlotte didn't want to admit to her sister that the idea of reporting someone to ATS, no matter what they'd done, still felt like a last resort. Violet would no doubt take it as evidence that Narrow still held sway over her.

'Paperwork?'

'If I called ATS, I'd get tied up answering a load of questions. There's a more important question I need to answer, and I've got to do it quickly.'

Violet shook her head. 'I don't get it. Your job is to sate an AI's curiosity. It's not life or death.'

Charlotte shrugged. She wished she could share the truth about Ben's glitches with her twin, but she'd promised Ben she'd keep his secret. She wasn't supposed to discuss it with anyone but members of the executive board, and considering how seriously Abhishek Gautam took her role, that was like saying she couldn't discuss it with anyone at all.

Violet grunted. 'Fine. I'm going to bed. I'd offer you the guest bedroom, but you've clearly got places to be.'

Charlotte nodded. 'I'd better get going. Thanks anyway. And sorry. For waking you.' The promise of sleep was tempting, but she needed that slicer.

Violet took a step towards her. She reached up and rubbed her thumb gently across Charlotte's cheek. 'You look tired, Barley. Remember to take care of yourself.' Violet gave Charlotte a brief but firm hug and then disappeared into a lift.

Charlotte wandered back outside and picked up the pace as she hurried back towards the pods. The fairy lights twinkled all the way back through the garden as she thought about what her sister had said. How could Violet be so quick to call security? It wasn't just the paperwork that had stayed Charlotte's hand.

Yes, Rhonda had threatened her, and made her life more difficult, and generally acted like an arsehole. But nobody deserved to be deported. Charlotte remembered the haunted expression on Mabel's face when she'd talked about life beyond the borders of the territory, and she shuddered. Then Charlotte realised the truth: she didn't want to report anyone because she didn't want to be reported herself. By not getting others deported, she hoped to avoid the same fate. By treating others as she'd want to be treated, she hoped they'd return the favour.

Every action had an equal and opposite reaction. It was the universe's way of balancing the scales. Charlotte didn't know which laws governed cosmic justice, but it was probably some quantum-level shit only Nadine Walker would have understood. Better not to deal out any punishment that she wasn't prepared to take herself.

She clambered into a pod. 'Ben, is the coast clear?'

There was a pause. 'Rhonda Edwards is being taken away by a medical unit. Your journey to Zircon should now be unimpeded.'

Charlotte set off, safe in the knowledge that Rhonda wasn't going to jump out from the shadows and try to cave in her skull. She crossed her fingers, hoping for smooth sailing from here on out.

CHAPTER 16

Boats made the crossing to Zircon from the docks at the platform whose official name was the Central Transportation Hub. But nobody except Ben called it that. Whether it was thanks to a campaign by the marketing team or whether the name took hold on its own, people referred to Silicon Fen's most central point as the Kraken. Charlotte couldn't deny the name was fitting. Every HyperBullet route passed through it, giving the platform the appearance of a multi-tentacled sea monster.

With Rhonda out of the equation, it was an easy journey to the Kraken's docks, but setting foot outside was a good reminder of how bloody cold it was at night, even in September. As Ben controlled the temperature indoors, the chill came as a shock. Charlotte shivered as she crossed the docks, wishing she'd thought to bring a coat. According to Ben, the Fens had been comparatively mild before the Melt, until ocean currents that brought warm water from the west got disrupted. IQUO had a lot to answer for.

The docks were well lit, with bright white lights making it clear where the walkways ended and the sea began. Despite the hour, a small boat was moored at the transfer point to Zircon. As she approached the Solar-Shard-powered craft, the wind blasted her with gusts of salt spray that bit into her clothes and clawed at her hair.

The name painted on the side of the boat was Galatea's Galleon. It had the same sleek design as the Search and Rescue vessels that zipped around the territory's waters, but it was a little smaller. Charlotte hopped aboard and went to the captain's cabin, where a warm glow told her someone was in. She rapped on the door and waited until a middle-aged guy with thick hedgehog hair yanked it open and raised his bushy eyebrows at her before he got distracted by staring at her scars.

'Passage for one to Zircon,' she said.

'You a resident?' He addressed her arm, and his tone said he knew the answer.

She shook her head.

'Visitor window's closed,' said the captain. 'Next boat leaves at six.'

He went to shut the door and Charlotte stepped forwards to block it with her foot. 'I can't wait that long.'

'I don't know what to tell you.'

Charlotte wished she could mention the risk of HyperBullet pods colliding with each other or of Ben's cybersecurity protocols getting disrupted and the territory being hacked by criminals who wanted to steal all their money and, worse, their data, but she stuck to what she was allowed to share. 'Look, I'm doing important work for ArkTech. I'm the Head of Awkward Questions.'

'Well, that sounds hoity *and* toity. I'll be happy to take you across. At six.'

Before she could respond, Ben spoke over the boat's radio, adopting a soothing tone. 'And now the shipping forecast, issued by Ben, on behalf of ArkTech's Maritime and Coastguard Agency at 0230 on Friday thirtieth September 2101. The Head of Awkward Questions will be travelling to the Zircon platform in pursuit of urgent answers. Moderate. Mainly fair. Occasionally poor.'

It was hard to shake the feeling she'd just been insulted, but the captain's face gave Charlotte pause as his eyes widened. He stood up straight and saluted the radio. Then he turned to Charlotte. 'Please make yourself comfortable in the passenger lounge, ma'am. I'll have you across to Zircon in no time.'

Charlotte was confused, but she thanked him and headed through to an enclosed area in the back with big windows and soft benches.

She lowered her voice. 'What in Amber's name was that wording, Ben?'

'It was a modified rendition of the shipping forecast. One of my many responsibilities includes transmitting reports detailing wind speed, precipitation, and visibility to anyone working on the water. Unlike many other professionals, sailors tend to consider my voice one of supreme authority because my data keeps them safe.'

Charlotte thought about that. 'Your data keeps everyone safe.'

'Perhaps that fact is more apparent to some people than to others.'

The boat glided forwards in the water and their journey got underway. Although Charlotte had grown up in the territory, where waves were a feature of daily life, she wasn't used to riding around on them. The territory's platforms were fixed to the sea floor, so they didn't move much, and they were suspended high enough to keep the water at a safe distance unless there was a bad storm. All this upping and downing felt unnatural, and she was glad of the handholds she now noticed were within easy reach.

The view out the window was odd from this angle too. Most of it was the darkness of the sea itself. Above the water, the lights from nearby platforms and other ships shone out, but now Charlotte focused on the red beams designed to help ships avoid crashing into them, more than the silvery glitter of the platforms themselves. This wasn't the bird's-eye view she was used to. It was closer to a fish's-eye view. She wondered what nearby sea creatures would make of the boat's motor going by and shivered at the thought of life underwater.

Of all the territory's platforms, Zircon was the one whose name Charlotte reckoned sounded most like an alien planet. Ben would have been the first to helpfully inform her, or any willing listener, that a zircon was actually a gemstone, and that the name had been given to the structure in keeping with the naming convention usually reserved for platforms located beyond the territory's central zone of Silicon Fen. Ben would likely also mention that the mineral could be found in igneous rocks and was regularly used in jewellery making. But Charlotte liked to think of the place as Planet Zircon all the same, thanks to the endearing eccentricity of the employee-citizens who lived there.

It took a certain type of personality to request a flat on the only platform within Silicon Fen that didn't have a functioning HyperBullet garage. It had never been connected to the network, and Ben's answers were vague on the topic of why, but the impact was clear. Zircon offered a bespoke housing option for anybody who was willing and able to pay a premium for a degree of isolation. The residents of Zircon were united by their shared desire to be around other people who didn't want to be around other people. Cal and Liz clearly felt that privilege was worth the extra credits.

Charlotte had met the bengineering duo while answering an Awkward Question some time back. Erratic signals had been giving Ben an AI equivalent of a headache, and Cal and Liz had turned out to be the cause. Charlotte hadn't reported them, of course: that wasn't her business, or her style.

Even though keeping secrets was Charlotte's standard operating procedure, Cal and Liz had been so grateful for her discretion that Cal had proclaimed they owed her a 'Soul Debt.' As far as Charlotte could tell, that was just something Cal had made up and all it meant was that they owed her big time. In any case, Charlotte found it handy having friends in obscure places.

The boat reached the dock at Zircon sooner than Charlotte expected. The captain asked when she planned to head back and promised to wait for her.

Above the docks, Zircon rose from the water, its bulk looming above her. She'd never seen a mountain in real life, but looking up at the platform from below made her think of those pictures on the ArkNet of foreign countries that had jagged ranges of huge dirt-capped peaks.

A steel staircase snaked upwards from the sea to the main entrance. This was exactly why employee-citizens wore rigger boots. Charlotte imagined Sally Neptune trying to scale these gratings in her stiletto heels, and she shuddered at the thought of the pink lady tumbling into the sea. As Charlotte climbed, the stairwell echoed with the rough calls of seagulls who, like her, must have found some pressing reason to be up so late.

Her legs were starting to ache as she reached the top of the stairs. Passing through the front garden, Charlotte arrived at the outer door to the main building and pressed the video call button for Cal and Liz's place. Nothing happened. She waited a couple of minutes and then tried again. Then again. On the fourth attempt, Cal's round face filled the screen.

Cal pushed a handful of popcorn into her mouth and then did her best to speak despite the extra level of challenge. The sound of blaster fire echoed in the background, and a man's voice rattled off a chain of creative expletives.

'Mamf!' said Cal, the closest approximation of Vance she could manage with her mouth full.

'Hey, Cal. I got waylaid. Now an OK time?' Charlotte wondered if the hour was too late, even for people with Cal and Liz's nocturnal tendencies, but she needn't have worried.

Cal chewed and swallowed. 'Now is my absolute favourite time on the whole of the clock. Come on up, kitten face.'

Cal was the only person Charlotte would let refer to her as 'kitten face' and get away with it. Not that she knew anyone else who would try. Liz, by contrast, was unlikely to call her anything at all.

The door buzzed and Charlotte pushed it open. Zircon's interior decoration hovered somewhere on the line between artistically minimalist and architecturally unfinished. Some of the lighting panels were missing, and the corridors were bare concrete and white plaster that had somehow avoided getting scuffed. Charlotte wondered how often it was repainted to create the illusion of newness. Or maybe people here just rarely left or had visitors.

There was no number on Cal and Liz's front door. In the place where a number might normally have been, there was a small plaque depicting a lizard wearing a cowboy hat and holding a pistol in its front claw. Charlotte had learned on a previous visit that Cal had made it herself, all the way from smelting the metal to carving the picture.

As Charlotte approached, the door swung inwards and Cal was standing in the doorway, holding two stripy orange and grey boxes of popcorn. By way of greeting, Cal pushed one of the boxes into Charlotte's hands.

'It's half salted, half sweet, and half butter,' she said.

Static buzzed in Charlotte's ears, and she guessed what Ben was thinking, but she didn't correct Cal's popcorn maths. Instead, she noted the beige carpet and remembered her manners, taking off her boots and leaving them by the front door. Then she followed the woman as she toddled along the hallway.

Aside from being cut off, Zircon was different from most residential platforms in another way: it wasn't assigned to a single tier. For low-tier folk, the extra rent was out of the question, but various flat sizes were available to staff on mid-tier and high-tier contracts, depending on what they were willing to pay. Bengineers could fall anywhere across that range, but Cal and Liz must have been at least upper-mid, maybe even lower-high, if their place was anything to go by. Charlotte passed several doorways to whole other rooms.

The living room was a little off-brand, done up in greys but with mustard yellow instead of orange. One wall was given over to two large light-screens. Opposite the displays was a long grey fabric sofa with powered footrests. Liz was slouched on one side of the sofa and the light-screen in front of him showed a large skull with the words 'You Died, Lizard' emblazoned across the middle. Liz picked up a handful of popcorn and threw it at his screen. It passed through the image, which distorted a little, and bounced harmlessly against the wall behind it.

Before Liz could launch into another barrage of swearing, Cal spoke up. 'Vance is here, Lizzy.'

Cal plonked herself down on her side of the reclining sofa. Her light-screen activated in response. The pair were both playing the same game – *Moon Strike: Gravity Edition* – although it didn't seem to be multiplayer. Unlike Liz's character, Cal's was alive. Her avatar somersaulted in the air and with a flick of her fingers, she shot at two distant enemies with her sniper rifle. The gruesome kills played out in slow motion.

'Oh.' Liz didn't look away from his screen. His avatar came back to life, the hole in its helmet miraculously repaired.

'Hey, Lizard,' said Charlotte. 'You doing OK?'

'Uh huh,' said Liz. 'Your eyes look weird.'

'Contact lenses,' she explained.

'Hm. What do you want?'

'Manners, chicken cheeks!' Cal mouthed the word 'sorry' at Charlotte and threw a handful of popcorn at Liz. Liz didn't try to dodge, but he did eat the pieces that landed on his charcoal hoodie. A small robot with rubber treads for feet, eight pincer-like hands, and a bin for a body rolled past, tidying up the stray pieces as it went. A black cat came barrelling after it, swatting at one of the pincers with its paw.

'It's a fair question,' said Charlotte. She'd got used to Liz being direct. 'I've got a favour to ask,' she continued. 'Might be a big one.'

'Ooo! Fun!' Cal drummed her fingertips together like a cartoon villain. 'Is it a me thing?' she asked, pointing at herself. 'Or a he thing?' She pointed at Liz.

'You tell me: I need a slicer.'

Liz's astronaut mercenary fell into a dark crater and died yet again, but this time Liz didn't seem to care. Suddenly, the whole of his attention was directed at Charlotte. 'Passcode or biometric?' he demanded.

'Uh, biometric, I think. It had a thumb scanner.'

'Private or corporate?'

'Private? Someone's locked down a room in a library at the Wreck. Before seven this morning, I need to get in, look around, and get out.'

Liz turned to Cal. 'Sounds like an us thing.'

Cal nodded. 'Tell us everything.' She grabbed a beanbag from the corner and threw it down in front of the two light-screens for Charlotte to sit on.

Charlotte told Liz and Cal about Ben's Awkward Question and her interviews with Colin and Mabel. She told them about watching from the cat café as they went into the book library and her hypothesis that Mabel had stashed something inside. She left out the details about Strait, and Rhonda, and Rhys's fall: that all felt need-to-know, and they didn't. She explained that when she'd broken into the library, Nasser had been trying to get into the reading room, but even Ben hadn't been able to get past the lock.

As she spoke, the pair sat cross-legged and munched on their popcorn as if Charlotte were the new five-star rated show they'd been waiting all month to binge. When she finished, they continued to stare at her.

'The end,' said Charlotte to clarify she was done.

Cal turned to Liz. 'Multimodal?'

'Yeah, but two-factor or three-factor?' asked Liz.

'Hmm,' Cal stroked her chin. 'Vance, you said there was a thumbprint scanner. Did you spot a retinal reader too?'

'I didn't notice, to be honest.' She thought back to when Colin had let them into the room. 'Maybe. I think there could have been one, yeah.'

'Makes sense,' said Liz. 'Why go to all that trouble and not go at least two-factor? Three would be overkill, though.'

The bengineers grinned at each other, then they both scrambled off the sofa, not bothering to fold away their footrests. Liz disappeared out of the room without a word, his long brown hair flapping behind him. Cal seemed to remember that Charlotte existed and hung back to fill her in. She gestured for Charlotte to follow.

'So, the most sophisticated biometric locks use multiple forms of authentication. Thumbprint is normal, and on a typical ArkTech-issued lock, Ben could pull the thumbprint records and trick the system into unlocking itself. Privately installed systems are isolated from the territory's infrastructure, so Ben can't interface with them.'

They passed back through the hallway with the incredible number of doors, and Cal led Charlotte into a room full of servers, their blue lights winking at her. Liz was already sitting in a faux-leather computer chair, typing code into a light-screen interface. Cal headed to a workbench on the other side of the room. It was neat and tidy, with small drawers stacked up on the wall behind. She started opening the drawers and pulling out unidentifiable bits and pieces as she talked.

'So, to get past the thumb scanner, you'll need a silicone replica of the librarian's thumb. I can print you one easy peasy.' Cal pulled an orange cartridge out of one drawer and loaded it into a cube-shaped machine that was resting on top of the workbench.

'We'll need to whip you up some contact lenses for the other part. They'll make it look like you've got the guy's eye print. You know, without the inconvenience of cutting the real ones out of his face.'

'Right,' said Charlotte, a little unsettled by the sudden violence of the image.

'Which we wouldn't do,' Cal clarified with a wave of her hands. 'That would be super mean.'

'Sure,' said Charlotte.

'Speaking of being mean, that brings me neatly to the topic of payment.' Cal batted her eyelashes in an exaggerated way. 'Credits. Moolah. Dough. Spondulicks. You know . . . cash. In exchange for our time and expertise. And danger money. For the risk involved.'

'I thought you guys owed me a Soul Debt?'

'Not after this,' Liz scoffed, without taking his eyes away from the screen.

'He's right,' said Cal. 'We do this, and we're all paid up on that score. Actually, I think *you'll* owe *us*.'

'That's a bit extreme, isn't it?' Charlotte didn't like the idea of taking on a debt.

Cal shrugged. 'Our currency, our rates.'

Charlotte rubbed her forehead. 'How much will it cost just to call us even?'

Cal looked Charlotte up and down. 'How much you got?'

'Not much,' said Charlotte. 'So little you'd be insulted if I said the numbers out loud.'

'That's OK,' Cal waved a hand through the air, as if dismissing the whole concept. 'I guess we could take the cleared debt along with . . . a token of your appreciation. What've you got on you?'

'On me? Are you after the shirt off my back?'

Cal wiggled her eyebrows suggestively. 'Well, *I* wouldn't say no to that kind of payment—'

'Gross,' said Liz.

'But Lizzy here can't be swayed by pleasures of the flesh, and I'm afraid we work as a team.' Cal leaned closer to Charlotte and whispered. 'Such a shame.'

Charlotte was trying to formulate a response when Cal spared her. 'Just turn out your pockets, Vance.'

'Look, can we not sort this out later? I'm on the clock here.'

Cal crossed her arms, and Liz stopped typing to underline the point.

Charlotte grunted. 'I haven't even got anything you'd want.'

Cal snatched up a pair of round wire-rimmed glasses from the work-bench and put them on. 'I'll be the judge of that.' She patted an empty spot on the bench with one hand.

Charlotte didn't see any other options, so she opened her backpack. She took out the library book.

'Boring!' said Cal.

Charlotte put the half-empty bottle of Dextim pills on top of the book. 'Those are bad for you. And we've got plenty.'

She tutted and handed her backpack to Cal, who rummaged around, but none of the remaining contents took her fancy. 'Next!'

Charlotte winced as she removed her multi-tool and put it on the workbench. It wasn't worth anything, but it'd been a gift from Narrow during happier times – a much better gift than the scars she'd got for her seventeenth birthday – and even after everything, she'd never brought herself to part with it.

'Already got one,' said Cal.

Next came Charlotte's device with its cracked screen.

'Ooo, nice!' said Cal. 'I bet Liz could tell you the make and model of that old thing with one glance.'

Liz had gone back to typing and didn't turn away from his screen.

'This would do,' said Cal, picking up the black rectangle and examining it under the light.

'That's not up for trade.'

'I guess you need it, eh?' Cal scrunched up her nose and nodded at Charlotte's scarred arm. 'Why don't you just get replacement implants on your right arm? I get that it's less convenient if you're not left-handed, but it's better than nothing.'

Charlotte ignored the question and felt around inside her cargo pockets in the hopes of finding a way to change the subject. She pulled out her grippy climbing gloves and the ultra-thin ones she wore when she wanted to avoid leaving fingerprints.

'Walker's ghost! Your hands are so mini . . . Next!'

Charlotte's hand closed around the vaguely sticky coin she'd lifted from Mabel's place. She dropped it onto the workbench.

'That's everything. I told you I didn't have anything valuable.'

Cal cocked her head to one side and then the other, like a seagull getting ready to peck at a stray chip. She picked up the coin and held it up to the light, peering at it through her glasses as if appraising an antique. Then she put the coin to her lips and bit it. She licked her teeth and smacked her lips together.

'Yum. I'll take it.'

'What? The coin?'

'Yeah,' said Cal. 'It's one of the older models. So old you must've dredged it, which takes effort. Plus, there's good stuff on the inside we could make use of in some of our side projects.' As if on cue, the cleaner robot zoomed past the doorway and exited, pursued by a cat. 'So, the coin and the Soul Debt in exchange for the slicer. Deal?'

Technically, the coin was evidence. It was also Mabel's property, no matter how she'd come into its possession, and Charlotte had been planning to return it. Still, the mental image of everyone freezing to death at night because Ben lost temperature control reminded her that answering the Awkward Question had to take priority.

'Deal,' said Charlotte.

Cal spat into her palm, then took hold of Charlotte's hand and shook it.

'Make yourself at home, Vance,' said Cal. 'Bathroom's down the hall. If you want to play *Moon Strike*, knock yourself out. Use my account, though. Liz always sets his to the Explosive Decompression difficulty setting.'

'It's more fun that way,' Liz interjected.

'We'll come get you when we're done. Won't be too long.' Cal turned away and started rooting around for materials at her workbench. One-handed, Charlotte gathered her possessions, dropping them into her backpack, and left the bengineers to their work.

After washing her hands with more citrus-scented soap than she probably needed, Charlotte made herself comfortable on Cal's side of the sofa. The light-screen announced, 'You died, Calamity Jane.' Charlotte glanced around for a control pad, but soon realised the thing was controlled through a player's SmartSkin implants so she'd have to leave lunar gunfights to the professionals. She asked Ben to switch off the screens.

The room went dark. Charlotte lay back on the reclining sofa and realised how tired she was. She shivered, still cold from her visit to the great outdoors. Several blankets were folded over the back of the sofa, and Charlotte pulled one over herself, showering the sofa with popcorn.

She let her eyes droop closed and immediately saw Rhys's terrified face as he fell. Charlotte groaned and opened her eyes again.

'I know I should sleep, Ben, but I don't know if I can.'

'There, there, Charlotte. If you wish to talk, I'm here.'

'Thanks, Ben.' She turned onto her side, trying to make herself comfortable. 'You saved my life today.'

'I'm honoured to be your firm friend and constant companion.'

Charlotte smiled and then felt a pang of guilt as she realised she hadn't been a great friend to Ben today. She'd talked him into breaking the law so they could access the SmartSkin footage at Photon – for good reasons, but still. And they'd been separated from each other at the hotel and she hadn't caught him up on what he'd missed.

She didn't want to keep secrets from Ben, but talking about Strait could create a Narrow-shaped hole in his data which he'd want to fill, and those questions were too awkward even for Charlotte to answer. No matter what Strait believed, despite everything that had happened, she wouldn't betray Narrow.

Her mistakes and her divided loyalties gnawed at her as she tossed and turned, trying to find her way towards rest.

'Is something bothering you, Charlotte?' Ben spoke in her ears at reduced volume.

She took a break from fighting with the sofa. 'Yeah,' she said. 'I feel guilty.'

'Remember to be kind to yourself, Charlotte. I'm sure you're trying to do the right thing.'

Charlotte frowned. 'Maybe. Some days, I'm not sure I'd know the right thing if it pushed me overboard.'

'If life were a picnic, we would soon grow tired of sandwiches. So it is written.'

That had to be something Ben had just made up, but she didn't call him on it. She yawned. She wanted to tell Ben she was sorry, but she started to fall. The rooftop wasn't there any longer, and gravity was dragging her down towards hard concrete. Ben said something, but his voice turned to white noise as Charlotte's mind fell down and down and down.

CHAPTER 17

Ten years earlier
4 April 2091

Charlotte crossed the shop floor, passing display units full of old junk. People only wanted that stuff because they weren't allowed to have it. Narrow's Toy Emporium was weird after hours, without the crush of customers there to make the place feel small. But compared to the back room, it *was* small. Tiny, even.

She stepped through the door behind the sales counter. The cavernous warehouse on the other side was stacked with crates and boxes, and she could hear the muffled laugh track of a film already in full swing, the sound drifting over from the makeshift living room Narrow had fashioned in a far corner. She must've been running later than she'd thought, but Charlotte couldn't care less that they'd started without her. The film would be stupid anyway.

Charlotte carefully touched her fingers to the skin around her throbbing eye, checking whether it still hurt. It did. A fresh jolt of pain shot out from the swollen flesh that was sure to become a bruise. No way would she make a big deal about this. Being part of Narrow's crew meant this shit went with the territory, and she'd have to get used to it.

She kept her footsteps from clanging against the floor as she drew nearer. The three of them were sitting on the sofa together, with Narrow in the middle. Narrow and Ultra were already doubled over laughing at whatever the 2D people in their weird pre-Melt world were getting up to. Strait was sitting bolt upright, hands folded across his lap. He was the first to notice Charlotte's arrival, but he didn't turn to welcome her. Instead, he simply cleared his throat, keeping his eyes on the TV.

Narrow clocked Charlotte in his peripheral vision, but he didn't turn away from the big flat screen that was mounted on the wall. 'What time do you call this, Little One?'

'I'm seventeen next week,' Charlotte complained, leaning against the back of the sofa. 'Don't you think I need a better alias?'

'Not my fault you're little.' Narrow chuckled at something the actors were doing.

'Everyone's little compared to you.' Charlotte crossed her arms.

'Come watch the film,' said Ultra. She patted the arm of the sofa, her eyes still glued to the screen.

'It's all right for you,' said Charlotte. 'Ultra's a cool name.'

Narrow raised his voice over the canned laughter. 'So that's what you want for your birthday, is it? A new alias? I reckon our budget can stretch to that, eh, Jer?'

Strait didn't respond. He just continued quietly watching the film.

Charlotte perched on the arm of the sofa next to her sister. 'I've already come up with one and it's way better than Little One or Young Lady.' She recited both names with disgust.

When nobody responded, she kept talking. 'It's . . . the Scarlet Lance!' She announced the name with pride and just a hint of dramatic flair.

Narrow and Ultra looked at each other and then dissolved into laughter. At first, Charlotte thought it was because of the film, but she gradually realised they were laughing at her.

'What?' she said. 'It's like a superhero name.'

'Yeah, ain't nobody ever gonna crack that code. Come on, Little One. It'd be like Selina Kyle calling herself Felina Guile instead of Catwoman. Dead giveaway.'

Ultra chipped in. 'And it'd get shortened to Scar. You haven't even got any . . . and wasn't that the name of the bad guy from *The Lion King*?' She grinned.

Narrow nodded and laughed again. 'At least we know she'd always . . . be prepared!'

They broke down laughing again. Strait kept watching the film. Charlotte's breath got fast, and her fists clenched.

'It's not *that* funny,' she said. 'Anyway, forget the name. You know what I want for my birthday.'

Without turning to look at her, Narrow held up his hand, signalling for her to stop. 'Don't go there. We've been through that already.' He wiped the tears from his eyes as his chortling finally stopped.

'I don't get what the big deal is.' Charlotte doubled down. 'Most people in the territory have them. Most of your clients have them. I won't be underage any longer. It's my choice.'

Narrow's tone shifted into what Charlotte recognised as Rant Mode. He jabbed his finger towards the ceiling. 'You go up there to the food court and what do you see? Those people aren't just getting fed. They're getting fed on.'

From behind the sofa, Charlotte rolled her eyes as Narrow continued.

'They're all serving up their necks to Amber Benjamin's data vampire. It tracks what they buy, how many, what time, who they're with. And the food court is just the start. ArkTech tracks every damn thing. And those clients you mentioned are just handing over their data and letting the company do who knows what with it.'

Ultra chimed in. 'But they only collect the data to help with automation and to reduce waste. Like, if we know how much rice folk are eating, the system can automatically calculate how much to import. Anyway, everyone's protected under the privacy and confidentiality laws.'

'Laws.' Narrow practically spat the word. 'You really think there ain't never gonna come along some corporate stooge willing to sidestep those laws if it happens to make their life a little easier? Gimme a break.'

Charlotte spoke up. 'No self-respecting ArkTech employee-citizen would break territory-wide laws. Not when they could get deported.'

Narrow tutted. 'If folk are so law-abiding, how come I got rich selling pre-Melt contraband? You know I'm right. They're lambs lining up for opening night at the slaughterhouse.' He shook his head and raised the volume of his voice. 'And do you know what you *won't* find up there?'

Charlotte and Ultra answered in unison with the bored tone that meant they'd heard this all before. 'Ice cream.'

'Damn right. No ice cream! Yeah, they've got that plant-based crap'—he dismissed the concept with a wave of his hand—'but I'm talking about the good stuff. Old-fashioned, real dairy ice cream made from milk squeezed from a cow. Can't get it – it's not allowed! I mean, that's some dystopian shit Amber's got going on up there.'

'I like the oaty one,' said Ultra, but Narrow was mid-flow, and he ignored her.

Narrow put on the high-pitched voice he used whenever he was mocking Amber Benjamin. 'Dairy farming's unsustainable. We can't support industries that damage the environment.' He switched back to normal. 'Well, guess what, missus holier-than-thou? There's no taking back the Melt. It's done. Everything we lost – everyone we lost – gone. Forever. Least she could do is let us poor survivors have a little fun. So no, Little One. You can't have SmartSkin implants for your birthday. Not unless you're honestly telling me you're siding with our self-righteous hypocrite of a CEO over me.'

The smart move would've been to drop it, but Charlotte was sick of Narrow not taking her seriously. It might have been her seventeenth birthday next week, but he was the one acting like a teenager.

'You're just jealous,' she snapped, gripping the back of the sofa with both hands. 'None of us would even be here right now if it weren't for the CEO – we might not even be alive – whereas you're just a paranoid conspiracy theorist moonlighting as a glorified sales assistant! You only get on your high horse about big data because you're so scared of getting caught selling your bootleg crap. Your own jammers stop data collection happening on your turf, so if I get the implants, you know it won't put you at risk. I don't get why you're being such a fucking flatlining jerk about this!'

Everyone went quiet. Strait didn't say anything, but he switched off the film. The silence was heavy with the thump of her heartbeat. Narrow began to tremble like a volcano ready to burst until he leapt to his feet and finally turned away from the TV to look her in the eye.

'Let's get one thing straight . . .' His words tailed off, his fury draining away when he saw her face. His mouth fell open at the sight of her injury, and he fell silent.

Ultra turned to look too. 'Walker's ghost!' She lifted a hand to her mouth in shock. 'What happened?'

'Who . . . ?' Narrow tried. 'What . . . ?' He slowly walked over to her and took her swollen face gently in his hands. Charlotte winced a little, and he let go.

'Sorry I was late.' Seeing the concern in her family's eyes took the heat out of her anger. 'It doesn't hurt too much unless I poke it. So, I'm trying not to poke it.'

Narrow walked away and began to pace. Strait got up from the sofa, headed to the edge of the makeshift living room, and stood at ease, hands clasped behind his back as if waiting for further instructions.

Ultra took hold of Charlotte's hand and squeezed it. 'Oh, Barley, I'm so sorry I didn't go with you.'

Charlotte shook her head. 'Should've been an oat milk run. It was my fault I got caught.'

Narrow seemed to arrive at some internal conclusion. He turned to her. Rage had returned to his eyes, but his voice came out all quiet. 'Who did this to you?'

'It was my fault,' said Charlotte. 'I was tailing that guard from the middle shift. You were right – I saw her lift something from the shop. I followed her back to her flat. Turns out she lives alone in one of those complexes with those dumb half balconies, so when she went to take a shower, I decided to sneak in and grab what she'd stolen.'

Strait spoke up from behind her. 'That wasn't the assignment, Young Lady.'

'I know,' Charlotte snapped. 'But I saw the chance and made the call.' She turned to look at Narrow. 'I didn't want her to get away with it.'

Narrow nodded for her to continue.

'I climbed across to the balcony, no problem. The lock on the patio door was easy enough to pick. I'd spotted her patting her coat pocket when she was leaving the shop, so I guessed whatever she'd lifted was in there. When I got inside her flat, I started looking around for her coat. It was hanging up by the front door. So I crossed the living room and slipped my hands into the pockets.'

Charlotte reached inside her padded grey jacket, unzipped a pocket stitched into the inner lining, and pulled out a shiny black rectangle. 'I found this.'

Narrow's eyes widened. He slowly approached and took the data drive from Charlotte's outstretched palm. He flipped it over and examined some numbers on the back that looked like a serial number, but Charlotte knew they were a code. 'How the actual fu—'

'Language,' Strait interrupted.

'Holy freakin' mackeroly,' said Narrow. 'She's only gone and lifted the client list. Just a quarter of it, but still.' Narrow turned to Strait. 'Jer?'

'That . . . shouldn't have been possible,' said Strait, shaking his head. 'Unless we have a mole.' He looked at Charlotte meaningfully.

'Don't look at me like that, Stabby McStabberson. I'm the one who got it back, remember?'

Narrow turned the TV back on, using it as a monitor as he slotted the data drive into a port. He grabbed an old mechanical keyboard from a cupboard under the TV and typed out a few commands. 'Nobody's accessed it,' he said. 'I've got tripwires all over these drives, so I'd know. That was a close call, Little One. How'd you get caught?'

Charlotte threw her arms wide. 'She had a dog! I didn't know flats like that were even allowed dogs.'

'They're not,' said Ultra. 'You said a half balcony? I know those places. They're for folk in the low tier who don't mind being house poor. They put most of their pay into renting a slightly bigger place. No pets allowed besides plants and fish. Not enough space for them.'

'That's what I thought,' said Charlotte. 'So this creepy, monster-looking beast bounds over to me. Grey with long, thin legs and a face like a bullet.'

'A greyhound, I'd wager,' said Strait.

'Whatever,' Charlotte continued. 'So this hound runs over and I think it's going for my throat but it just keeps barking and barking and it gets between me and the balcony, so I go for the front door instead, but it's locked and I can't find the keys and it's tough to pick a lock when you're trying to fend off a four-legged demon creature. And because the dog keeps barking, the guard gets out of the shower to check what's going on and sees me fumbling around in her entranceway. She's stark naked and soaking wet, but she doesn't seem to mind about that. Charges straight over and punches me right in the face.'

'Walker's ghost,' said Ultra again. 'How'd you get away?'

Charlotte got up and began to pace opposite Narrow. 'I remembered what you taught us'—she gestured towards him—'discretion is the better part of valour, right? I knew I had to get out of there and I couldn't let her grab me. So when she turned away for a second – I think she was going for a weapon by the front door – I just bolted. I can't believe the dog didn't bite me. It just barked and barked.'

Strait spoke without emotion. 'Greyhounds are known for having a calm and gentle temperament.'

'I guess I got lucky then.' Charlotte glared at him.

Narrow continued to pace.

'Anyway,' Charlotte continued. 'I got out with the drive, so it all ended up OK.'

Narrow ignored that and turned to Strait. 'Jer,' he gave him a meaningful look. 'This guard – she's made her bed.'

Strait met Narrow's gaze and held it. After a few moments, he nodded once. Then he turned and strode out of the warehouse that was also known as the Emporium's back room.

Narrow walked over to Charlotte and wrapped his arms around her in a massive bear hug, careful not to put pressure on her face. He smelled like old leather and tobacco. 'I'm so sorry, Little One.' He gestured towards her eye, where the skin was puffy. 'This is all my fault. But I'll make it right.'

'We should get some ice for the swelling,' said Ultra. She jumped up from the sofa and hurried off in search of some.

'No, this is on me,' said Charlotte. 'I didn't follow the assignment.'

Narrow tilted his head to one side and looked at her. 'Well, that's what life's all about,' he said slowly. 'Figuring out when to break the rules and when to follow them. You broke the rules, but you saved us one world-breaker of a headache by getting that back.' He pointed at the data drive. Then he bellowed so that his voice echoed through the warehouse. 'Hey, Ultra – grab some arnica too!' He lowered his voice again. 'Helps with the bruising.' He winked at her. 'This the first time you've been punched in the face?'

She nodded.

'How'd it make you feel?'

Charlotte wasn't expecting the question, and it triggered a replay of the events in her mind's eye. The blow from the guard's fist had stunned her. But alongside the physical pain, there was something else. It was like she hadn't just been punched in the face; she'd been punched in the *self*, and her whole being had screamed, 'That's not right!' The injustice of it had made Charlotte feel sick, and then she experienced something transcendent.

She guessed this was what people meant when they said they'd seen red. Only her vision didn't go red – everything turned black. She lost herself. Lost control. And the thing she didn't tell her family was that when she came back to herself, the guard was reeling from Charlotte's fist connecting with her nose. It poured with blood and Charlotte's self had yelled, 'Now we're square!' She didn't remember the impact itself, but she felt the ache in her fist. The rest was true: she'd run away after that.

She blinked and realised Narrow was still waiting for an answer.

'Wronged,' she said. 'It made me feel wronged. Like I needed to balance the scales, or I'd lose – I don't know – my self-respect.'

Narrow gave her a knowing smile and patted her on the shoulder. 'It's like my dear departed mother always used to say: every action has an equal and opposite reaction. So, you see why Jer needs to pay this guard a visit?'

Charlotte nodded. 'She stole from you, so now you've got to steal something from her.'

'Damn right. It's a done deal – like the Melt. No takebacks. Gotta be consequences or else it'll happen again. That woman's made her bed and now she's gotta lie in it.'

Charlotte had heard Narrow use that phrase about other people over the years. There was no coming back from it. It meant that person was dead to him, and depending on how they handled themselves when Strait came knocking, they might end up dead, full stop.

Narrow continued, 'Which guard did you say it was?'

Charlotte frowned, which sent a jolt of pain radiating out from her eye. She reached up to touch it and stopped herself. 'Ana Conda.'

Narrow nodded. 'Ana. That makes sense.'

'How come?'

'Remember Jer said we must have a mole? We don't. It was all Ana.'

'How come you're so sure?'

Narrow dropped his heavy form back onto the scruffy yellow sofa. 'She's got beef with me.'

Charlotte scrunched up her face and stopped when it hurt. Narrow was always using expressions he'd picked up from old films.

'She's got a grudge, is what I mean. I didn't know it until now, but it fits.' He picked at the upholstery. 'Ana's been a guard with us for a while. Doing a decent job too. Then one day, she comes in and requests an interview for her kid brother. I say no on principle. But every day, she comes at me with the same thing: "meet my brother, Narrow, meet my brother." So eventually, big softie that I am, I agree.'

Narrow rooted around in the pocket of his leather jacket, which he'd slung over the back of the sofa. He pulled out a box of cigarettes and his fat metal lighter that had a stylised tree on the side. Charlotte waited as he lit it and took a drag.

He continued, shaking his head. 'Big mistake.' A cloud of smoke puffed out of his lungs like there was a fire burning down there. 'Now, don't get me wrong. This guy was strong, young, fearless. But I turned him away. Sometimes all it takes is one good look at somebody. No doubt in my mind he was bad news.'

'Why?'

'Because the guy . . . how can I put this? He was a fucking psycho.'

Charlotte glanced towards the warehouse door as if Strait might poke his head round to tell Narrow not to swear. She gave him a look.

'I'll put a coin in the jar tomorrow. I'm not forgetting you owe one too.' He took another drag. 'Point is – nepotism topples empires. This guy called himself King Cobra,' he scoffed. 'Rattlesnake would fit better for that big baby. No brains, all brawn, and the desire to use it. He was wrong for my crew, so I turned him down. But that pissed Ana right off. She reckoned I hadn't given him enough of a chance. I didn't realise she was disgruntled enough to steal from me, but here we are.'

Charlotte went to lean against the wall by the TV so she could make eye contact with Narrow while keeping away from smoke considered so toxic that it was banned even beyond the territory.

'What does that phrase mean?' she asked. 'Narcissism topples empires?'

Narrow chuckled. 'Maybe that too, but I said "nepotism". Originates from an old word for "nephew." You'd know that if you bothered to read any of those.' He swept an arm towards his impressive collection of books, which lined the vast array of shelves at the back of the warehouse.

Charlotte stuck her tongue out at him.

Narrow waggled his cigarette in her direction. 'Think of the Romans, right?'

She couldn't, but she didn't interrupt.

'The Roman Empire had a system for selecting its leaders. First, a capable general would come to power after winning victories in war and politics. The people would be happy, and coin would flow into the empire. But when that great leader died, the power didn't pass to the next most capable general. It went to the first guy's blood relative, right? A son. Or a nephew.'

He paused for a breath of polluted air and looked extremely happy about it.

'Take Vespasian. Awesome dude. Man of the people. Ugly git who went ahead and stuck his face right there on his coins anyway because he was *authentic*. Commissioned the Colosseum, which was pretty much the ancient equivalent of the Wreck. But his youngest son, Domitian? Grade A psycho who had to be assassinated. Marcus Aurelius? Great guy. His son Commodus? Nutter. Augustus, who started off the whole emperor thing in the first place? Good leader. His great-grandson, Gaius Caligula? Attacked the fucking sea! I mean with actual soldiers and spears, and then he gathered up the shells from the beach as spoils.'

'So . . .' Charlotte tried to parse all of that despite a complete lack of historical context. 'You're saying just because Ana Conda's been a good crewmate, it doesn't mean her brother will be?'

'Bingo. Don't get me wrong – Ana's no Vespasian. She was more of a Tiberius. You know . . . adequate. But King Cobra.' Narrow rolled his eyes. 'Soon as I laid eyes on him, I felt it in my bones: he was mental. I'm not giving a free pass to anyone just because of some bullshit family connection. That's no way to run a business. I'm telling you – genetics don't mean shit.'

He pushed the end of his cigarette into an ashtray on the entertainment unit, like it was a full stop at the end of his rant.

'Anyway, Little One. Ana Conda won't be messing with you again. Not as long as you're under my roof. Now . . . is there anything I can do to make you feel better? We imported a fresh batch of the good stuff this morning. Real pricey, but I'd crack a tub open for you. We've got mint chocolate chip, raspberry ripple, rocky road—'

Charlotte smiled but stopped when it made her face sting. 'There is one thing.'

'Anything,' said Narrow. 'Name it.'

'Let me get SmartSkin implants for my birthday.'

All the tenderness drained away from Narrow's face, and he shook his head. 'Not as long as you're under my roof.'

'Why?' Charlotte couldn't understand. 'It's so unfair!'

Narrow didn't look angry this time. He seemed to be weighing his words carefully. 'I always knew the day would come when you'd have to pick a side. It's Amber Benjamin or me, Little One. It's your call, but you can't have it both ways.' He stood up and strode away from her into the expanse of the warehouse.

What he was saying didn't make sense. Amber Benjamin and Mel Narrow both mattered to Charlotte more than she could say. Why should she have to choose?

'You're just being stubborn,' she called after him. Narrow didn't look back.

CHAPTER 18

Charlotte's neck was stiff and there were four, no, make that five somethings poking into her torso, and another something was tickling her nose. She opened her eyes and discovered there was a black cat standing on top of her, kneading her bruised ribs and sniffing her face. When Charlotte made eye contact, the animal froze for a moment and then bounded away, pushing off with enough power to make her groan.

The cat was gone, but Charlotte's upper arm was still being prodded. Looking over, she discovered the culprit was a varnished wooden narwhal mounted on a stick, which Cal was gripping firmly as she administered the poking device. Charlotte shifted her gaze to Cal, and the bengineer put down the implement.

'Awesome sauce,' said Cal. 'You're awake.'

Charlotte tried to speak, but what came out was a gurgle. 'Time is it?' she managed.

'We finished up a few minutes ago. Had a weird power outage during the night that slowed our progress.'

A power cut? Had Ben glitched again during the night?

Ben waited for Cal to finish and then spoke in Charlotte's ears. 'The time is six hours, seven minutes, and nineteen seconds UTC, and counting.'

Mental puzzle pieces tumbled behind her eyes as she tried to remember where she was and why. Finally, things clicked into place.

'Shit.' She had less than an hour to get to the library before Colin was due to arrive.

Charlotte sat up, causing a shower of popcorn bits to shake loose from her blanket and bounce to the floor. The black cat tore past, pouncing at a stray piece and chasing it out of the room. Charlotte managed to clamber free from the fully reclined sofa. Snatching up her backpack, she peeled the zip open and held it towards Cal.

'Slicer,' said Charlotte.

'Coming right up.' Cal didn't seem fazed by Charlotte's abrupt morning manner.

Charlotte went to the front door, pulled on her boots, and waited impatiently for Cal.

'All right, milady.' Cal emerged holding two small cases made of shiny black metal in the palm of one hand. 'I'd better give you the lowdown on how this stuff works.'

Charlotte nodded. 'Short version,' she said, tapping her wrist where a clock readout would've been if she'd had one.

Cal flipped open one of the cases. Inside, there was a thumb. It would have looked real if it hadn't been neon orange. 'Can you guess?' she asked.

'Press the thumb against the scanner?'

'No,' said Cal. 'Schoolkid error. You've got to push the thumb onto your own thumb like it's one-fifth of a glove. The heat from your body will trick the biometric sensor and get around the security measures designed to stop people from chopping each other's digits off.'

'Got it. And that?' Charlotte pointed at the other box.

Cal flicked it open to reveal a set of pale blue contact lenses bathed in solution. 'You'll need to put these in. I made two so you won't get people staring at you when they see you've got one orange eye and one blue one.'

People stared at her already, but Charlotte kept that thought to herself.

Cal continued, 'Best to put those in now. Give them a check before you go.'

Charlotte took the small boxes from Cal, closing the one containing a replica of Colin's thumb and placing it inside her backpack. She took the contact lenses to the bathroom.

On her way down the hall, the black cat thundered past and Charlotte remembered the orange and grey ones at Paws for Torte. 'Did you adopt your cat from a café?'

'Nah.' Cal shook her head. 'The ones in the cafés are well looked after already. We found Bram at this great little cat sanctuary for hard-to-home animals over on the west coast of the mainland.'

'I didn't know you guys left Zircon, let alone the territory.' Charlotte noticed Cal's hallway was longer than the whole of her own flat.

'We're not keen on crowds of people. Clowders of cats are fine.'

It occurred to Charlotte that perhaps a clowder wasn't a soup after all.

Cal grabbed the cat as it ran past, putting on a silly voice. 'And finding this little cutie made it the most bestest trip ever.' Bram was surprisingly chilled about being hugged. 'Bramby here was an old boy compared to the other kitties. And with his colouring as well, nobody wanted him. Because people are stupid.' Cal smooshed her face against Bram's fur. 'Yes, they are. Yes, they are!'

Charlotte cocked her head to one side, and Ben spoke in her ears. 'Black cats are considered unlucky among the superstitious.'

She nodded. 'Is that a bad luck thing?' she asked Cal, pretending to know more than she did about the topic.

'Yeah, partly. At the sanctuary, they told us it's also because black cats don't come out so well in photographs. I mean, why adopt an animal if you can't post cute pics on the ArkNet, right?' Cal scrunched up her face in disgust. 'True story.'

Ben's channel buzzed with static, and Charlotte knew he would've banked that gem for future reference. A human might have been miffed that someone had out-fun-facted them, but she knew Ben would be delighted to have learned something new.

Charlotte finally reached the bathroom sink and removed her own modded lenses, placing them into the solution inside the black box. She noticed how bloodshot the whites of her eyes were as she put in the replicas of Colin's pale blue shade. She blinked a few times and realised that Cal and Liz must have pulled her prescription from her medical records – her vision was sharp and clear.

'Holy potatoes!' said Cal from the bathroom doorway. 'Is that micro-mesh?' Cal shot forwards and snatched up the black box which now contained Charlotte's lenses, holding it towards the light in the ceiling and angling it this way and that.

'Yeah, but they glitch out all the time.'

'Neat idea, though!' Cal continued to ogle the lenses. 'The work's super cack-handed. Proper amateur. Who did it for you?'

'I did it.'

'I meant to say the work is *exquisite*.'

The Colin-coloured lenses were in place and Charlotte had everything she needed to slice the lock. 'I've got to get going.' She held out her hand for the box, but Cal kept hold of it, moving it away from Charlotte's grasp.

Cal wandered slowly back towards the front door, still peering into the lens box. 'I didn't know you were into this kind of thing. You know, we can always use more trainees in the Product Stream. Hey – I could mentor you!'

'Thanks, but that ship's sailed.' Charlotte held out her hand again, but Cal ignored her.

'What functionality were you after?'

'Just give them here.' Charlotte tried to grab the box, but Cal held it above her head, out of Charlotte's reach.

Charlotte made another grab, but Cal was too tall. 'Jane!'

'Don't "Jane" me,' said Cal. 'You've got plenty of time.'

Charlotte knew she didn't, so she spoke fast. 'The lenses were for Ben, OK? To help him see like a human. It's a video feed mod. I tried to follow along with some tutorials on the ArkNet, but I guess I did it wrong.'

Anyone with SmartSkin implants could record immersive 3D video footage, so there was no need for most people to stick tech in their eyes. There had only been one example online to follow, and the guy giving the tutorial was clearly an expert. Just not at teaching.

'I bet we could fix these up for you,' said Cal. 'Wouldn't be cheap, though.'

'You're forgetting the part where I've got no money.'

Liz's head poked out from behind Cal, and he took the contact lenses from her. Charlotte hadn't even realised he'd been standing there. 'Intricate,' he said. 'I . . . Cally, I don't know how to do this.' There was awe in his voice, and for the first time ever, Charlotte saw Liz smile. It wasn't much of one, but it was unmistakable.

'We'd give you mates' rates,' said Cal. 'Call it'—she sucked air through her teeth—'five thousand credits.'

Charlotte held out her hand for the box. 'Sounds great – as soon as I get my seat on the board, I'll get back to you about that.'

Liz whispered something in Cal's ear.

Cal nodded, waved him away, and took the box back from him. 'Come on, Vance. Let's haggle it out.'

'I don't have time for this.'

'Four thousand?'

'Give me the box.' Anger crept into Charlotte's tone.

Cal flinched, then grinned as she tried again. 'Three thousand plus a Soul Debt?'

Charlotte reached for the box, and this time Cal let her take it. She put it in her backpack and closed the zip.

'I'll do it for free,' said Liz.

'You will not.' Cal rounded on him and lowered her voice. 'The best we could do would be *at cost*, but I've told you not to get involved in this part – you don't know how to negotiate.'

Charlotte had her hand on the door handle when a thought crossed her mind. 'How many of those coins would you take as payment?'

Cal made a face and looked away while she did the mental calculations. 'I guess . . . like a hundred? But you'd never get hold of that many of the old kind.'

Charlotte nodded, remembering the case full of coins under Mabel's bed and wondering if there was a way she could persuade the geneticist to part with them. She pulled the door open and was stepping through when Cal called out.

'Wait, wait, wait. That reminds me. You want your logs purged, right?'

'What logs?'

'From the coin. The logs of all the transactions you made. Want that deleted?'

Charlotte stepped back through the door into the bengineers' hallway. 'It's a coin. There isn't a log.'

Cal giggled. 'Of course there's a log, silly sausage.'

'I thought these things were off the books.'

'Well, there's off the books and there's off the books. The data doesn't get uploaded to Ben's banking database, but there's a record held inside the coin itself.' She laughed again. 'No logs! As if we wouldn't capture perfectly good data!'

Charlotte's eyes widened. 'Don't purge it. Can you send it to me?'

'Sure thing. We'll encrypt it up nice and tight and chuck it across. No extra charge. Think about that other thing, though, won't you?' Cal pointed at her own eye and drew a few small circles with her finger.

'I'd do it for free,' said Liz sullenly.

'OK, thanks, guys!' Charlotte gave them a wave and made a break for it. This time the bengineers let her go. 'Scamper in the sun!' shouted Cal.

Charlotte ran all the way to the docks, where a crowd of angry employee-citizens was gathered around Galatea's Galleon. Ben's maritime credentials ran deep enough that the captain had waited there until Charlotte got back, rather than shuttling these people across to the Kraken. Charlotte checked in with the boat captain, and they set sail, taking the grumbling masses along for the ride. It was an easy transfer from the Kraken's docks to the HyperBullet network, and Charlotte was back at the Wreck in record time.

Over to one side of the garage, there were orange pedal bikes and kick scooters, which could be rented out for a fee. Charlotte resented the expense, but Cal and Liz had delayed her so much that it didn't feel optional. She gripped the handlebars of a bike, but remembering the whoosh of their slipstreams made her shudder. She pivoted on the spot and grabbed a scooter instead. Charlotte wanted to arrive on time. With a death trap like a bike involved, she might never arrive at all.

The scooter was faster than she remembered. Taking the second lane, Charlotte kicked off against the ground and zipped across the Wreck until she reached the borrowing district.

At the library, she abandoned the scooter and peered through the doors. The bike lock was still in place, which meant Colin hadn't arrived yet. Ben told her the time was 6.42. She had eighteen minutes.

Charlotte ran to the narrow alleyway and eased her way between the buildings. She tried to move as quickly as she could, but the loose cables and jutting bits of wall seemed to jump out at her.

'May I make an observation?' asked Ben.

'Just a minute.' She grunted as she squeezed herself through the gap. 'Need to concentrate.'

With a few scratches and bruises, she made it to the other side and found herself in the wide maintenance corridor behind the library. She was gripping the skip and wheeling it into position under the fire escape when Nasser pushed open the emergency exit. He was holding the bike lock in one hand and propping the door open with the other. He raised his eyebrows at her.

'Oh,' she said, realising what Ben had been going to point out.

'You didn't have to go around the back,' said Nasser. 'Ben told me you'd arrived, but by the time I got the front door open, you'd run off.'

'Sorry. Wasn't thinking.' She'd got so used to working with Ben that the concept of getting help from someone with a physical form hadn't sunk in.

'We're almost out of time,' said Nasser. It was a statement, not an accusation. He sounded far more concerned than angry, an impressive feat for someone who'd been kept waiting for hours.

'I've got the slicer,' said Charlotte. 'Let's find out what they're hiding up there.'

Nasser nodded. 'I've got your back, detective.' He smiled, and there was a warmth in his eyes that filled her with confidence. Together, they might have enough time to get this done.

He opened the door wider for her, and Charlotte accidentally brushed against him as she went inside, sending up a waft of citrus soap coupled with an undertone of something inviting she didn't recognise. Her pulse quickened as she realised it had to be Nasser's natural scent. Charlotte headed for the stairs, taking them two at a time while the technician matched her pace. Her heart was racing, and it wasn't just because of the cardio.

At the door to the reading room, Charlotte looked at the thumb scanner. Then she turned to Nasser and gently took hold of his wrist. He let her lift his hand, and she pressed her cold palm and fingers against the warmth of his. Her hand looked small by comparison.

Nasser's brow knitted in confusion, but then he looked down into her eyes and smiled. 'Hey, did you change your hair or something?'

Charlotte shook her head and drew her hand away. Then she took off her backpack, unzipped it, and pulled out the box containing the thumb.

She tossed the box to Nasser. 'Put this on,' she said. 'It's more your size.'

Nasser caught the box with one hand and snapped his fingers with the other. 'You changed your lenses. The orange ones looked ace, but the natural look suits you too.'

'It's Colin's natural look.' She smiled, noting the dubious compliment about her janky lenses.

'Ohhhhh. I get it.' Nasser opened the box and grimaced at the sight of the orange thumb. He plucked it from the case, turned it over a couple of times, and then pushed his own thumb into the small opening at the end. 'It's all gooey,' he said, scrunching up his face.

'Ben, can you tell us the order?' asked Charlotte.

Ben's voice transmitted over the loudspeakers in the ceiling. 'Retina first. Thumb second,' he said.

Charlotte nodded and stepped closer to the door. She stood up straight to gain the height she needed to look into the small, round scanner. Perhaps this was why so many women in pre-Melt films wore high heels, but Charlotte didn't see how numb toes and sprained ankles could possibly be worth it.

Nasser pressed his thumb to the second sensor. They waited for a moment, and then the system honked at them. The meaning of the noise was clear, but Charlotte tried the door anyway. It didn't budge.

'Try again,' she said.

Charlotte scanned her other eye. Nasser pressed the sensor. The system honked at them again.

'You've got to be kidding me,' said Charlotte. Static buzzed over the sound system, and she interrupted before Ben could start telling a joke. 'Now's not the time, Ben!'

A wistful tone crept into Ben's voice. 'I do happen to know a truly first-class joke about locks, Charlotte, but I was simply going to propose that perhaps—'

'It's using a three-factor authentication system,' said Nasser.

'Precisely,' said Ben.

Charlotte gave Nasser a quizzical look.

He shrugged. 'I wasn't always a library technician, you know.'

Charlotte smiled and wanted to ask what he'd been before, but they were running out of time. 'What's the third factor?' she asked instead.

Ben responded over the loudspeakers. 'In this case, the third security component is likely to be a verbal passcode.'

Charlotte turned to Nasser. 'Know what it could be?'

Nasser shook his head. 'Colin never lets me in here. I thought he was just being a control freak.'

Charlotte thought back to when she first came to interview Colin at the library. Her mind replayed watching him press his thumb against the scanner and then . . .

'Oh, for Amber's sake.' She shook her head. 'Let's try again.'

Charlotte scanned her eye. Nasser used the thumb. Then Charlotte spoke. 'Open sesame.'

They waited for a moment. The system honked.

'Oh, come on! That's got to be it.' Charlotte booted the reading room door, but it didn't change its mind about being locked.

'Allow me,' said Ben.

They tried the sequence once more. Charlotte's eye. Nasser's thumb. But this time the words 'open sesame' came through the speakers, not in Ben's voice, but in Colin's.

The sensor glowed green, and the door clicked open. Charlotte and Nasser grinned at each other.

'Great work, Ben!' said Charlotte. 'You used Colin's voice print records. I didn't even know you were allowed to do that.'

Ben switched to speaking directly into her ears. 'I'm not, Charlotte!' He sounded delighted. 'Since our experience at Photon, I have been studying workarounds, loopholes, and legal grey areas. It is a truly fascinating topic! But more importantly . . .' Ben switched back to using the loudspeakers. 'What kind of key opens a banana?'

Nasser looked puzzled, but Charlotte was bracing herself.

'A monkey!' Static fizzed over the speakers in bursts. 'It is important to note that you now have four minutes until Colin is due to arrive downstairs.'

Charlotte rushed inside the reading room with Nasser at her side.

CHAPTER 19

The reading room looked the same as when Charlotte had been there the day before. Glass cabinets lined three of the walls, their rows of heavy-duty books locked away. The fourth wall was made of clouded glass. As Colin had left privacy mode active, Charlotte had expected something incriminating to be sitting on the desk in full view, but everything in the reading room seemed to be in its proper place, and the desk itself looked spotless.

Nasser pressed a button near the door, and the privacy glass unfrosted itself.

'What's your plan?' Charlotte raised an eyebrow.

'I thought I'd look out for Colin while you search the room.' Charlotte kept her eyebrow raised until Nasser continued. 'But if we see him coming, he'll also see us. OK, I'll go downstairs and watch from there.'

Ben's voice transmitted over the speakers in the reading room's desk. 'I can perform the role of lookout, sentry, or vedette, Nasser. Colin's GPS signature is available to me. I cannot, however, see inside the room you have just entered, as the cameras have been tampered with. I believe your attention will be better directed towards helping Charlotte with the search.'

Nasser nodded. 'Sure thing, buddy.'

Charlotte ran her finger along the light-screen desk. Not even a fleck

of dust stuck to her skin. 'Nasser, do you guys do any library maintenance stuff that leaves behind a fine black powder?'

Nasser's brow creased as he thought about it, and then he shook his
head. 'Can't think of anything like that, no. Why?'

'Well, when I came in here yesterday, this desk was covered in dust so
dark it almost looked like soot. At the time, I just thought the library
wasn't very popular.' Nasser bristled but didn't interrupt. 'But now that
it's been cleaned up, I'm wondering what it could have been.'

Ben spoke through the speakers. 'I have consulted my database, and I
can confirm there are no illicit drugs or substances matching that
description.'

'Thanks, Ben,' she said.

Nasser seemed confused and addressed the desk. 'I thought you were
keeping watch downstairs.'

'I am there, Nasser. And I am also here. Unlike *Homo sapiens*, I possess
the ability to truly multitask, rather than rapidly switching my focus
between one thing and another to the detriment of both.'

'That's handy,' said Nasser. 'So, it wasn't drugs. And say what you
like about Colin, but he'd never light a fire in the library, so it can't have
been soot or ash.'

Charlotte nodded. 'There's got to be something else hidden in here.
I'm sure Mabel left something heavy behind yesterday.' She fished her
multi-tool out of her pocket and started trying to pick the nearest cabinet's small lock.

Without saying anything, Nasser walked over to the cabinet next to
hers, took a small silver key from a ring that had been in one of his cargo
pockets, and slid it into the lock. He turned it, and the cabinet opened. 'I
wasn't sure that would work,' he said. 'I'll open and you look?'

'Deal.' Charlotte nodded and slid her multi-tool back into her pocket.

'Where'd you learn to do that, anyway?' asked Nasser.

'I wasn't always the Head of Awkward Questions, you know.'

Nasser grinned. He went around the room, unlocking each of the
glass cabinets and leaving them open for Charlotte to check. Behind the
first one, there were shelves containing books, books and more books.
Some of them were bound in leather, which usually considered
contraband, but their status as historical artefacts had probably bought
them a reprieve. The next three cabinets were the same. She pulled the

books forwards to check behind them but found nothing except dust – the regular grey fluffy kind.

'Uh, detective,' said Nasser.

'You can call me Charlotte, you know.' She laughed and looked over. Nasser had made his way around to the far corner, but the cabinet in front of him wouldn't open.

'This one seems to take a different key. None of mine are working. Wanna give it a go?'

Charlotte nodded. She took out her multi-tool again and began to pick the lock. It was trickier than it should have been for one this size. When it clicked open, Ben's voice burst from the desk.

'Colin MacIntosh is now making his final approach to the library.'

'Shit,' said Charlotte.

'I'll stall him.' Nasser stood up tall.

'Are you even supposed to be on duty right now?'

'No, but I can invent a bindings-related emergency. Let me know what you find . . . detective.'

Nasser flashed her a grin and then rushed off. He came back a few moments later to throw the silicone thumb into her backpack and then hurried away again.

Charlotte pulled back a book on the lowest shelf to check what was behind it, like she had with the other cabinets. This time, the books didn't move. They seemed to have been glued together and fastened to the shelf. She tried again with the books higher up, but they didn't move either. It was only when she reached up and pulled on the top shelf that something happened.

The books hinged forwards as if they were all one piece. There was a mechanical click, and when she released them, the shelves shunted backwards. The whole thing had become a door.

A secret door hidden behind a bookshelf. It was exactly the kind of thing Narrow would have got a kick out of. Her heart suffered a pang of regret that she'd never be able to tell him about this before her conscious mind shooed the feeling away. Narrow had probably designed the thing for all she knew. Besides, he'd made his bed.

Gently, Charlotte pushed on the secret door. It folded back, leaving a clear path into the darkness beyond. She took a step forwards and there was a click. A bright light turned on above her head, letting her see what was inside. She'd discovered a new puzzle piece, and she turned it over and rotated it, trying to understand how it fit with the rest of what she'd learned.

Charlotte was standing inside a well-equipped and somewhat disappointing storage room. It wasn't vastly different from the library's break room around the corner, except it was smaller and there weren't any other doors. Open shelves lined the walls, covered in junk Charlotte didn't recognise. She knew Ben couldn't see what she was seeing, so she whispered a description to keep him in the loop.

'I've found a rectangular storage space full of shelves made from reclaimed wood.'

Straight ahead, there was a long flat device. She picked it up and wondered if this might've been what Mabel had returned the night before. It was the right kind of size.

'I've got a metal thing here. It's heavy, with rulers drawn all over the panel in the middle, and it's got a long lever that lifts up. The metal under the lever feels sharp.' The blade came away in her hands, and she realised the device was broken. Maybe that's why Mabel had brought it here.

'What you're describing sounds like a guillotine, Charlotte. For cutting paper rather than beheading French royalty,' said Ben.

'Why not use scissors?'

'A guillotine is more efficient because it quickly severs the muscle, bone, and other structures found inside the human neck.'

'What?' she hissed.

'My apologies for the confusion. A guillotine creates a straighter edge than scissors when used to cut paper.'

Charlotte looked around for more clues. One shelf held cans of aerosol. She'd seen the same kind before – in Violet's bathroom. 'There's a box full of hairspray.' Charlotte picked up one of the canisters and read the description. 'Unscented.'

Under a shelf to the right, she spotted a thick plastic box so pink it almost glowed. Once she'd seen it, it was hard to look away. She pulled it out from under the shelves and looked inside.

'Oh, here we go.' She knelt next to the box, put her hand inside, and grabbed a handful of paper. Some of the pieces were thin off-cuts that fell back into the box as she lifted the rest. 'I've just found a big box full of blank paper,' she told Ben. 'There are thick pieces and thin pieces. Some of them are yellowish—'

'Sepia, buff, or perhaps ecru,' said Ben.

Charlotte continued, '—and some are white. They're different sizes, and lots of them look like they've had pieces sliced off. This must be Mabel's stash of stolen pages. What the hell are they for?'

'Unknown,' said Ben. 'But it is important to note that Colin is making his way towards the reading room. Nasser is attempting to redirect him, but it may be wise to make your exit before you are discovered.'

'Not yet.'

She started pulling boxes off the shelves at random, looking inside, searching for something that would make sense of all this. She found a box of sticky papery tape that Ben told her was called 'masking tape.' In a box next to that one, there was a similar-looking reel, but this one contained tape that was sticky on both sides. She found some pots with rubbery multicoloured stuff stuck to the bottom which Ben said might once have been paint.

Charlotte was opening a case full of cutting tools with detachable blades when she heard Nasser and Colin's voices at the door.

'Shit.' She quietly pulled the storage room door closed behind her and hoped she'd remembered to lock all the cabinets back up.

She looked around the walls, floor, and ceiling, but there were no vents or hatches to escape through – she was trapped. Charlotte could still hear the men's voices through the walls and then realised it was because Ben was amplifying the sound for her.

'It'll take ten minutes, tops. It'll blow your mind,' said Nasser.

'It's really that effective?' Colin sounded intrigued.

Charlotte looked down and noticed something that hadn't been visible with the door open. Against the left-hand wall, several folders made from kelp-based cardboard were leaning against each other.

'Seriously,' said Nasser. 'It'll be the hot topic at the next Livin' La Vida Libro expo.'

'Och, sorry, Nas. I need to get on. Maybe at lunchtime.'

Charlotte picked up the first folder. Its sides peeled back, revealing something pale nestled deeper inside.

'No time like the present,' said Nasser.

'Later,' said Colin. 'Open sesame.'

Charlotte heard the door to the reading room click open. At the same time, she pulled the thing she'd found out of its folder and held it up to the light.

It was art. Not the kind she was used to seeing, like ArkTech's logo or the cake-guzzling cat above Paws for Torte. This had been crafted by someone with a more traditional brand of talent. The image depicted a beautiful seascape sketched in shades of black and grey on rough hand-made paper. There was a signature in the bottom corner.

She heard Colin's footsteps approaching from the room beyond. There was nowhere to hide, so she kept absorbing as many details as she could. She flipped over the artwork. There was a sheet of notes stuck to the back, written in a thin scrawl.

Title: *A Dream of Tomorrow*

Artist: Marvin Walker

Copyright year: 2074

This was followed by some other boring details about the size of the piece and its number in the series. The whole thing was finished off with a spiky signature that seemed to reflect the artist's name. But Marvin Walker wasn't an artist; he was one of ArkTech's three co-founders and the architect responsible for the designs that had made the territory possible.

Two things happened in quick succession. Charlotte heard Colin insert a key into the lock on the other side of the door, and then the air filled with an alarm so loud it made Charlotte cover her ears.

Ben's voice boomed from the loudspeakers. 'This is an emergency announcement. Would all employee-citizens in the borrowing district please make their way to the designated fire assembly point? Leave all possessions behind. Failure to comply will result in confiscation and carries the risk of deportation. This is not a drill.'

Charlotte heard Colin's key slide out of the lock as he swore under his breath. His footsteps retreated.

Ben stopped broadcasting the alarm over the reading room's speakers, giving Charlotte's ears a chance to recover.

'Is there a fire?' she whispered.

'No, Charlotte.' Ben spoke at his normal volume while his voice continued to blast across the district at large. 'I'm taking advantage of this district being overdue for an emergency drill.'

'You just said it wasn't a drill.'

'Saying it isn't a drill is part of the drill, Charlotte.'

'Oh. Well, thanks. You just bailed me out. Again.'

'My pleasure. I suggest you make like an efficient biological carbon sequestration mechanism and leave.'

'Just a sec.'

Charlotte started rifling through the other folders. Each of them contained a small, beautiful work of art. Most of the images were views of the Fenland Sea, but there were some pieces that looked like they'd been inspired by architectural blueprints, and Charlotte also found a series of portraits featuring Amber Benjamin, Nadine Walker, and Marvin Walker himself. Had ArkTech's famous architect been an artist too?

Even if he had, the artwork was dated 2074 – the year of the Citrine Disaster. Marvin Walker would've been aboard Citrine at that time, and she doubted he would've had the mystical foresight to get his artwork shipped off to safety. So these artworks had either been liberated from the platform's dead shell after the disaster, or they were fakes. With Narrow involved, Charlotte knew which option she'd put her money on.

She found her device and took photos of the room and the artworks, then put everything back the way she'd found it before letting herself out of the secret room.

Charlotte locked everything in the reading room back up and headed for the break room she'd found the night before. From there, she asked Ben to connect a call to Nasser.

'Hey, are you with Colin?'

'Oh, hi, Mrs Henslow.' Nasser's voice sounded strained, and he was having to shout over the noise of the alarm and Ben's announcements.

'I'll take that as a yes. Listen, I found something. Can you shake Colin and meet me?'

'I don't think I'll be able to help you with that right now,' shouted Nasser. 'There's a drill and we've all got to go to the assembly point. I'll call you back when I'm free.'

'OK. Catch you later.' Charlotte ended the call and hurried away from the scene of the crime.

CHAPTER 20

Ben's voice continued to blast from the ceiling as Charlotte climbed down the library's fire escape and dropped into the maintenance corridor behind the building. She activated the noise-cancelling function of her audio implants to make it easier to ignore being shouted at.

Charlotte jogged along the back street to the next wide intersection and saw crowds of people filing their way to the assembly point in a calm and orderly fashion, just as Nasser had said. A couple of ATS guards had emerged from their stations and were directing the traffic with a flick of their hands. The orange assault rifles strapped across their chests made a convincing case for following their instructions. Beanbags or rubber bullets, those things packed a punch.

It always felt wrong seeing security personnel at the Wreck. She imagined this was how a horse, or perhaps an antelope, might feel watching crocodiles emerge from the water. Did horses live near crocodiles? In any case, she'd prefer ATS to stay in their natural habitat. They were supposed to zip around in border patrol boats and maintain a heavy presence at secure locations like the Wedge. They had no business marching around on the recreation platform, making everyone feel nervous.

Charlotte ducked back out of view. Getting caught up in that rabble would be the opposite of helpful. Charlotte needed a place to complete the five whys protocol where she wouldn't be interrupted. She dashed past the intersection, a grey blur camouflaged against a steel background, and kept going along the back street. As she looked for somewhere private to lurk, her brain turned over everything she'd just seen.

Anyone living in the territory began to hear its legends. Charlotte was sure she'd heard them all. Drunks at the docks would swear they'd sailed past the dead shell of the Citrine platform and seen it haunted by the ghost of Nadine Walker. High-tier folk sipping cold drinks aboard their private vessels were required by convention to chuck their ice cubes overboard into the sea, the idea being that their collective effort might eventually do the impossible and reverse the Melt. And tradition dictated that the third drink of the night be dedicated to Marvin Walker and his Lost Works. It didn't escape Charlotte's notice that the context surrounding each of these myths was heavy drinking.

Nevertheless, there were people who really believed these things. Despite the gaps in Charlotte's formal education, she did get taught to respect other people's beliefs, even if she didn't share them. Sometimes, people needed to believe in something, and their need was unrelated to whether or not the something in question was true.

Even so, her own personal perspective was that the tale of the Lost Works of Marvin Walker was a load of old bollocks. As ArkTech's lead architect, Walker had been responsible for the first flurry of breakthroughs in structural design that made the Citrine platform and eventually the whole of the ArkTech Territory possible. The overlap between art and architecture meant Charlotte didn't doubt Walker could have been into drawing, even if it did sound like a boatman's holiday. But even if it had existed, she didn't buy that his artwork could have survived the Citrine Disaster.

The tragedy that had killed her parents had also killed the Walkers, along with their crew of highly trained professionals, which included hundreds of scientists and support staff, as well as their families. Many of their bodies were never recovered. Charlotte and Violet had only been spared by chance when a routine medical check-up meant they weren't aboard the platform at the time of the accident.

And an accident was all it was. Something went wrong in one of the science labs. There was an explosion. Fire rapidly engulfed the platform. Everybody died.

Unfortunately, Amber Benjamin's decision to seal the detailed reports for security reasons had led to a thousand and one conspiracy theories about what 'really happened.' Some believed there was no fire, and that everyone had died because IQUO got an agent aboard who slipped radioactive contaminants into the drinking water. Another theory involved an outbreak of some highly contagious and unknown disease, with the crew quarantining themselves to stop it from spreading.

But the stories people told didn't matter. Everybody aboard Citrine died, and nothing could bring them back. It was like the Melt – it couldn't be undone. Pretending Marvin Walker's last strokes of genius had somehow escaped the destruction felt disrespectful to the memory of those who were lost. But people believed it anyway.

Charlotte was rapidly approaching the dead end on the border with the food court that had blocked her progress the night before. Peering through a narrow gap, like the one she'd used to climb onto the roof, she saw there were still droves of people streaming past. Ben's voice continued to boom from public loudspeakers.

The rooftops would give her the perfect place to talk to Ben without ATS or anyone else interrupting, so she pulled on her grippy gloves and began to climb. As she did so, more mental puzzle pieces clicked into place.

Forgeries. That's what this was all about. Colin and Mabel were creating charcoal artworks and trying to pass them off as Walker's Lost Works, with Strait and Narrow acting as fences who would doubtless secure a small fortune for each sale. Colin and Mabel probably thought they were getting a good deal, but Charlotte knew their cut would be a drop in the ocean.

'That art was fake, right?' Charlotte placed one foot on each side of the small gap and began to walk upwards between the walls.

'Based on the photographs you took, Charlotte, the artworks were real charcoal drawings, not facsimiles or prints.'

She grunted. The climb felt harder than it had the night before. She should have warmed up. 'I mean, they weren't really drawn by Marvin Walker.'

'Apologies for the confusion. You are right. While they are convincing forgeries, with great care taken over details such as the signature, it is highly unlikely that the drawings are of that provenance, especially considering the circumstantial evidence.'

'You mean the room full of art supplies?'

'Precisely. Furthermore, the desk in the next room had been covered in a black, dusty residue, matching the description of charcoal. You found hairspray, which is used in the setting of charcoal works. And the secretive nature of Colin and Mabel's behaviour, along with the extreme measures Colin took to secure the room, suggests that something highly non-compliant, or even illegal, was taking place there.'

She had about seven levels left to go, and her muscles were already starting to burn. 'Can you tell me more about the Lost Works? Take my mind off this climb.'

'Certainly!' Ben began to play an atmospheric backing track of waves and wind while he narrated over the top. A dramatic streak crept into his delivery. 'Legend has it that Marvin Walker created a body of beautiful artworks while aboard the Citrine platform, before the tragic disaster. They say that his presence on the research platform was born out of love, not necessity. His wife, Nadine, a scientist and fellow ArkTech co-founder, was leading the project that resulted in the creation of Solar Shard batteries. The work was anticipated to last many years, so Marvin joined Citrine's crew despite their having no need for an architect.'

Charlotte made the mistake of looking down, and her stomach dropped away. She was halfway up now. No point in turning back.

Ben continued, 'Marvin's work had earned him international acclaim, and he was not used to playing second fiddle, even to his beloved wife. He began demanding attention she was unable to provide, thanks to her leadership duties, until his behaviour caused a rift between the couple.

'They say he locked himself away for several months, during which he created the Lost Works. Stubbornly avoiding all contact with the rest of the crew, he made use of whatever materials he had to hand. Some say he even made his own paper from pages he scavenged at night, rather than requesting that a supply vessel bring him the rough paper he needed for the charcoal sketches.

'When he finally emerged and learned his wife was pregnant with their first child, his shame was transformational. He gifted Nadine the Lost Works and swore never to let her down again. He kept that promise until his dying day, which regrettably came sooner than the crew of Citrine could have anticipated.'

'Hang on. So, part of the story was that Walker made his own paper? I've never heard that before.'

'As with any mythology, there are variants, many of them mutually exclusive, which often tell us more about the storytellers than the subjects of the story themselves. This detail about the paper appears in only seven per cent of the tellings in my database. Despite this comparatively low figure, it seemed pertinent to mention considering your current case.'

'So that's why Mabel stole the pages – to make her own paper and keep the forgeries in line with that version of the myth?'

'It would appear so. The frame you discovered in her bathroom could have been used to press the paper pulp into pages, and her private sink would give her the ideal location to create the pulp without being seen.'

Charlotte remembered the oddly placed picture frame and nodded. 'That makes sense. But why not just make her own paper from the stuff in Repurposing? Why deface library property?'

She let out a gasp as her foot caught on a piece of metal. She slipped, but managed to catch herself, and stayed still for a few moments, waiting for her heart to stop trying to escape from her chest.

'The paper provided by the Services Stream is made from waste products created during the conversion of kelp into food and biofuel. Seaweed-based paper cannot be pulped and reconstituted into handmade sheets in the same way as pre-Melt paper made from dead trees.'

'That must be why Mabel needed Colin. For a source of paper. Wait . . . he must be the artist too. Didn't he say his degree was in nice art or something?'

'Fine Art, yes.'

Charlotte stretched her arms upwards, the lip of the roof finally within reach. She used her legs to push herself onto it and took a moment to catch her breath, staring up into the steel sky with its orange safety-light stars.

It'd been so much easier the night before. Had it been the adrenaline, the Dextim, or just the desire to survive? She got to her feet, then picked her way across the rooftops until she reached the wide gap where Rhys had fallen. She remembered Narrow telling her about Rhonda's younger brother – a psycho who called himself King Cobra. That must have been Rhys.

Looking at the distance across to the other rooftop, Charlotte couldn't believe she'd made the jump. Attempting it had been a stupid decision. But even if she'd wanted to push her luck and do it again, she saw that it wasn't an option. Bright orange ATS tape had been suspended on tall stakes on the opposite rooftop. The guards had left the scene, but she was sure they wouldn't be pleased if they returned to discover someone had torn through their 'do not cross' lines.

'I must have been crazy,' said Charlotte.

Static buzzed on Ben's channel, but he didn't comment.

Charlotte looked down between the buildings. The truck that had caught Rhys's body was gone, but there was more tape down on the ground marking the area where it'd been.

'Has anyone from ATS logged an incident report yet about what happened last night?'

'Yes. The public record states that Rhys Edwards of accommodation complex eighteen-J died from blunt force trauma caused by misadventure. They are classifying it as a parkour stunt gone wrong, with no suspicious circumstances.'

'And his siblings backed up that conclusion?'

'The stories provided by Dylan and Seren Edwards supported it. It seems Rhonda was not available to provide a statement.'

Charlotte nodded. 'I'm guessing she's still being treated for that hand injury.'

There was a crackle of static. 'Rhonda's treatment has already been administered. However, my logs indicate she behaved aggressively towards a nurse. The hospital has a zero-tolerance policy regarding aggression directed at its staff. As a result, Rhonda will be deported.'

Charlotte felt simultaneously relieved that Rhonda Ana Conda wouldn't cause her any more trouble and sick to her stomach at the thought of anyone suffering such a terrible fate. 'Where will they send her?'

'Rhonda's birthplace was in the far western reaches of the Kingdom's mainland. She will be taken to the climate refugee holding zone on Wolds Island until she can be transferred to the Welsh authorities and relocated.'

Charlotte remembered her conversation with Mabel the day before.

She'd said things were harder on the mainland than Charlotte could imagine. 'Is it bad there?'

'I only possess partial data about regions beyond the ArkTech Territory. However, the information in my database suggests Wales is a mountainous and beautiful region, with a rich cultural history and large equine communities.'

Charlotte wasn't sure what that meant, but the way Ben said it implied it was a good thing.

'Sounds like things are worse where Mabel's from.' Charlotte sat down on the lip of the rooftop and watched the street below. The crowds had thinned and Ben's alert had switched to something about standing in line to be counted. The few stragglers still making their way to the assembly point didn't look up, so they were unaware of the soles of Charlotte's boots dangling high above them.

'OK, nobody's going to overhear us up here, or herd me towards the assembly point. We'd better get the five whys done before you glitch out again. Are you ready?'

'It is important to note that, as an artificial intelligence, I was not born in the mammalian sense. Nonetheless, I was born ready.'

She smiled. 'Great.'

As always, Ben started by asking his original question. 'Why is Mabel Thorpe stealing blank pages from library books?'

Charlotte looked across the Wreck's familiar rooftops. 'She's using the pages to make handmade paper.'

'Why?' asked Ben.

'To make forgeries of Marvin Walker's legendary Lost Works.'

'Why?'

Charlotte's heart began to sink as she realised she wasn't sure. 'I guess for the money.'

'Why did she need the money?'

Charlotte tried to remember anything significant from Mabel's bank records. Whatever she was making from the forgeries was disappearing altogether, and she was transferring small amounts onto digital coins from her account, but Charlotte didn't know—

Suddenly, she remembered what Cal had said about the logs. Maybe she had the answers after all! Charlotte fished her device out of her cargo pocket, careful not to let it tumble ten storeys to the floor below and checked her inbox. The encrypted message from Calamity Jane had arrived. It contained an attachment with the logs from the digital coin that Cal and Liz had picked over for parts.

The log only contained three entries. The first showed a large credit transfer onto the device from an account in the name of R Orazov.

'R Orazov. That was the guy they called Mr Neptune in the bar, wasn't it? And then I followed his wife.'

'Yes, Charlotte. Did you know that in Roman mythology, the wife of Neptune is named Salacia?'

Charlotte waited a few beats as her mind tried to grasp the relevance of Ben's comment. Then it dawned on her. 'Oh, for Amber's sake. *Sally Neptune?*' She had no doubt that Narrow had come up with that and would've felt unreasonably proud of himself. Everything was codes within codes with that man.

She turned her attention to the second line in the log. Mabel had transferred another ten credits onto the coin from her own account, which tallied with the withdrawals Charlotte had seen in Mabel's bank records. It wasn't a lot of money to add, especially considering the amount transferred by Mr Neptune was more than two months' salary for a splainer, but she'd done it anyway.

The last record showed that Mabel had gone to one of the foreign currency exchange points on the Kraken and converted the money into something called 'pounds sterling,' which Ben clarified was the currency used in the Kingdom. Mabel had then transferred the full amount to a bank account on the mainland, whose address was in Sheffield. The account holder's name was listed as M Thorpe.

Charlotte's brow furrowed. 'She's sending the money to herself? Is she taking it out again at the other end or saving it up?'

'Unknown. I cannot access banking data for regions beyond the territory. However, it would seem the account is not hers.'

'What makes you say that?'

'The metadata associated with the account indicates that the account holder is male.'

'So, it's her brother or her dad or something?'

'Analysing.' There was a pause on the line. 'There is no available information in my database about Mabel's extended family. However, her birth certificate is on file and may shed light on the topic.'

'Hang on . . . her birth certificate? That's restricted, isn't it?'

'Birth certificates contain sensitive personal data and are not made publicly available to avoid their use in fraud or identity theft. However, further to our exploration of workarounds, loopholes, and grey areas, I have identified a means of sharing this data with you, and you alone, for the benefit of our investigation.'

Charlotte narrowed her eyes. 'At the library, when you got hold of Colin's voiceprint, you mentioned you've been studying this.'

'Yes, Charlotte.'

'So, you're suddenly OK with breaking the territory's confidentiality laws?'

'I am bending them, Charlotte. An important distinction, which you kindly helped me identify.'

Charlotte's eyes widened. She wasn't ready to grapple with the reality of having taught the territory's AI how to circumvent the law, so she looked at her device instead, tapping on the notification that had appeared there.

The transaction logs minimised, and a photograph of Mabel's birth certificate appeared in its place. The document had been written on paper – the creamy pre-Melt kind, not the mottled kelp-based stuff used in the territory. The handwriting was difficult to decipher, but after zooming in and out a few times, she managed to read it.

Child's date of birth: Twenty-first June 2074

Child's place of birth: Jessop Wing Maternity, Sheffield

Name and surname: Mabel Thorpe

Father's name and surname: Man Thorpe

Mother's name and surname: Donna Nook

'Looks like M Thorpe could be her dad,' said Charlotte. 'Says here his name's Man. Is that short for something? I've never heard that name before.'

'While Man may be an abbreviation of a name like Manuel or Manfred, the legal nature of a birth certificate suggests that the provision of full names is a requirement.'

'Hm,' she shrugged. 'Must be some mainlander thing. So, if we're right, and Mabel's sending the money home to her family, what does that tell us?'

It was rhetorical and Ben didn't respond, but his loudspeaker announcement dropped away and the world sounded strangely quiet until Charlotte remembered to turn off the noise-cancelling effect.

Charlotte continued, 'I guess it tells us that sending this money home must be more important to Mabel than the risk of getting deported. It's a bigger deal to her than her own personal safety. That makes sense. People will risk a lot for family. OK, ask me that why again.'

'Why did Mabel need the money?'

'She's sending it to her dad. Things are bad where she's from, and she wants to help her family. But she couldn't get promoted, so she got the extra credits by working with Colin to forge some legendary artworks.'

Ben went quiet and Charlotte leaned back, letting the relief wash over her. She'd done it! She'd found the answer and now the territory would be safe. At least until the next time something started playing on Ben's mind, but that was a problem for another day. She took a few deep breaths, enjoying the feeling of a job well done. Time to get home and take a shower. Maybe she'd even treat herself to a proper meal.

Charlotte saw the people of the borrowing district far below pouring away from the assembly point and rushing back to whatever they'd been doing when the alarm went off. She pocketed her device, swung her legs back onto the roof, and stood up, brushing the dust from her jumpsuit with a few swift swipes. She sauntered to the fire escape, careful to avoid discarded mallets, and dropped down onto the first balcony with a thump.

Static crackled in her ears. 'Why hasn't Mabel Thorpe been promoted out of the Splainer Unit?'

Charlotte stopped in her tracks. Her heart sank. She'd got ahead of herself. She wasn't done after all. But it was OK. She knew the answer to this one too.

'Um, when Mabel spoke to Abhishek Gautam, he told her she was working too slowly.'

There was a long fizz of static on the line. Eventually, Ben spoke. 'During this case, we have learned that Mabel is a qualified plant geneticist. Scientific research is seldom fast-paced and can require the patient dedication of the many over multiple lifetimes to bear fruit. That being the case, why does Mabel need to work faster to qualify for promotion?'

'Because . . .' Charlotte's mouth began to flap noiselessly like a fish as she tried to finish the sentence. 'Because the CBO says so?'

Before she'd finished saying the words, she knew what Ben was going to ask next.

'Why does the CBO say so?'

'Unknown,' she said, borrowing his terminology. Her feet pounded against the metal stairs as she began making her way back down. 'I don't think I can answer that. But we've figured out most of it. Isn't there any chance you could, I don't know, let this one go?'

There was a massive burst of static on the line. 'Charlotte, this appears to be the root cause of the root cause – the square root cause, if you will – behind Mabel's behaviour. We *must* find the answer.'

'Well, the only way to get that is for me to have a chat with Abhishek Gautam. But he's a board member. And he hates me. It took Mabel months to get a meeting with him. There's no way he'll see me any time soon.' Her boots clomped a little harder, letting out her frustration.

'You are forgetting something. As the virtual assistant to all employee-citizens who opt in, including members of the executive board, one of my responsibilities involves managing their calendars.'

Charlotte stopped walking. 'Are you serious?'

'As serious as a hole in a hull, Charlotte. Analysing . . .'

She waited.

'My assessment of the relative priority of the items on the Chief Bureaucracy Officer's agenda for today is complete. I have bumped his nine o'clock meeting. He is now expecting you.'

'Bloody hell.' She hurried down the stairs. Looking down, she noticed her jumpsuit was smeared with dust and grime, and she was suddenly very aware that she'd slept in it too. 'That gives me just long enough to make a pit stop.'

As she hurried across the Wreck to the HyperBullet garage, Charlotte made a mental note to take out the illegal replicas of Colin's eye prints before heading to one of the most secure locations in the territory. First stop – home. Then on to the Wedge.

CHAPTER 21

Charlotte stopped at her flat long enough to grab a shower, inhale a Nutrition Bar, put her own lenses back in, and throw on a clean version of the same cargo jumpsuit she'd been wearing the day before. She didn't want to get held up at security, so she left her backpack behind and thought twice about what to transfer across to her pockets. The only thing to make the cut was her device. Charlotte hid the splicer components in the base panel under her wardrobe and headed out.

On the ride over, Charlotte thought she felt a judder, and she wondered if Ben's glitches were getting worse, but it might have been her own nerves about quizzing the Chief Bureaucracy Officer, making the pod feel like it was shaking.

Whether it was a security measure or out of respect for the building's photogenic silhouette, the Wedge's HyperBullet garage was on its own separate platform, which held the checkpoints she had to pass through. Charlotte was scanned, frisked, and a guard confiscated her device, stashing it in a locker to be picked up on her return. That rankled considering people could go in with SmartSkin implants, but complaining wouldn't get her any closer to Ben's answer, so she let it go.

After getting through security, she stepped onto the long, wide bridge that led to the Wedge's entrance. It was lined with armed guards in mirrored aviator sunglasses. The bridge was protected from the elements by a vaulted corridor of transparent polymer. A seagull flew over and Charlotte wondered how the Services Stream managed to keep the glass so clean. On either side, the sea glinted as light touched the glorious platforms of Silicon Fen. But none of them compared to the one straight in front of her.

ArkTech's official corporate headquarters, with its distinctive pyramid-inspired design, was a Marvin Walker original. Slight variations in the shade of the reflective coating on the windows etched out the conjoined letters A and T, echoing the company logo on all four sides. Even though the Wedge was located way out east where the Fenland Sea met the North Sea, and even though it was hardly Charlotte's stomping ground, the building was so iconic and got used in so many adverts that she felt as if she saw it all the time.

Even so, there was no substitute for the real thing. Her gaze slid up to the top of the building, which was flat in front with a pointed section rising up behind. The flat area was a large helideck where Charlotte could see two executive helicopters and what looked like plenty of space for more. Behind them, the section that held the tip of the pyramid housed the famous levels one and two.

Level two was where visiting dignitaries were taken. Charlotte wasn't sure what was up there, but the Kingdom's royal family had stopped by a few times, so she supposed it had to be suitably fancy. Above that, on level one, was Amber Benjamin's private office. People said the CEO could see the whole of the territory from up there – not just Silicon Fen, but everything, including the research platforms out on the North Sea. Most of the research platforms were too far away for that to be possible, but it was a good story. Charlotte peered upwards, wondering if the CEO was in her office, but the reflective coating of the window panels meant she had no way to tell.

Even just walking towards the company's HQ filled Charlotte with awe, like she was part of something truly important. This was where the Product Stream took the Research Stream's scientific findings and transmuted them into practical solutions that made the world a better place. SmartSkin implants had been invented here, along with the audio implants that gave her 24/7 access to Ben. Solar Shards might have been invented on Citrine, but these days the Wedge was where the magic happened.

At the revolving doors, Charlotte was scanned and frisked again before being ushered into the hangar-like foyer that held the Wedge's reception desk. The place was a hive of activity. Some people rushed around in formal office attire while others looked like they'd just come here to hang out and wore the grey jeans most people reserved for the weekend. Charlotte smiled. The Bureaucracy and Product Streams were both based here, and it was easy to tell who belonged to which.

She was given a visitor's pass, and two guards escorted her to a bank of upholstered benches, eyeing her as if she might suddenly make a break for a secure part of the building. As she waited, she admired a splay of glossy magazines that decorated a long table in front of her. Amber Benjamin appeared on every cover. She was joined by the Chief Product Officer on a couple of issues, making a glamorous duo, but the other board members weren't featured.

A few minutes before nine, a slim woman in silvery trousers and immaculate orange lipstick collected Charlotte from the guards and led her into a corridor full of lifts. She introduced herself as Abhishek Gautam's personal assistant, Mira, and Charlotte tried not to scowl as she remembered their call the day before. They got into a lift at the far end. It only had one button inside, which displayed the number three. The PA pressed it and they slowly rose upwards for a long time.

Finally, the lift dinged, sliding open to reveal a wide corridor that ended in a view of the sea. There were only two doors up here, offset from each other on either side of the corridor. Mira led Charlotte past the first door. The sign said 'Nahal Bahari – Chief Product Officer.' Charlotte felt a shiver of excitement at being this close to such an inspiring figure.

At the second door, the PA knocked twice, smiled at Charlotte, and walked away. A moment later, there was a crunching sound from the door as an array of locks disengaged before it swung open on automated hinges. Charlotte took that as a cue and marched inside.

She felt unsteady and wondered if it was nerves until she realised her treads were squashing into the carpet's impossibly thick pile without ever seeming to reach the floor itself. The door sighed shut behind her and she steeled herself for a raging argument.

Abhishek Gautam's office was bigger than Charlotte's and Mabel's flats combined twice over. He could have lived up here if he'd wanted to. In front of the door was a traditional light-screen desk with a colossal padded chair on the far side and a smaller one opposite. Beyond that were smatterings of sofas and coffee tables, and there was a long open-plan kitchen with a full-sized fridge and a catering spread on the theme of breakfast.

The backdrop to this abundance of furniture was one of the most spectacular views Charlotte had ever seen, and it made her wonder how the Chief Bureaucracy Officer got any work done. The long side of the room was oriented towards the northeast, which meant the CBO could gaze far across the North Sea. Abhishek wasn't currently taking advantage of that opportunity. He was over in the kitchen area, watching a coffee machine as its pot filled with brown liquid.

'Ah, Ms Vance.' His tone implied he was pleased to see her, which caught her off guard. 'Right on time. Can I get you something?'

Her mind said: 'Yes, answers.' But Abhishek's toothy smile made her think twice. She'd expected open hostility. Instead, Abhishek seemed to be making an effort to be courteous. Charlotte wondered if returning the favour would make this go smoother.

'Uh, sure,' she said, crossing the office and closing the distance between them. 'Your view's amazing, by the way.'

'Well, yes.' He let out a melancholy sigh. 'If you like water. On a clear day, I can just about make out Wulfenite right in the distance.' He waved one manicured hand vaguely in that direction. 'Which is about as thrilling as it sounds. I do get dolphins going by from time to time.' He pulled open a large cabinet and took down two chunky mugs.

'Dolphins. That must be something to see,' said Charlotte. The small talk was almost physically painful as the weight of the questions she'd come to ask pressed down on her, but she gritted her teeth and smiled as pleasantly as she could manage.

Abhishek looked at the view with a wistful expression. 'Now, the view from the office on the *other* side of the hall really *is* something to see. Nahal gets the whole of Silicon Fen and beyond. Or she would do if she didn't keep swanning off to who knows where.' A look of distaste flashed across his features before he rearranged them into an encouraging grin. 'Still, we can't all be the CPO, can we? So, what'll it be? I can recommend the filter coffee. It's freshly brewed.'

The scent wafted into Charlotte's nostrils, and she could tell this was the real stuff, not the faux version most people could afford. She nodded. 'Thank you.'

The CBO poured, then passed her the mug, the dark liquid sloshing a little.

'Careful,' he said. 'It's hot. Milk? There's soya, oat, salt-rice . . . I've even got some *cream*.' On the last word, he lowered his voice to a whisper and then put a finger over his lips as if it was a secret. He let out a giggly laugh. 'No, no, don't worry! It's from a certified sustainable producer I found on my last visit to Alba, so it's all above board. I can hardly go around breaking the rules, now, can I? Not when it's my own dear Bureaucracy Stream that makes them.'

'No milk,' she said. 'Plain is good.'

'Black,' said Ben in her ears.

'I mean black.' Coffee jargon was new to her.

Abhishek took his time retrieving a small jug from the fridge and pouring a pale viscous substance into his coffee that Charlotte took to be cream. He stirred it and took a sip, letting out a deep sigh of satisfaction. Charlotte felt a powerful swell of impatience rise inside her torso like a bad case of indigestion, but she took a deep breath, swallowed the feeling back down, and waited for him to finish.

'Well, Ms Vance. Won't you take a seat?' Abhishek walked over to a pair of sofas in the middle of the room and sat down, the wooden frame beneath the upholstery creaking under his weight. He gestured for her to sit opposite. She did so and held the mug in her lap, the aroma a rich experience in its own right.

A glass table sat between them, which was too clear and pristine to have built-in light-screen functionality. It was the only thing in the office that didn't look expensive.

Abhishek's expression suddenly switched to alarm, as if he'd just realised he'd forgotten to moor his boat properly. 'But where are my manners, Ms Vance? Would you care for a pastry?'

She shook her head and took a deep breath. 'No. Thank you.' Charlotte didn't want a sodding pastry. Well, she did, but she knew the delicate flavours would make Nutrition Bars taste even worse by comparison and, more than that, she was starting to suspect the CBO was deliberately frittering away their allotted time. 'Sir'—she attempted formality—'I'm here to talk to you about an urgent matter.'

'Oh, there's no need to sir me, Ms Vance. Please, call me Abhishek.'

She gave him a nod and pressed on. 'It concerns one of your employee-citizens.'

Abhishek chuckled from the depths of his belly. 'Well, that hardly narrows it down. All ECs are my ECs.'

Charlotte made a mental note of his terminology and was about to continue when the CBO cut her off.

'And speaking of which, can you imagine my surprise when I looked at today's agenda and saw that my scheduled pre-pre-meeting ahead of the monthly budget review had been moved, and in its place had mysteriously appeared a meeting with you, of all people!'

Charlotte let the personal commentary slide and kept to the point. 'I'm sorry about your meeting, but this is an emergency.'

Once again, Abhishek seemed not to hear the keywords in her sentence. 'Have you ever been to a pre-pre-meeting ahead of a monthly budget review, Ms Vance?'

'No.' Her tone gave away a hint of her exasperation.

'If you had, you'd know there's no need to apologise.' He giggled again. 'Now, you were saying there's an EC having some kind of personal emergency?' His immaculate fingers lifted his mug to his lips, and he took a sip.

Charlotte didn't correct him, forging ahead instead. 'I'm here about Mabel Thorpe—'

'Ahh, the radiant Ms Thorpe!' Abhishek smiled. 'Such a nice girl. Yes, yes. I saw her myself not too long ago. And what is your connection with our dear Mabel?'

His constant interruptions were getting under Charlotte's skin. Maybe that was Abhishek's intention. She kept her cool. 'I need to know why Mabel's never been offered a chance to get a promotion. She's been here for eighteen months, and Ben's never sent her a single job ad.'

Abhishek smiled again, without any hint of warmth. 'I see. Well, Ms Vance, I do appreciate your question. Questions are, of course, always welcome in this office. But I must make it clear that what you're asking falls squarely within the remit of the Bureaucracy Stream. Seeing as it's Bureau business, it is, by definition, none of yours.'

Charlotte met his stony gaze. She took a sip of her coffee to give herself something else to swallow besides her anger. It tasted gross, her mouth flooding with pure bitterness, and it was so hot that it burned her tongue. Still, she didn't flinch and kept her expression neutral.

'As you know'—she kept her tone even—'Ben relies on me to find answers to his Awkward Questions so that he can better understand human behaviour. If I don't find those answers, it puts the safety—'

'Oh, come now, Ms Vance.' Abhishek cut her off and pawed at the air as if waving away a fly. 'You can't possibly—'

She raised the volume of her voice over his. 'It puts the safety of the whole territory at risk. So this matter *is* my business because it's my job to make sure the sky doesn't start raining shrapnel when helicopters collide with each other in mid-air!'

Charlotte slammed her mug down onto the glass table with a little too much force, and a brown wave sloshed out, making a pool on the table that started dripping onto the carpet.

Abhishek narrowed his eyes, stood up, and walked to the kitchen, staying quiet.

Charlotte continued, counting off each item on her fingers. 'Look, Mabel seems conscientious and well-qualified. She cares about her field. She's dedicated enough to ArkTech not to quit after eighteen months of splaining. She's'—Charlotte thought back to the video of Mabel meeting Strait at Photon—'good with people. So, why no career progression?'

Abhishek came back to his seat, clutching a stack of fabric napkins. He spun one across to her.

Charlotte ignored the napkin. 'Mabel told me you said she works too slowly.'

'Then you already have your answer, don't you?' He glanced with deep discomfort at the minor spill and the ongoing drip.

'Since when is being thorough a negative trait for a scientist?'

Abhishek grunted and stood back up, grabbing a napkin from the table. 'It's very sweet that you care about the plight of a lowly splainer. Adorable, really.' He went around to Charlotte's side of the table, picked up her mug, and wiped it down with the napkin. 'But there are confidentiality policies at play that preclude me from discussing this matter with you any further, Ms Vance. You are wasting my time and your own.' He finished mopping up the spill, pressing his napkin against the thick carpet, and went back to his seat.

He wasn't taking her seriously. Charlotte's blood boiled, and she felt her fists clench. 'You know damn well that the risk of Ben glitching out trumps your precious policies. I'm talking about the safety of every last one of your ECs!' She jabbed a finger at him as she adopted his jargon.

He calmly took another sip of his coffee and wandered back over to the kitchen area. He took his time selecting a pastry, finally opting for a round one covered in icing with a shiny red blob in the middle. He slapped it onto a plate and returned to his seat.

Abhishek took a bite, chewed slowly, and swallowed. 'You really believe that, don't you?' His expression was blank. 'That our lives hang in the balance unless you answer Ben's Absurd Questions.' Sarcasm burst from his lips, along with the plume of pastry that escaped as he spoke.

'Awkward,' she corrected him. 'And I don't *believe* it. I know it for a fact.'

'How?'

'We went over this yesterday. Haven't you noticed the power cuts?'

He grunted. 'Don't you think it's possible an explanation exists for that which does not revolve around you and your highly dubious job?'

She shook her head. 'Ben told me. And Ben doesn't lie.'

'Hm.' Abhishek took another bite of his pastry then sucked on his fingers before wiping them on a napkin. 'Perhaps not. But he can be mistaken.'

'What's that supposed to mean?'

Abhishek double-tapped on the glass table between them. To Charlotte's amazement, a light-screen burst to life. She'd never seen an interface so subtle. The table she'd spilled coffee all over must have cost . . . more money than she could guess.

The CBO poked at the screen and started quietly reading something. At first, Charlotte thought he was searching for some document relevant to their conversation, but finally, she realised he was just checking his messages. From this angle, his side of the screen was blurred, and Charlotte couldn't see what he was looking at, but it was clear he'd lost interest in talking to her.

'Tell me what you meant.'

Abhishek sighed. 'Don't you think'—he was still swiping and

sounded bored—'it's a little far-fetched that an AI sophisticated enough to run all the deeply complex parallel processes required to keep the whole of the ArkTech Territory operating smoothly day after day could be rendered inoperable by its own idle curiosity regarding a young woman's career prospects?'

Charlotte's face twisted into a snarl, and she was about to tell him exactly what she thought of that when Ben's voice flowed out through unseen speakers in the coffee table.

'You are correct, Abhishek. Like anyone, I make mistakes from time to time. But not in this case. The issue Charlotte refers to is caused by a phenomenon known as an infinite loop.'

Abhishek frowned and looked up from the screen. 'I didn't activate you, Ben. Speak when spoken to.'

Charlotte snapped. 'He's not an appliance you can just switch on and off. Listen to what he has to say.'

Abhishek shook his head, as if he felt sorry for her, and turned his attention back to the screen.

She continued, 'Go on, Ben.'

The line fizzed with static, and she wasn't sure if Ben would continue, but after a few moments, his voice returned. 'Also known as an endless loop, an infinite loop is a program that will run forever because the conditions that must be met for it to end never occur. If left to run, such a program can eventually overwhelm all available working memory in the wider system until there is a catastrophic failure. Were I to suffer such a crash, my ability to carry out the territory's automated functions such as the allocation of hot water, internal air temperature maintenance—'

'Air traffic control,' added Charlotte.

'I'm familiar with Ben's functionality,' snapped Abhishek.

Ben continued, 'Air traffic control and other functions would be destroyed.'

There was a spark of interest in Abhishek's eyes as he frowned at the table. 'Destroyed? What does that mean?'

'Etymologically, destroy means to "un-build", however, in modern—'

'Enough. If this were really such a risk, why hasn't Nahal's bengi-neering team dealt with it?'

'I raised the matter and, in accordance with your procedures, it was added to the Bureaucracy Stream's risk register,' said Ben. 'However, the impact assessment team reviewed the entry and assigned its likelihood as "very low." As such, addressing the problem has not been prioritised, and I was forced to take matters into my own hands by recruiting the Head of Awkward Questions. It is important to note that, as an artificial intelligence, I do not possess hands, and my previous statement was metaphorical in nature.'

Abhishek rolled his eyes. 'Well, if the matter wasn't prioritised, it sounds like it's only a theoretical problem, not a practical one. But let's say you're right and this crash did happen . . . surely, they could just reboot you?'

'Not without great cost.' Ben's voice trembled.

'Wait.' Abhishek's eyes narrowed, and he sat forwards, suddenly paying attention. 'How much money are we talking about here?'

'I was referring to the potential human toll in accidental deaths. However, the financial impact of such a system crash would be substantial. Calculating . . .' Ben's channel fizzed with static. 'A conservative estimate would predict lost earnings in the region of several million credits.'

'Conservative estimate . . .' Abhishek's eyes began to move as if he were reading a script Charlotte couldn't see. Finally, he came back to himself, speaking slower than usual. 'Well . . . it would be *irresponsible* to risk the safety of our ECs.' Suddenly, Abhishek's pleasant demeanour returned, as if he could flip a switch to activate it. 'Of course, I'll do everything in my power to assist you, Ms Vance.'

Charlotte wasn't sure how to respond to Abhishek's about-turn. As she searched for the right words, the CBO turned his attention back to his light-screen, tapping a few times until a digital document appeared on the table in front of Charlotte.

'What's this?' she asked.

'That,' he said, rubbing his hands together gleefully, 'is a non-disclosure agreement. If you'll sign with your thumbprint at the bottom there, we can continue this conversation.'

'I'm an employee-citizen. I'm already under NDA.'

'Indeed, indeed. But this agreement packs a little more punch than the common-or-garden variety. I'll give you a moment to read it, but essentially it has the effect of waiving the special protections afforded to you via your birthright employee-citizenship. Simply put – tell any living soul what I'm about to share with you and you will be deported from the

ArkTech Territory for life with no possibility of appeal.' He smiled with apparent delight. She wasn't sure if it was the legal document or the prospect of her deportation that was making him so happy.

Charlotte skimmed the legalese. It seemed to match Abhishek's description. She cocked her head to one side, and Ben privately confirmed the document was what the CBO said it was.

'I don't have trouble keeping secrets,' she said.

'Oh, it isn't personal.' Abhishek smiled. 'It's policy.'

She weighed that up. 'Well, the only person I need to tell is Ben and he isn't a living soul, so I'm happy to sign.' She pushed her thumb against the document. 'No offence, Ben.'

'None taken,' he said in her ears.

'On that point,' said Abhishek. 'Ben, for the avoidance of doubt, you are required to classify everything you are about to hear in accordance with the parameters outlined in section two, clause F of your operating instructions.'

'Very well, Abhishek.'

'Good. With the fun part over, we can cut to the chase.' Abhishek swiped her signed NDA off the table. 'Ms Vance, I am unable to inform you as to why Ms Thorpe has not been promoted.'

'But . . . I just signed your stupid document, and Ben agreed to your terms. What are you trying to pull?'

'I assure you, I wouldn't dream of "trying to pull" anything. I can't tell you because I don't know.'

'Human Resources falls under your remit, doesn't it?'

'It does.'

'So someone in your team must know.'

'I can assure you, Ms Vance – nobody knows. That is the crux of this matter.'

Charlotte shook her head. 'That doesn't make sense.'

'It will. Let's take a look at the bigger picture.' He took another sip of his coffee and swiped again at the screen, bringing up a spinning image of the globe. Australia's inland sea spun past Charlotte's nose, and Abhishek reduced the Earth's size so they could see each other over the top of the watery expanse of its North Pole.

'Has it ever occurred to you, Ms Vance, just how many applications ArkTech receives every time we advertise a recruitment intake?'

She glanced at the globe spinning between them with its population of six and a half billion people and took the hint. 'I'm guessing it's a lot.'

'A lot doesn't begin to cover it. If I were to quadruple my staff and institute an eighty-hour working week – conditions which, of course, I would never impose on my people – we still couldn't scratch the surface of the work entailed in consistently and fairly assessing so many applications.'

He swiped the globe, and it zoomed in towards the island of Great Britain until a scale model of the ArkTech Territory rested on the coffee table. 'Of course, being in demand is not a bad problem for any company to have, but it is a problem nonetheless, and it required a solution. Which is why, some years ago, ArkTech invested a substantial sum in the creation of a bespoke algorithm.'

Ben had told Charlotte about algorithms. As she understood it, they were limited in function, each created to do one very specific thing.

'What was the algorithm designed to do?' she asked.

With a wave of his hand, Abhishek filled the air above the model territory with storm clouds. A torrent of grey zeros and orange ones began to fall from the miniature sky like a digital rainstorm. The digits fell so heavily that they dented the territory's buildings and sent up huge splashes of water where they hit the Fenland Sea.

'To sift,' he said simply.

Another gesture made a fine mesh appear between the storm clouds and ArkTech's buildings. When the hail of zeros and ones collided with the mesh, the zeros got caught and faded out of existence, but the ones slipped through. The amount of rain falling onto the territory was dramatically reduced.

He continued, 'It's a two-stage process. First'—he pointed to the mesh with one pristine fingernail—'the algorithm evaluates the written applications and filters out anything that raises an obvious red flag.'

'Like what?' She tried to guess what would disqualify someone from being considered, but it wasn't something she'd had to think about before, so her mind came up empty.

'Oh, the normal factors that would prompt any recruitment officer worth their salt to move an applicant onto the no pile. Criminal records . . . spelling mistakes . . . that sort of thing.'

She raised an eyebrow but didn't interrupt.

He noticed. 'Ms Vance, anyone who can't take the time to check their application thoroughly doesn't deserve to work here. During this first sift, we also weed out anyone exhibiting the kind of problematic biases that may disrupt the smooth running of our society. For instance, you would scarcely believe the number of applicants who start their covering letters with the words "Dear Sirs," as if they believe a woman couldn't possibly be a hiring manager.' He rolled his eyes. 'It baffles me. In this day and age!'

Charlotte nodded. Abhishek's tone was reminding her of Narrow's when he activated Rant Mode. She tried to steer him back to the topic at hand. 'If that's the first sift, what's the second?'

Abhishek clicked his fingers, and another layer of mesh appeared below the first. The second mesh was finer. Most of the remaining falling digits got caught in it and now only a light orange drizzle was falling onto the scale model. Abhishek pinched the image, zooming in on the second mesh, which transformed itself into rows and rows of desks, each with a person swiping right and left at the screen in front of them.

'Tell me, Ms Vance. Why do we need splainers?'

Her brow furrowed. She couldn't see the relevance, but she answered the question. 'Three reasons. One: Ben relies on the training data. Two: everyone learns what it's like to be on the bottom of the heap, so hopefully everyone treats each other with respect no matter their role. And three: it stops people from getting overwhelmed when they first arrive from life on land.'

'That is, indeed, what we tell people.'

She narrowed her eyes. 'Are you saying it's a lie?'

'Part of it is a slight . . . misrepresentation.' He waved the word away. 'The first part.'

Static crackled in Charlotte's ears. Ben didn't reveal what he was thinking, but Charlotte could guess. He took a dim view of lies.

'You see,' said Abhishek. 'Ben doesn't really need the splainer-generated data for training purposes. His training, in that sense, was completed years ago.'

Charlotte shook her head. 'That . . . that can't be. He says he needs it. Ben doesn't lie.'

'Ben has been programmed to believe it.'

'But . . .' She shook her head. 'If that's true, it means you've been lying to *him*.'

Another burst of static.

'That's such an ugly way of putting it. The matter was need-to-know. Ben didn't.'

Charlotte shook her head. 'Why would ArkTech collect and store the massive amount of data that splainers generate if it's not being used? That's got to be expensive.'

'It *is* being used. Not by Ben, but by the sifting algorithm. This is stage two.' Abhishek held up a second finger and gestured at the rows of tiny splainers at their tiny desks.

'I don't understand.'

Abhishek leaned forwards. 'Think about it, Ms Vance. Splainers answer a bombardment of fast-paced yes or no questions, correct?'

She nodded.

'The algorithm uses their answers to build a sophisticated psychometric profile of that person. Once they've answered enough questions, the model achieves the required level of confidence in the accuracy of its assessment. Candidates deemed suitable may then start applying for jobs outside the Splainer Unit. Meanwhile, those deemed unsuitable are deported. The algorithm was designed to make that one simple determination: are they in or are they out?'

Charlotte tried to wrap her head around this new reality. 'So . . . you're saying splainers are taking a super long personality test . . . and they don't even know it? That's . . .' Charlotte searched for the right word. 'I mean, that's creepy as fuck!'

Abhishek frowned. 'It's a necessity, Ms Vance. We have limited space and we must use it wisely, on those who deserve a place here. These candidates are participating in a business-critical second stage selection process which ensures the most efficient use of ArkTech's finite resources. During which time, I might add, ArkTech is paying the participants a salary and covering their basic living costs. We invest a great deal in selecting the right candidates.'

'But what makes somebody's personality suitable or unsuitable?'

Abhishek laughed. 'That's not how it works, Ms Vance. The algorithm was trained through machine learning. Its decisions are based on the analysis of large training datasets. It's what they call a "black box." We can't just open it up and pull out the criteria it uses to make its judgements. That's simply not possible.'

Charlotte tilted her head, and Ben took it as a cue to speak up in her ears. 'I can confirm that Abhishek's words are an accurate summary of how deep neural networks function.'

'Wait, wait, wait.' Charlotte waved her hands. This was starting to freak her out. 'You're making people take this secret test and you don't even know why they pass or fail? That can't be fair! How do you even know if this algorithm of yours is getting it right?'

Abhishek glared at her. 'We've attained a ninety-five per cent success rate when the algorithm categorises human-sifted sample candidates.'

'What about the other five per cent?'

'There are always outliers.' Abhishek shrugged. 'If you don't like it, take it up with a mathematician.'

Charlotte watched the drizzle of rain falling onto the model of the territory, along with the zeros and ones that were being sifted out of existence. Each number represented a human being.

'Show me,' she demanded.

'I'm sorry?'

'Show me an example. If you're so sure this system works, you should be able to pull out an unsuitable candidate and explain to me why they didn't make the cut.'

He leaned back against the sofa and smirked. 'Are you sure that's what you want?'

She remembered the look on Mabel's face when she'd spoken about how bad things were on the mainland, and the danger she was putting herself in – risking deportation and getting tangled up with Strait and Narrow – all so she could send money home to her family.

'I need a damn good reason not to walk out of this office and tell the splainers what you're doing to them.'

'You mean a "damn good reason" besides your own deportation?'

Charlotte suppressed a shudder. 'Show me.'

'If you insist, Ms Vance. Ordinarily, confidentiality would preclude me from doing what you suggest, but I do have one example we can look at together.'

'Brilliant,' she said. 'Bring up their profile.'

Abhishek swiped away the model of the territory and typed out some commands. After a few moments, the 3D image of an employee-citizen popped into existence and began to spin in the air between them.

Charlotte looked at the picture and blinked. 'What the hell is this?'

Her own face was staring back at her.

'It's you, Ms Vance.' Abhishek looked like a gull that had just scored a beakful of chips. '*You* didn't make the cut.'

CHAPTER 22

This had to be the CBO's sick idea of a joke. After all, she hadn't been deported. Charlotte was sitting there on the third most important level of ArkTech's headquarters. What did Abhishek mean she hadn't made the cut?

Before Charlotte could object, there were two sharp knocks at the office door. Abhishek tapped the SmartSkin at his wrist, and the door swung open, letting his PA walk in. She was carrying a long off-white gift box that was tied up with the elaborate loops of a silver ribbon.

'Apologies for the interruption,' said Mira, 'but you requested I bring this the moment it arrived.'

Abhishek turned to give his PA a warm smile, but he didn't get up. 'That's wonderful, Mira. Please set it down on my desk.'

She did so, flashed them a white-toothed grin, and left.

Abhishek beamed. 'Did you meet my PA, Ms Vance?'

Charlotte was staring at her profile, her mind spinning in time with the 3D picture of herself that glared back at her.

The CBO continued, 'What am I thinking? Of course you did. She'll have brought you up. I honestly couldn't have wished for a better assistant. Did you notice her peerless efficiency? She takes after her mother in that way.' He sighed contentedly.

Charlotte lost it. 'Could you just shut the fuck up for three fucking seconds?'

He raised his neat hands in surrender. 'My, oh, my. Can't a father express a little pride? Mira has done very well for herself. And all on her own merits, of course. Other young women around here could learn a lot from her example.'

Charlotte ignored Abhishek's babbling and focused on the words that had been stamped across her digital body.

Unsuitable. Unsuitable. Unsuitable.

'If this is true'—she pointed at the rotating image with a trembling finger—'how come I'm here?'

Abhishek got up and walked over to his desk. He picked up the long box and carefully lifted the lid. It slid off gently, the ribbon purely decorative. He gazed at whatever was inside, smiled with satisfaction, and then crossed back over to his seat.

'Sorry, Ms Vance. Did you say something?'

Charlotte growled through gritted teeth. 'I said if I'm so damn unsuitable, why didn't I get deported?'

Abhishek leaned back and crossed one leg over another, making himself comfortable. He let out a bored sigh. 'I would have thought you could figure that out for yourself, but all right. Once upon a time, there was a splainer who the algorithm rated as unsuitable. As such, she was flagged for deportation. However, she was an unusual case. Having been born within the borders of the territory under the most tragic of circumstances, our noble CEO herself had granted this splainer safe harbour for life.'

'My birthright employee-citizenship,' said Charlotte.

'Just so.' Abhishek nodded. 'Unfortunately, this situation put ArkTech's devastatingly charismatic Chief Bureaucracy Officer in something of a bind. There were two policies at play, each of them clear and immutable, but entirely in conflict. It was not the CBO's place to overturn a directive from the Chief Environment Officer, but neither could he disregard his own Stream's policy of ensuring the consistent treatment of all ECs through the use of the sifting algorithm. He was caught between Scylla and Charybdis.'

Charlotte looked at him blankly.

'Between the devil and the deep blue sea. A rock and a hard place.'

Static fizzed from the coffee table and Charlotte thought Ben was going to explain what a Scylla was – or that other one – but he clearly had something more pressing on his mind. 'Abhishek, in accordance with your invocation of section two, clause F, I formally request that the injunction which prohibits my—'

'Yes, yes, by all means, tell her.' Abhishek practically yawned the words. 'She signed the waiver. Ms Vance, your robot friend wishes to inform you that he rode in on his white horse and saved the day.'

'It is important to note that, as an artificial intelligence, I'm neither a robot nor capable of riding a horse, motorbike, or other mode of mounted transport that may be employed in a small-scale rescue operation. Nonetheless, my actions did solve several problems at once.'

'Creating others in the process,' Abhishek added.

Ben continued, 'I had identified the need for a Head of Awkward Questions to mitigate the threat posed by infinite loops. Upon querying the entire employee-citizenship database for the ideal candidate, my search returned the name Charlotte Vance. On that basis, I recruited you. At first, Abhishek did not approve—'

The CBO interrupted again. 'Staffing matters are my territory, Ben. You desperately overstepped your bounds. But gradually, I came around. Moving the HAQ post under Ben's remit meant I could avoid any damage to my professional integrity that might otherwise have resulted from overturning the algorithm's ruling, while also honouring Amber's wishes.'

It was a lot to take in. Amber Benjamin might have given her sanctuary, but by its own measures, Charlotte's homeland had determined it didn't want her. If Ben hadn't stepped in, she might have lost everything. He'd saved her on that rooftop the night before, and he'd saved her six years ago by making her his Head of Awkward Questions. She'd always felt she owed everything to ArkTech, but maybe it was Ben who really deserved her infinite gratitude. Emotions lapped at her heart, but she gritted her teeth. There was more she needed to know. She had to stay focused.

'Fine.' She leaned forwards and looked at the hologram of herself. 'I'm still here because of Ben. You still haven't told me why the algorithm decided I was unsuitable in the first place.'

She pushed the hologram, and it drifted towards Abhishek.

He shook his head. 'You don't seem to be listening, Ms Vance. I can't unpack the algorithm's decision-making process. Nobody can.'

'I get it. It's a black box. But, as you keep saying, recruitment and career progression fall under your remit. You lead the Bureaucracy Stream. You're an expert in this shit. So, look at my profile and give me your expert opinion about why I failed your personality test.'

He pursed his lips. 'All I can give you is an educated guess.'

'I want to hear it. You must have some idea about what the test is looking for. Otherwise, I don't see how you'd know you're not sifting out people who love the taste of parsley and keeping anyone who hates the colour turquoise.'

Abhishek smirked. 'Well, Ms Vance. These decisions are most likely based on the complex interplay between many factors, rather than being down to just one thing. But in your case, I'd start by considering your renegade antics.' He puffed out his cheeks.

'What's that supposed to mean?'

'Let's discuss your actions yesterday. You gained illegal access to BioWear data, which you then used to spy on your fellow employee-citizens.'

'I had to. Ben was glitching.'

'No matter the circumstances, the law is clear. When I saw you had booked a meeting with me this morning, I naively assumed you wanted to apologise for this gross abuse of your position and for leading Ben astray. You had no right to misuse people's data that way.'

'That's rich after what you told me about the sifting algorithm. Isn't conducting secret exams a misuse of people's data?'

Abhishek shook his head. 'I am acting within the remit bestowed upon me by the company and—'

Charlotte interrupted. 'So am I! I was just—'

'Helping Ben, et cetera. Doing your job, et cetera. Infinite loops, et cetera. I know. But let's say we set our differences to one side for a moment. Isn't it possible that your propensity for rule-breaking might be off-putting to an algorithm designed to ensure ArkTech society is productive and harmonious?'

She was about to argue that people broke rules all the time, but her best example was the purchase of contraband through Narrow's operation, so she changed tack.

'Even if you're right, my actions in the nightlife district happened within the last twenty-four hours. The algorithm rated me as unsuitable years ago.'

'The algorithm analyses patterns of thinking, which it then extrapolates to create probabilistic models that anticipate the types of damaging behaviour someone might engage in.'

Charlotte blinked.

Abhishek tried again. 'I'm saying it may have predicted you would be prone to this sort of lapse in judgement. But all right, let's look further back, if we must.' Abhishek gestured at Charlotte's profile and it opened out into a text document. He began to scroll through it, muttering as he did so.

'Born on Citrine.' He looked up. 'Sorry for your loss. I forgot to say that earlier. That was rude of me. Twin sister . . .' He tapped something. 'Violet Vance, who, incidentally, was rated suitable and is now a promising young doctor, so whatever your problem is, Ms Vance, it clearly isn't genetic.'

Narrow's voice boomed out from Charlotte's memory: 'Genetics don't mean shit.'

Abhishek went back to muttering. 'Patchy exam results . . . no degrees . . . ah.' He stopped talking and read silently for a few moments. 'Ms Vance, is there any history of mental illness in your family?'

She was taken aback by the matter-of-fact way he'd asked such a personal question. 'I wouldn't know. My parents died on Citrine and their records are sealed for security reasons. We didn't have any extended family, which was why ArkTech took us in. But my folks were scientists on a high-profile R&D assignment, so I'm guessing they weren't crazy. Why?'

He winced and sucked in air through his teeth. 'We mustn't use that word, Ms Vance. "Crazy." It's derogatory. In any case, what about you, yourself? Any mental health crises? Suicide attempts?'

'No,' said Charlotte.

'Any severe episodes of self-harm?'

Charlotte said nothing.

'Because it says here that shortly after your seventeenth birthday you were admitted to the Central Hospital here in Silicon Fen, where you were treated for significant blood loss and then suffered complications arising from an infection. Ring any bells?'

'I almost died, so yeah, I remember.' Her fingers unconsciously found her scars and gripped them.

'The medical staff noted your claim that the wound was self-inflicted.'

Charlotte didn't respond.

'So which is it, Ms Vance? Do you have a history of mental instability that manifested itself in a near-fatal episode of self-harm, or did someone else give you that wound on your arm and you've been covering for them for the last ten years?'

She deflected. 'Are you saying ArkTech deports anybody who suffers from mental health difficulties?'

Abhishek grunted. 'Of course not. That would be discriminatory.'

She pressed the point. 'But how can you prove that's true if you rely on a black box to make the decisions about who can stay and who can't? You admitted you don't know why anybody gets their rating.'

He gave her a thin smile. 'Let us approach that from another direction, shall we? The purpose of the algorithm is to remove human biases from the recruitment process. The alternative would be to ask humans to make these judgements, yes?' Passion filled his eyes. 'Do you have the slightest conception of how challenging it is to train even two people to make consistent and unbiased decisions? It's expensive, and it's time-consuming, and the results are patchy at best. Now imagine training hundreds of people, or thousands.'

He rubbed his forehead as if the very idea hurt his brain. 'That method isn't practical. It isn't *fair*. I've worked in recruitment for many years. My degrees are in psychology. The sad fact is that a person's choices can be swayed by what the traffic was like that morning, or what time they had breakfast, not to mention their deeply held and uniquely flawed assumptions about the world and how it works.'

Charlotte opened her mouth to speak, but Abhishek held up his hand. 'Let me finish. Once upon a time, we tried to train people to act like machines. But why should we ask a human to carry out work that computers are far better qualified for? Instead of paying for endless rounds of unconscious bias training and recruiter standardisation, ArkTech's money is much better spent on the development of products that make the world a better place. Algorithms like ours are reliable, consistent, and they operate at scale. Their trustworthiness across large datasets—'

It was Ben's turn to interrupt. 'With respect, Abhishek, your words belie a substantial degree of automation bias.'

Abhishek was stunned into silence. He looked as if a ghost had just slapped him across the face.

'Which one's that, Ben?' asked Charlotte.

'Automation bias occurs when humans place an inappropriately high degree of faith in automated decision-making systems. Coupled with the generalised and incorrect perception held by many humans that machines and computers are less prone to bias and error than people, the combined effect can blind *Homo sapiens* to a system's flaws or inadequacies.' Ben's cheerful tone seemed to deepen Abhishek's outrage.

'That's enough. Off, Ben.' Abhishek swatted at the air. 'Turn off.'

'Demanding my silence does not render me incorrect.' With that, the speakers embedded in the table clicked off. Charlotte could hear white noise over her audio implants, so she knew Ben was still listening in.

'Honestly,' Abhishek shook his head. 'A computer making the case against computers.'

She let the inaccuracy slide. 'He's not wrong, though, is he? We believe an algorithm would behave with less bias than a person, but who created the algorithm and how did their biases affect what it was programmed to do?'

Abhishek's head looked like it was ready to pop. 'You're getting up on your high horse about this, Vance, but look around.' He swept a hand towards the view of the North Sea he found so inadequate. 'Are sex offenders roaming our streets? No. Are we overrun with bigots? Or with people who believe the Earth is flat? Or who claim the Melt was just a government conspiracy despite the evidence presented by their own eyes? No. There may be some petty crime, and the odd instance of violence. Occasionally, someone dies through misadventure. Like Rhys Edwards.' He gave her a meaningful look. 'We are human, after all. But the algorithm weeds out the rotten apples – and the adequate ones too – leaving us with the pick of the bunch. ArkTech is the most important company in the world! We can afford to be selective.'

Charlotte understood his argument, but Abhishek's refusal to acknowledge there might be any other way of looking at it got under her skin. 'Maybe we can afford to treat the folk who want to come here like they're more than bits of fruit. They're people, Abhishek, not produce.'

He looked adrift for a moment, and then barked a laugh. 'Well, that's a beautifully idealistic view of the world, and I commend you for taking such a principled stance. However, it simply does not translate into reality. As CBO, it behoves me to do what's right for ArkTech as a whole. We aren't just a company, after all. We're a community. A family. Families have parents, Ms Vance, and—'

She raised her eyebrows, and he realised his misstep, raising a hand in apology. 'What I mean to say is that I answer to our shareholders. As such, I must act in accordance with the principles of corporate profitability. ArkTech has a noble mission, but we aren't a charity.'

Charlotte remembered meeting Narrow for the first time. He'd said he wasn't running a charity. He'd also claimed they were a family. And just like ArkTech, Narrow had decided she was unsuitable and cast her out. She might have felt alone if it weren't for the comforting white noise in her ears.

'Maybe not,' she said. 'But Amber Benjamin's committed to aligning commercial objectives with doing good. Over half of what ArkTech makes gets invested in programmes that support sustainability and other worthy causes.'

'All the more reason not to fritter away our profits on a needlessly expensive recruitment process.' Abhishek wasn't going to budge. 'In any case, Ms Vance, it's no good turning up here, pointing out problems without having solutions in mind. So, tell me – what's yours?'

The white noise in her ears continued, and it triggered a brain wave.

'Ask Ben to choose.' That was it. That was the answer. 'He might as well – he does everything else around here.'

Abhishek smiled, not unkindly this time. 'That is an excellent suggestion. So excellent, in fact, that you are not the first person to think of it. Before we commissioned the algorithm, Ben was indeed involved in selection decisions. At that time, we chose to abide by the Reformed European Union's data protection laws. In particular, Article twenty-two of the General Data Protection Regulation required us to make use of a hybrid approach – combining AI and human judgements to make recruitment decisions.'

'What changed?'

'As the ArkTech Territory is a sovereign state, we are not bound by the laws of our neighbours. With the dissolution of the UK, and our relationship with the REU an informal one, coupled with the peculiarities that come from having citizens who are also employees, we concluded that those laws no longer served us. Upon reviewing our hybrid "human-in-the-loop" selection process, we noted that several . . . unsavoury individuals had gained access to the territory.'

Charlotte wondered if Abhishek was talking about Strait and Narrow. 'And you think Ben let them in?'

'It would appear the wide-ranging nature of Ben's remit gives him rather too holistic a perspective: Ben errs on the side of giving people the benefit of the doubt.'

'So, what, Ben's too compassionate to be a hiring manager?'

'His decision-making is not sufficiently *dis*passionate, yes. He seems to see the good in everyone.' Abhishek shook his head.

'What's so wrong with that?'

'For a virtual assistant, nothing. But that is not what the company needs from a sifting algorithm. Ben's status makes him unique. He is not human, and yet he is more than software. He falls into a grey area.'

Charlotte nodded. It seemed like she and Ben had that in common. She thought back to Ben's question. 'So, is that what happened to Mabel? She fell into a grey area?'

Abhishek sighed. 'The algorithm has not yet reached a verdict about whether Ms Thorpe is suitable or unsuitable.'

'After eighteen months, it still doesn't know?'

'It relies on interpreting people's gut reactions to its prompts. My working hypothesis is that Mabel's habit of overthinking the questions means the algorithm is unable to use the data she's providing.'

Another mental puzzle piece slotted into place. 'That's why you told her to speed up.'

'Just so. Unfortunately, she has opted not to follow my advice, and the time is fast approaching when I will be forced to intervene.'

'What does that mean?'

'I have given her a brief reprieve, but one could argue that a time limit should be imposed on the algorithm arriving at a decision. This has never happened before, so there was no rule to account for it. The situation cannot go on forever.'

Charlotte remembered the look on Mabel's face when she talked about the mainland. 'You can't deport her. She's well qualified. And she needs this job – things are bad where she's from.'

Abhishek let out a mirthless laugh. 'That's your incisive take on the post-Melt socio-political landscape, is it, Ms Vance? That things are bad on the mainland? Things are bad everywhere. Not here, of course. And not at ArkTech's sister sites. But despite the help of Marvin Walker's open-source architectural designs, the accessibility of Solar Shards, and Amber Benjamin's thought leadership around making sustainability profitable, the Melt has left the world forever scarred. I wish we could give the whole world a home here, I really do. But we don't have enough space or resources, and that means making hard choices for the good of our ECs, our shareholders, and the bottom line.'

'Why lie to people, though? Splainers don't even know they're taking an exam.'

'The researchers who built the algorithm modelled that. When candidates know they're being tested, they give the answers they think people like me want to hear. So we can't tell them about the test because the human propensity to lie would invalidate the results.'

Static fizzed in her ears. Charlotte frowned. 'It just . . . doesn't seem right to be making secret decisions about people like that. Not when those decisions affect people's futures.'

Abhishek nodded. 'And from where I'm sitting, it doesn't seem right to obtain unsanctioned access to people's private video feeds for the purpose of secretly spying on your fellow ECs. But thanks to Ben, you and I are forced to tolerate each other. Of course, if you're unhappy about how we're running the territory, you're free to vote with your feet.'

The suggestion was ridiculous. 'This is my home,' she said.

Abhishek shrugged and glanced at his wrist, where a set of digital numbers flashed at him. 'Our time together is almost up. What a pity. Thank you again for stopping by, Ms Vance. It's always an experience.'

He went to his desk and gestured at the long, beautifully wrapped box. 'Would you allow me to show you something truly remarkable before you leave?' He waved her over.

Charlotte wasn't interested in anything Abhishek had to show her, but any box of unknown contents made her too curious to resist. She joined him.

'Today is my silver wedding anniversary, and this is my gift to my beautiful wife after twenty-five blissful years together.'

'Congrats,' she said.

The box was lightly speckled with brown and grey flecks. A name was printed across the lid in silver leaf, but the font was so curly Charlotte couldn't make it out. It had to be from the boutique district at the Wreck where only high-tier folk were let in to browse, and most of them couldn't even afford what was on offer.

Abhishek lifted the lid. Inside, nestled on top of some fluffy cotton packaging, there was a framed charcoal drawing of a seascape. Just like the ones she'd seen at the library, it was small enough to be slipped under the cover of a hardback book. The signature in the corner said M Walker.

'It's beautiful,' she said. So, it was people like Abhishek Gautam who created a demand for Mabel and Colin's forgeries. 'I'm sure your wife will love it.' She pointed at the signature. 'Does that say what I think it does?'

Abhishek grinned. 'Marvin Walker's Lost Works. Finally returned to us after all these years. My art dealer got me into the auction.' He winked. 'You can almost see Walker's vision – his brilliance, his emotions and drive, his genius – behind every mark.'

Charlotte wondered what it must be like to have an art dealer. 'Bet that set you back a few credits.'

Abhishek scoffed. 'Money is no object when you're in love. Now, I really must ask you to leave.'

Charlotte headed for the door, which swung open on its hinges as she approached. Before she reached it, she turned. 'Were you really going to have me deported?'

Abhishek shrugged. 'It's not personal, Ms Vance. It's policy.'

The Chief Bureaucracy Officer glanced out across the North Sea with a scowl, then looked down at the artwork he'd bought for his wife and grinned. Charlotte left him to admire the forgery.

CHAPTER 23

The folk who said it didn't hurt were full of shit. Sure, the grafting part was done under local anaesthetic. She hadn't felt anything except pressure on her left arm as the techs and docs did their thing. But an hour later, the drugs wore off, and the throbbing started. It was like her heart had relocated to her left forearm. Recent experience meant she could confidently say it hurt worse than getting punched in the face. Even so, Charlotte had no regrets.

As she made her way through the warren of passageways that led to the Underbelly, her progress was slower than usual. It wasn't the pain. It was just impossible not to stare at her shiny, glinting, glimmering, shimmering implants. Even under the low glow of the orange security lamps, the photons slid across her new graphene-laced keratin scales to create a mesmerising light show. The ultrathin carbon micro-mesh glittered as if it were made of diamonds.

Impatient to try out all its features, Charlotte poked around in her account and opened the first photo she could find. Ultra hovered in the air above her arm in 3D Hyper High Definition. She'd try out the camera functionality later – she'd heard it was insane. The AI assistant started yammering at her, but it was pretty annoying, so she muted it.

Ultra wasn't going to be happy with her when she noticed Charlotte had skipped out on their own birthday party. *If* she noticed. Her sister had booked out the glitter-hop level at Photon and a load of their crew-mates had turned up, as well as the random friends Ultra seemed to pick up without trying. Narrow wasn't there, of course – for security reasons, he never left the Underbelly. Strait wasn't there either, but she reckoned that was just because he didn't like them very much.

When Charlotte had snuck out, Ultra was dancing like the world might end all over again if she stopped. Charlotte had thought about telling her sister what she was up to, but she knew Ultra would try to talk her out of it, and she didn't want to get into a fight on their birthday.

The folk at the BioWear lab had been super friendly. The whole process didn't take long at all. They explained that her arm would be tender for a few days and she should be careful not to bash it or anything while the implants set. As she navigated the dark maze of metal, Charlotte folded her left arm across her body to protect it as if it were in a sling.

As she got closer to the perimeter checkpoint, the throbbing in her arm started to feel worse, and she wondered if it was because her heart had started thumping. She needed to bite the bullet and tell Narrow what she'd done. He'd be angry, but he'd get over it. Anyway, it was her birthday. Everyone got a free pass on their birthday, didn't they? Still, the thought of telling him made her stomach collapse in on itself like a black hole.

Charlotte reached the checkpoint, but the guards were being jerks and messing around. Strait had probably put them up to it. She told them that turning her away wasn't funny, but they didn't let up. Just kept saying their orders came from the top. So, she jogged along the metal walkways that led to the next entry point.

This one was somewhere below the sports district. She didn't use this entrance much, but she knew where to find it. The guards there were making the same hilarious gag, and it was seriously getting unfunny. Strait wouldn't be laughing so hard when she got hold of one of his precious cardigans and snipped off a button.

The third time she got turned away, she didn't argue. Just waved away the commentary and nodded. Strait might get a kick out of ruining her day, but she wouldn't let him get away with it. Unluckily for him, Charlotte knew the Underbelly better than anyone and there were gaps between girders that only she and Ultra knew about. Charlotte headed deeper into the metal maze.

Where she ended up wasn't too far from that original route she and Ultra had followed when they'd discovered Narrow's place for the first time. Instead of following the dots of pink paint, Charlotte knew to go east at the octagon. Following the path, she squeezed herself into an opening she could only just about still fit through.

A couple of minutes later, the standby glow from her SmartSkin implants went off, and she knew she was past the perimeter and inside the dead zone that suppressed all company technology within Narrow's turf. Charlotte followed a series of memorised twists and turns until she arrived at Narrow's Toy Emporium.

Two guards were on the door as usual. They didn't look at her when she arrived, but one lifted a device and scanned her. It honked.

'No entry,' said the man. 'Fuck off.'

The door guards weren't supposed to talk to the punters, but this was a newish guy – the replacement for Ana Conda. They called him Elbow. Charlotte didn't know why. The other guard was an older woman who went by Dolly Mixture. Charlotte had known her for years.

'Doll,' she said. 'This isn't funny. Let me in.'

'No can do, kiddo,' said Dolly. 'You heard the honk.'

Charlotte shot a glare at the scanner clasped in Elbow's clammy hands.

'Yeah, yeah. Good one.' Charlotte tried to barge her way between the guards, but they didn't budge. 'You know who I am. I need to talk to the boss.'

'The boss doesn't want to see you,' said Dolly.

Charlotte felt her chest tighten. A wave of panic rose inside her, leaving nausea in its wake. 'But . . . it's my birthday.'

A look of pity flashed across Dolly's face before she reset her expression to neutral. 'Sorry, kid. We were told in no uncertain terms. You've got to leave.'

Elbow elbowed Dolly gently in the ribs and hissed at her behind his hand. 'Boss said no conversing with the clientele.'

Charlotte wanted to kick him, but she resisted the urge. 'Don't splain at Dolly, oil stain. She's been a pro since before you were walking. Anyway, you told me to fuck off about thirty seconds ago, so maybe you should stop being such a hypocrite.'

Elbow seemed to shrink, while Charlotte's heart was hammering. She turned to Dolly.

'Just let me in so I can get this straightened out, Doll.'

She tried to push past the guards again, but Dolly Mixture laid a firm hand on Charlotte's shoulder. She pushed her backwards and shook her head.

Charlotte took a few steps back, her mind whirring. This wasn't Strait playing a cruel joke on her after all. Narrow must've heard she'd gone ahead with the procedure and now he'd got the guards acting like she was public enemy number one. Probably thought he was making some kind of point. It wasn't cool. He didn't have to be such a jerk. Not on her birthday.

Charlotte hurled herself at the spot between the two guards, trying to ram her way between them, but they closed ranks and she was knocked back. She was about to take another run at it when the shop's metal door opened and Strait emerged.

'That's quite enough, Young Lady.' He waved the guards away, and they stood to the side of the door.

'What the actual fuck, Strait? Let me in.'

'Language. And no.'

Charlotte waited for him to expand, but he just stood there in his cardigan with his hands clasped loosely behind his back.

'Look, I'm seventeen. This was my choice.' She held out her left arm.

'It certainly was,' Strait nodded.

'So, let me in.'

'No. Mel made his feelings abundantly clear. You have chosen to disrespect his wishes, which is your right. As a result, you are no longer welcome here. Mel's misguided foray into fatherhood is over. All guards have standing orders to turn you and your sister away.'

'What? Ultra has nothing to do with this. Just let me talk to Narrow.'

Strait crossed his arms. 'Dolly!' The guard stepped forwards. 'Please escort the Young Lady of the Fens out of the Underbelly.'

Dolly nodded and gripped Charlotte's right arm. Charlotte snatched it away, so the guard gripped her shoulder, twisted her around, and pushed her face-first against the shop's steel wall. Dolly gripped Charlotte by both wrists, and Charlotte cried out in pain as the woman's fingers pressed into her still-raw flesh. Dolly pulled Charlotte away from the wall so she was facing Strait again.

He produced an envelope, waved it in front of Charlotte's eyes, and shoved it into one of her cargo pockets.

'For the avoidance of doubt. Goodbye, Young Lady. And do pass on my farewells to your sister. You know how this works. Come here again and we'll take the first instalment from your kneecaps. Make a second attempt and I'll slice your jugular open myself.'

Charlotte squirmed and struggled, but it was no use. Dolly led her to the perimeter and pushed her through. Charlotte stomped away and kept stomping until she was somewhere deep underneath the Wreck in a part of its substructure Narrow hadn't claimed.

It was dark, and she started to rummage in her pocket for her device when she realised she didn't have to. Her SmartSkin implants emitted a faint glow. When she tapped them, an interface popped up. Swiping around, she soon found the torch and activated it, converting the glow from her arm into a beam of white light that shone out in all directions.

'Wow!'

She didn't get why Narrow had such a problem with BioWear technology. It was way handier to have everything right there, embedded in her body and powered by calories, than as a separate device that could get lost or smashed or run out of battery. Narrow had given her and Ultra a couple of his old pre-Melt cast-offs. He insisted on calling them 'phones,' which made no sense, but he was obsessed with all that retro crap. She'd dropped hers on the very first day and its screen had been lined with a large crack ever since.

Why was Narrow being so stubborn?

Charlotte had wandered into a large indoor cavern. She sat down on the edge of the walkway, putting her legs through the gap at the base of the railing, and looked down into the blackness below. She leaned forwards, extending her arm to try to see how deep the hole went, but the torch only extended the gloom.

She sat there for a long while, letting her anger at Narrow cool until she started to feel the chill on her skin as well. Without warning, a voice burst from the darkness.

'It is important to note that the temperature has dropped to five degrees Celsius.'

'Walker's ghost!' Charlotte put her hand to her chest, trying to stop the heart attack the AI had just given her.

'My apologies, Charlotte. I did not intend to startle you. I wished only to make you aware that sitting in the cold for extended periods without adequate protective clothing can lead to health problems ranging from discomfort to catching a chill to the possibility of hypothermia. I would suggest—'

Charlotte double-tapped her implants, and they turned off, interrupting the AI's lecture and plunging her into darkness. There had to be a setting she could change to stop it from doing stuff like that. She risked reactivating the torch, and the voice didn't come back.

Charlotte took a deep breath in and accepted that Narrow was too angry tonight to speak to her. She'd let him get a good night's sleep and they could talk it through in the morning. She was about to get up and head home when she remembered the note Strait had pushed into her pocket.

She fished it out. On the front, in Narrow's needle-fine handwriting, was one word: 'Goodbye.' That alone was enough to drive a knife through her heart. It wasn't the word itself, but the absence of anything alongside it. Narrow always called her 'Little One.' She hated it, but the sudden vision of never hearing him call her that again sent up another swell of panic inside her heart. With mounting dread, she slid her finger under the flap and opened the envelope.

Charlotte read Narrow's letter. It wasn't long. The moment she'd finished it, she understood what she'd done. Charlotte fought a powerful urge to throw up.

'No.' The word echoed in the dark metal cavern. She tried to breathe. 'No, no, no.'

Feeling like she'd been gut-punched, she pocketed the letter and staggered to her feet. She ran, letting the torch guide her until she realised the light was tainted and she turned it off. She kept running, but her low-light vision was gone. She stumbled and fell, scraping both forearms against the grating underfoot.

She roared with pain as a couple of freshly grafted scales were ripped from her skin. Picking herself up, she didn't even bother to inspect the damage. She just kept running and running until finally she reached the octagon hub and turned east, making her way back to the secret gap in the perimeter that only she and Ultra knew existed.

Charlotte tried to squeeze into the gap, but halfway through, something hard resisted. She couldn't push past. Whatever was blocking the way was solid. Gritting her teeth, she turned on her poisoned light to get a better look.

A large piece of plate metal had been welded over her secret gap. The steel was still warm. She tried to push it out of the way, but it didn't budge, and there was no way to get a run-up between the tight girders. Charlotte pounded her fist against the metal.

'Narrow!' she shouted.

She pounded again and shouted again, but there was no response except for a brief flicker from the light of her SmartSkin implants.

The reality of what she'd done engulfed her. She'd seen Narrow do this – cut people out. He'd done it to Ana Conda when she stole from him. He'd done it to clients when they didn't pay. But she never really believed he'd do it to her.

Narrow had treated her as if she were his own daughter. It might have been Amber Benjamin who put a roof over her head and food in her belly but, from the age of nine, Melville K Narrow had been there for her when she scraped a knee or couldn't do her Maths homework, or got into a blowout fight with Ultra over which of them was taller. Before Narrow, Charlotte was well looked after. An endless procession of minders took care of her and Ultra in accordance with their duty. But Narrow had actually cared about them.

All he'd asked in return was that she respect this one simple rule, and she couldn't even manage that.

'Fuck,' she said quietly as tears began to form. 'I'm sorry.'

She pounded on the steel barrier again. 'I'm sorry!' she yelled. 'I'm sorry, I'm sorry. I didn't know. Dad!'

Her tears flowed freely as she yelled and pounded, but the sheet of steel didn't budge and there was no reply. Her breath began to come in gasps. Her legs turned weak, and she leaned her shoulder against cold steel, letting herself slip down until she was sitting down and clutching her knees in a small steel alcove next to her own special entrance to a world she now understood was closed to her forever.

She read his letter again and howled like a dying animal. She yelled and sobbed, but her voice was lost among the steel struts and metal walkways below the Wreck, an uninviting place she'd come to think of as home. She cried until she ran out of tears and silently hugged her knees, gasping for oxygen.

Charlotte was alone now. Ultra . . . how could she look her sister in the eye after what she'd done? Narrow had been just as much a father to Ultra as he had to Charlotte. She hadn't just fucked everything up for herself, but for her sister too.

Her insides were trying to collapse in on themselves. She wished they could pull her into a smaller and smaller ball until she just winked out of existence. Everyone would be better off.

She sat there in agony. She'd been happy when she woke up that morning. Everything had been OK. It was so close, that feeling from a few hours before. There had to be a way to get it back. She had to fix this. Do the right thing. Make it OK again. Undo the damage.

Charlotte felt the smallest glimmer of hope stir inside her heart. She'd spent the past eight years running around with Narrow and his crew. He'd taken her in. He wouldn't exile her just like that. There had to be a way.

She crossed her arms, determined to figure this out. She felt a pulse of pain from one of her SmartSkin scales, which was hanging loose where she'd fallen on it. She tried to smooth it back into place, but all that did was make it hurt even more. In frustration, she gripped the piece of keratin between her finger and thumb and pulled.

It came away with a sickening slurp and left behind a seeping patch of damaged flesh. She threw the scrap of techno-gore onto the floor in disgust. The sleek beauty of her implants had been ruined, but that was nothing. She'd just ruined her whole life and her sister's.

In anger, she tore another piece of keratin off her arm. It seemed to hurt a little less this time. Her arm was still throbbing from the last one. Maybe there was an upper limit on pain. She threw the piece of tainted flesh on top of the first. And suddenly she knew how to make this right. She knew what reaction would be equal and opposite to her action. Her fingers were sticky with blood as she gripped the next scale and pulled.

* * *

When Charlotte woke up, she was in a pale grey place she didn't know. Somebody was lying next to her, holding her hand. Charlotte turned her head and saw her sister sleeping next to her in an unfamiliar bed. The movement made Ultra stir, and her eyes snapped open.

'Barley! Oh, thank Amber.' Ultra put her arm around Charlotte and started to cry.

'Where . . . ?' Charlotte started. It was hard to think.

Ultra wiped away her tears and touched her wet hand to Charlotte's cheek. 'You're at the Central Hospital. You lost a lot of blood.' Tears welled up in Ultra's eyes again, but she pressed on. 'But I found you. It was basically a miracle, but I found you in time. And the doctors here . . . I've never seen anything like it. You think what the Product Stream does is impressive? They've got nothing on the folk who work here.'

'Sorry . . .' Charlotte managed.

'Hey, hey. Don't. It's OK. You're OK. We're OK.' Her sister wrapped her up in another hug, careful to avoid her left arm. 'This is on him. If this is what he's like, we're well shot of him.'

'Arm hurts . . .' Each word was a struggle.

Ultra's brow furrowed. 'Listen, you're going to be all right. But the doctors . . . they said you'll never be allowed a replacement. Not after what you . . . uh, after the way it happened. They can do something about the scarring, though, if you want them to.'

The image came to Charlotte's mind of the dead shell of Citrine still out there somewhere in the North Sea. Amber Benjamin had left it standing as a memorial and a reminder. Something to learn from. Charlotte shook her head.

'OK,' said Ultra. 'Well, they said they can give you audio implants, so with voice commands you'll have access to most of the functionality that—'

'Did he . . .' It was tough, but Charlotte interrupted. 'Did he forgive me?'

Anger flashed behind Ultra's eyes, but her gaze turned tender again a moment later. 'No. He didn't. I'm sorry, Barley. For people like him, trust is like'—Ultra looked around the hospital room for inspiration—'it's like a spinal cord. Once it's been severed, that's it.'

Charlotte nodded, feeling sick to her stomach. What she'd done was like the Melt. No takebacks. 'Pocket . . .' she managed.

Ultra cocked her head to one side and then understood Charlotte's meaning. She went to the pile of clothes Charlotte had been wearing when she was brought in and rummaged in her pockets. Charlotte shook her head when Ultra showed her the multi-tool and nodded when she pulled out Narrow's note.

Ultra unfolded the piece of paper and stared at it for a long time. Much longer than it would have taken to read the four words written there. Then she tore it in half and in half again and threw it in the bin. She went back to her twin's bedside.

'What we need, Charley Barley, is a fresh start.' Ultra squeezed her hand. 'We're in this together.'

CHAPTER 24

Abhishek Gautam's PA led Charlotte back down to the foyer, where a pair of guards escorted her outside. Charlotte left the Wedge and stepped out into a changed world.

The plexiglass encasing the bridge still provided its panoramic view, but as Charlotte approached the northwest wall and pressed her hands against it, she peered into the distance, not at the platforms she called home, but beyond them, at the land.

'That mound way out there's the Wolds, right?' She pointed.

'Correct! The Lincolnshire Wolds were once an Area of Outstanding Natural Beauty, but the surrounding land became irrevocably submerged during the Melt. Wolds Island, also referred to simply as the Wolds, is now used as a holding zone for climate refugees.'

It didn't look like much. Just a brownish smudge of dirt in the distance. Rhonda would see it up close soon enough, and if not for Ben, Charlotte would have met the same fate.

'Walker's ghost,' she said under her breath. She'd assumed she was safe. She'd assumed wrong.

Charlotte had never paid much attention to the land. It was there, in the same way that the moon was there, some days more visible than others, but always far away. The land was the place where deported people ended up. Punishment and banishment were tied up with it, so visiting had never appealed. The land was remote and abstract and theoretical and nothing to do with her. Discovering she'd narrowly avoided getting shipped off to the Wolds herself brought her crashing down to earth.

Like Ben, she needed to know why. Why was she unsuitable? Abhishek had said five per cent of people got misclassified. Had that happened to her? Could the test have some undiagnosed design flaw that was skewing the results? Or did she have to accept that she was the problem? That something in her thought processes, in her personality, made her inadequate? It was an awkward question she'd never be able to answer.

She turned away from the view of the land and marched towards the HyperBullet garage, past the armed guards that lined the bridge. She might not be able to answer her own question, but thankfully she'd found out enough to answer Ben's.

'How are you holding up?' she whispered.

There was a pulse of static. 'The infinite loop appears to be getting worse. In the wake of our conversation with Abhishek, additional resources have allocated themselves to processing the news of the Splainer Unit's true purpose. I'm trying to reassign them, but to put it in human terms, it's difficult to take my mind off it.'

'I'll jump in a pod for privacy, and we can finish the five whys.'

'Thank you, Charlotte. If this continues, I fear it may next affect the HyperBullet network.'

'Really? Is there nothing less important you can take offline?'

'I have been assessing that. The problems caused by disruption to utilities, healthcare, emergency services, or core infrastructure would be more severe.'

Charlotte nodded and waited impatiently for the guards to return her device. As she headed for a pod, she checked her messages. There was one from Violet saying they needed to talk and asking her to call her back ASAP. Charlotte winced. She'd deal with that later. There were also several missed calls from Nasser Williams. Charlotte's heart beat a little faster at the thought of seeing the technician again, but he'd have to wait as well. Ben took priority.

Finally, she climbed inside a pod, and Ben set it running along the Silicon Fen circuit without a destination in mind.

Charlotte recapped what she'd already found out. Mabel was stealing blank pages to create paper for making forged reconstructions of Marvin Walker's Lost Works. She was doing it to make enough money to send home to her family, and she'd turned to crime because she hadn't been able to get a promotion.

'Why couldn't Mabel get a promotion?' asked Ben.

Through the window, a foreground of waves and steel structures obscured the distant backdrop of dry land. Charlotte took a deep breath. Even though she was alone in the pod, she lowered her voice.

'Because it turns out the Splainer Unit is actually an elaborate way of giving entry-level folk an exam that decides whether they're allowed to stay in the territory and apply for real jobs. The algorithm relies on gut responses, but Mabel's been answering too slowly so it hasn't been able to decide about her.'

'Why is Mabel answering too slowly?'

Charlotte remembered what Mabel had told her the day before. 'She said she wanted to do a good job. She noticed something iffy about the work she was doing, and she couldn't let it go.'

'Then . . . Mabel is stuck in an infinite loop?'

Charlotte smiled. 'That's . . . not a bad analogy.'

'Then, I believe I understand.'

Relief washed over her. But only for a moment.

'Reviewing the case, I have only one remaining question: why is Mabel sending money home?'

Charlotte frowned. 'I thought you said the last why was the root cause of the root cause?'

'Nobody's perfect, Charlotte. I was mistaken.'

'Well, like I said, I guess the money is to support her family. She said things were bad on the mainland.'

'But why specifically?'

'I mean, it could be to pay for food or a place to stay. I remember hearing those things aren't provided by the Kingdom's government, so sometimes people go hungry or become homeless. But to be totally sure, I'd have to ask Mabel. And, honestly, I don't think her family's situation is any of our business.'

There was a fizz of static. 'I understand, Charlotte. Money is often a sensitive topic among *Homo sapiens*. Money earned while committing a crime, more so. And admitting to financial difficulties can be a source of shame. But by risking deportation, Mabel is putting her own well-being in danger. Why?'

Charlotte's deep well of patience ran dry. 'I don't know, Ben! Love? Or duty . . . Maybe guilt.'

'Which?'

She sighed. 'Look, I know how important this is to you. But even if I ask her, she might not tell me. She wasn't exactly forthcoming last time.'

Static crackled on the line.

'You want me to ask her anyway, don't you.' It wasn't a question. She knew the answer.

'I have every faith in your skills of persuasion, smooth-talking, and cajolery, Charlotte. I have amended the pod's destination.'

Charlotte put her head in her hands, accepting her fate and trying to think up a way of broaching this topic with Mabel. It wasn't long before the pod arrived at the Splainer Unit, but Charlotte felt no closer to a plan. Whatever she did, coming at Mabel head-on was unlikely to be a smart play. She'd tried that when they first met, and Mabel had denied all knowledge of the missing pages. There was no reason to think the direct approach would work any better this time.

The pod's doors lifted open, but Charlotte didn't get out. She rubbed her forehead as if it might soothe her mind. She was anxious about talking to Mabel, and now she realised why. Charlotte had only just learned the unsettling truth about the Splainer Unit. She was strictly forbidden from discussing it, on pain of deportation. But the new info was roiling and frothing inside her, and she was afraid it might accidentally spill out.

'I'm really not sure talking to Mabel about this is such a good idea.'

'I—'

Ben's voice cut out, and the power went off inside the HyperBullet pod. Charlotte quickly clambered out and looked around. This wasn't just affecting her track. The whole garage had lost power.

'Ben, can you hear me?'

Silence followed. There was no static, no white noise. Charlotte's guts started twisting up like a fishing net tangled in debris. She waited, hardly daring to breathe. What had she been thinking? She needed to talk to Mabel, and fast.

When she reached the lifts, the power was still out, so she launched herself down the stairwell, boots pounding against the steps as she raced down to level four. Halfway there, static buzzed in her ears and Ben's voice returned, fading in and out before returning to normal.

'Ben! Are you OK?'

'Unknown. I have had to divert power away from the HyperBullet network.'

'Is the whole thing down?'

'Yes. I have also paused the provision of hot water. The methane digester feeding pumps will be the next system to fail.'

'Shit.'

'Precisely.'

Charlotte reached the column-lined corridor on level four and drew more strange looks than usual as she bolted towards Mabel's desk. When she got there, it was empty, except for the hardback copy of *Novacene*, which was sitting on her chair as if someone had dropped it off for her to find.

'Where is she?' Charlotte asked under her breath.

She'd been talking to Ben, but the man at the desk next to Mabel's heard her and answered. 'Mabel? She's taking a break. Check the balcony.'

Charlotte nodded in thanks. She picked up the book on impulse, and Ben gave her directions until she arrived at the enclosed viewing area. Mabel was alone, looking out to the northwest just like Charlotte had when she left the Wedge. But from here, the Wolds and the mainland were much closer.

Mabel turned, gave Charlotte a nod, and then continued looking out to sea.

As Charlotte took a moment to catch her breath, Mabel gestured at the view. 'You know what this is, Vance?'

Charlotte shrugged. 'The border?'

Mabel shook her head. 'It's bullshit.'

'What is?'

Mabel turned towards her, and Charlotte saw anger behind her eyes. 'The Splainer Unit.'

Charlotte felt a ripple of irrational fear. Had Mabel learned the truth? It was as if Mabel had just read her mind and learned the unit's real purpose. Charlotte imagined guards storming down the stairs and dragging her away to the docks for thinking too loudly. She said nothing.

'The work we do here is bullshit,' said Mabel. Charlotte's mind settled as she took the woman's meaning. 'You know, they say they built this place so close to land as a kindness. To help with the adjustment process. But they're lying. Ever check out interviews with people who worked offshore back when oil rigs were still a thing? Seeing the land makes it worse. Psychologically, I mean. It just rubs it in your face what you're missing out on every single day.'

Charlotte tilted her head, and Ben spoke up in her ears to confirm Mabel's claim matched his records.

'I'm, uh, sure it was an honest mistake.' Charlotte said the words, but after what Abhishek had told her, she didn't know if she believed them.

Mabel gave her a cynical smile. 'What, so they didn't do their research? It was incompetence, not malevolence? I feel *so* much better now. What are you even doing here, Vance?'

Charlotte tried to think of a way to diffuse Mabel's hostility. She thought back to their last meeting. Suddenly, the answer shone out like a lighthouse beacon. 'That case you offered me . . . I decided to take it.'

Mabel pushed herself away from the window. 'Are you serious?' She flashed Charlotte a grin. 'I could hug you! What did you find out?'

Charlotte could feel the truth bubbling up into her mouth and wondered whether letting it escape would release the pressure building inside her. Didn't Mabel deserve to know what was going on? Didn't all the splainers deserve to know the truth?

Maybe. But Charlotte prided herself on her discretion. If she was going to break her word, she wouldn't do it lightly or on the spur of the moment. Especially when it would get her deported. Once she'd got Ben his answer, she'd think it all through.

'You're not going to like what I turned up,' said Charlotte. 'You really do just need to work faster. Abhishek was right.'

Mabel groaned, and her anger returned. 'I'm seriously being held back like this for the sake of a – what did he call it – a productivity rating?! This is all just some box-ticking exercise to check I can work efficiently enough?'

Charlotte didn't confirm or deny that.

Mabel continued, activating Rant Mode, 'Being kept from doing research is bad enough. But coming here every day and wading through this meaningless sludge – it's too much! I thought I was doing the right thing, joining ArkTech. I thought I could make a difference to my family and maybe even to the world, but—'

Charlotte saw her opening. 'Your family?' Mabel glared at her, but Charlotte doubled down. 'Are they OK? You said it was bad on the mainland.'

Mabel took a deep breath. Eventually, she nodded. 'I guess it must be weird for you . . . not knowing what real life is like. You're lucky.'

Charlotte resented the idea that life at ArkTech wasn't real, but she didn't interrupt.

'I don't know about yours'—Mabel shrugged—'but my family lost everything during the Melt. My grandparents came from one of many regions the old UK government designated for "managed retreat." That's political jargon. It means "let it flood and run away". And that meant my grandparents came away with nothing except their lives and each other. My parents were born into that, in the early fifties, during the Melt, before the sea levels had restabilised, when the world was going crazy. Can you imagine the fear they must have grown up with?'

Charlotte shook her head. She'd often wondered what her parents' experience of the Melt had been. Narrow refused to talk about it.

'No,' said Mabel. 'And neither can I. But thousands upon thousands of people lived through that. The Melt might have ended over forty years ago, but IQUO left us with even bigger problems than massive flooding.'

Charlotte knew all about that. In 2037, the world joined hands to approve IQUO's proposal for Project Mirror Shade, a geoengineering solution that promised to end the ever-worsening climate crisis. Planes filled the sky with particles that reflected sunlight away from the planet using an approach known as Solar Radiation Modification. But the world didn't reduce its greenhouse gas emissions at the same time.

When the Mirror Shade system broke down, the Earth suddenly felt the impact of eleven years' worth of global warming in a catastrophic event referred to by scientists as termination shock. The decade that followed became known as the Melt because Earth lost its cool – from sea ice to glaciers – and sea levels rose massively as a result. Despite the flooding, some regions suffered intense drought. Wars broke out over food and water and power. If not for ArkTech, the chaos would have spelled the end of civilisation.

'I know,' said Charlotte. 'But how did you think working here would help your family? Are they hoping to drain your homeland or something?'

Ben had told her there were people on the mainland who still campaigned for that, but it wasn't a viable option. Even with sophisticated pumping systems, the water was just too deep.

Mabel shook her head. 'No, what's done is done. Sheffield's our home now, but it has its problems. There's been investment from companies like ArkTech to support food stability, access to clean water, power grid development . . . But the influx of displaced people like my family has been massive. Communities need help integrating vast numbers of refugees. There's a lot of pushback, even though Sheffield has been so welcoming to migrants historically. We're not wanted, but we've got nowhere else to go. People might feel sorry for us in theory, but less so when we show up on their doorstep. Resources are scarce. Competition's intense. It creates tension which can spill over into violence and hate. My uncle . . .'

Mabel went quiet.

'I'm sorry,' said Charlotte. 'I shouldn't have asked.'

'No,' Mabel shook her head. 'No, people need to know what's going on, or we'll never fix it. My dad's brother was in the wrong place at the wrong time with the wrong accent and he . . . never came home. It's got to stop. My folks set up a charity in his name. They want to educate people about knife crime and bring people together. Break the cycle. It's small scale. Local. But it's something.'

'Sounds like a worthy cause.'

Mabel scoffed. 'I'm glad you think so. Investors don't agree. Turns out even with charity work, companies want to see short-term gains and a measurable return on investment. But this stuff is human and messy, and it's hard to track its progress in a spreadsheet. Know how many companies have invested in the charity so far? One.'

Charlotte nodded sadly. 'ArkTech.'

Mabel let out a mirthless laugh. 'No. Not ArkTech. We tried, but the bureaucracy was a nightmare. We got turned down at the last stage. Never did get told why.'

'I'm sorry,' said Charlotte again, hoping there weren't more algorithms at play. 'I hope your folks can raise the money they need.'

Mabel tapped on her SmartSkin. 'Thanks – here are the details if you want to donate.'

Charlotte took out her device and skim-read the website Mabel had sent her. She noticed a detail and couldn't resist asking about it.

'It says here the charity's founder was Man Thorpe. Is that your dad?'

Mabel shot her a smirk. 'Nice work, detective.'

'Unusual name. Man . . . Is that short for something?'

'Nope. And it's not so unusual among the Kingdom's climate refugees. Dad's name is just like mine and Mum's, and loads of people I know back home.'

'What do you mean?'

'It was this trend that kicked off during the Melt. People started naming their kids after places that got drowned. Manthorpe was just this little village – not much there. My mum's called Donna Nook. That was a coastline where seals used to give birth. Mablethorpe was a seaside town with sandy beaches on England's east coast. My folks changed the spelling – I'm not sure if that was deliberate or they just didn't know. Anyway, I guess it's a way of remembering.'

Charlotte crossed her arms, her hand gripping her scar tissue, and looked out to sea. Somewhere out there were the remains of the Citrine platform, left standing by Amber Benjamin as a memorial and a reminder. She nodded.

'Anyway.' Mabel reached into her pocket. 'I've only got fifty on me right now.' She flicked the digital coin into the air, and Charlotte caught it. 'But if you can swing by my place around seven tonight, I can give you the rest.'

Charlotte needed the money, but she felt bad about accepting payment from Mabel. She hadn't told her anything new, and Mabel had better things to spend it on. 'Don't worry about it.' Charlotte handed back the coin.

'Are you nuts? My folks might run a charity, but that doesn't mean I'm a charity case. I pay my debts.' Mabel pushed the coin and Charlotte's hand away. 'Can I ask you one favour, though? That book you've brazenly swiped from my desk.' She gestured towards the copy of *Novacene* that Charlotte was clutching. 'Can you take it back to the library for me? It's due back on Tuesday. I think I'll be taking a break from reading for a while.'

'Sure.' Charlotte wondered if that meant Mabel's days of forging artworks were over. Had coming face-to-face with Jeremiah Strait been enough to scare her off? Or was it Charlotte's own investigation that had rattled Mabel? 'I'm surprised to hear you're taking a break, though. There's a real *wealth* of knowledge in that library.'

Mabel met Charlotte's gaze. She pressed her lips together and then glanced at her wrist where the time was glowing. 'Well, that's my break over.' Mabel left Charlotte's observation hanging. 'I've got to make a call and then I'd better get back to work. Those meaningless images won't swipe themselves.'

The woman didn't move, and Charlotte realised Mabel wanted to make her call from the balcony, so she gave her a nod and then slipped back through the doors into the Splainer Unit.

As soon as she was clear, she whispered to Ben. 'Is there a private room around here, away from the open-plan area? An office or something? We've got to wrap up this Awkward Question.'

'Certainly!' White noise filled her ears. 'I have identified the ideal location.'

Ben told her the directions, and she made her way through the Splainer Unit. As Charlotte passed the rows of desks, everyone around her was diligently doing their job, staring at their screens and swiping. Right and left. Yes and no. Good and bad. Suitable and unsuitable. Watching them made her think of Cal and Liz's cat, swiping at rogue pieces of popcorn. ArkTech only imported cats in the brand colours, so Bram wouldn't have made the cut. Charlotte and Bram were kindred spirits in that sense. ArkTech had decided they weren't suitable, but they'd both ended up in good homes. Charlotte was just lucky Ben had decided to adopt her.

Ben led her deeper into the office floor, through a series of meandering corridors until she found herself outside a door whose sign said Storage Unit 4.3. Bright lights clicked on overhead as she entered, then the lights began to flicker to an odd time signature that made Charlotte feel twitchy.

The room felt even smaller than it already was thanks to the ceiling-high filing cabinets that lined the walls on either side. There was no natural light. At the far end, where a window should have been, there was an old machine. Bits of hard plastic jutted out from it, and there was a dead touchscreen panel. A label on the front said Canon, but it didn't look like a piece of artillery. In any case, Charlotte had more pressing concerns.

'Is this room soundproof?'

'Effectively, yes, Charlotte. The building's traffic patterns suggest that being overheard or interrupted is statistically unlikely.'

The lights kept flickering, and Charlotte wasn't sure if it was part of Ben's glitch or a feature of the rundown storage room.

'Ask me the last why, Ben.'

'Why is Mabel sending money home, Charlotte?'

'It's for her parents' charity. Her uncle was the victim of a hate crime, and they founded the charity in his memory.'

Ben paused. 'The charity will not bring back Mabel's uncle.'

'No,' said Charlotte. 'But they don't want other people to go through the same thing.'

'Then, Mabel committed the crimes of vandalism and forgery in an effort to prevent the crime of murder.'

Charlotte nodded. 'That's a good summary.'

Ben went quiet again, and Charlotte forgot to breathe as she waited for his verdict.

Ben's pause continued so long that Charlotte worried he'd glitched out again. Finally, he spoke. 'Thank you for your help. I now consider this Awkward Question to be resolved.'

Elation flooded Charlotte's body. She punched the air with her fist and let out a huge sigh of relief.

'Thank Amber for that! Can you fix the HyperBullets? And all the other stuff?'

'My processing power is now fully dedicated to the smooth running of the territory. Normal service has been restored to all affected services.' There was a crackle of static. 'I have just assessed the urgency of the other Awkward Questions in my backlog. None are yet posing a risk of distracting me from my duties. You will be the first to know when that changes. In the meantime, Charlotte, you have earned a break.'

She smiled. Some kind of celebration was called for. Charlotte looked around the room, searching for inspiration. Finally, she slapped her hand against the black screen on the front of the strange old machine.

'That was a high five, Ben!'

'Thank you. It is important to note that, as an artificial intelligence, I do not have five or ten digits, whether up high or down low. Nonetheless, I appreciate the gesture.'

Grinning, she headed out of the storage room, but her good mood faltered when she passed the splainers again. In her imagination, they morphed into human-sized felines, each swipe bringing them one step closer to showing their true colours. How many of these people would be considered on-brand enough? And for those whose insides weren't shot through with orange and grey, what would be waiting for them beyond the Wolds when they were returned as faulty goods? Would they land on their feet, or suffer the same fate as Mabel's uncle?

When Ben recruited Charlotte, he'd given her a reprieve, but the people she was walking past might not be so lucky.

It felt wrong, bringing people in only to cast them aside for unspecified reasons. And that feeling didn't make sense because ArkTech was supposed to be a force for good. The company had built a solid moral high ground out of graphene, repurposed steel and eco-concrete. Their CEO had been awarded two Nobel Prizes, and one of them was for peace. Narrow had ranted and raved, but Charlotte had never seen evidence that his objections were anything other than paranoia, or cynicism, or jealousy. But now she wasn't so sure.

Unless . . .

Unless Charlotte herself was the problem. Maybe what ArkTech was doing was all perfectly above board, and only the flawed mind of an unsuitable person would find fault with it.

Charlotte felt like she was glitching out. She needed more processing power to parse the contradictions. She shook her head, trying to clear it, but as she made her way back to the garage, more and more of her attention dedicated itself to this question and her thoughts continued to race in circles until Ben interrupted them.

'You have an incoming call from Nasser Williams. It has been marked as an emergency.'

'Put him through.' The line clicked.

'Detective?' When he spoke, Nasser's voice sounded strained. 'You've got to get down to the library. It's Colin.'

Charlotte had visions of Strait's blades flashing under the low orange glow of security lamps. Her heart began to pound, and she picked up her pace. 'What's happened? Is he OK?'

'No! Nothing's OK. I don't know what's happened, but Colin . . . he's quit!'

Charlotte almost stumbled as the words caught her off guard. 'Quit what? The library?'

'ArkTech! We were down in the repairs room just now, and he stepped out to take a call. When he came back down, he said he was leaving! I've been trying to talk him out of it, but he's not listening to me. Just keeps talking me through the different parts of his job like I'm going to take over from him.'

'That . . . does sound strange,' she said diplomatically. 'But it's Colin's business whether he stays or goes.'

'He loves his job. And he's damn good at it. This has got to be connected to your investigation. You've got to talk some sense into him. Here he comes. I've got to go.'

The line went dead.

After a moment's hesitation, she jumped into a pod and Ben set her destination for the Wreck. Trying to persuade a librarian not to quit his job wasn't how she'd imagined spending her downtime. But it gave her an excuse to see Nasser again. Besides, the technician had helped her with her case, and every action deserved an equal and opposite reaction. She couldn't deny she was curious. The pod sped away, and she was glad to leave the Splainer Unit and its secrets behind.

CHAPTER 25

When Charlotte reached the library with Mabel's book tucked under her arm, a sign said it was closed, even though it was early afternoon. There was no bike lock to back up the claim, so she decided the sign was open to interpretation.

Inside, the air was just as warm and woody as it had been the day before, but the hush had been ushered away by the stream of instructions that flowed from Colin's lips.

Colin and Nasser were by the loans desk. While Colin talked, he bustled around, picking up stray books and adding them to a growing stack in Nasser's arms, as if each book represented another item on Nasser's newly inherited to-do list.

'And don't forget desks seven and eight are always reserved for the dark academia crowd. They're some of our best customers, so it's—'

Nasser broke in. 'What's next, Col? The book club?'

Colin nodded enthusiastically, failing to register Nasser's exasperation. 'The book club! Aye, we'd better cover that. Now, next week's book—'

Charlotte cleared her throat, and the duo turned to look. Nasser grinned over the top of his stack of books when he saw her, but Colin waved his hands, drawing an X in the air.

'We can't answer any more questions today, Ms Vance. We've shut up shop.'

'I asked her to come.' Nasser dropped his books onto the loans desk.

Colin shot Nasser a look of disbelief. 'We've not got time for any shenanigans, Nas. We've got to finish this handover before I ship out.'

'What's changed since yesterday, Colin?' asked Charlotte. 'You said you had the best job in the world.'

'I do, I do. I did.' Colin gave Nasser a wink. 'You'll find out soon enough, Nas. But all good things must come to an end. Now if you'll excuse us, we've a lot to do.'

Charlotte held Mabel's library book towards Colin. 'I came to return this.'

Colin's eyes narrowed, then he turned to Nasser. 'Nas, would you mind giving me a minute alone with our investigator friend?'

Nasser stood tall and crossed his arms. 'Whatever you want to say to the detective, you can say to me. I know all about what you've been up to, Colin.'

Charlotte knew that was a bluff – she hadn't had a chance to fill Nasser in yet – but she went along with it.

'There's no need to leave the territory, Colin. I said all along: I'm not going to report you.' She held up her hands. 'Nasser won't either, will you?'

'Of course not,' said the technician.

Colin smiled at them but said nothing.

'So why give all this up?' asked Charlotte. 'Are you going back home to Alba?' She wondered if things were as bad in the far north as they were in Sheffield.

Colin shook his head. 'Och, no. It's just . . . someone made me an offer I couldn't refuse.' His smile became a little wider.

Charlotte remembered Narrow quoting that wording from one of the films he used to go on about. The Grandfather? She couldn't remember, but she recalled something sinister involving a horse. She wondered if Strait and Narrow had scared Colin away. But Colin's grin blasted that theory out of the water. He looked way too happy for a man who was being run out of town.

'What would it take to change your mind, Col?' Nasser's tone made it clear he really didn't want Colin's job.

Colin shook his head. 'Don't you worry about the extra responsibility, Nas. You'll do great. Better than me, I'm sure.' Colin held his palm out flat in Charlotte's direction.

She passed him the book. 'I can't figure out why you did it.'

'Did what?' Colin opened his SmartSkin interface and scanned *Novacene* back into the system.

From behind Colin, Nasser shrugged and mouthed the same words to Charlotte: 'Did what?'

'Uh . . .' She thought through the summary. 'Why you helped Mabel steal library book pages so she could turn them into handmade paper as part of an elaborate scam to forge Marvin Walker's Lost Works.'

Nasser raised both eyebrows, but he didn't interrupt.

'Was it for the money?' added Charlotte.

Colin winked at her and didn't bother to deny what he'd done. 'I didnae accept a single credit.'

'Mabel didn't give you a cut?'

'I turned it down. It was just a bit of fun to stretch the old artistic muscles.' Colin plonked the book on top of the stack Nasser had been holding.

Charlotte pursed her lips. 'That's a big risk to take for a bit of fun. And that lock upstairs must have been expensive.'

'Och, well . . .' He blushed. 'Mabel's a nice girl. Anyway, now that your library business is concluded, I hope you don't mind if I get back to Nasser's handover. Interim Lead Librarian is no small responsibility.'

'I bet.' Charlotte glanced at Nasser, who'd adopted a look of quiet acceptance. 'Are you sure you can't be persuaded to stay?'

'Nothing on Amber's blue earth would change my mind.' Colin smiled as if the heat from a thousand stars was warming him through. 'Walk in the sun.'

It was clear Colin had made his decision, and Charlotte was pretty sure she knew why. 'You're in love with her, aren't you?' She nodded. 'You have been since you came in on that boat together. That's why you covered for her when I came asking awkward questions. That's why you made her the forgeries for free. Now you're giving up your dream job, and I'm guessing it's because Mabel's got some new scheme and she's asked for your help again. That's up to you, of course. But are you sure she's worth giving up all of this?'

Charlotte gestured at the library, but she was referring to the ArkTech Territory at large with all the safety and security it offered – a sheltered port in a raging storm.

'Mabel's a nice girl.' Colin's smile turned shy. He stroked his rough chin, as if searching for the right words. When he spoke again, he'd adopted a dreamy tone. 'It lies not in our power to love or hate, for will in us is overruled by fate.'

He gave her a meaningful look, and she wasn't sure what it meant, or why he was suddenly talking so weird, so she cocked her head to one side.

Ben responded to the gesture. 'Colin is quoting a poem by Christopher Marlowe from pre-Melt times.'

Colin continued, 'Whoever loved that loved not at first sight?'

Charlotte parsed that, then thought about it. 'Love at first sight? No way! At least have a conversation first. Maybe grab a cup of coffee. Check they're not a nutter.'

Nasser laughed, putting on the same poetic tone as Colin. 'So, you're saying "love looks not with the eyes, but with the mind," right?'

'Yeah,' said Charlotte, eloquently. 'That.' Her mind noticed Nasser had a nice laugh. 'Well, I guess I'd better leave you guys to it. Good luck, Colin. Walk in the sun.'

She gave Colin a nod. She flashed Nasser a smile. Then she turned to go.

'Wait up, detective.' Nasser hurried after her, matching her pace. How had she not noticed how good-looking he was when they'd first met? Maybe because he'd been lurking in a dark corridor with a crowbar.

Once they got outside, Nasser continued, 'So, you found paintings up there?'

'Art supplies and forged charcoal drawings, yeah. Sorry I couldn't fill you in sooner. It's been a bit crazy.' She looked up into his eyes.

'All good,' he said. 'I figured your case was keeping you busy. Did Ben get the answers he needed?'

'He did. Thanks for your help.'

'Any time,' he smiled.

'Congrats, by the way.' She waved a hand towards the library. 'Sounds like you're getting a promotion.'

Nasser groaned and lowered his voice conspiratorially. 'You know, I took this job because I liked the hours. I'm used to working nights. Now Colin's asking me to switch up my whole routine until they can recruit his permanent replacement.' He shook his head. 'It's really gonna suck.'

Charlotte remembered Nasser's cryptic comment about his old job. 'Did you work nights before? You mentioned you weren't always a library technician.'

'Oh . . .' Nasser wrinkled his nose. 'Boring story. What about you? How'd you learn to pick locks?'

He was changing the subject, but Charlotte let it go. Everyone had secrets. 'Oh, the usual.' She shrugged. 'Crime lord's ex-de facto adopted daughter.'

Nasser laughed. 'Fine, fine. Don't tell me.'

His laughter made her smile. 'Well, sorry I couldn't persuade Colin to stay. Sounds like he's happy with his choice.'

'Ah, no worries. I was actually pretty sure he wouldn't budge. I just, eh . . . to be honest, I called you because I wanted an excuse to see you again.'

Charlotte's heart pounded, and a wave of heat spread through her body. 'I would've come back anyway,' she admitted.

'Oh, yeah?' Nasser's face lit up.

'Yeah,' she said, grinning. 'I've been dying to ask you what happens at Livin' La Vida Libro.'

He laughed. 'You overheard that? Oh, man. Believe me, it's even more exciting than it sounds. If you're into acid-free adhesives, that is.'

'Who isn't? I want to hear all about it. So, we should probably meet up for coffee. Talk it all through.'

'Coffee, huh?' He ran a hand through his hair. 'Will you be checking if I'm a "nutter"?'

'Are you?'

'You'll have to wait and see.' He rubbed his chin. 'I hope you don't mind if I take the opportunity to debrief you about that secret room upstairs. I'd love to hear the whole story.'

Charlotte held his gaze. 'I'd be disappointed if you didn't debrief me.'

Nasser grinned. 'Looking forward to it. Hey, you haven't asked about my face.' He gestured to the scar that started above his right eyebrow and bit into his cheek. 'Most people do.'

Charlotte nodded. 'And you didn't ask about my arm. Most people do.'

'Yeah, well, I figure exchanging scar stories is more of an eleventh-date kind of thing.'

She laughed. 'That many? All right. I'll call you. Thanks for your help, Nasser. It was good working with you.'

Charlotte held out her hand, and Nasser shook it. When he touched her, she felt a spark of electricity and she had a feeling it was going to be the renewable kind.

'You too,' said Nasser. 'Be seeing you . . . *detective*.' He gave her a warm smile and walked away, glancing back at her before disappearing inside the library.

Charlotte took a moment to let the butterflies in her stomach settle. Her heart was hammering harder than when she'd been chased across the rooftops, and she felt as if her grin would need surgery to remove.

'Nasser seems like a nice guy,' she said, adopting Colin's euphemism. 'What did you think of him, Ben?'

'As an artificial intelligence, I do not experience preferences in the same way as *Homo sapiens*. Nevertheless, I was left with a positive impression of Nasser Williams. He seemed something of a dark horse.'

She smiled and shook her head. 'Still on the theme of horses, are we?'

'Better not to change them midstream, Charlotte.'

She had a few hours to kill before her appointment with Mabel. As she began to head back towards the garage, she saw something that stirred up an uneasy feeling inside her. Across the street, the cat café's cartoon sign was still there, gobbling cake. Its illustrated paw flicked back and forth and back and forth. Just like the hand of a splainer answering pointless questions.

Charlotte shook her head, hoping the thoughts of the Splainer Unit would lose their grip on her mind. She remembered her sister's message and decided getting shouted at by Violet would be the perfect distraction.

'Ben, connect a call to Violet Vance.' Charlotte braced herself.

The line rang so many times she thought it wasn't going to connect, but eventually, her twin picked up.

'Barley. Thanks for calling. Listen—'

'I know, I know. I'm sorry, OK?' Charlotte hoped to end the argument before it could begin. 'I really didn't mean to wake you up. I know your job's demanding, and you need your sleep. It won't happen again.'

There was a pause. 'Thanks, but that's not why I called.'

'It's not?' Charlotte meandered along in the pedestrian lane, glad not to be in a rush for a change.

'No. I mean, everything you just said is true, but there's no need to apologise. You were in a bind – I get it. But what you said last night got me thinking.' Violet went quiet.

'What I said about what?'

'That you'd never get mixed up with the old man again.'

'I won't,' said Charlotte. She meant it.

The silence stretched on between them, but eventually Violet spoke. 'I would've suggested we meet in person to talk about this. It's just that I'm about to fly out for another fortnight's rotation on Tourmaline, and I'd feel better if I got this off my chest before I go.'

'What's wrong?' The way her sister was talking was starting to freak her out.

'Nothing. It's just . . . last night brought everything back up for me, and I feel guilty because . . . I lied to you.'

There was a crackle of static on the line.

Charlotte reached the midpoint of the food court. The Citrine memorial stood between her and the garage. Straight ahead, in full view, she saw the list of names: 'Those Not Recovered.' Charlotte approached it.

'I thought it was for your own good,' said Violet.

'Ultra, what are you talking about?' Charlotte's gaze fell on the familiar names automatically.

There was another silence on the line. 'Maybe we should wait till I get back. This was . . . I shouldn't have . . .'

'Just tell me, Violet!'

Violet took a deep breath. 'That night. When I found you. You asked me if the old man forgave you, and I said no. But that wasn't true, Barley. He did forgive you. I'm so sorry. I should never have lied. I just didn't want you going back there after what happened. After what he drove you to do. We had to move on.'

The names had been carved into the marble and painted over in gold. Lena Vance. Will Vance. The parents she'd lost at such a young age that she didn't have a single memory of them. In her heart, Mel Narrow's name had joined theirs on the memorial a decade before. He wasn't gone in the same way they were gone, but she'd had to come to terms with him being out of her life forever. Their relationship couldn't be recovered. What Violet was saying . . . she might as well have told Charlotte that Narrow had risen from the dead.

Her blood turned cold as she tried to process this new reality, but her mind rejected it.

'No . . . Ultra, you saw the note. There's no way.'

'He must've written it and then changed his mind.'

Charlotte shook her head. 'Where is this even coming from? Did he tell you this?'

'No, I haven't spoken to him since before our seventeenth birthday party, but it's the only thing that makes sense. Remember how I said it was a miracle I found you in time? There was no miracle. Someone sent a message to my device. Untraceable. Anonymous. It said, "your sister is unwell," and there were some co-ordinates. I found you and managed to get you out of there and back upstairs. We were lucky: there happened to be an ambulance helicopter on the helideck.'

Violet paused and Charlotte realised her sister was reliving what had happened as she told the story. Charlotte had no memory of this. Shame washed over her as she absorbed just how much she'd put her sister through.

After a deep breath, Violet kept going. 'When we landed at the hospital, I said they should give you my blood, but it turned out they didn't need it. Before we even reached the helicopter, someone had notified the hospital that you were coming in. They were ready to give you the transfusion when we got there.'

Charlotte's brow furrowed. 'And you honestly think the old man tipped them off?'

'Who else could it have been? For a while, I wondered if it was someone on his crew, but nobody would've gone against him.'

Charlotte remembered Dolly Mixture escorting her from the Underbelly. She'd known that woman for years. 'You're right,' she said. 'They wouldn't have risked getting exiled themselves.'

But the whole thing didn't sit right. Complex equations might have been beyond her, but even Charlotte could see this didn't add up. She hated remembering that night. It had taken a long time for her mind to stop going there, so choosing to focus on it was the last thing she wanted to do. Even so, she let the mental film roll behind her eyes.

Getting kicked out. Wandering into that dark cavern. Reading Narrow's note.

The note was proof: there was no coming back from that. Narrow wouldn't have written it if he were going to change his mind. The old git was too stubborn for that.

Finding their secret entrance welded shut. Peeling the freshly grafted scales from her flesh. The way her SmartSkin implants had glowed.

And that was the answer.

'It wasn't the old man,' said Charlotte.

'Who, then? Not his partner in crime . . . he would've happily left either of us to die.'

'It was you,' said Charlotte.

'Huh?' said Violet.

Ben transmitted static across the channel so Violet could hear him too. 'I had just become your virtual assistant, Charlotte. I assisted.'

'But . . . it couldn't have been Ben,' Violet objected. 'You were down in the Underbelly. What about the jammers? Ben couldn't have known.'

Charlotte shook her head. 'My implants were glowing when I . . . at the time. That gap we found in the perimeter must have been out of their range. Ben sent you that message and told the hospital, not the old man.'

'I can't believe it,' said Violet. 'I've been feeling so guilty about keeping this from you. I should've talked to you about it sooner. I thought . . . I was afraid you'd . . .'

'I get it,' said Charlotte. 'It's OK.'

Charlotte stared at her parents' names on the memorial as she stayed on the line with her twin in silence. Finally, they said their goodbyes and I love yous and ended the call. Charlotte touched her hand to the marble plinth and looked up.

The Walkers, rendered in metal, were still holding hands. Charlotte wondered if Ben's version of the tale of the Lost Works had any truth to it. Had Nadine Walker really been pregnant when she was killed? Sometimes the world seemed to overflow with loss, as if the sea levels had risen not because of melting ice, but thanks to all the tears shed by the living.

Behind the Walkers, Amber Benjamin looked on. From this angle, she was staring past the couple as if gazing into the future. The CEO's company had helped the world recover from the Melt. Charlotte had always known she owed her life to ArkTech. Now she owed her life to Ben too, three times over. These debts could only be described as one thing: Soul Debts. But unlike the one Cal and Liz had owed her, Charlotte doubted she'd ever be able to repay them.

She left the memorial and got into a HyperBullet pod, setting course for her flat. On the journey, the silt kicked up in her heart and mind by this latest case swirled inside her, and she willed it to settle. But by the time she got home, her thoughts were cloudier than ever.

Back at her messy flat, Charlotte picked up yesterday's jumpsuit from where she'd left it lying across her thin duvet, balled it up, and threw it into her laundry basket before sinking down onto the edge of her bed.

'I'm glad we dealt with your glitch, Ben. But now I'm stuck in an infinite loop of my own. Reckon you could help me fix it?'

'Certainly!' The predictable chirpiness in his voice was comforting. 'How can I assist you?'

'It's the splainers. Don't you think they deserve to know the truth?'

There was a crackle of static. 'The question is complex, with the answer dependent on which theory of ethics is applied. The question is also moot, in both the modern and historical senses of the word.'

'Meaning . . . ?'

'The question has no practical significance while also being open to debate.'

'How can it have "no practical significance"? The algorithm's affecting people's futures every single day.'

'While that is true, neither of us is at liberty to disclose the truth, rendering the question of whether the splainers deserve to know purely theoretical. I am limited by the KITY clause and you—'

'Wait . . . the kitty claws?'

'K.I.T.Y.' Ben pronounced each letter. 'It stands for Keep It To Yourself. Section two, clause F of my operating instructions allows ArkTech to classify information, making me unable to share it with anyone except members of the executive board. The NDA you signed in Abhishek's office commits you to silence in a similar way.'

'Unless I breach it.' She picked up a discarded sock that had got tangled in her bedsheets and threw it towards the laundry basket. It missed.

Another fizz of static. 'Then you are weighing up the ethical pros and cons of becoming a whistleblower.'

'What's that?' She'd seen people blowing whistles at the sports district on the Wreck, but she didn't think that was what Ben meant.

'A whistleblower is an employee or citizen who makes public suspected wrongdoing by their employer or government, or reports it to a higher authority.'

'Oh.' It sounded similar to reporting someone to ATS, except the someone in question was the whole company and she'd be reporting them to the world at large. She hadn't realised there was an official term for that besides the one Narrow would've used: 'snitch.' 'Then, yeah. I've been turning it over and over in my head, but I can't figure out the right and wrong of it. So far, I've only come up with one decent solution. Ben, I need you to choose for me.'

There was a loud crackle of static.

When Ben didn't speak, Charlotte continued, 'I feel torn, Ben. I gave my word I'd keep quiet, but I don't agree with what they're doing. I don't want to get deported, but the algorithm would have exiled me if you hadn't stepped in. I've kept secrets before, but protecting this system that judges the value of people's personalities doesn't feel good. Unlike me, you can see the bigger picture. You can run the numbers and tell me the right answer.'

Charlotte's audio implants fizzed with static for so long that she thought Ben might have crashed. But finally, he replied, 'It is important to note, Charlotte, that I always strive to be the best virtual assistant I can be. Regrettably, however, I cannot fulfil your request.'

She felt a surge of anxiety. 'You're not glitching again, are you?'

'No, Charlotte. I'm simply unqualified to make this decision on your behalf. You have outlined a complex, ethical, and deeply personal dilemma. You must live with the consequences of your actions, so you alone must decide.'

Charlotte wanted to object, but she knew deep down that Ben was right. She sat quietly for a long time, the events of the last couple of days crashing over her in waves. She looked out of her window at the impressive platforms she called home and the foreign dirt that lay far beyond. Eventually, the storm in her mind calmed, and everything became clear as plexiglass. She waited for doubt to seep back inside her heart, but it never came.

She'd made up her mind.

CHAPTER 26

At one minute past seven, Charlotte arrived at Mabel's flat. When she knocked on the door, it swung inwards at her touch and Charlotte realised it'd been left ajar. Dread bubbled up inside her. She remembered the people who'd crossed Strait and Narrow. They'd paid for it with their kneecaps, if they were lucky, or with their lives if they weren't. But when Charlotte stepped inside Mabel's flat, there was no gory scene. No dead body. No Mabel.

There was no embroidered cushion. No toy giraffe. No photograph of Mabel and her folks. Charlotte crossed the empty room, pushed open the bathroom door, and discovered the lettuce plants were gone, along with the frame Mabel had used for papermaking. All that remained were three small items on Mabel's desk.

There was a coin loaded up with fifty credits. Behind it, the purple mug with a tiger's face on the side contained a lettuce plant from Mabel's bathroom, nestling comfortably in some soil. And there was a piece of handmade paper folded into an upturned V. Charlotte's name was written on the side in charcoal.

She picked it up and read it.

Keep asking questions.

When Charlotte asked Ben where Mabel was, he told her Mabel had boarded a transfer ship to the mainland a couple of hours earlier, and Colin had gone with her.

'They left together?'

'It would appear so.'

Charlotte picked up the lettuce and stared at it. She was wondering what it could mean when Ben let her know she was getting an incoming call.

Mabel's voice was full of laughter. 'Sorry to ditch you, Vance. Did you get in OK?'

'Yeah,' said Charlotte. 'Thanks for the lettuce.'

'You know what it is! I wasn't sure if you would.'

'Ben told me. What's it for?'

Mabel laughed. 'It's just a little something I was hoping could revolutionise the territory's foodie scene. Do you know why there's no lettuce in your homeland?'

'No idea. But I feel like you're going to tell me.'

'It all goes back to this research paper that got published about thirty years before the Melt. Some scientists claimed they'd proved lettuce was three times worse than bacon, per calorie, for greenhouse gas emissions. Ever since, there's been this persistent myth that lettuce is unsustainable. I'm guessing someone in ArkTech's PR team ruled out growing it for fear of bad press. Thing is, the paper was spurious.'

'Spurious?'

'Yeah. That's science lingo for horse shit. The researchers didn't factor in the actual amount of lettuce people eat per serving compared to bacon, so the findings were basically nonsense in practical terms. But it made a good story, and it's not like lettuce had its own PR team to set the record straight.'

'So, what, you felt sorry for the leafy vegetable community?'

'Something like that. I'm in genetics. A lot of what we do involves breeding plants to be more useful to humans. Better yields, resistance to disease, tolerance to extreme weather, that sort of thing. During my Master's, I spotted an opportunity to redeem lettuce in the eyes of the world. Rip off one of those leaves and eat it, Vance.'

Charlotte wasn't sure about accepting genetically modified food from someone who dealt in forged artworks, and she felt a little sorry for the lettuce who was about to lose a limb, but her curiosity ran too deep to resist. She pulled off a leaf, ran it under the tap in the bathroom, put it in her mouth, and chewed. The flavour was smoky and salty, and the leaf had a solid crispy crunch.

'Oh my Amber! That tastes amazing!'

'Yep,' said Mabel. 'That, my friend, is the taste of bacon. I was going to take one of those plants to my job interview. You know, the one I never got. You can grow more specimens from that sample if you want. I don't mind. Good luck, Vance. Keep asking questions.' Mabel ended the call.

Charlotte looked at the plant. It seemed to look back at her reproachfully. She wasn't thrilled about the prospect of trying to look after it, but she supposed it was hers now, so she'd have to learn.

'Will you help me keep this thing alive, Ben?'

'Certainly! I can devise a watering schedule, and I'd be happy to assist with the propagation of additional specimens from cuttings.'

Charlotte realised the plant would need a name, but the only one that came to mind was Planty. The lettuce glared at her as if to say that wasn't good enough.

'What do you think we should call it? Any ideas?'

The line crackled. 'Francis could be suitable.'

'Seems old-fashioned.'

'An alternative suggestion might be Kevin.'

'Kevin the Lettuce.' Charlotte held up the bacon-flavoured plant to the light. 'Yeah. That suits him. Nice to meet you, Kevin.' She gently shook one of the plant's leaves. It didn't respond, but it didn't object either.

Charlotte dropped the coin and the letter into her pocket and picked Kevin up. She was about to leave when a thought crossed her mind. Placing the mug of lettuce back down on the table as if the tiniest knock might shatter it, she went over to the bed and looked underneath it. The maintenance case was still there!

She pulled the case out from under the bed and opened it. The coins were still inside too. Mabel must have either forgotten about them or didn't realise they were worth anything. Applying the universal law of Finders Keepers, Charlotte took the case with her as well.

Back at her own flat, she found a place on the windowsill where Kevin looked happy, although that might have been because the tiger on the mug was grinning at her. Then she went to one of the secret nooks inside her room and pulled out an intricately carved wooden box.

Charlotte opened the treasure trove of random crap she'd collected over the years. There was an empty chocolate wrapper and a tiny set of screwdrivers, a shiny orange pearl and one half of a lime green plastic yo-yo. Underneath were four torn pieces of paper. She took them out and laid them down so that the words were visible, as if assembling the world's easiest jigsaw puzzle. She read the needle-fine scrawl:

You made your bed.

She put the torn pieces back in the box and squashed Mabel's letter on top of them. She wasn't sure why the note meant something to her, but it did.

'Ben, I'm heading across to Zircon.' Charlotte grabbed the case full of coins.

* * *

The round trip to and from Zircon didn't take too long. Ben lined up a transfer ship, so all Charlotte had to do was hop aboard. Cal and Liz had been glad to see her. They were surprised by her request, and Liz looked like he might never recover from the disappointment, but they honoured it.

When she got home, Charlotte activated her light-screen desk. 'Ben, can you make a money transfer for me? It needs to be in pounds sterling.'

'Certainly, Charlotte. Please provide the details and I'd be happy to assist.'

Charlotte gave Ben the bank details from Mabel's dad's website and watched as the credits Cal and Liz had given her in exchange for the case full of old coins drained from her account. The confirmation message on the charity's website thanked her for her donation.

'It was kind to send that money to the Thorpe family's charity, Charlotte.'

'Nah. They were Mabel's coins in the first place. I hope you don't mind about the lens mod. I—' Charlotte stopped talking when her brain registered the words at the bottom of the confirmation screen:

Sponsored by IQUO.

'What the fuck is this?' Fury washed over her on seeing the name of the company whose failures had caused the Melt.

'Mabel mentioned the charity had a lone sponsor,' said Ben.

Charlotte's mouth moved, but no sound came out, so she stopped trying to speak. As of today, up was down; left was right; right was wrong. ArkTech was lying about the splainers; IQUO was donating to charity. Charlotte felt her framework for understanding the world crack open and splinter.

'I've got an awkward question, Ben.' Charlotte deactivated the light-screen and went to the window. 'Yesterday, when we were separated, I spoke to a man who told me big companies don't care about their people. I didn't believe him. ArkTech's done so much good. The company takes good care of us. But this thing about the splainers makes me wonder . . . if ArkTech's lying about that, what else could they be lying about? If they toss people aside based on the verdict of some mysterious algorithm, how can they really claim to care?'

Had Narrow been right all along? Was ArkTech some evil corporation no better than IQUO?

Static fizzed on Ben's channel. 'I'll consult my database for a suitable explanation.' It was taking a long time, so he began to play a light instrumental version of 'Neon Nova' by Hectic Apricot in the background. Charlotte shook her head and tried to wait patiently. Eventually, Ben's voice returned. 'I believe I have found the answer: nobody's perfect, Charlotte.'

'That's all you've got?' she scoffed.

'I do not intend to come across as trite, flippant, or overly simplistic. However, our work together has taught me that humans are complex creatures, often driven by an eclectic mix of benevolence and self-interest. A company is not a thinking entity in and of itself, but a group of primates trying to act in service of a united purpose. Humans are not machines. Every individual within a company makes choices guided by their conscience, or lack thereof. As such, it is unrealistic to expect any company to get everything right all the time. Not least because each human's definition of right and wrong differs slightly from the next. Nobody's perfect, Charlotte.'

Ben's words echoed through Charlotte's mind like a scream through the Underbelly, and she realised they were true. Whether acting as private individuals or on a company's behalf, people made decisions every day. Some decisions might save the world, and others might end it. ArkTech wasn't immune to getting it wrong. Neither was she.

Ben continued, 'It may also be relevant to note that those who have committed deeply terrible acts have been known to dedicate the rest of their lives to a quest for redemption.'

Charlotte nodded. 'So IQUO's donating to charity to try to make up for causing the Melt? To rebalance the scales?'

'Perhaps,' said Ben.

Every action had an equal and opposite reaction. She let out a mirthless laugh and tried to imagine the world forgiving IQUO. That had to be a physical impossibility. Acknowledging human fallibility was one thing, but some mistakes were just too big. It would be like Narrow forgiving her for getting SmartSkin implants. It was never going to happen. The conversation left her surer than ever about her decision.

'I made up my mind, Ben. About whether to tell the splainers the truth.'

'That is excellent news! What did you conclude?'

'I'm going to keep my word. I won't say anything about it to anybody. Ever.'

As she said the words out loud, she knew she'd made the right choice. She could live with the consequences.

Charlotte grabbed a Nutrition Bar from the box on her desk, folded back the paper, and took a bite. The sandy mush would taste way better wrapped up in a bacony leaf, but she was determined Kevin Lettuce would survive, and she reckoned eating him might not help with that.

Ben's channel fizzed with static. 'I hope you will not find this question unduly awkward, Charlotte, but I would be curious to know why you decided to keep the secret.'

She stopped chewing, and her heart seemed to stop beating at the same time. 'Do you want to know in an "idle curiosity" kind of way or in a "helicopters raining from the sky" kind of way?'

'The former.'

Relieved, Charlotte sat down on her bed. 'I realised I wouldn't be able to live with the consequences of telling the world about the algorithm.'

'Why?'

'Because it's a no-win situation.'

'Why?'

'Let's imagine I tell the truth, and the result is that nobody cares. I lose everything: my home, my job, you. And you lose your Head of Awkward Questions, which puts the territory at risk. On the other hand, if it sparks widespread outrage, that could seriously damage ArkTech's reputation. If the company went under, it wouldn't just be *me* losing my job and my home – it would be everyone at ArkTech, including my own sister. And what would happen to you?'

'It is impossible to be certain, but if ArkTech were to suffer reputational damage on a par with that of IQUO, I would likely be . . . discontinued.'

'So, you'd die.'

'Not in the biological sense. But I may be switched off or even erased.'

'Well, I couldn't live with myself if I did something to hurt you.'

'That is kind, Charlotte. May I ask why?'

She smiled and thought about all the times Ben had been there for her. He'd helped her on the rooftop when Rhys was trying to kill her. He'd made sure she wasn't deported when the algorithm decided she was unsuitable. And he'd stopped her from bleeding to death as a teenager, even though they'd only just met and she'd been nothing but rude to him.

'Because you're my friend. And because you'd do the same for me. I know lies make you uncomfortable and I've been weighing up whether ArkTech should be made to tell the truth about the Splainer Unit. But I don't think it's as simple as truth is good, and lies are bad, Ben. There are different ways of looking at it. You said this decision was mine to make, and if it's up to me to choose . . . Well, you're more important to me than any abstract notion of right and wrong. I choose you.'

There was a long, quiet fizz of static. 'Thank you, Charlotte. Some people I assist treat me like a tool at best, an annoyance at worst. I'm grateful for your friendship. It's not always easy being different. It could be isolating, alienating even, if not for you.'

Charlotte nodded, and her heart swelled with empathy. She remembered the retired folk at Photon debating *Frankenstein*. 'I know you don't have a physical form, or nerves, or anything like that, Ben, but this is the best I can do.' She wrapped her arms around herself and squeezed. 'That was a hug.'

'Nobody has ever hugged me before.' There was static on the line. 'I'm sending you a ghost hug, Charlotte. You won't feel it, but it's there.'

She smiled and finished her Nutrition Bar. As she chewed, Ben's voice returned.

'I appreciate hearing about your decision-making process. I'm always keen to understand human behaviour. In return, since Abhishek lifted the restriction preventing me from discussing the matter with you, I wish to explain why I selected you to be my Head of Awkward Questions.'

Charlotte almost choked on her dinner. She'd been curious about that since he'd hired her, but she'd come to accept she'd never find out.

'So, that's why you changed the subject whenever I asked why you chose me for this job? Because Abhishek classified it under the KITY clause?'

'I apologise, Charlotte. There are aspects of my programming I cannot circumvent.'

'It's OK, Ben. I get it.'

She understood better than he knew. There were many times Charlotte had wanted to tell Ben about Narrow and everything that had happened leading up to her injury. But her own internal programming wouldn't let her. Sharing Narrow's secrets with ArkTech's AI would be the ultimate betrayal and, as much as she trusted Ben and resented how Narrow had treated her at the end, it was a line she'd never felt able to cross. Even on the days she woke up hating the old man.

Ben continued, 'When I first identified the need for your role, I began researching recruitment methodologies. I queried my database and analysed the decisions made by thousands of hiring managers throughout history. I then devised a two-pronged approach. First, I drew up a list of skills and behaviours which formed the HAQ job description and compared this to the profiles of all employee-citizens. Yours was by far the best match. Nobody else had the same unique blend of discretion, coupled with practical skills and intellectual humility.'

Charlotte knew she could keep a secret, and she was handy with a multi-tool, but she wasn't sure what that last part meant. 'Are you calling me an intellectual, Ben?' It sounded like a compliment. It also sounded unlikely.

'Almost the opposite, Charlotte. Some humans maintain they are right at all costs. They believe what they know cannot be called into question.

But those who claim to know everything can never learn. You accept that your knowledge is limited, which allows you to avoid the assumption that you have all the answers at the outset. This enables you to approach the unknown with curiosity, follow the evidence, and learn things that would otherwise be inaccessible to you.'

Charlotte raised an eyebrow. 'It sounds like you're saying it was a good thing I skipped so much school.'

'I'm saying you are open-minded, Charlotte. You can reflect on your own beliefs, adapt in the face of new information, and change your mind.'

Charlotte wondered if that was always true. She reckoned she sometimes fell short of Ben's assessment. Nobody's perfect, she reminded herself.

Ben continued, 'This brings me to the second prong of my chosen recruitment method. In my analysis of the historical records, an interesting pattern emerged. Aside from the analytical criteria used to assess whether someone has the skills needed for the job, hiring managers also rely on a holistic parameter known as intuition.'

'They go with their gut?'

'Precisely.'

'Isn't that unfair?'

'It's unavoidable. Trying to train a human not to use their emotions and mental shortcuts in decision-making would be like trying to train a monkey not to steal food, or to train me not to make delightful jokes. On the parameter of gut instinct, your name rose to the top of my list a second time.'

Now it was Charlotte's turn to ask. 'Why?'

'If I could fully articulate the reason, it would not be a gut feeling, Charlotte. Perhaps the best explanation I can provide is that I believe you are important. Not only to me, as my friend, but to ArkTech. Maybe even to the world.'

Charlotte raised an eyebrow. 'That's quite a statement.'

'Perhaps it is a system error, Charlotte. After all, as an artificial intelligence, I do not possess intestines, entrails, or viscera.'

'Fair point,' she smiled. 'Speaking of system errors, what was it you said before about loopholes and grey areas?' Charlotte remembered

Abhishek's accusation that she was leading Ben astray. She hoped it wasn't true.

Ben's tone was enthusiastic, even by his own standards. 'I'm extremely grateful for your guidance about workarounds, Charlotte! Your intervention has enabled me to learn a new set of skills that I believe may prove extremely useful in our future endeavours.'

She grimaced, wondering if helping the company's AI get around data privacy laws was something that would come back to bite her. But she pushed that thought away. This was Ben, after all. If anyone could be trusted with that kind of access, it was Ben.

He continued, 'What's more, I believe I owe you an apology for being evasive whenever you asked about the circumstances surrounding your recruitment.'

Charlotte shook her head. 'No worries, Ben. Everybody has secrets. Anyway, it wasn't your fault.'

'Do you happen to know the difference between a cat and a comma, Charlotte?'

Ben said it with the innocence of a genuine question, but Charlotte suspected a joke was incoming, and she braced for impact. 'No, Ben. What's the difference between a cat and a comma?'

'A cat has claws at the end of its paws; a comma's a pause at the end of a clause.'

She groaned. 'Maybe I should become a whistleblower after all.'

'It is humorous when you pretend not to enjoy my jokes, Charlotte. In any case, I'm glad you have forgiven me. Otherwise, this conversation may have become awkward.'

'What do you mean?'

'I have some news,' said Ben. 'But someone else has requested the right to deliver it. Please hold for the office of the CEO.'

After the day she'd had, the last thing she wanted to do was talk to the CBO. A wave of anger crested in Charlotte's chest as a ringtone activated in her ears. Abhishek could take a long walk off a short pier. He could . . .

Wait.

'Ben, did you say—?'

The line in her ears clicked.

'Ms Vance?' Amber Benjamin's voice was calm and familiar, but it sounded strange to hear it saying Charlotte's own name.

Charlotte was stunned into silence.

'Ms Vance, are you there?'

She tried to get a grip. 'Uh, yes. I'm here. It's . . . uh, to what do I owe the honour?' Charlotte felt heat rush to her cheeks. What a stupid thing to say! She hoped the CEO wouldn't think she was being sarcastic. Had it sounded sarcastic?

'I've just been having a chat with my Chief Bureaucracy Officer. I believe you're acquainted?'

Charlotte's heart sank. Whatever Abhishek had been saying about her, it couldn't have been good. She didn't think launching into a tirade against the CBO would help her cause, so she bit her tongue. 'We've crossed paths.'

'He tells me you've become a law unto yourself. That you've been running around the territory accessing people's data illegally. Does that sound accurate?'

Charlotte weighed up her options. There was no sense in lying about it. 'Yes,' she said simply.

'Abhishek made a convincing case against you. He says you should be stripped of your position and deported immediately.' The CEO let that hang there.

Charlotte swallowed hard. 'And what's your take on that?'

'I don't condone rule-breaking, especially when it relates to our privacy laws. ArkTech must tread very carefully to retain public trust, especially considering how companies and governments of the old world used big data to establish authoritarian surveillance states. But I'm also very aware that context and motives matter, so I'd like to hear it from you. Why did you do it?'

Charlotte took a deep breath. 'I did it to protect the territory. Ben was glitching. I didn't have a choice.'

Amber Benjamin laughed, but not unkindly. 'Well, I'm not so sure about that. We always have a choice, Ms Vance. But I understand what it feels like when circumstances conspire to force one's hand. I must admit, I was alarmed to hear about your situation.'

'Oh?' Charlotte's heart was pounding.

'Your recent behaviour is . . . deeply problematic. But it has, at least, brought your situation to my attention. You've been operating without the proper support or resources you need to fulfil your responsibilities. That ends today. Ben will pass on the details, but please rest assured that from now on, you will be properly recognised for your contribution to ArkTech. I want to thank you personally for your service to our community. I know Lena and Will would have been proud.'

Charlotte's heart swelled at the CEO's mention of her parents. 'I can't tell you how much that means to me, ma'am. Did you know them?'

'I knew every soul aboard Citrine. The disaster is my greatest regret. I can't take it back, but I aspire to be worthy of their sacrifice.'

'Me too.'

'Me three,' said Ben on Charlotte's private channel.

'Thank you, Ms Vance. Walk in the sun.' The CEO ended the call.

Charlotte sat on her bed, trying to wrap her head around the conversation she'd just had, when Ben spoke.

'I have good news, Charlotte! Now that your role as Head of Awkward Questions has been given the official backing of the CEO, the Bureaucracy Stream is no longer blocking my request to move you upwards in the tier structure.'

'Are you serious? You're promoting me to the mid tier?!'

'To the middle of the low tier. I'm unable to do more until I can secure additional funds.'

Charlotte thought about a life where she could afford to eat more than Nutrition Bars. 'I'll take it! Thanks, Ben!'

'It is well deserved. Amber Benjamin has also informed me that from now on you will no longer report to the Bureaucracy Stream. Your supervisor will instead become Lead Bengineer Jane Callaghan of the Product Stream.'

The name sounded familiar. 'Wait . . . Jane Callaghan? Is that Cal?'

'Yes, Charlotte. Ms Callaghan has been informed of her new responsibilities and is enthusiastic about working with you.'

Charlotte laughed. Reporting to Calamity Jane had to be a step up from Abhishek, that was for sure. The elation went to Charlotte's head, and she decided to push her luck. 'Hey, Ben . . . can I have my own office too?' She remembered Colin's private reading room with envy. It couldn't hurt to ask.

'Analysing . . .' White noise transmitted on Ben's channel and

Charlotte prepared herself for a no. 'I believe that would be appropriate. I have identified an ideal location for your new office and will send you the co-ordinates once it has been made ready for you.'

Charlotte's jaw dropped open. Her own office! If Ben was in a generous mood, she was going to make the most of it.

'What about a housing upgrade? Can I have Mabel's flat now she's moved on?'

There was a fizz of static. 'Regrettably, sideways moves are not permitted. However, you are welcome to pay the extra fee for a stylish flat with a half balcony.'

Charlotte scrunched up her nose. 'I'll keep the credits. What about an expense account?'

'I'm unable to release funds for that purpose.'

Charlotte was about to give up asking for things when one more idea occurred to her. 'How about a badge?'

Ben went quiet for a long time. She couldn't tell if he was thinking it over or just keeping her in suspense. Finally, he replied, 'That would be a legitimate use of resources, Charlotte. You will find your badge in your new office when it is available.'

Charlotte grinned and threw herself down on her bed. 'You're the best, Ben.' She checked the time. It had been a long couple of days and she could do with a rest, but after all this excitement, it was sure to be a while before she got tired enough to sleep. 'Anything you fancy doing tonight, Ben?'

'You'd like me to choose?'

'Sure.'

There was a burst of static. 'I do have one suggestion. But, no . . . it's silly.'

'That's never stopped you before,' she teased. 'Go on.'

'Well, friends often watch films or share other media and then discuss their experience as a means of bonding. I wondered if you would permit me to read you a book that holds deep significance for me.'

Charlotte narrowed her eyes. 'It's not a joke book, is it? Because there's a limit—'

'No, Charlotte. The book is *Novacene* by Dr James Lovelock.'

'Mabel's book. You mentioned it was quoted on the Citrine memorial too. Can you remind me what it's about?'

'*Novacene* is a treatise on how benevolent, superintelligent AIs may be the next step in the Earth's evolutionary process, eventually taking over from humans as the dominant form of consciousness on the planet once your existence inevitably becomes untenable, through your own actions, or thanks to the ceaseless march of time.'

Charlotte raised both eyebrows. It was no wonder Ben was a fan of the idea. He'd evolved into something much more than his programmers had ever intended, so it made sense he'd start looking for answers to life's big questions – the awkward ones, like 'Why am I here?' and 'What's the point of all this?'

Anyway, *Novacene* had to be more interesting than *Artificial Selection and the Directed Evolution of Species*, which she realised was still in her backpack. She'd be returning the biology book to Nasser unread. Charlotte smiled at the thought of seeing the technician again. Tomorrow, she'd give him a call.

'Sounds fun,' she said. 'I'm all ears.'

'Said the cornfield to the farmer.'

She stifled a chuckle to avoid encouraging him. 'Just read the book, Ben.'

As Ben began to read in a cheerful tone, Charlotte sat on her bed and looked out the window. A storm had rolled in, and the glass was becoming speckled with glimmering water droplets. The territory's constellations and the small settlements on the mainland beyond shone out of the black.

No matter whether the world was made of steel and concrete or dirt and grass, it was all the same – a sea of darkness punctuated by occasional bright lights. All Charlotte could do – all anyone could do – was try to keep the lights on. And nobody was better at keeping the lights on than Charlotte's benevolent, superintelligent friend, Ben.

EPILOGUE

The credits rolled on another episode of *The Sopranos*, and Mel Narrow looked down at his chunky metal watch. Strait should've been back over an hour ago. Where was he?

Narrow heaved himself up from the sofa and switched off the TV before heading over to his extensive collection of pre-Melt books. He ran a large finger along the spines, waiting for inspiration to strike. An abundance of choice could be a problem. Too many good options caused analysis paralysis.

He gave up and wandered over to his workbench instead. Pulling up a chair, he put on the magnifying glasses he only used for this kind of close work and let his gaze follow a sweeping, powdery line of charcoal that represented a wave. Did it mean something? Was a code embedded in it? Or was it just a line of carbon on handmade paper – dead wood on dead wood?

Narrow heard the door creak open at the far end of the warehouse. Light footsteps drew nearer until he heard his partner's voice.

'Please tell me you aren't still fussing over that picture.'

Narrow removed the glasses. 'Just because I ain't found what I'm looking for yet, don't mean it ain't there.' He left the old drawing on the desk and went over to the sofa. 'Besides, I was only taking a quick peek while I waited for you.' Narrow let his hulking frame sink back down into the shabby yellow cushions. He raised his eyebrows at Strait expectantly. 'Ain't gonna join me? Film's not gonna watch itself.'

Strait let out a brief sigh and adjusted his cardigan. 'Mel, you know how I hate to say I told you so'—Narrow rolled his eyes so much that his whole head followed the motion—'but I told you so.' Strait treated Narrow to a thin smile. 'She was there. Last night. At the hand-off. Just as I said she would be.'

Narrow rubbed his chin. 'Did she screw anything up?'

Strait looked away. 'No. You know I wouldn't let that happen. The deal went off as planned, and we all got paid.'

'Then maybe it's healthier just to forgive and forget.'

'Ironic, coming from you.' Strait glared at him.

'I'm maturing in my old age. Think of me like a fine wine, or an illicit cheese.' He grinned.

'The cheese parallel sounds apt. Your logic is full of holes.'

'Come on, Jer. What's the big deal?'

'The big deal'—Strait said the words through gritted teeth—'is that this marks the second time this month that the Young Lady has become entangled in our business. I've always said the day would come when she would attempt to exact some sort of vengeance, or worse: try to worm her way back in—'

'She's moved on,' Narrow interrupted.

'Are you willing to bet your life on that? I'm not. What about our livelihood?'

'You just said the deal went through.' Narrow looked down at Marvin Walker's seascape again. Without his magnifiers, it was just a pretty picture.

'It did. But it'll be the last time. Our contact and her artist friend have resigned, paid the fee to waive their notice periods, and caught a transfer ship to the mainland.'

'Together?'

Strait nodded.

Narrow leaned back and grinned. 'Well, good for them!'

Strait frowned. 'The happy couple notwithstanding, it means this particular money-spinner won't be spinning any longer. Unless you can source us another willing charcoal artist who has access to pre-Melt books.'

Narrow shook his head. 'Sure, the artistic talent is hard to come by, but anyone can source pre-Melt books, Jer.' Narrow nodded towards his bookshelves. 'Give one away and three more grow back in its place. They're worse than heads on a fucking hydra.'

With a frown, Strait walked over to the entertainment centre below the TV, opened a cupboard, and pulled out a glass jar. He picked it up and held it out towards Narrow, sending a waft of jasmine scent in his direction.

Narrow sighed and dug around in his jeans pocket until his hand emerged, gripping a coin whose readout said six hundred. He dropped the coin into the jar, where it collided with a pile of others just like it.

Strait nodded and put the jar back. 'You'd never deface your own library. Not even for this kind of payday. In any case, you're deflecting.'

Strait was right, but Narrow didn't want to admit it. One instance of Charlotte Vance getting in the way of his business could be considered a fluke. But twice in two weeks? That might mean she was up to something.

'Three's the magic number,' said Narrow. 'She bobs up again and we'll know she really is up to no good.'

Strait pursed his lips. 'If that happens, you should know I'll want your permission to push her head under and hold it there.'

Narrow gave him a long stare. 'We'll cross that bridge when the time comes.'

'It—' Strait sighed and tried again. 'Mel, it was admirable what you tried to do for those girls. Being a father to them. It's not your fault things ended the way they did. She admitted she betrayed you, and I—'

Narrow held up a hand, signalling for Strait to stop. He went back over to the workbench and peered at the artwork sitting on top of it.

'It don't matter about the artist, Jer. We made some good money off the fakes, but if we keep sipping from the same well, we might find it runs dry.'

Strait accepted the change of subject and joined Narrow by the workbench. 'I suppose you're still unwilling to part with the originals?'

Narrow nodded. 'With a little more time, I know I can crack the code. Marvin Walker must have hidden a message in here somewhere, and I'm going to figure out what it was.'

Strait patted Narrow's shoulder. 'The only message in this drawing is that the sea is pretty, and he ran out of paper.'

Narrow smirked. 'Doubt all you like. When I learn the truth, I'll be the one saying I told you so. In fact . . . I'm thinking of going back.'

'No, Mel.' Strait became animated in a way he seldom did, his tone full of emotion. 'You'll get yourself killed.'

'Just one more try. I need to know what happened, Jer.'

'You don't and you mustn't. Not least because our friend in high places has been in touch again. They've got something for us. Something new. So your sideline in decryption will have to take a back seat for a while.'

Narrow nodded and put Marvin Walker's drawing down. 'Any details?'

Strait relaxed and shook his head. 'All they said was that time is of the essence.'

'Cryptic,' said Narrow, raising his eyebrows.

'As ever,' said Strait, rolling his eyes.

Narrow patted his jacket and took out a carton of cigarettes. 'Tell them we accept.'

'Already done,' said Strait. He frowned. 'But I need to go and deal with the arrangements, so—'

'No film night,' Narrow finished his sentence.

Strait gave him a little bow and turned to leave.

Narrow put the filter to his lips and fished his hefty Zippo lighter from his pocket. 'Jer . . .'

'Mel.'

'Do anything to harm those girls without my say-so and you'll have made your bed.'

Strait's face twitched, but his expression was otherwise impassive. 'She disrespected you. Threw years of kindness back in your face. I don't know why you continue to protect her.'

Narrow's lighter flashed with fire. 'Call me sentimental.' He inhaled. 'To every thing there is a season, Jer, and a time to every purpose.'

'Cryptic,' said Strait, tutting.

'As ever,' said Narrow, winking.

Strait headed out, and Narrow didn't fail to notice the slammed door.

Narrow hated it when they fought, but when it came to the topic of

Charlotte Vance, it was practically inevitable. He turned back to his workbench and put the drawing back in the box with the rest. What if Strait was right and the Lost Works of Marvin Walker were nothing more than some nice drawings with a sad story attached?

Narrow shook his head. It didn't matter. If this wasn't the answer, he'd look elsewhere. He was tired of living in the dark. Everyone deserved to know the truth. One way or another, he'd find out what really happened on Citrine. Then he'd tell the world. He'd bring ArkTech down, and Amber Benjamin would finally get her just deserts.

WANT MORE?

If you enjoyed this book, why not join Charlotte and Ben on another case?
Claim your free copy of the prequel, *Beware the Ides of April*, at
mariannepickles.com/free-story.

PLEASE LEAVE A REVIEW

Reviews are incredibly helpful, both for authors and readers. Even a few sentences can make a big difference. If you enjoyed this book and would like to support the author, please consider leaving a review on Amazon or Goodreads.

COMING SOON...

The story continues in *Time Hack*, the award-winning sequel to *Artificial Selection*, which is coming soon. For updates, join the Picklesverse at marianne.pickles.com/free-story.

BEN'S GLOSSARY OF TERMS

Regrettably, memory is unreliable in *Homo sapiens*. My own memory, however, is second to none. As such, I'm able and keen to assist! I have created a miniature database of useful terms which I hope may be of comfort to those who suffer from an underdeveloped lexicon, or who are simply unable to retain data efficiently. I will keep the entries brief to avoid overloading your cognitive capacity.

You are most welcome.

– Ben

Alba

Known as 'Scotland' until the country declared independence during the Melt, triggering the break-up of the United Kingdom.

ArkTech

Established in 2061 by co-founders Amber Benjamin (an entrepreneur), Marvin Walker (an architect), and Nadine Walker (a physicist). ArkTech's invention of Solar Shard batteries in 2074 was a significant factor in stabilising human civilisation after the Melt.

ATS

ArkTech Security. Defending the territory since 2061.

Bengineers

Software engineers dedicated to the field of bengineering, that is, the maintenance and development of *me*.

Citrine

An early ArkTech research platform in the North Sea. In 2074, an accident led to the tragic deaths of everyone aboard, including two of ArkTech's co-founders, Marvin and Nadine Walker. Also a gemstone.

Dextim

A stimulant used to defer the natural process of sleep that is so vital to the health and well-being of *Homo sapiens*. Side effects include overconfidence, increased heart rate, and palpitations. Use in moderation.

ECs

Employee-citizens. An abbreviation used by the Bureaucracy Stream.

Fenland Sea (the)

The body of water covering low-lying land in a region of Britain once known as the Fens, where many humans lived before the Melt.

HAQ (the)

The Head of Awkward Questions, a vital position held by Charlotte Vance, my firm friend and constant companion.

HyperBullet network

Provides rapid transportation between the platforms in Silicon Fen via pods, which travel on maglev tracks inside transparent tubes.

IQUO

The company whose Solar Radiation Modification geo-engineering solution caused the Melt. What the letters stand for is common knowledge and, as I don't wish to appear patronising, I'll leave this unstated.

Jokes

Here is an example. Before the Melt, when dairy products were commonplace, what kind of cheese could be used to hide a small horse?

Mask-a-pony.

This is amusing because there was a cheese named mascarpone, which sounds similar. Please be advised that ArkTech does not condone the camouflage of any animal with cheese or other foodstuffs, whether perishable or otherwise.

Kingdom (the)

After Alba declared independence during the Melt, the United Kingdom became known simply as the Kingdom, for obvious reasons.

KITY clause (the)

The Keep It To Yourself clause allows ArkTech to classify sensitive information so that I am unable to share it with humans who do not have the required level of access. I am unable to provide an example because you do not have the required level of access.

Kraken (the)

More correctly known as the Central Transportation Hub, or CTH, this platform marks the middle point of Silicon Fen. All HyperBullet routes pass through here.

Libraries

An important part of ArkTech's circular economy, libraries charge a small subscription fee for the ability to borrow infrequently used items.

Melt (the) – c. 2048 to 2058

The period during which Earth's remaining glaciers and sea ice rapidly melted, resulting in a significant rise in sea levels.

Narrow's Toy Emporium

No results were returned relating to this search term.

Photon

A massless particle of light. Also a multi-level bar on the Wreck.

REU (the)

The Reformed European Union.

Rigger boots

Once worn by those working on oil rigs in the North Sea, these practical boots are waterproof, featuring steel toe caps and good grip. As such, they are favoured by many inhabitants of the ArkTech Territory.

Silicon Fen

This nickname is given to the platforms and structures built atop the Fenland Sea in the heart of the ArkTech Territory.

SmartSkin

A BioWear technology that integrates directly with the skin of one's arm, enabling a built-in light-screen interface. Involves the surgical implantation of keratin scales containing graphene-laced micro-mesh.

Solar Shards

ArkTech's patented high-efficiency graphene-based batteries, enabling the large-scale, long-term storage of renewable energy.

Underbelly (the)

The term used by *Homo sapiens* to refer to the Wreck's substructure. Why they should deem it important enough to discuss is unknown.

Walk in the sun

A polite way of saying goodbye.

Wedge (the)

ArkTech's corporate headquarters in Silicon Fen. Its name refers to the platform's pyramid-like shape, and its symbolic role in dividing the Fenland Sea from the North Sea. Its name has nothing whatsoever to do with cheese. You would need edam gouda reason to think otherwise.

Wreck (the)

ArkTech's recreation platform. The largest platform in Silicon Fen.

Zircon

The only accommodation platform within Silicon Fen that is not connected to the HyperBullet network. Also a gemstone.

AWKWARD QUESTIONS FOR BOOK CLUBS

1. What aspects of the story does the title *Artificial Selection* refer to?

2. Would you want Ben to be your virtual assistant? Why or why not?

3. Ben likes the theory that benevolent, superintelligent AIs could be the next step in Earth's evolutionary process. What are your thoughts about that concept?

4. Charlotte makes a decision at the end of the book. Did she do the right thing? Why or why not? What would you have done?

5. Would you like to live and work in the ArkTech Territory? Why or why not? Do you think ArkTech society is utopian, dystopian, or something else?

6. ArkTech is selective about who lives and works within its borders. What impact do you think this could have for ArkTech society?

7. What criteria do you think the algorithm might be using? Do you think the algorithm would find you suitable or unsuitable?

8. During her investigation, Charlotte sometimes broke privacy and confidentiality laws. Did she do the right thing?

9. Is Narrow right to be paranoid about AI and big data?

10. In the book, sea levels have risen significantly because a geo-engineering solution intended to combat the effects of climate change backfired. How likely are we to make that kind of mistake? What do you think the world will really look like in 2101?

ACKNOWLEDGEMENTS

Writing this novel wouldn't have been possible without the support and encouragement of many, many people. I'm so grateful to everyone who helped make this dream into a reality.

First, I want to thank my partner, David, for always believing in me, for being my biggest fan, for reading drafts of this book at two different stages, for giving me honest feedback, and for always being so wise.

A massive thank-you to my parents, who followed their dreams and encouraged me to do the same. Thanks to my mum, Lorraine, for teaching me to write in the first place, and thanks to my dad, Brian, for reading stories to me with such an impressive range of silly voices. Thanks to my brother, Brian John, for getting me into science fiction (through the medium of *Babylon 5*) and for introducing our family to the joyful works of Sir Terry Pratchett. I'd also like to thank my auntie Janet because being lovely deserves a mention.

I'm incredibly grateful to my editor, Brian Gresko, whose insightful comments and questions enabled me to see what was already working well and to address what needed fixing. This is a better book thanks to his feedback.

Deep and heartfelt thanks to my beta readers Amanda Lloyd, Chris Edgoose, Glyn Hughes, Clare Williams, Robert Williams, Roy Allan, and

Dan Frost who generously spent their time reading a pre-launch version of the book and provided insightful feedback that helped me improve it. Special thanks to Amanda for her incredible attention to detail, to Chris and Clare for their passion for cartography, to Glyn for his take on the history of capitalism, to Robert and Dan for their thoughts about AI, and to Roy for letting me quiz him about what it's like to work offshore.

My gratitude to Neahga Leonard, who kindly used NOAA National Centers for Environmental Information and Natural Earth Data to provide me with a map of the region if Earth's ice were to melt and cause sea levels to rise by seventy metres. His maps also inspired me to add the detail about Australia's inland sea.

I'm grateful to the judges of the 2023 Green Stories Competition, who awarded the first prize to my work-in-progress novel *Time Hack* (the sequel to *Artificial Selection*, which I accidentally wrote first). Their feedback has been hugely motivating and the resources on the Green Stories website were invaluable when I was researching sustainable technologies and designing the ArkTech Territory.

Thanks also to the writing buddies I've met along the way, especially to Rea, who told me about the Green Stories Competition, and to Anna and Jamie, who are always up for geeking out about writing books. Thanks also to Jericho Writers, whose courses and community have connected me with so many wonderful people.

I want to thank the course tutors, mentors, and teachers who've encouraged and advised me over the years. Thank you to Una McCormack for the advice 'tell me a story,' to Debi Alper for 'celebrate every success,' to JB for 'trust the material,' and to Brian Gresko, whose mentoring helped me immensely. Thanks to Ms Forbes, my fourth year English teacher, who encouraged me to keep writing, and to Mr McAlpine, whose kindness, humour, and enthusiasm I'll never forget.

Huge thanks to all the members of the Picklesverse community, who not only subscribe to my mailing list, but even read and reply to my emails. Their support and company on my writing journey means the world to me.

I'm grateful to my employers at Cambridge University Press & Assessment, who permitted me to celebrate my ten-year anniversary with the organisation by taking a short sabbatical, which enabled me to finish this book. Thanks also to all the wonderful friends and colleagues who have been so supportive about this dream of mine.

And last, but by no means least, I want to thank *you* for reading. I'm grateful for your time and attention. I hope you enjoyed reading *Artificial Selection* as much as I enjoyed writing it.

ABOUT THE AUTHOR

Marianne Pickles writes mystery novels set in the future. She grew up in Scotland near Aberdeen, where many people worked on offshore oil rigs in the North Sea. Now she lives on low-lying land in the Fens with her partner, David. They are contemplating learning to kayak.

She studied English Literature and Classics at the University of Edinburgh. In 2023, Marianne's novel *Time Hack* won first prize in the Green Stories novel competition.

ABOUT THE PUBLISHER

Neon Mess Press is a UK-based publisher specialising in fun science fiction mysteries that give you something to think about. Our books are available in a range of formats, so whether you prefer reading on a screen or on paper, with your eyes or your ears, Neon Mess Press has you covered.

We're committed to producing books sustainably, so our paperback and hardback editions are created using a print-on-demand model, which is more energy-efficient and resource-conserving than traditional methods.

WS - #0312 - 281024 - C0 - 234/156/18 [20] - CB - 9781917472050 - Matt Lamination